# L O U D E R
# T H A N
# W O R D S

*Edited and with an Introduction by*

# W I L L I A M   S H O R E

*Vintage Books*

*A Division of Random House, Inc.* / *New York*

# LOUDER THAN WORDS

●

*22 Authors Donate*
*New Stories to Benefit*
*Share Our Strength's*
*Fight Against Hunger,*
*Homelessness And Illiteracy*

A VINTAGE ORIGINAL, DECEMBER 1989
FIRST EDITION

Library of Congress Cataloging-in-Publication Data
Louder than words : 22 authors donate new stories to benefit Share
  Our Strength's fight against hunger, homelessness, and illiteracy /
  edited and with an introduction by William Shore.—1st ed.
    p. cm.
  ISBN 0-679-72157-6 : $8.95
    1. Short stories, American.  2. American fiction—20th century.
I. Shore, William.  II. Share Our Strength.
PS648.S5L68  1989
813'.0108—dc20                                    89-40138
                                                       CIP

Book design by Chris Welch
Manufactured in the United States of America
10  9  8  7  6  5  4  3  2  1

# CONTENTS

# ACKNOWLEDGMENTS

More than most books, an anthology, by definition, owes its existence to the talents of many people. In this case the twenty-two fine writers who donated their stories have first claim on my gratitude. What follows is their work. My own efforts to recruit, organize, correspond with, and review the final products of each fall more appropriately under the category of pleasure.

The enthusiasm and energy I sought to provide over the last eighteen months can take a project like this one just so far, and then no farther. There comes a point at which skill, judgment and experience are needed. Fortunately, Robin Desser, my editor at Vintage Books has all three in abundance. She has been a great friend whose advice and encouragement did much to shape the ultimate version of this book.

This book is just one of Share Our Strength's many endeavors to support the fight against hunger, homelessness and illiteracy. And while it happens to be associated with my name, the hardest work in that organization is done by an incredibly dedicated full-time staff to whom I am particularly grateful. Meghan Hays and Richard Wagner, as recent additions, share responsibility for our growth. Debbie Shore, Joann Shepherd, and Cathy Townsend have stuck with this effort from the very beginning and demonstrated a level of commitment that has made a profound impact. Together, the five of them are Share Our Strength and the principal reason it exists and thrives.

Finally, a special thanks to my wife, Bonnie, who in countless ways has enabled both Share Our Strength and me to become what we've become.

# INTRODUCTION

Share Our Strength (SOS) was established in 1984 to raise funds for hunger relief through the American food and restaurant industry. It has since become a broad-based non-profit vehicle for channeling creative talent and energy in a variety of fields toward those in need.

Over the past year SOS has provided more than one million dollars to food banks and homeless shelters in sixty cities, as well as to international famine relief and development overseas. The funds are most often used to improve kitchen equipment, transport excess food products, train volunteers, and to support agricultural enhancement projects in the developing world. In many American cities SOS funds ensure that literally thousands of pounds of healthful, nutritious, nonsalable food will be shared by soup kitchens and homeless shelters, instead of just being thrown away.

Financial contributions to our organization from several well-known writers inspired the idea that there ought to be a vehicle for writers to do more than simply contribute dollars to a cause they believe in. There ought to be a way for them to contribute *through their craft*.

We conceived and proposed a writers' committee on which participating writers would contribute one previously unpublished short story to an anthology from which profits would be donated to antipoverty organizations fighting hunger, homelessness, and illiteracy. I was surprised by the quick and generous responses: from those of Louise Erdrich and Anne Tyler, who immediately telephoned their support, to that of Lee K. Abbott, who enthusiastically replied: "Hell, yes, count me in

... If anything I do can end this national horror, then I will have accomplished more with this story, in practical terms, than any I have written before."

The contribution of these participating writers has been generous indeed. So that the maximum amount of funds could be raised, the stories donated to this anthology were also made available to magazines and literary journals and have appeared in *The New Yorker, Ladies' Home Journal, Mother Jones, Antaeus, Shenandoah, The Georgia Review,* and many others.

Ultimately the writers who have contributed to this anthology have given something of much greater value than money. They have given of themselves. Contributing author Michael Downing put it best when he wrote, confirming his participation: "I thank you for the privilege of giving away something of value. I typically find myself writing rather inconsequential checks which I try to inflate with good will and best wishes. It is a joy to know that my contribution's value will appreciate because of your work and the contribution of others."

This volume, which we hope will become the first of many, stands as a tribute to the idea that helping others can be one of the most eloquent forms of self-expression.

—William Shore
Executive Director, Share Our Strength

# LOUDER

# THAN

# WORDS

# A WOMAN LIKE A

# FIELDSTONE HOUSE

O

*Anne Tyler*

T HAT WAS THE YEAR she turned squeamish—
1936. Up till then she'd been a tough and gritty little girl, the
kind of child who gleefully sprinkled salt on garden slugs and
stuck firefly tails to her knuckles for rings. But during her
twelfth birthday party, which was held out of doors, she was
stung by something unseen and she carried on about it far longer than was reasonable (as all three of her brothers informed
her) and afterward behaved timidly around insects, garter
snakes and even her brother Peter's pretty orange salamander
with the tiny, cool, humanlike hands who lived in a pie plate
full of water under the front porch.

So imagine her distress when she discovered, later in
May, a great number of mysterious round holes the size of
snake holes scattered through the backyard. They were so precisely formed that they might have been made with the staff of
a beach umbrella, but of course they couldn't have been. (The

beach umbrella still lay in its wintering place behind the coal furnace in the basement.) Her brothers said the holes must be, oh, something or other, gopher holes, maybe; who knew; who cared. But then her father told her they were exit doors for locusts. Cicadas, actually, he said, but here in Baltimore everyone called them locusts, seventeen-year locusts; and yes, this would be the year for them, as a matter of fact. He was surprised to see how quickly they had come around again. Last time, he told Corey, he had been in high school. He had not even kissed a girl yet, not even held hands with one. He looked at Corey's mother when he said this, in a wondering, slightly abstracted way, and Corey's mother laughed, but he did not. He was silent for a moment.

Then he went on to explain how the pupae crawled out of the dirt where they had lived for seventeen years and how they climbed the first available vertical object (your leg, if you stood still long enough) and wriggled free of their shells and turned into big black flying insects who mated and died in a matter of weeks, leaving their eggs to mature in turn seventeen years later. He presented this as a miracle of nature. He used the same tone of voice Corey's mother had used earlier in the spring when she was introducing the facts of life. But Corey was repelled by that description of their climbing the first available vertical object. She imagined how they would feel: burrlike, barnaclelike, clinging with their prickly feet to her bare leg.

That whole summer, therefore, she behaved in an edgy, old-maidish manner whenever she was outdoors. Sent to retrieve the morning paper, she stayed on the sidewalk and leaned far, far over to fish the paper from the grass. Waiting at the streetcar stop, she hopped up and down continually like someone who needed to go to the bathroom. She did this even after all the horny beige shells were emptied; she did this even after the locusts had started zooming through the air in their clumsy, barging fashion, slamming into the windshield of her father's Hudson and buzzing like a million giant zippers. There was no question now of their choosing one of Corey's wiry white legs as a shedding station, and yet still she went on hopping. Her mother said, "Corey, what on earth . . . ?" and in public, looked around embarrassed and whispered, "Stand still, sweetie." But Corey couldn't stand still, not for the life of her.

Then one day—oh, it must have been June, mid-June or so—she realized the locusts were gone. There were a few black carcasses at the edges of the sidewalks, their bright red, mappin eyes filmed over now, and a few empty shells fastened to the tree trunks, but no more locusts. For a while, she went on hopping anyway. It was a kind of superstition. Then gradually she stopped. She began to allow her family to open the car windows again when they went for their Sunday drives. She no longer ran her fingers apprehensively through her straw-colored fan of hair after the briefest trip outdoors, or shook out her skirt, or examined the soles of her sandals. And by September (when Minella Smith had moved in across the alley and they'd started their secret club, the Jewels), Corey had forgotten that the locusts had ever existed.

She was hanging diapers out back when she noticed that one of the clothesline poles had collected some sort of clustery growths around its base, and when she bent for a closer look she said, "Why!" They were locust shells, or pupae, or whatever you want to call them. She recognized them instantly. The sight gave her a swooping sensation. The year was 1953, she was twenty-nine years old and she had a husband and three children, and yet here were these crisp little shrimpy things come all the way from her twelfth summer. She took a clothespin from her apron pocket and poked at one of the pupae and it fell to the ground, unresisting. She went over to the other pole—actually a maple tree—and found them even thicker there. Her youngest, Dudley, held one clenched in his chubby, creased fist and his mouth was poised expectantly. "No, no, Dudley! Dirty!" she told him, and she slapped it out of his hand. She could see it was going to be a long summer.

Her husband was a New Englander, transplanted. (He'd been switched to the Baltimore branch of Northeastern Life back when Corey worked there as a secretary, and she had instantly fallen for his bright red hair and bashful smile.) When she told him about the locusts, he claimed he had never heard of such a thing. "Seventeen years?" he said. "They wait underground for seventeen years and then mate and die in just weeks? Isn't that kind of inefficient?"

"Well, maybe I've got it wrong," Corey said. "Maybe there's some in-between stage that I don't know about."

There wasn't, though. When her parents came over for Sunday dinner, she asked her father and he said it was just as she had remembered. They spent that whole long time underground.

The shells began to empty, and then the trees began to droop with what looked like heavy black fruit. "Ugly things!" her friend Marilyn said. (Marilyn was transplanted too, from someplace out west.) "This is like a horror movie," Marilyn said, but Corey—no longer so squeamish—merely laughed and continued trying to peel a lacy, iridescent wing from Dudley's tongue. She felt like an old-timer; she was almost showing off. "Wait a few days till they gather their strength," she told Marilyn. "Wait till they start dive-bombing you."

"Ooh! Do they bite?"

"No, but they're such poor fliers, they kind of stagger through the air and bang into people."

"Maybe I'll summer in Europe this year," Marilyn said languidly. But she was only joking; she was nothing but a beautician at the Princesse Beauty Shoppes.

As for Corey's two older children—Danny, who was six, and Virginia, who was eight—they thought the locusts were their own personal playthings. They collected seething mounds of them in Mason jars. They tied threads to them and let them zoom in circles like domestic animals on leashes. Corey supposed she ought to put a stop to this (locusts were God's creatures too) but somehow she didn't. She had enough to do these days just chasing after Dudley. And she was so weary of locusts by now—their bitter, musky smell, which she had not remembered from last time; and the messy snippets of branches that littered the ground after they had slit the bark to lay their eggs; and above all, their ceaseless racket. Her friend Marilyn called them the Jug Band. "Oh, the Jug Band is hot tonight!" she'd say. "There's a guest soloist on the steel tub." Then she demonstrated the Locust Walk: scurrying along on her spike heels with her collar clamped tight around her neck to guard against a locust's falling inside her blouse. And the Locust Stomp: that crazed dance you saw passersby performing when they all at once discovered an unexpected hitchhiker in their hair. And the Locust Exit: slapping smartly at the screen door before she stepped outside so they wouldn't fly up and zoom into her when the door slammed shut again. She was a card, that Marilyn—all sharp angles and peroxided curls and red lipstick, long red nails, tight red skirts and swinging ear-bobs; the kind of person who didn't mind looking like a fool from time to time if it would make other people laugh a little bit. Corey's husband thought she was sort of cheap, but Corey got a real kick out of her.

Only in the few hours before dawn now was there any peace. The rest of the time the air was frantically busy, so filled with noise you had to raise your voice to be heard. Those locusts that were far away made a zinging sound like tires on a wet highway, while the closer ones buzzed like chain saws, and there was another kind—a whole separate species, the newspaper said—that gave an unpleasant, rising scream. All these sounds competed, insistently. Lying in bed at night, Corey would ask, "How can they keep this up? Wouldn't you think they'd get tired?"

"Maybe they work in shifts," Ben told the ceiling. Then he tossed irritably on his pillow and said, "If only we had air-conditioning, we could close the windows."

The people across the street had put an air conditioner in their bedroom—something that astounded Corey, for she associated air-conditioning with major department stores and those movie theaters that advertise "It's Cold Inside!," each letter dripping blue icicles. Also, she felt there was something dank and shallow about air-conditioned air. "I like to catch the breeze," she told Ben. "I like that moment at night when everything all at once cools down."

"What breeze? What moment?" he asked. "Lately it's been hot as Hades the whole night through." Then he said, "The fact is, you're just not a person who feels the heat."

"I feel it," she said. "It just doesn't *get* to me. It has to be hot for weeks and weeks before it really gets to me."

"You're like my grandma's old fieldstone house," he told her. "It takes a while for the weather to sink through to you."

And then he laughed, because at heart he really was a good-natured man, and he turned to face her and rested a hand on her breast. His warmth traveled instantly through the thin cotton of her nightgown. Outside, the Jug Band sawed away, filling the night with clatter.


She was hauling two bags of groceries out of the car trunk because Dudley, bless his soul, had completely emptied the fridge in the day and a half he'd been home from college; and what did she see but a large black locust sitting on the curb. It had a sort of stunned look, she thought. It was utterly motionless, and when she nudged it with the toe of her sneaker it moved over slightly but it didn't fly away. She wondered if these modern fertilizers or pollutants or whatever had had some harmful effect. She wondered why her first inkling of the locusts' arrival had been this adult specimen and not the usual beige shells—although, coming up the front walk with her groceries, she saw the shells everywhere, so evidently it was just that she'd been unobservant. Her husband had undergone major surgery a couple of months earlier (but he was doing fine now, just fine), and Corey often had the feeling that she had missed out on spring this year.

While she was putting the milk away she asked Dudley, "Did you see the locusts?"

"Locusts? Sure," he said. He was hunkered over the table in his pajama bottoms—at eleven o'clock in the morning—spooning cornflakes into his mouth and reading the sports section.

"Last time they were here you kept trying to eat them," she said.

This didn't disgust him as much as you would expect, or maybe he wasn't listening, because all he said was, "Huh," and he went on reading. She thought of how he'd looked beneath the clothesline—his round little face and fat fists and his cap of soft blond hair. It didn't seem to be the same person. She couldn't make the connection.

She went out to the sun porch. Ben lay on the couch with his head at a funny angle—it gave her a turn, for a second—but as soon as she entered, his eyes flew open and he struggled to sit up higher against his pillow. He said, "How was the outside world?" and she said, "Oh, very nice," and smoothed the plaid afghan over his legs. Since the operation he'd been cold all the time. He wore a flannel bathrobe even on this warm June morning.

"You'll never guess what," she said. "The seventeen-year locusts are back."

He said, "Everybody knows that."

"They do?"

"Where have you been? Locusts in the paper, locusts on TV—"

"Well, *I* never saw."

"They're running into problems with all the new malls and developments," Ben said. "The land that's been paved over

since 1953. The locusts bump into solid concrete when they try
to crawl out of the ground."

"Well, good riddance," Corey said, but without much em-
phasis. At the mention of 1953, her mind had veered. She
thought of Marilyn in her tight red skirt, performing the Locust Stomp. "Oh," she said, "where must Marilyn Holmes be
now? Remember Marilyn? I haven't thought of her in years."

Her husband merely closed his eyes.

"The children were still little then and my parents were
still alive," she said. "Dudley was still in diapers. Now it's Hilary who's in diapers, and I don't envy Virginia for a minute
trying to stop her from putting those nasty creatures in her
mouth."

"Oh, well, they're protein," her husband said.

Corey made a sick noise, but only because he expected
her to.

As it turned out, it wasn't Hilary who ate locusts (she
was fastidious, for a baby) but Corey's new gray kitten, Calvert. Calvert had just reached the stage where everything was
a game—the crocheted ring swinging from the window shade,
Ben's feet fidgeting beneath the afghan—and by the time the
locusts were in full force, he must have thought he was in
heaven. First thing every morning, he was waiting at the
kitchen door begging to be let out onto the patio. Even if Corey
opened a tin of cat food—that fishy-smelling, expensive brand
that Calvert used to gobble down—he would just sniff it and
walk away and mew again at the door. "Go, then," Corey told
him, and she opened the door and he darted out and right away
pounced on a locust. When he batted it with his paw it churred
at him like an angry squirrel, and his ears perked forward with
interest. He nudged the locust playfully across the flagstones
and then he ate it up, rustle-rustle. All that June he ate locusts
like potato chips. His freckled tummy grew round and tight.
And every morning new locusts awaited him. They were buzzing with energy now, no longer torpid as they had first seemed
to Corey, but still they were no match for Calvert.

That was the summer Dudley dated Denise—a Towson State student with the figure of a Barbie doll. (And the IQ too, Corey often felt.) Dudley and Denise hung all over each other, nuzzling and whispering. They had little secret jokes that they never thought to share with Corey. Squeezed together on one side of the supper table, leaving Corey the entire length of the opposite side, they jabbed each other in the ribs and laughed until they squeaked. "What's so funny?" Corey demanded. Dudley didn't deign to answer. Denise said, "Oh, nothing," and wiped her eyes and sat up straight, but the obvious downward pull she gave the corners of her mouth showed she was only pretending to grow serious.

Once, at one of these suppers, Calvert sprang into Denise's lap and Denise said, "Ick!" and pushed him off. "Repulsive!" she said. "He's packed full of locusts."

"In Africa, locusts are a perfectly acceptable food," Dudley told her.

He was joking, for all Corey knew, but one thing led to another and eventually he bet five dollars that Denise wouldn't eat a wing. Well, to make a long story short, she took him up on it. There was a ceremony in the kitchen; much was made of Denise's accepting a rainbow-hued wing on a dinner plate, slathering it with mayonnaise, then holding her nose and closing her eyes and gulping the thing down whole. She gagged and took a hasty gulp of iced tea. Then she held out her palm. "Five dollars, please," she said in a singsong voice. Corey rolled her eyes and went to see if Ben had touched any of his tray.

That wasn't the end of it, either. A week or so later Dudley started saying that a wing was nothing, no test at all, as easy to eat as cellophane. "The question is," he said, "can you manage the entire beast." They argued about this for several days, and the price climbed from twenty dollars to fifty. But by the time Denise said she might do it (just maybe, was how she put it), the locusts had disappeared. They had vanished while everybody was looking the other way, and when Denise and Dudley went out hunting they found just a few half-desiccated corpses. The air was unsettlingly quiet, and Calvert was hunched on the flagstones looking as mystified and bereft as if he had lost his last friend.

She was taking her usual morning walk when her eyes chanced to fall upon the most peculiar sight. There in the yard with the privet hedge (she didn't know the people's names; they were new folks from out of town) was what appeared to be a statue of the Madonna. "My goodness," she said out loud. Then she looked around to make certain no one had overheard her talking to herself.

Were these people Catholic, or what? Up till now, the neighborhood had been so restrained and tasteful. She patted the pockets of her cardigan, hunting her bifocals, which she should have been wearing all along except the nosepiece pinched. She put them on and blinked and then laughed. It wasn't a Madonna; it was a freshly planted tree swaddled in white cheesecloth. She was getting as blind as a bat.

While she was standing there a young woman came out of the house, click-clicking in high-heeled shoes. She was a professional sort, wearing a suit and carrying a briefcase. "Morning," she called to Corey.

Corey said, "I was just . . ."

But then it seemed too much trouble to explain that whole misunderstanding about the Madonna, so all she said was, "I see you've covered up your little tree."

"Japanese cherry," the woman said. "Yes, my husband thought we ought to. Some people say when a tree is that young it can suffer a lot of damage."

"Damage?" Corey asked.

"From the seventeen-year locusts; you know they slit the bark when they lay their eggs."

"Oh, yes," Corey said.

Then the woman opened her car door and got in, and Corey walked on.

She was supposed to exercise a minimum of twenty minutes each day—strict orders from her doctor after she'd suffered her latest heart attack—but this morning she quit early and went home, not striding briskly as she usually did but strolling thoughtfully. At the edge of her own yard she clutched her skirt in front of her and bent at the knees to pick up the paper. She opened it out as she walked toward the door. Nicaragua, Persian Gulf . . . Her eyes went to the top of the page for the capsule weather report. It was going to be warm and sunny. Thank the Lord. She was so tired of wearing this everlasting cardigan.

When she opened the door there was a sense of movement someplace toward the rear of the house, but she knew by now it was nothing; only the too-tidy, too-quiet, uninhabited rooms suddenly jerking awake again. In the kitchen she set the tea-kettle to boil and poured herself a bowl of bran flakes. "Milk," she said, heading toward the fridge. Then the telephone rang. She crossed the room to lift the receiver. "Hello?"

"Mom?"

It was Virginia, making her usual check-up call. Corey felt behind her for a stool and sat down. She said, "Morning, sweetie."

"How're you feeling?" Virginia asked.

"Why, fine! Just fine! How are *you*?"

"Did you have your walk?"

"Yes, I just now came back from it," Corey said.

"Twenty full minutes?"

"Oh, at least," Corey said, because Virginia was one of those people you always had to be humoring and reassuring. "It was a lovely day out and I just had a fine time," she said. An image of the little tree came to her mind. She considered telling the joke on herself about the Madonna but decided, once again, that it was too much trouble, and anyhow Virginia might interpret it as some sign of infirmity. Instead she said, "Did you know the locusts are due this year?"

"Yes, I heard," Virginia said. "Elise is having a fit. She keeps asking if we can leave town till it's over."

Elise was Virginia's youngest—Corey's favorite grandchild. Corey smiled. "You should tell her how much fun you and Danny used to have," she said. "Remember how you collected them in bottles? Made them zoom around on leashes?"

"*I* did that?"

"You most certainly did."

"I don't have the faintest recollection of it," Virginia said.

Then the kettle started whistling and Corey had to hang up.

In the afternoon Elise dropped by. She often walked the five blocks from Virginia's. She said, "Did you hear about those big bugs that are coming?"

"Oh, they're not so big as all that," Corey told her.

"In the paper they looked enormous."

"They're only about this long," Corey said, and she held a thumb and forefinger two inches apart. Elise shuddered. Corey said, "And they'd never harm you. All they do is make a hubbub."

"What kind of hubbub?" Elise asked.

Corey said, "Oh . . ."

Then all at once, looking into Elise's sharp little freckled face, she felt how very odd it was that this child had not even existed the last time the locusts were here. But the thought lasted only a second. Of *course* she hadn't existed; she was barely thirteen years old. Corey said, "It's a sort of rattling sound," and she demonstrated by whirring her tongue against the roof of her mouth. It wasn't exact, but it was close enough.

As it happened, 1987's was a much heavier infestation than any of the earlier years'. Or maybe it just seemed so to Corey. Two or three times a day she slapped locusts off the screen doors with the flat of her hand ("The Locust Exit," she heard Marilyn say from long, long ago) and then stepped outside to sweep their dead and dying bodies from the sidewalk. Even those that were still alive allowed themselves to be tumbled around, pushed off the concrete, heaped in buzzing piles on the grass. She swept them from the flagstone patio and thought of how Calvert used to enjoy stalking them as a kitten. Calvert had grown up and turned into a lean, bored, grumpy tomcat and finally died of old age, but Corey could still picture his soft kitten paws batting locusts and his ears perking forward so curiously whenever they churred at him.

Mrs. Jefferson, who came on Thursdays to help with the heavy cleaning, told Corey there were no locusts whatsoever down in the inner city. "Must be it's because we don't have no trees," she told Corey. "But you know the saying, don't you?"

"What saying is that?" Corey asked.

"The locusts sticks only to neighborhoods that is rich and unreligious."

"Well, *I'm* not rich," Corey said, "and I go to church every Sunday, so what does that prove?"

"It's only a ignorant saying," Mrs. Jefferson told her.

Then why repeat it, Corey wanted to ask. But didn't.

Her eyesight was giving her fits and the ophthalmologist couldn't work her in till August, so often she just let the morning paper stay rolled in its rubber band till Elise stopped by in the afternoon and read it to her. Elise wasn't much for hard news but she read out scraps of human-interest stories, all about Princess Di and such. She read every word about the locusts, because they continued to horrify her. (Any time she stepped outdoors, she wore a head scarf. Her daily walk—or run—to Corey's was an act of heroism Corey very much appreciated.) "Listen to this," she said. "There's three separate species; you can tell them apart by the sound."

"Yes, seems to me I've heard that," Corey murmured, stirring her tea.

"Some company's put out a bumper sticker: Every Seventeen Years Is Too Often."

Corey laughed.

"A rumor's going around that scientists at Hopkins will pay a thousand dollars for a blue-eyed locust. But that's all bunk, the paper says."

"Blue-eyed! All's I've ever seen is red."

"And here in the food section—ooh! Gross!"

"What's that?"

"Recipes."

"Recipes for *locusts?*"

"You put them in a jar in the freezer in order to kill them."

"Goodness."

"Then you toast them and roll them in salt and serve them as hors d'oeuvres."

"Are you making this up?"

"It says right here in the paper! Honest! Says you can crumble them over your ice cream, too."

Corey wondered why the talk always came around to eating these creatures. Why did that cross everybody's mind? "I knew a girl who ate a wing once," she said. And at that moment Denise might have been lolling at the kitchen table with them, giggling till she squeaked and then sternly pulling down the corners of her mouth, although Corey hadn't thought of her in years and Dudley was married to a very nice woman named Laura. She sighed. Elise said, "Grandma? Are you all right?"

"Why, I'm just fine!" Corey said.

It was true what they said about sons: They left you. Dudley lived in California and Danny had moved so often that Corey sometimes had to stop and think before she could say where he was now.

By the middle of June, just when it was beginning to seem that the locusts were here to stay, they started thinning out. The nights grew quieter. Corey could turn off the air-conditioning and open the bedroom window. Elise could arrive at a normal pace—not hammering up the sidewalk with both hands clamped to her head scarf. "See there?" Corey told her. "You lived through it. They're almost gone. Next time you see a locust you'll be thirty."

"I'll never be thirty," Elise said.

Corey only smiled.

In July she went to Ocean City for two weeks with Virginia and Ted and the children, and when she came back not even the carcasses remained; only a few empty shells stuck to the tree trunks. Although once in late September, opening the double doors off the sun porch and preparing to wash their glass panes, she was startled to find a single locust clinging to one screen. But it was dead, as she discovered when she put on her bifocals and stepped closer. It was held in place only by its brittle legs, no doubt, and could have been knocked loose by the slightest tap of her fingers. For some reason, though, she let it stay. She washed the panes with newspapers dipped in hot water, the way her mother used to do, and she dried them with a chamois cloth. Then she stood for a moment gazing out at the locust before she gently swung the doors together and slid the bolts shut.

# HOSTAGE

O

*Joyce Carol Oates*

B Y   T H E   A G E   O F  fourteen Bruno Sokolov had the heft and swagger of a near-grown man. His wide shoulders, sturdy neck, dark oily hair wetted and combed sleekly back from his forehead like a rooster's crest, above all his large head and the shrewd squint of his pebble-colored eyes gave him an air unnervingly adult, as if, in junior high school, in the company of children, he was in disguise, yet carelessly in disguise. He wore his older brothers' and even his father's cast-off clothing, rakish combinations that suited him, pin-striped shirts, sweater vests, suspenders, bulky tweed coats and corduroy trousers, cheap leather belts with enormous buckles, even, frequently, for there were always deaths in those big immigrant families, mourning bands around his upper arm that gave him a look both sinister and holy, to which none of our teachers could object. He was smart; he was tough; the natural leader of a neighborhood gang of boys; he carried a switchblade knife, or was believed to do so. He had a strangely scarred forehead—in one version of the story he'd overturned a pan of boiling water on himself as a small child, in another version his mother in a fit of emotion had overturned it on him. He spoke English with a strong accent, musical, yet mocking, as if these sounds were his own invention, these queer eliding vowels and diphthongs, and he had remarkable self-confidence for a boy with his background, the son of Polish-Russian immigrants—out of bravado he ran for, and actually won, our ninth-grade presidency, in a fluke of an election that pitted our teachers' choice, a "good" boy, against a boy whom most of the teachers mistrusted, or feared. Even when Bruno Sokolov spoke intelligently in class there was an overtone of subtle mockery, if not contempt, in his voice. His grades were erratic and he was often absent from school—"family reasons" the usual excuse—and he was famous for intimidating, or harassing, or actually beating up certain of his classmates. His play at football and basketball was that of a steer loosed happily among heifers, and when, as our class president, a black snap-on bow tie around his neck, he addressed the rowdy assemblage from the stage with the aplomb and drawling ease of a radio broadcaster or a politician, shrewd eyes glittering with a sense of his own power, we felt, aroused, laughing at his jokes, a shiver of certitude, rippling among even the dullest of us like a nervous reflex through a school of fish, that we were in the presence of someone distinctive; someone of whom, however we might dislike him, we might be proud.

I didn't know him. I didn't belong to his world. Though my family lived only a block or so from his family in a neighborhood of row houses built in the 1890s and hardly renovated since that time, my grandparents had emigrated from Budapest in the early 1900s and Bruno's parents had come from Lublin, a Polish city near the Russian border, in the early 1930s, and that made a considerable difference. And I was younger than Bruno, younger than most of my classmates—I had been skipped a grade in elementary school, a source of obscure pride and shame to me—so that if he happened to glance toward me, if his squinty amused stare drifted in my direction, there was nothing, it seemed, on which it might snag. I was small, I was brainy, I was invisible. For my part I observed Bruno Sokolov scrupulously, in classes, in the school corridors, making his way down the stairs, pushing ahead in the cafeteria line, actions he seemed to perform without thinking, as if the very size of his body had to be accommodated, his needs and impulses immediately discharged. Even to be teased by Bruno Sokolov was an honor of a kind but it was not an honor casually granted, for the Sokolovs, poor as they were, crowded into their shabby row house with its rear yard lifting to a railway embankment, nonetheless took themselves seriously; they were displaced tradesmen, not Polish peasants.

The immigrants' world retained its taxonomical distinctions of class, money, power, "breeding." In America, you were hungry to move up but you had no intention of helping others, outside the family, to move up with you.

The places where imagination takes root . . . There was an oversized winter coat Bruno Sokolov wore in bad weather, Cossack-style, navy blue, with upturned collar, deep pockets, and frayed sleeves, the mere sight of which made me feel confused, light-headed, panicked. There was the back of Bruno's big head, observed slantwise from me in English class, the springy oily dark hair often separating in quills, falling about his ears, and every few weeks a fresh haircut, done at home, crude and brutal, shaved at the neck. There was the sound of his suddenly uplifted voice, ringing and abrasive, often drawling in mockery, the give-and-take, foulmouthed, of young adolescent boys, and my immediate sense of alarm when I heard it, but also my envy: a sharp stabbing envy that cut me like a knife: for of course Bruno Sokolov never spoke my name, even in derision. He gave no sign of knowing it.

The infatuation was hardly love, not even affection, for I often fantasized Bruno Sokolov dying, a violent cinematic death, and took a vengeful pleasure in it; but there was about my feeling for him that sense, common to love, of futility and wild optimism conjoined, a quickening of the pulse even at the very instant that the quickening, the hope, is checked: *No. Don't.*

Midway in the school year when we were in ninth grade Bruno's father died a strange and much talked-of death and I waited for weeks to tell Bruno how sorry I was that it had happened, approaching him, one day, in the corridor outside our homeroom, with an aggressive sort of shyness, and Bruno stared down at me with a look of blank surprise as if a voice had sounded out of the very air beside him, a voice wrongly intimate and knowing. He was taller than I by more than a head, his height exaggerated by the springy thickness of his hair and the breadth of his shoulders. The shiny-smooth skin of his scar, disappearing under his hair, was serrated and would have been rough to the touch. His eyes were heavy-lidded from lack of sleep or grief and he stared at me for what seemed a long time before saying, with a shrug of his shoulders, "Yeah. Me too." And that was all.

My heart was beating rapidly, wildly. But that was all.

Even by the standards of our neighborhood Mr. Sokolov had died an unusual death. He was a large fleshy man with deep-set suspicious eyes and bushy but receding hair that gave him a perpetually affronted look; he dressed formally, in dark tight-fitting suits with old-fashioned wide lapels, starched white shirts, dark neckties. He and two brothers owned a small neighborhood grocery with a meat counter, a real butcher's shop as my mother spoke of it, and Mr. Sokolov so dominated the store, took such edgy excitable antagonistic pride in it, that many customers, including my mother, were offended by his manner. In Bruno's father Bruno's coarse sly charm was mere coarseness; he was in the habit of issuing commands, in Polish, to his brothers, in front of customers; the neighborhood belief was that he wasn't quite "right in the head"—and certainly the dislocations of language made for constant misunderstandings, and constant misunderstandings made for what is called, clinically, paranoia, that sense that the world's very tilt is in our disfavor, and that nothing, however accidental-seeming, is accidental. Mr. Sokolov's short temper led him into arguments and even into feuds with neighbors, customers, city authorities, local police; he was tyrannical with his family—three sons, two daughters, a wife who spoke virtually no English; he was driven to fits of rage when his store was vandalized, and burglarized, and police failed to arrest the criminals, or even to give the Sokolovs the satisfaction that they were trying to find them. (All this was "Mafia"-related. It was an open secret that the small neighborhood tradesmen were being extorted or were engaged in some elaborate process of attempting to resist extortion.) Mr. Sokolov died, in fact, defending his store: he was hiding at the rear when someone broke in, and he attacked the intruder with a meat cleaver, but was himself shot in the leg, and when the man ran limping and bleeding out into the alley Mr. Sokolov pursued him with the cleaver, limping and bleeding too, and shouting wildly in Polish . . . and somehow Mr. Sokolov and the other man both disappeared. A trail of their commingled blood drops led to an intersection close by, then stopped. Police theorized that a van had been parked there, and that Mr. Sokolov was taken away in it: he was missing for several days, the object of a much-publicized local search, then his body, or rather parts of his body, began to be discovered . . . floating in the canal, carelessly buried at the city dump, tossed into the weedy vacant lot behind St. John the Evangelist Church, to which the Sokolovs belonged. The murderer or murderers were never found and twenty years later, long after Bruno Sokolov himself had died, in Korea, one of his cousins ran for mayor, and narrowly missed winning, on the strength of a passionate campaign against "organized crime" in the city.


On Saturday mornings in all but the worst winter weather I took two city buses downtown to the public library, where, in a windowless ground-floor room set aside for "young adult" readers I searched the shelves for books, especially novels, the search invested with a queer heart-stopping urgency as if the next book I chose, encased in its yellowing plastic cover, *YA* in tall black letters on its spine, might in some way change my life. I was of an age when any change at all seemed promising; I hadn't yet the temperament to conceive of change as fearful. I didn't doubt that *the* book, *the* revelation, awaited me, no matter that the books I actually did read were usually disappointing, too simplistically written and imagined, made up of characters too unswervingly good or bad to be believable. It was the search itself that excited me . . . the look and the feel of the books on their bracketed metal shelves, the smell of the room, a close, warm, stale mixture of floor wax, furniture polish, paper paste, the faint chemical scent of the middle-aged librarian's inky-black dyed hair. Sometimes the very approach to the library—my first glimpse of its Greek Revival portico and columns, its fanning stone steps—aroused me to a sickish apprehension, as if I understood beforehand that whatever I hoped to find there I would not find; or, by the act of finding it, making it my own, I would thereby lose it. The library was further invested with romance since every second or third Saturday I caught sight of Bruno Sokolov there too . . . and one day when I was sitting on the front steps, waiting for the bus, Bruno stooped over me unannounced to ask, in his oddly breezy, brotherly manner, what I'd checked out, and to show me what he had—adult science fiction by Heinlein, Bradbury, Asimov. Did he have a card for upstairs? for adult books? I asked, surprised, and Bruno said, "Sure." Another time he showed me a book with a dark lurid cover, a ghoulish face with red-gleaming eyes, Bram Stoker's *Dracula*—he hadn't checked it out of the library but had simply taken it from a shelf and slipped it inside his coat. Not stealing exactly, Bruno said, because he'd bring it back, probably. "The kind of stuff I like, it's things that make you think, y'know, the weirder the better," he said, smiling and showing big damp yellowed teeth,

"—stuff that scares you into thinking, y'know what I mean?" His eyes were heavy-lidded, his lips rather thick, the lower lip in particular; the curious scar high on his forehead gleamed with reflected light. I saw with surprise his thick stubby battered-looking fingers clutching the book, dirt-edged nails, the knuckles nicked and raw, as if he hurt himself casually without knowing what he did, or caring. Or maybe his hands were roughened from work at the grocery. Or from fighting.

"Yes," I said, looking up at him, "—I know what you mean."

I watched him walk away, my eyes pinching, following his tall figure in its forward-plunging impatient stride until he was out of sight. *Thief,* I thought. *I could turn you in.* It was only the second or third time we'd spoken together and it would be the final time. And I guessed he didn't know my name. Or even know that he didn't know.

It wasn't long afterward, on another Saturday morning, in late winter, in the library, downstairs, alone, emerging from the women's lavatory—that place of ancient toilets with chain-activated flushes, black-and-white-checked tile encrusted with decades of dirt, incongruously ornate plaster moldings—I heard someone say in a low insinuating voice, "Little girl? Eh? Little girl?—where're you going?" and was crudely awakened from my brooding trance, the usual spellbound state in which I walked about, when I was alone, in those days, dreaming not so much of Bruno Sokolov or one or another boy I knew as of the mysterious stab of emotions they aroused, the angry teasing hope they seemed to embody, and I'd just pushed through the heavy frosted-glass swinging door and saw, there, a few feet away, in the cavernous poorly lit corridor—this was in an alcove, not far from the young adults reading room—one of the hellish sights of my life: a man approaching me, smiling at me, intimate, derisive, accusatory. I had vaguely recalled this man following me down the stairs but I must have told myself, if I'd told myself anything, that he was simply headed for the men's lavatory. "Little girl—c'mon *here,*" he said, less pa-

tiently. Did he know me? Was I expected to know him? I had
seen him around the library and on the street outside, dressed
shabbily yet flamboyantly in layers of mismatched clothing,
overcoat, sweaters, shirt, filthy woollen scarf wound around his
neck, unbuckled overshoes flapping on his feet; he was one of a
number of oldish odd-looking and -behaving men who haunted
the library, in cold weather especially, spending much of the
day in the reference room, where they made a show of reading,
or actually did read, the daily newspapers, turning the pages
harshly, as if the world's events filled them with contempt.
Sometimes they dozed, or muttered to themselves, or drank
from pint bottles hidden in much-wrinkled paper bags, or forgot where they were, the precariousness of their welcome, and
addressed someone who didn't know them and who quickly
edged away. If they caused much disruption one of the librari-
ans, usually a stocky woman with pearl-framed glasses (whom
I myself feared for her air of cold authority), ushered them
outside, and shut the door behind them. Upon rare occasions
police were called but I had never actually seen a policeman
arrive.

But here, now, today, for no reason I could guess or
would ever be explained to me, one of these men had followed
me downstairs to the women's lavatory, speaking excitedly,
scolding me, now walking straight at me as if he meant to run
me down. He grabbed hold of my arm and wrestled me back
against the wall, and the things I was carrying—my little beige
leather army surplus purse, an armload of library books—went
flying. I saw his coarse-veined face above me, and his white-
rimmed rheumy mad eyes, felt his whiskers like wire brush
against my skin, and must have screamed, though I don't remember screaming, and he panted, and cursed, and spoke to me
with great urgency, now dragging me to the doorway of the
men's lavatory, where, I suddenly knew, he would assault me,
keep me hostage, kill me—there was no hope for me now. Had I
not read of such horrors hinted in the newspaper, or heard of
them, whispered, never fully articulated . . .

Yet I might have escaped my assailant, had I squirmed, ducked under his arm, twisted free. He outweighed me by more than one hundred pounds but I might have escaped him and run upstairs screaming for help except that I could not move; all the strength had drained from me. It was as if the mere touch of an adult, an adult's terrible authority, had paralyzed me.

But we were making noise, and the noises echoed in the high-ceilinged space. And then the frosted-glass window of the door to the lavatory shattered and fell in pieces around us. By now the librarian from the young adult room had emerged, and another woman was poking her head around a corner staring at us incredulously, and someone cried out for the madman to leave me alone, and the madman shouted back in a rage, and how many minutes passed in this way, or was it merely seconds, while I crouched unable to move yet trembling violently in a crook of a stranger's arm, breathing in the odors, the stench really, of his desperate being, a sharp smell of alcohol, and dirt-stiffened clothing, and I might have thought of praying, I might have thought of God, but all thoughts were struck from my brain, like shadows in a room blasted by light, and even the thought that I would be held hostage and mutilated and murdered and shamed before all the world had not the power to make me fight as I might have, and should have fought.

A number of people had gathered, but were shy of approaching us. The librarian with the pearl-framed glasses was trying to reason with my assailant, who, gripping me hard, with a kind of joy, kept saying, "No! No! No you don't—stay away!" His arm was crooked around my head, his elbow pinioning my neck, I half crouched in an awkward position, the side of my face against his coat, the rough material of his coat, and my hair bunched up fallen into my face; I did not think I was crying, for I had not the space or the breath for crying yet my face was wet with tears, my nose ran shamefully as a baby's—and all the while we swayed and lurched and staggered together, as in a comical dance, which, having begun, we could not end, for there was no way of ending, no way of escaping the corner we had backed into. Several times the word *police* was uttered and several times the madman threatened to "kill the little girl" if any police should so much as appear. Shouts and cries burst about us like birds' shrieks echoing in the passageway and then dipping abruptly to silence. My assailant had pulled me into the lavatory, the outer area of sinks and tall narrow mirrors and naked light bulbs, identical to the women's lavatory, it seemed, yet a forbidden space, and I was able to think clearly, for the first time since the madman had grabbed me, *He will have to kill me now to prove he can do it.*

And then the door was pushed open, and Bruno Sokolov appeared, crouched, unhesitating, moving swiftly—he had shoved his way past the witnesses in the corridor, paying no attention to them, drawn by the excitement, the upset, the prospect of a fight, not knowing who I was until he saw me and perhaps not even knowing then, for there wasn't time to think; in describing what happened I am trying to put into words quicksilver actions that took place within seconds, or split seconds: Bruno fierce and direct as on the basketball court when he deliberately ran down another player, pulling the madman off me, yanking him away, the two of them screaming at each other, cursing, like men who know each other well, and there was Bruno of a height with my assailant fending off the man's frenzied windmill blows, the two of them now struggling by the sinks, Bruno punching, stabbing, kicking, a blade flashing in his right hand, and blood splashing on the floor, thick sinewy worms of red splashing on the tiled floor . . . Bruno had taken out his switchblade knife, and Bruno was using it, in wide sweeping furious strokes, cursing the man, saying repeatedly, "Die! Die! Die!—shit-eating old bastard!" though the man had fallen to his knees shrieking in pain and terror, trying to shield his head with his arms. And there was Bruno in a pea-green army surplus jacket, bareheaded, sweating, crouched above him like a madman himself, his face so doughy-pale and dis-

tended in rage I would not have known it, eyes shining with
moisture, "Die! *Die!*" with each stroke of the knife . . . but
now I ran out of the lavatory and into the corridor, where
someone caught me in her arms and walked me hurriedly down
the hall to a cubicle of an office, the door shut, locked, a call
placed to the emergency room of the closest hospital, the word
*assault* uttered, and I saw it was the librarian with the pearl-
framed glasses now as solicitous of me as a mother. And I
knew I would be safe.

My assailant was a man of fifty-eight, an ex–mental patient
now living on a disability pension from the U.S. Navy in a
downtown hotel for transients. He did not die from Bruno
Sokolov's attack but he was in critical condition for some
weeks, semiconscious, and when conscious rarely coherent, unable to explain why he had assaulted me or even to recall that
he had done so. Nor did he remember the junior high school
boy who'd stabbed him with a wicked eight-inch switchblade
knife, wounding him in the chest, belly, groin, arms, and face.
His memories, such as they were, were concentrated upon late
childhood spent in a rural settlement in western Pennsylvania
half a century ago.

Following this much-publicized incident things were never the
same again for Bruno Sokolov. As a minor who had, in a sense,
behaved heroically, he was not formally charged with any
crime (possession of a deadly weapon, for instance, or "ag-
gravated assault") and naturally witnesses testified in his behalf: he had rushed into the lavatory and thrown himself on
the madman in order to save me, and then he had fought him,
nearly killing him, in self-defense. (So I testified too. So I told
everyone. Though I always knew that in the strictest sense it
wasn't true.) But a juvenile-court judge placed him on six
months' probation, during which time he was obliged to seek

psychiatric therapy and to register as an outpatient at a state psychiatric facility, and the shame of that connection so qualified the glamour of Bruno's heroism, and what, literally, he had almost done—*killed a man! stabbed an adult man to death with a switchblade!*—that, in school, he became increasingly withdrawn and sullen, even among his pals, given to unpredictable displays of temper and childish violence, and his grades sharply declined, and he had to resign his class office, and there were intervals when he simply stayed away from school, and the psychiatric therapy was extended for another six months, and there were difficulties in the Sokolov family, and Bruno ran away, tried to enlist in the army, but failed, and came back home, working in the grocery after school and on Saturdays, and through the summer, and in the autumn, in high school; it could never have been the case that this hulking moody overgrown boy might have run for, let alone won, one of the class offices, nor was he on any of the sports teams, hardly a schoolboy any longer but not a man either, bored, ironic, and truculent, out of scale in our classrooms and in our corridors, slamming his locker door shut as if he meant to break it . . . and should a textbook fall from his hand he'd be likely to give it a kick, but not out of clowning high spirits and not inviting you to laugh sharing a joke because there was no joke, only Bruno Sokolov's dangerous eyes shifting like water under wind, and then he'd be gone, no backward glance, hardly more than a tight ticlike grimace to acknowledge the tie, the bond, the secret between us, unspoken, that we were kin almost as blood relatives are kin who have virtually nothing to do with each other publicly and do not in a sense "know" each other at all, a phenomenon common with schoolchildren though perhaps not limited to them. *It's because of me,* I would think, staring after him, *what he is now—my fault.* Though at more sober moments I understood that what Bruno Sokolov had done had nothing to do with me, or no more to do with me than it had with the ex–mental patient he had nearly killed.

By sixteen Bruno Sokolov had quit school, by seventeen

he had joined the army, by eighteen he'd been shipped overseas to die within a few months at the Battle of Taegu, Korea. Pvt. First Class Bruno J. Sokolov, his photograph, tough-jawed, squinty-eyed, hopeful, in the evening paper. And the other night I dreamt of him, a boy thirty-four years dead, remembering in the dream what I'd forgotten for years that none of his friends had ever called him "Bruno" but always "Sokolov" or "Sokki"—"Sockie"—a harsh sibilant magical sound I had yearned to have the right to say, shouting it in the street as others did, and he would have turned, and he would have seen me, and he would have raised his hand in recognition. As if that might have made a difference.

# HERE IN TIME

# AND NOT

O

*Lee K. Abbott*

T HE TIMES I TOLD this story of first love while
it was going on, I screwed it up—its parts mismatched, its time
haywire as that in nightmares or its people like made-up creatures from storybooks and not the flesh and type O blood they
are in my household. I got it wrong because I did not, could
not, see them—my oldest son (about whom this mostly is), my
wife, Darlene, my littlest son Craig John—as one friend and
neighbor, Fudge Walker, says is right, which has to do with a
pal's sympathy and (so he says) a Martian's disinterest.

Fudge Walker, who is our golf pro and affects a sports-
man's view of human activity, claims love is itself a game, by
which he means that it involves risk and rewards and common
happenstance; but he's on his third wife now and tries damn
hard to look at the funny side of what can be won and lost in
love. My in-laws, who heard Buddy's story last Xmas when we
visited their ranch in Roswell, say love is a fine thing

("Hunky-dory," my jolly father-in-law's words were, "Jim dandy") and very useful, which is wisdom you evidently achieve after thirty-plus years you have no desire to look back on too suspiciously. My wife, whose own first love was a 216-pound high schooler named Wicks, doesn't say much on the subject, but there are times—when we are watching something drippy on TV or when she is tired and loose-minded from cocktails—that I suspect she is thinking of a Letter Club president more gentle than we expect all-district outside linebackers to be.

My own view—the one I arrived at joylessly in my Buick on Interstate 25 outside of Socorro, about 150 miles north of the town of Hatch where we live in New Mexico—is that first love has only a little to do with what Hallmark rhymes about, or how our glands make us hop, or what is invented to entertain the wishful thinker we now and then are; the point of first love is to hurt us, deeply and permanently.

Buddy, my son, knows this now. I saw the truth of it in his face and arms and blue eyes one night last week after he'd broken up with his girl friend.

"It will get better," I said, which was one overused line that occurred to me. I told him, yes, that he'd laugh about this one day, that he'd survive—all the lines that are standard and important, parent to child.

"I don't want to talk about it," he said.

We were at my kitchen table, me reading the *Sun News* to find out how dumb some Americans had been that day, and him flipping through the tenth-grade mathematics he's supposed to be sharp enough to master. Polynomials were not on his mind, I could tell. Rather, he was wrought up with bitterness and grief, his brain collapsed sideways and not in any way ready for the silly $x$'s and $y$'s numbers sometimes are.

"It hurts like hell," he said finally. "Is that what you want to hear?"

. . .

Her name is Stacy and she became Buddy's girl friend during the fall last year, when he was an entirely adequate shooting guard for the Alameda Junior High School Falcons. Though nothing like my own first love—Leonna Allen, now a registered nurse who lives in Lubbock, Texas—Stacy was as perfect and sure of herself as every first love appears to be; and, as I have told Buddy, he went for her as I, in eleventh-grade history, went for Leonna Allen—which, in the moon-June-swoon poetry I learned, is described as tumbling and falling and being, well, rent with life. Something opens up in you, I have decided. A vessel, or a cavity, or an organ, and for a while thereafter you are a rocking-chair philosopher who sees significance in all the objects and rigamarole and ideas you bump into day by day by day. Sofas have meaning, as do what is eaten by the two of you and how the weather whirls. Everything is secret, and you are made so strong—by words and touch and smell—that you wonder why you were so weak without it.

That's what Leonna Allen did to me. Tall (Stacy is medium) and thin (Stacy is thicker through the shoulders) and quiet (Stacy is, like me, a blabbermouth), Leonna sat behind me in Mrs. Sutherland's class, and one day she tapped me on the back to ask me to name again the British kings and queens whose order we'd studied; and suddenly—there is no other word that recollects the thunderclap love is—I was absolutely smitten. My past (which had my father and his heart attacks, and my mother and her alcoholism) vanished completely; and my future (which has come to have property and wealth) seemed impossible. I had only what Darlene calls an eternal moment: electric and weird, physical as fistfight.

In the old story this is, Leonna Allen did not love me back. She loved Rodney Tate, a senior with a car and pocket money and, from my view, nothing remotely intellectual on his mind.

"What happened to him?" Buddy asked at a basketball game.

Rodney Tate had gone to Vietnam, I thought.

"He died, right?"

(No, I was able to answer the other day, Rodney Tate did not die, for he resides now in Houston and is himself married to a woman with a cheery telephone voice and manners enough to humor someone like me pestering about the past.)

"Did you hate him?" Buddy asked.

Unlike now, when it is possible, even healthy, to loathe the cheaters who govern and disappoint us or the bad guys who maim and murder and violate the rule of innocence we ought to live by, I hated no one. Or I hated—which is the bottom half of passion, I think—only me, particularly that me who traipsed after Leonna Allen like a scrawny, milky-eyed hound dog looking for food. I drove by her home when I could, night and day; or I'd beg my friends, Jimmy Bullard and Mike Runyan, to drive me by so I could see which lights were hers and if, from the signs a house can give, she would ever love me. I even gave her my letter sweater with the big red-and-blue H I earned for being a good-humored duffer on a golf team of bookworms and two kids who didn't make the swim club.

"I can't do this, Archie," she said. "You're sweet to ask, but it wouldn't be right. I have a boyfriend."

I had lugged it to school in a fancy box, and it had no meaning if she did not wear it.

"Honest, I understand," I told her. "What about when the weather gets cold?"

She accepted it, I think now, because she appreciated if not the sweater itself, certainly the feeling it stood for. She respected it as I, and the folks I intend to line up behind in the hereafter, respect the symbols that are hereabouts important: wedding bands, the starchy collar Reverend Ellis wears, the badge my old buddy George Toomer has for being sheriff—all the things smart-asses in the big world giggle at and have figured out how to make money from.

Buddy had symbols, too. Last year, he gave record albums to Stacy, U2 and Tears for Fears and Hoodoo Gurus, whose lyrics talked about the place he lived in and were themselves the sentences he felt. On her birthday in September, he gave her a Longines watch, whose purchase he'd mowed lawns and caddied for. It only told time—no special features like dates or what hour it is in Moscow—but it stood for something: for why he used Jade East cologne and why he kept his room more picked up than usual and why he wouldn't let anyone but his mother trim his hair. It wasn't sentimentality, which is what dummies say emotion is; it was sentiment, which is the opening and closing of you and the marvel that anything about you—your hands or sloppy legs—works and maybe gets better.

The day after he bought the watch, I tried to discuss this observation with him while we fixed a window in the garage. For five minutes I went on with the oooo-la-la and dizziness these feelings were. "Ain't it grand?" I asked. "Don't you feel like a million bucks?"

Buddy gave me a look that came from the bottom of him: "C'mon, Dad, leave me alone."

With his hair flopped over one eye and five pimples on his cheeks, he looked too young for the adventure he was on.

"I can tell you what to watch for," I said.

He shook his head. "Maybe later, okay? Not now."

So the window was repaired and the watch delivered, and I got to observe—as maybe Rodney Tate had observed me—and wait.

Love turns you into a son of a bitch. What I did not see in me years ago, but what became clear in the example that was my son, is that love—the weight and density it is, even the private lingo it has—shifts and twists the world away: time becomes wretched, topsy-turvy and wrong; nothing about you fits; even our gizmos—the stove, the car, the TV—fail to do what they should. You are exiled and cross-hearted, hiking uphill when everyone else you see is running down. My own father, who is dead and probably golfing in the dry purgatory he believed in, said he came close one time to beating the holy stuffings out of me in the days first love made me brutish and proud.

"For your own good," my father said after this incident ended. "You'll thank me one day."

In history, this happened two weeks after Kennedy was killed. I was sixteen, my father sixty, and on the Saturday I am concerned with we were alone in our living room (the one, fittingly, I now own and into which my son only goes to pout in the darkness). My father was practicing his putting stroke, sending ball after ball across the carpet toward a water glass he'd put in the dining room. "It's Red Mather on the eighteenth green," he was saying, whispering as if there were ten million in TV land to hear him. "This for the Masters and lasting goddamn fame." He had a match in an hour and was dressed in a fashion a certain lovestruck youngster had no tolerance for: white Nutonic spikes, slacks the green that garbage trucks come in, a yellow shirt I have dreamt about once or twice.

"The crowd is hushed," my father was saying. "You can hear a you-know-what drop, you know?"

For too long he stood over his putts, serious as a surgeon, and for too long I listened to one click after another. I was waiting for Leonna to call; we'd planned to drive to the new mall in Las Cruces thirty miles away, and I wanted to be with her, not in my living room watching my daddy pretend he was Orville "Sarge" Moody (just as, in more recent times, Buddy has wanted to be with Stacy and not on the couch listening to his own father pretend he was wise like "Dear Abby").

I could hear everything that day (which is only one sense love sharpens): Ugg Mackey's collie dog yapping, a man on KOBE radio saying who Oswald was, my own heart going clomp-CLOMP. I had no place to put my hands, or my feet. I could not read the *Life* magazine in my lap, or make real its wild full-page pictures. Yes, I checked the phone—once, twice, three times—and dashed outside to look up the street for the signals nature owes those in love. But I could see only flaws: tarnished silver, a crack in the marble coffee table, a portrait of us that made us look crooked and a little bit like criminals.

"I've had just about enough of you," my daddy said at last.

This could have been the man in the moon yammering, and I felt a need to be silent and wide-eyed.

"C'mere," he said. "Sit your butt down."

He had the mayhem-filled face of the welterweight he'd been at Dartmouth College a million years ago, so I did as ordered.

"When are you going to grow up?"

Those were his words—which were enough like mine, that time we were fixing the window, to be scary—but they blew by me that day as dumb as the wind. I was concentrating, instead, on the thwack thwack his putter made in his hand, and how he seemed to be taking up most of the light in the universe.

"This won't do," my daddy was saying. "This is how a stray dog behaves. Next you'll be outdoors bawling."

I regarded him the way a human regards a bird that can chatter a paragraph or two of English. There was a defense I tried to make—a justifying of my ups and downs, a speech that accounted for the special chemicals and hopes running in me—but my father wasn't hearing any of it. The lawyer in him was going, wearing a path back and forth in front of me. There was stuff I needed to know, he was saying. The mechanics of boy and girl. Pubic hair and puberty. About how to bait your hook, which was his semiwise metaphor for the catching and keeping of love. Yelling and pacing, he drew me pictures of the uproar I stood in. "It is war," he said. "It is commerce," he said. And more: hubbub and sweet talk and slack-wittedness and shilly-shally that topples you away from goodness.

He informed me of the running down love was, the hollow clank you notice when it one day stops. It was a building up, he said, and a tearing down. Love, the thing he was talking

about and the way he was talking about it, was only jibber-
jabber, a language we either learn or shut our goddamn
mouths about.

"You understand?" he said.

His face was red, his putter in the air like a war club, and
my head went "yes" for one solid minute, I swear.

"Good," he said, and at the end of a special scene in my
life, my father brought that putter down, yanked it out of the
air in a fury and whacked off a corner of our marble table the
size of an emperor's dinner dish.

"Now, that," he began, giving me the wink he was famous
for, "is something real to fret about."


For the three months after Buddy fell in love, instead of butting in and checking up, I kept watch over the steady rise and
fall of my here and now. I pushed my memories aside, as we
push aside questions we are yet too boneheaded to answer, to
attend to the ordinariness of bill paying and to what is normal
come-and-go in our town of five thousand. For Xmas, I took an
Electra out of my showroom and parked it in my driveway for
Darlene to ooohhh over; on New Year's, a party at Tommy
Gaddy's ranch, I danced an ancient cha-cha-cha with Harriet
Feltman and received for my efforts a knee sprain and two
dozen hostile expressions from her husband Marv; in February
I fired my disk brakes expert for stealing tools and for using
marijuana in the storeroom behind Parts. For three months, I
say, I kept out of my mind any thoughts of Stacy and Buddy
and the modern reflections they were of my long-gone Leonna
and the distant me.

"You're a sick man," Fudge Walker told me more than
once during this time. "What you need is a good drunk and
five hours of golf."

When I was small and only absorbed with the idea of the
rooting-tooting cowboy I wanted to be one day, my mother
(this was much before my father shipped her up to Las Vegas

to live with folks addicted to glue and pills and laundry pencils
and vodka) used to insist that memory was a door—"a goddamn portal," her exact phrase was—to a room we entered like
burglars or the otherwise naughty-minded. "You don't dare
stay too long," she said. It is spookhouse, she said, and crypt
and Oz and nailed-up closet—an idea she inherited, it is clear,
from her lanky insurance-selling father and the oddball Louisi-
ana swampland Presbyterianism he practiced. It is corny, I
know, cheap as anything secondhand sold to us as new; but for
me, as for all who accept cheapness as one fact of life, it works.

The other day, for example, in my office, my shades
drawn, my phone disconnected, what business I had (a new car
inventory, mostly) swept into a corner, I entered that room,
through the "goddamn" it is, a zillion times. I saw, and won
again, my first serious fistfight (with the offensive dufus Phil-
lip Trafton was); I saw the first car I drove, a Ford Fairlane
500, and another I, drunk, raced off a highway overpass; I saw
a stubbly cottonfield I lay in during a graduation party and
awakened again to the sight of my pal Les Fletcher hanging
out of the top of his convertible and steering with his bare feet;
I saw, and felt again, the important breasts of Mary Jo
Griggs, and watched her pat my hands as if to say I'd survive
the need of her. Most important, I stumbled again into that
storehouse my damaged mother grew moony over and saw,
shiny and real as my own bald head, what is now a three-year-
old image of Leonna Allen, Texas registered nurse.

This was at the Pan-American Center at New Mexico
State University, a good university whose not-good basketball
team was—on the night I peeked into again—taking on the
dribblers and giants from the University of the Pacific. Buddy
was with me, partly overwhelmed by the ten thousand scream-
ers around us, and on the way back from the concession stand
I saw, and was frozen by the coincidence that fate is, this
Leonna I once upon a time loved. "Lordy," I said. "Wait."
This is an old moment, like the noisy minutes in a bad movie or
the har-de-har-har of the community theater that Darlene

regularly drags me to. I want to say we made contact—through eyes and beating hearts?—but we did not. I want to say a spotlight or two shone on us, but they did not. Instead, I found my way back to my seat, my feet like a puppet's, my head whipping left and right trying to find her and not, at the same time, dump my cherry Coke in the lap of a fanatic Aggie.

"What happened to you?" Buddy said when I sat down.

On the court, California's black men were clobbering ours. In the stands, the fans were all worked up and angry, but higher up and to the right, maybe where all crackpot visions are, was flesh and hair and voice I once thought worth crying for.

"Leonna Allen," I said, pointing.

Buddy gave a look-see. He appeared serious. Then baffled. Then blank, like a fish. He'd heard the name before, but it was only a sound, like Zulu to an Eskimo, and not full of power and time and pain. So I told him.

Right there, amidst the riot defeat is and at a volume inconsistent with the privacy shame is, I gave him my history: the beginning and petered-out end it had, the songs I played for her (which were Lesley Gore and whiny as the pound-bred puppy Buddy currently has), the barbells I lifted to puff me up, the rented dinner jacket (with cummerbund) I wore to cotillion. Because these events and feelings are as much features of my permanent record as the numbers America makes you get and the names your parents have, I dumped the whole scribbled-on folder of me in front of him: the one sister-brother kiss we had in the marriage booth at the FFA fair, the shine her hair was, the singsong hello she had, what the bottom of me did when she made clear that Archie Freeman Mather was not at the center of the circle she was drawing. Then, winded by the effort, I asked, "You understand?"

He was bored. He was only book-smart. He was twelve. His old man was lunatic.

"Sure," he said. "Geez," he said. "Uh, thanks," he said.

And that would be all, I knew. Until his own life had been

split, or burned up, or razed by the necessary catastrophe love is.

And so, after I came out of that unhappy funhouse of memory and before I discovered on I-25 what I was truly meant to know and to say about Buddy's first love and mine, I screwed up. I sought, at fitting times and not, to put my two cents in. At the dinner table, as the green beans went round and the conversation became the high-octane chitchat we enjoy, I'd hear a comment about women—or failure, or what an elected dingdong in Santa Fe had said—and, given the two-plus-two-equals-five thinking I had, I'd see a way, wrong as cussing in church, of moving our talk to the subjects of youth and love. I'd sputter, drop my fork with a bang, hum as the self-important do; and Darlene, former Zeta Tau pledge chairperson and Dona Ana County rodeo champion, would raise her tough eyes to mine and say, "Don't." In the TV room, hearing Hollywood's description of the battleground between boys and girls, I'd sit up like a judge, slam my mouth into gear; and my wife, with her master's degree in sociology and yellow belt in karate, would say, "Archie, don't." I heard that word, whispered and wailed, in the bathroom, in my smoky den, in the living room, on the patio. It reached me by phone, by note taped to the refrigerator, and once by Bucky Gridley (who approached me at the Fourth of July picnic to say, "Darlene says don't"). I even heard it one Saturday in August when Buddy and I were in the garage tending to the riding mower: I had stopped, a look to the eyes that is three-quarters schoolmarm; I had thought to say, once and for all, Whoa and Stop and Watch Out.

Then Darlene hollered at me. "Don't you dare," she said. She was indoors, at the kitchen sink, her face half out the window, and my eyes went first to Buddy, who was greasy-fingered and sure enough happy, and then to the horizon, which was flat and empty and dark. "Archie Freeman Mather," she exploded. A dishcloth was waving. "Why don't you just leave him alone? He doesn't need to hear from you right now."

So I told other people, the near and not-so-near to me. I told Fudge Walker when we were at the Las Cruces Country Club—specifically the nineteenth hole, which is golf for booze and bullshit—about how Buddy would have his heart ripped from him by Stacy Jean Toomer, first girl friend. I told Fudge Walker, who was sloshed enough to listen and mumble affirmatively, about Buddy and the clumsy, inevitable two-step the end of his love would be. There would be phone calls and silences, eyeballs that flipped in and out of focus. In one week there would be giddiness, jokes whose humor rises from the belly of us; in the next, there would be that comic book stormcloud that forms over the head in ugly times. It was an old story, I said, the ooooppps and aaarrgghhh of it, her lines and actions as familiar to me as his.

It was February, and I was talking to Harvey and Ella Sweem, who'd come in for a Skylark; then it was March, and I was telling Billie Jean Maxwell at the Farmers and Merchants Bank. "It's happening," I said, not at all pleased to be right. "You watch and see."

When it was time for woe, I say, woe came. As did—like the order A, B and C are—merriment and messiness and calamity. Buddy charged out and crept back, dragged out and hurtled back. In a manner that did not surprise, he was yappy and tight-lipped, generous as a poor man and stingy as a banker. It was, as my dead father liked to say, frick followed by frack. *If This,* I remembered from the philosophy I had dropped at SMU, *Then That.*

Then the end announced itself. This was a Wednesday, in the late evening. Darlene was in our bedroom, reviewing the work she does for our county welfare office, Craig John was asleep and I was in my paper-strewn study, trying to see how much money I had. I heard the door and Buddy's footsteps and then my own voice say, "Well," which is one idiot word that occurs when knowledge comes our way.

Because, for all purposes practical in the melodrama this

is, I was my son himself—just removed from him by years and
more brooding—I knew what was on his mind. As I had been
when Leonna Allen directed me to step over yonder, please, and
never come back, Buddy, except for one or two nasty thoughts,
had shut down. He was saying "God damn" to himself. And
"Christ." And "Jesus H." He was outraged—he'd been bush-
wacked, cheated and stomped. "Shit," he was saying. "Damn."

The kitchen door went crash, and I heaved up, told my
legs to get moving. Halfway to the garage, where Buddy was
heading, his Schwinn bicycle was flopped over, and I was going
past a sweater I should have pulled on. My head was half here
in time, half not. Part of me—the part that votes yellow-dog
Democrat and tends to the buy-and-sell of living life—was
watching another part, that which was itself once young and
silly and in a hurry to grow up.

"Don't come in," Buddy said, when he heard my hand on
the knob. "Just go away. You have nothing to say to me."

In there were tools it takes years to get the sense of, and
trunks, and junk—bottles, rags, tin cans, stuff it takes three
moves to accumulate. He was still, I knew, maybe studying
himself, maybe taking hold of the anger in him.

"I know what you're going to do," I said.

Between us was a standard hollow-core door, nothing at
all to jam your fist through when everything has let you down.

"Yeah, you know everything," he said. "Just go away."

I'd done the same thing, I told him. Only it was my bedroom door, the one he slams when there is something personal
to be tended to.

"So what?" he said. "Big deal."

Overhead was darkness, black upon black upon black, and
way off a dog was howling to come in.

"You could bust a knuckle," I said, trying to be sensible.
"Maybe your wrist."

A light had gone on inside, and the scrape of a boy's feet
setting themselves.

"That means six weeks in a cast," I said. "No baseball."

"Who cares?" he snapped.

One of us had to do something, I told myself. A gesture had to be made, so I made it. I turned away, reminded myself where my wallet was, my car keys, how best to get to the hospital. I took one step, as if wobbling on a high wire, and another, all the while arranging what I'd say, in a minute or two, to Darlene about the connection between self-mangling and the excellent condition love is.

I like stories with morals, stories that say, "Here is the line and you may not cross it"; stories, written by anyone in the anywhere we live in, that make clear the hole the inner life pokes in the outer. Primitive though it is, I like stories with folks you can root for (as you root for those in your own towns to be heroes and heroines). I like strength for the strong, ruin for the ruinous. Yet now—it is Thursday, P.M. (mountain time), 1987—your story teller can't say what it is he knew when these events were, well, fresh and not so picked over by memory. Time moves not forward, I think, but round and round and round, until, when the heart is involved, there is no now, or then; there is only turmoil with you in the center of it, like a stick.

I had my own end, in the backasswards report this is, well before Buddy put his fist in my garage door. I had been in Albuquerque, at a convention, and was on my way home. Ours was the postcard spectacle of sunshine New Mexico is the standard for, high heavens that discourage those words the "Range" song sings of. On my radio was the polite redneck music I go for, what can be yodeled through the nose about betrayal and getting caught. For a time, as I drove south, I had the feeling that those passing by me, high speed or not, were, whatever their station or point of view, my friends. I'd wave, or tip the Hibs and Hannon ten-gallon hat I wear out of town, and in answer would come a tractor-trailer's toot or what tourists from New Jersey think is a buckaroo's howdy.

As forward-feeling as are winning gamblers, I took note of my age, which is forty, and accepted the content I am. I thought of the fat I ought to lose, and the sweat involved in losing it. I thought of striped ties to look dandy in, and ostrich boots that take eight months to make, and how charitable the outlook of the homeward bound is. And then, nodding over the notion of how much more than tissue and gore and skeleton we are, I thought of Buddy and what terrible event awaited him.

The floor fell out of me then, plank by plank by plank. Stunned—is there another word that says how dumb we wiseguys can instantly become?—I took the one, two, three deep breaths my mother said were vital in crisis. "Geez," I said, the same expression my son used the night he heard my confession in Aggie land. "Well, I'll be damned," I said and pinched myself wide awake to pull off the road like a responsible citizen. I switched the radio off, put my car in neutral, cranked down a window, tried to light a cigarette. Left and right and front and back of me stretched the desert I like so much, a wrinkled, scrub-dotted outland not so inhospitable as many imagine. Ahead, down a dip or two, lay the towns of Socorro and Truth or Consequences, and way, way off—where it was already less light—was my home in Hatch. I was thinking of Buddy, the skinny he is and the too tight jeans he wears. He was in love now, I was thinking, and would not be one day. He was happy now, and would not be one day.

"Lordy," I said. It was a word which had no meaning, just a sound to be made in a big, empty place. I had a thought about love, which made no sense, and another, about the pieces to be picked up afterwards. "Okay," I told myself. "Five minutes," I said. I had a cigarette to smoke and one or two more facts to know, then I'd put my car in gear, stop thinking, and go home.

# THE FARTHER

# YOU GO

O

*Richard Russo*

**I**'VE CUT ONLY A couple of swaths when I have
to shut the damn thing down because of the pain. It's not dag-
ger pain, but deep, rumbling nausea pain, the sort that seems
to have as its source the center of my being. There are those
who think that a man's phallus *is* the center of his being, but I
have not been among them until now.

Inside the house Faye has heard me shut the mower off
and come out onto the deck to see why. She shades her eyes
with a small hand, scout fashion, to see me better, though the
sun is behind her. Ours is a large yard and I'm a long way off.
"What's wrong?" she calls.

I'd like to tell her. It's a question she's asked off and on
for thirty years, and just once I'd like to answer it. "My dick
is throbbing," I'd like to call out, and if we had any neighbors
within hearing, I believe I would, so help me. But there are no

neighbors. We've bought the two adjacent lots to prevent them. Regrets? I've had a few. I mow their yards and my own.

"Nothing," I call to Faye. It's my standard line. Nothing is wrong. Go ahead, try to find something wrong. If something were wrong, I would say so, I constantly assure her, always amazed at how this lie springs to my lips. I have never in my life told her when anything was wrong, and I have no intention of telling her about my throbbing groin now. She has already spent a thousand dollars we didn't really have on a riding mower because of the doctor's insistence that I not overdo after the operation. It has not occurred to her that, to a man recovering from prostate surgery, sitting on top of a vibrating engine may not be preferable to gently guiding a self-propelled push mower. I cannot blame her for this failure of imagination because it had not occurred to me either until I was aboard and in gear.

I start up the mower again and cut a long loop back to the base of the deck, stopping directly below her and turning the engine off for good.

"You're finished?"

"You can't tell?" I say looking back over the yard. I appear to have cut a warning track around a fenceless outfield. I'm now sitting on home plate.

"Why are you perspiring?"

It's true. There is autumn in the air, and no reason for me to be sweating, cast about as I might. "It's a beauty," I say, slapping the steering wheel affectionately. "Worth every penny. How much was it again?"

"I just got off the phone with Julie," she says.

This does not sound good to me. Our daughter seldom calls without a reason. She and her husband Russell owe us too much money to enjoy casual conversation. They are building a house half a mile up the road from our own. "Where?" I said last year when Faye broke the news that they'd purchased the lot. "Here? In Connecticut? In Durham?" I was certain that some trust had been violated. Could it be that we had loaned them the money without a distance clause in the contract? We had been prudent enough to ensure against neighbors on either side, but we were so focused on the idea of strangers that we failed to take into account relatives. Another failure of imagination.

Faye bends over the railing and holds out to me a delicate hand, which I take, half grateful, half suspicious. "I know this is the last thing in the world you need, but I think you should go over there. Today," she adds, in case there is any doubt in my mind that whatever this is about, it is serious.

"What," I say.

Now that she has my attention, she is reluctant to do anything with it. She is looking for the right way to say it, and there is no right way. I can tell that by looking at her.

"Julie says . . . that Russell hit her."

I am shocked, though I have known for some time that their marriage is in trouble. To make matters worse, Russell has recently quit a good job for what he thought would be a better one, only to find that the several large loans needed to start the project he's to direct have not been approved as expected. It could be weeks, he admits. Months.

"I'm not sure I believe Russell would hit Julie," I tell Faye.

"I do," she says in a way that makes me believe it too. When my wife is dead sure, she is seldom wrong, except where I am concerned.

"What am I supposed to do. Hit him?"

"She just wants to see you."

"I'm right here."

"She thinks you'll be angry."

"I *am* angry."

"That she didn't come to see you in the hospital. She feels guilty."

"She didn't know I'd be grateful?"

"She thought you'd be hurt. Like you were. Like I was."

"Thirty years we've been married and still you confuse me with yourself," I tell her. "I didn't want Julie at the hospital. I didn't want *you* at the hospital. Heart surgery might have been a different story."

"There are times I think you could use heart surgery. A transplant maybe. This is our daughter we're talking about."

"One of our daughters," I correct her. "The other one is fine. So is our son."

"So is Julie."

I would like to believe her, but I am not so sure. Before the wedding I had wanted to take Russell aside and ask him if he knew what he was doing. In time Julie might have turned out as well as the other two, but she wasn't ripe, somehow, it seemed to me. Not ripe for the colleges she'd been in and out of. Not ripe for a husband. Not ripe for adult life.

And I am not ripe for intervention. My daughter may not be an adult, but she's been acting like one—getting married, having houses built, borrowing money. And I don't, on general principle, like the idea of trespassing once people have slept together, because they know things about each other that you can't, and if you think you're ever going to understand what's eating them you're a fool, even if one of them happens to be your own daughter. Especially if one happens to be your own daughter.

"We cannot tolerate physical abuse," Faye says. "You know I'm fond of Russell and it may not be all his fault, but if they are out of control, we must do something. We could end up wishing we had."

I would still like to argue the matter. Even as Faye has been speaking I have been marshaling semivalid reasons for butting out of our daughter's marriage. There are half a dozen pretty good ones, but I would be wasting my breath.

"Julie thinks they should separate. For a while, anyway," Faye says. "That makes sense, to me. She wants to insist, and she wants you to be there."

I am not thinking of Julie now, but of my own parents. If

I want your help I'll call you in, I remember telling my father
in the early days of my own marriage when we had no money
and things seemed a lot worse than they were. Maybe it is that
way with Julie and Russell. Maybe things seem worse than
they are. I wish for that to be the case, almost as fervently as I
wish I had not been called in. But I have been.

I start out on foot. I tell Faye that the exercise will do me
good, but in truth I don't want to sit on top of another motor.
Julie and Russell's house is only half a mile up the road and
until the operation I was running two miles a day, though usually in the opposite direction. Seeing their house rise up out of
the ground has been an unsettling experience, though for some
time it did not occur to me why, even when I saw the frame.
Only when the two decks, one front, one back, were built did it
dawn on me why they have used my contractor. My daughter is
building my house.

"Well of course they are," Faye said when I told her
about my suspicion. "You should be flattered."

"I should?" I said, wondering exactly when it was that I
stopped being the one to see things first.

"Theft being the sincerest form of flattery. Besides,
they're a mile away. It's not like people are going to think it's
a subdivision."

"Half a mile," I said. "And what bothers me is that Julie
would *want* to build our house."

Their mission tile is already visible, but halfway up the
hill I have to stop and let the nausea pass. Off to the side of the
road there is a big flat rock that looks like a feather bed. I go
over to it and stretch out. It takes every ounce of willpower I
have not to unzip and check things out. Instead, I lie still and
watch the moving sky. When I finally stand up again, I am not
sure that I can make it the rest of the way, though this is the
same hill I was running up a few months ago when I was
fifty-one. Now I am fifty-two and scared that maybe I won't be

running up any more hills. The doctors have told me they got
what they were after, but I am aware of just how little similar
assurances meant in my father's case. After the chemotherapy,
they sent him home with a clean bill of health and he was dead
in two weeks.

Nevertheless, I do make the top of the hill. Up close, the
house looks like a parody, but that's not Julie's and Russell's
fault. They have simply run out of money, their own, ours, the
bank's. The grounds are not landscaped and the winding drive
is unpaved. There are patches of grass and larger patches of
dirt. Not wanting to ring the doorbell, I go around to the back,
hoping to catch sight of Julie in the kitchen. I want to talk to
her first, before Russell, though I have no idea what I will say.
I am hoping that in the last half hour she will have changed
her mind about inviting me into their lives. Maybe I will see
her in the window and she will flash me a sign. I wonder what
a go-back-home sign looks like. I'm willing to interpret almost
anything as meaning that I should go back home.

When I get around back, I remember there are no steps
up to the deck, which is uniformly three feet off the ground all
the way around. I am looking around for a makeshift ladder
when Julie comes out onto the deck, closing the sliding glass
door behind her. Except for not knowing how to join her up
there, my plan is working.

"I didn't think you were coming," she says.

"Hand me one of those deck chairs," I tell her.

She does and I step up onto it. When she offers a hand, I
take that too, my other one on the rail to hoist myself up. Julie
is wearing a peasant blouse and when she leans over I see that
she is wearing no brassiere. There have been other times when,
against my will, I have been subjected to the sight of Julie's
bare breasts, and I wonder if her casual attitude toward them
might be one of the things between her and Russell. He may
not like the idea of his friends becoming so intimately ac-
quainted with her person over the onion dip. According to
Faye, Karen, our oldest, has always kept one lone brassiere

around the house for our visits. There is much to be said for hypocrisy.

"He's asleep on the sofa," Julie says. "Neither of us slept much last night. He finally zonked."

She smiles weakly and when she turns full face, I get a better view of her eye, which sports a mouse. The cheek beneath is swollen, but so is the other, perhaps from crying. Her complexion, which a year ago finally began to clear up, is bad again. Suddenly, she is in my arms and I can't think about anything but the fact that she is my daughter. I'm not going to be much good at blaming Russell, but at least I am certain where my loyalties must be, where they have always been.

Finally, she snuffs her nose and steps back. "I've gotten some of his things together. He can pack them himself."

"You're sure about this?"

"I know I should be the one to tell him . . ."

"But you want me to," I finish for her. "Stay out here then."

She promises, snuffs again. I go in through the sliding door.

I know right where to find Russell. It's my house they're living in, after all, and their sofa is right where ours is. Russell, in jeans and a sweatshirt, is sitting up and rubbing his eyes when I come in. Oddly enough, he looks glad to see me.

"Hank," he says. "You don't look so hot."

"You're the first to notice," I tell him. He wants to shake hands and I see no reason not to.

"I shouldn't be sleeping in the daytime," he says with what sounds like real guilt.

Or punching my daughter, I consider saying. But there is no need to, because it's beginning to dawn on him that my unexpected appearance in his living room is not mere happenstance. He peers out through the kitchen window. Julie's blond head alone is visible on the deck outside.

"So," he says. "You're here to read me the riot act."

I am suddenly aware of just how absurd the situation is. "Russell," I say. "I'm here to run you out of town."

"What do you mean?"

"I mean I'm going to give you a lift to the airport."

"You can't mean that."

"Russell, I do."

A car pulls up outside and we both look to see who it is, probably because whoever it is will upset the balance of our conflict. One of us will have an ally. I do not expect it to be Faye, but that's who it is, and when Russell sees, his face falls, as if my wife's mere presence has convinced him that I am fully vested and authorized to run him off his own land.

When Faye rings the bell, I open the door and tell her to go around back and join Julie. She wants to know how things are going. I say I just got here. How could I have just got here, she wants to know. I tell her to go around back.

"This is nuts," Russell says.

There's nothing to do but agree with that, and I do, but I tell him that Julie has gathered some of his things and that he should go pack them. Russell looks like he can't decide whether to cry or fly into a rage, but to my surprise he does what he's told.

When he's gone, I realize that with Julie and Faye out back, I have no one to talk to and nothing to do. It seems wrong to turn on the TV or browse through their books. I can hear Russell in the closet in one of the bedrooms. I figure he's looking for either a suitcase or a gun. I sit down to wait, then remember something and get up. Julie has helped her mother up onto the deck and is crying again. I study the two of them before going out. From the back they look remarkably similar, like sisters almost. I look for something of myself in Julie but can find little. When Faye spies me looking at them, I join them on the deck.

"How much do you have in your checking account?" I ask Julie.

She blinks.

"How much?" I say.

"Not a lot," she says. "There's never a lot. A hundred dollars maybe."

"Write me a check," I say. "I'll take him to the airport."

"You want me to pay for it?" Julie says.

"You want *me* to?"

"Hank," Faye starts.

But I am not about to budge on this one. I'll loan her money later, or give it to her if I have to, but if she wants Russell on a plane, she's going to experience at least the appearance of paying for it.

The checkbook is in a drawer in the kitchen and Julie returns with it. She hates the idea, but she writes the check anyway. I look it over, put it in my pocket.

"He's over there in the window staring at us," Julie says. "Don't look."

I don't intend to.


It's forty-five minutes to Bradley International. I tell Russell to take it easy. After all. It's not like we're trying to catch any particular plane. Where I will send Russell is one of the many things we have not discussed. Why he has struck my daughter is another. More than anything, I am afraid he will tell me, because I don't want to know what is wrong with my daughter, what went wrong with their lives together.

I know too much already. Knew, in fact, when I saw my house taking shape on their lot. Knew that it wasn't Russell's idea, that if he'd had his way he'd have been living in New Haven in an apartment, spending their money in restaurants, on the occasional train into New York, the theater, a cruise around the island, maybe. The sort of thing you have a ticket stub to show for when you're finished. Left to himself, it would take him a decade or so to want something more permanent, and even then it would be against his better instincts. He didn't need a house right now and he certainly didn't need a replica of mine. When we drove away, he hadn't even looked back at it.

I know all this better than he does. He probably imagines that what is between him and Julie is more immediate. He may even think he's a bad lover or a bad person. I doubt he likes what he's thinking as the Connecticut countryside flies by and recedes behind us like a welshed promise. I have asked him if he would mind driving and he's said why should he. Why indeed. It's his car.

"It's funny," he says finally when we hit I-91.

"Please, Russell," I beg him. "Don't tell me what's funny."

"Why not?"

"Because it won't be."

"What's funny is I'm relieved . . ."

"See what I mean?"

"No, seriously," he says. I suspect he doesn't really know what *serious* means, though he's learning. "Ever since last night I've been trying to figure some way to punish myself. Now I can leave the whole thing in your capable hands. You're about the most capable man I've ever known, Hank. I don't mind saying it's been a bitch competing with you."

I can't think what to say to this, but I have to admit, now that I've heard him out, that it *is* funny. "I hope you won't misconstrue my running you out of town as not liking you, Russell."

We both smile at that.

"Were you and Faye ever unhappy?" he says.

"Together or separately?"

"Together."

"Sure."

He thinks about this for a minute. "I bet that's not true," he says. "I bet you're just saying it for one of your famous philosophical reasons, like happiness just isn't in the cards for human beings, the sort of thing guys like you say to

college students in your late afternoon class before you go
home and spend a happy evening in front of the television."

There is a curious mixture of wisdom and naïveté in this
observation, and it makes me even sadder about putting Russell on a plane.

"Julie always says that's what she had in mind for us. To
be as happy as you guys."

Once again I am aghast at how little my own daughter
knows me, what a desert her imagination must be. What can
she see when she looks at me? When I look at myself the evidence is everywhere. I know now why she did not come to see
me at the hospital. It was the nature of my operation. It isn't
that she couldn't imagine me with cancer. She couldn't imagine
me with a dick. That I am a man has somehow escaped her,
which is why she doesn't think about bending over in front of
me in her peasant blouse. And maybe it's worse than that. If
she has never thought of her father as a man, can she imagine
herself as a woman?

Russell's car rides smoothly enough, but like most small
Japanese models there is low-level vibration that comes from
being close to the earth and the buzzing engine. The nausea
that I felt atop the lawn mower is returning. I close my eyes
and will it away, hoping that Russell will think I'm asleep.

"The good thing is I know now I can't make her happy.
That's what hitting her meant, I think. It's what I was thinking when I hit her. That I'd never make her happy. It pissed
me off because it was something I thought I could do."

"You're very young, Russell," I tell him.

For some reason this observation angers him and he looks
over at me as if he's thinking about hitting *me*. "You can be
one cold son of a bitch, you know that, Hank. You're just the
sort who'd kick a man out of his own house, take him to the
airport in his own car, put him on a plane, and figure he had a
right to. The only reason I'm going along with this shit is because you look half dead. One little poke in the stones and I
could leave you along the side of the road for the undertaker."

"There," I say after a respectful moment of silence. "I guess you told me."

Bradley is crowded and we have to take the shuttle from a distant parking lot to the terminal. Then we walk a little and I begin to feel better again. I wait in line at the ticket counter, Russell behind me with his two suitcases.

When it's my turn an earnest young woman wants to know how she may serve me. How do people keep such straight faces, I wonder. "Where can you go for a hundred dollars?" I ask her. "One way."

"Sir?"

I repeat my question.

"Lots of places. Boston. Albany. Philadelphia. New York."

"Nothing west of the Mississippi?" Russell asks.

She shakes her pretty head. The farther you go, the more expensive it gets. This is life, she seems to imply.

"Too bad, Hank," Russell says.

"How about Pittsburgh?" I suggest, noticing that there is a flight leaving in half an hour. I think of a woman I know who lives there, or did once. We met at a convention a dozen years or so into my marriage. My one infidelity. She had been recently divorced and we made love more or less constantly for three days. Then she returned to Pittsburgh and I to Faye and I never heard from her again. For several years I stopped going to academic conventions, afraid she would be there and that I would prove faithless a second critical time. Lately, though I feel no real desire for her, she has been on my mind.

"Pittsburgh;" Russell shrugs. "Why not?"

There is only twenty-five minutes until departure, so we head for the gate.

"You can split if you like," Russell says. "You have my word I'll get on the plane."

In fact, I don't trust him. In his shoes I would not get on the plane. Or maybe I'd get on and then off again, circling back to the gate lounge to watch whoever was seeing me off wave to the departing plane. I intend to see him on the plane and to see it airborne. If he wants to get off then, it's his business.

Blessedly, the gate is not far. I am not looking forward to driving back home. I almost asked Faye to come with us, but that would have left Julie alone. It occurs to me it's not just the drive I'm dreading.

"When you get there," I say, facing Russell, "let me know how to contact you. We'll need your signature to get you and Julie out from under the house."

"Sometimes I think it's the house that killed us," Russell admits without much conviction, as if this is one of a dozen equally plausible explanations he's considered in the last twenty-four hours.

"At least you don't have to go back to it," I say.

He admits this is good. "I wish you'd let me take the car," he says suddenly. "It's really not fair that I should end up in some strange city and not even have a way to look for a job. I mean I've been a shit and everything, but . . ."

In truth, I have not thought of this. Failures of imagination abound. And now that he's brought the unfairness of it to my attention, I know I cannot put him on the plane.

"I swear to Christ," he says. "If you let me have my car, I'll go far away. Farther than Pittsburgh."

Right now, he seems about the most generous human being I have ever known. After all, he doesn't need my permission. The keys I am holding are his keys. They fit the ignition to his car. It dawns on me that only a combination of generosity and deep guilt can account for the fact that he has put up no fuss. By hitting Julie he has unmanned himself, lost everything but kindness. And I am suddenly sure he will do as he says.

A voice comes over the intercom saying that those needing assistance will be boarded first, then passengers with small children. I hand Russell his keys.

"I didn't mean that about you being a cold son of a bitch,

Hank," he says as we make our way back from the gate to the main terminal. "And you're not half dead."

"And you would never poke me in the stones," I add.

At the sliding doors we shake hands again and I watch him with his two soft suitcases all the way across the huge parking lot. I don't feel too badly about him. Almost anyplace he ends up will be better for him than where he is.

I am holding the airline ticket to Pittsburgh, which I will have to cash in. Then I will have to call Faye and admit to her what I've done. She will have to come fetch me. It seems too much to ask. Of either of us.

So instead I head back to the gate. I get there just in time to see the flight to Pittsburgh airborne. "You're too late," says a young man in a red blazer sporting an official insignia.

"I guess so," I tell him. In fact, there's no doubt about it. Odds are that she is no longer in Pittsburgh. She is probably married again by now, not that it matters, really. I only wanted to see her at some restaurant with half-moon booths where I could tell her about my surgery. For some reason I am convinced that my brush with death would matter to her and that I would feel better after confessing to someone that I fear the nausea, that I think of it as prophetic, a sign that some terrible malignancy remains. I remember her body and the way we made love, and I hoped that she would remember my body too. Maybe she would be afraid for me in the way I want someone to be afraid.

Back in the terminal I feed coins into a pay phone, dial, and let it ring a dozen times before hanging up and trying Julie's number, which does the same thing. I'm too tired to be sure what this means. Probably Faye has made Julie take a sedative. Maybe I have caught Faye in transit between houses. I wait a few minutes, try my house again, wondering if I have forgotten our number.

Whoever I am dialing is not home. I go outside onto the terminal ramp and am about to ask a taxi driver how much it would cost to drive me to Durham when Faye pulls up right in front of me. I get in.

"I got to thinking about it and realized that you'd give him the car," she says.

I look at her, wondering if she can have also intuited that I just missed getting on a plane to Pittsburgh, that I had a lover fifteen long years ago who I want to tell things I can't tell my wife.

"You think I don't know you after thirty years?" she says, as if in answer to my unspoken question.

"Not intimately," I tell her.

"Hurry up and mend then," she says.

Night is coming and most of the trip back is dark, but the car is warm and there will be no harm if I fall asleep. Faye knows how to get us home.

# THE OCCASIONAL

# PIGNOLI TART

O

## *Ann Hood*

EVERYWHERE TINA went, she smelled cannolis.
The odor of their sweet cream filling seemed to stick to her, to
follow her around. Sometimes, she'd be somewhere and the
smell would hit her so strongly that she'd feel dizzy. In bed at
night, Tina would try to count how many cannolis she had
served that day. Everybody that came into Amadeo's Bakery
ordered them. Except in March, around St. Joseph's Day.
Then there would be a big surge in zeppoli. And, occasionally,
someone might order a pignoli tart.

Tina's mother worked behind the counter at Amadeo's.
She was the fastest cannoli filler in Manhattan. People stood
around the counter just to watch her squeeze the cream out of
the floppy pastry bag and into the empty shells. Her mother
loved an audience. She would line up a dozen or more shells on
the counter and challenge, "Who's going to time me, huh?"
Tina could no longer watch as her mother, wearing the short

pink Amadeo's uniform, paraded up and down behind the rows
of ricotta cake and zuppa inglese, waving the pastry bag like a
banner.

There was a crowd around the counter now. Tina wiped
off a table and put the fifty-cent tip in her apron pocket. Two
new customers sat down immediately.

"Do you speak English?" the woman said in a slow exaggerated voice. She wore a T-shirt with the logo from *Me and My
Girl* emblazoned across it, a man dressed like a king, leaning
against a lamppost.

Tina took out her order pad and stared at the woman.

Someone at the counter yelled to Tina's mother: "Way to
go, Bernie!"

Without turning around, Tina could picture her mother
shooting the cream filling into the shells.

The man at Tina's table said to his wife, "The guidebook
recommends the cannolis here." His shirt was bright yellow,
with a polo player on it. "In fact," he added, "they're famous
for their cannolis."

His wife craned her neck to see the action at the counter.

Someone shouted, "Fourteen in forty seconds!" Everyone
in Amadeo's applauded.

"This is so exciting," the woman said. "I feel like I'm in
Italy."

The man read aloud from his guidebook, *New York Now.*
"Amadeo's, in the heart of SoHo, is famous for its cannolis.
These delicious pastries are always freshly filled in front of the
customer with a homemade sweet cream filling. They are an
excellent accompaniment to cappuccino."

"Well, then," the woman said.

"Two cannolis," her husband said. He also spoke loudly
and slowly. "And two cappuccinos." He held up two fingers
with one hand, and pretended to hold a cup and sip from the
other.

"Cappuccini," Tina said. "The plural of cappuccin*o* is
cappuccin*i*."

She walked over to the counter to place her order. Her mother was drinking an espresso and talking to one of the customers. On the bib of her apron, Bernie had pinned a button with a picture of Bozo the Clown on it. There was a red line across his face.

"I remember when this was all part of the Village," Bernie was saying. "There was no SoHo then. I lived my whole life here, I never heard of no SoHo."

"Really?" the customer said. His chin and shirt were dusted with powdered sugar from his cannoli. "That's fascinating. A little local folklore."

"Two cannolis, two caps," Tina said.

"Did you see me do fourteen in forty?" Bernie asked her. "Personally I think it was a little faster."

"Much faster," the customer said.

"Did you watch?" her mother asked again.

"Of course," Tina lied. "You looked great."

Bernie turned back to the man at the counter. "You know," she told him, "I've done it on TV. 'Live at Five.' 'The Morning Show.' Shows like that. Especially in summer, around the San Gennaro Festival. Promotional stuff for the bakery." She wiped the powder from the counter. "Yeah," she said. "I'm the best."


"You didn't watch, did you?" Bernie said to Tina as they walked home.

"I did. I watched."

They walked past a gourmet shop, a Japanese boutique, an art gallery. Tina stopped in front of a brightly lit restaurant and watched through the window as a bartender handed a tray of slushy pink drinks to a waitress.

"I ate in there once," she said. "I had pasta with pine nuts and gorgonzola." She didn't tell her mother that it had cost a week's tips for that dinner. "It was delicious," she said. "Maybe some night I'll make it at home."

"Gorgonzola cheese in macaroni?" her mother said. "I never heard of it."

"Just because you've never heard of it doesn't mean it's not good."

"Damn," her mother said. "I forgot to call the Shanghai Express for your father's pork buns."

"Call now," Tina said.

"You know how he gets if he doesn't get his pork buns."

"So call now."

Her mother stared into the restaurant. In thick pink paint it had Spanky's Bar and Grill written in one corner, with a shiny silver star underneath.

"I'll call," Tina said. "You want to wait here?"

"I'll come in," Bernie said. "See what all the fuss is about."

The pay phone was in an alcove at the front of the restaurant. The telephone was made of clear plastic and the inside workings were fluorescent pink and green. Behind them, Frank Sinatra sang "Luck Be a Lady" above the noise of the crowd. There were two women on the telephone, passing it back and forth between them.

"How about London?" one of them was saying.

The other one grabbed the phone from her. "London. Please."

"We've got to hold," the first woman said. She was very tall with a long blond ponytail and silver parachute pants that fell in soft folds around her hips and legs.

Bernie touched Tina's arm. "Let's go call someplace else," she said.

"I'm sorry," the second woman said. She had on a hat that looked like a rum cake from Amadeo's. "We're stewardesses and we have to call in for our flight assignments for tomorrow."

"Can you pick where you go?" Tina asked them.

"We can request a place," the blond one said, "but they don't have to give it to us."

"We know these guys in London," the other one explained.

"You know what?" Bernie said. "We can call from home."

The girl with the hat that looked like a rum cake held up her finger as if to say wait. "Oh," she said into the phone. "Okay. Thanks."

"What?" Tina said when she'd hung up.

"Rome," the girl said. "Sorry to hold you up."

"Rome?" the blonde moaned. "Again?"

Tina watched as the two girls walked back to the bar.

"How about that, Ma?" she said. "Pick up the phone and someone tells you you've got to go to Rome. How do you like that?"

"I'd like to pick up the phone and order those pork buns. That's what I'd like."

"Where do we ever go? Amadeo's and back. Period."

"We go lots of places," her mother said.

"Like where?"

"I don't know. Brooklyn. To visit Aunt Lily."

Tina leaned against the shiny black wall. "Right now I could throw up," she said. "I can smell cannolis and they're making me sick."

"They wouldn't know a cannoli if one came in and introduced itself. Believe me. All you smell is those girls' perfume. Very heavy."

Tina looked at her mother, at the thick fuchsia lipstick she wore, and the Bozo pin, and the tiny piece of lace she had bobby-pinned in her hair.

"What if we don't go back, Ma?"

"Back where? The bakery? Home? Where?"

Tina shrugged. "I don't know. What if we just took off somewhere?"

"Tina, sweetie, that takes money. Something we don't have. Those girls in there aren't getting a free ride you know. They're working all the way to Rome."

"Ma," Tina said, "next week I'm going to be twenty-four years old and I've never been farther than Brooklyn."

"Every place looks the same," her mother said. "Believe me."

"You don't know that. Where have you ever been?"

Tina watched the blond girl in the silver pants at the bar. She was bending backwards, like a gymnast, her long ponytail sweeping the floor.

"I've been somewhere," Bernie said.

"Where?"

The girl lifted her legs high into the air, the silver material ballooning out around her.

"Atlantic City. Your father and me went there once. This was years ago. They had a big boardwalk and little stores that sold seashells and hot dogs. And there was the boardwalk and the sand and the ocean. It smelled like Coney Island. Like things were frying."

Now the girl was lifting her arms too, standing, completely, on her head.

"You know what, Tina?" Bernie said. "It looked just like Sheepshead Bay. Only with big hotels. In fact, Sheepshead Bay is nicer."

Tina dialed the number for Shanghai Express. "Six pork buns," she said. "To go."

Tina could remember a time when her father wouldn't eat Chinese food at all. He said the restaurants used cat meat. "Give me a good bowl of spaghetti any day," he used to say. When Tina was ten, her father got sick. He used to be a baker at Amadeo's. His specialty was wedding cakes, multi-tiered creations covered with tiny silver candies or elaborate sugared flowers and topped with bells and doves and a marzipan bride and groom. Once, for Amadeo's daughter's wedding, Tina's father made a cake suspended atop four sugared columns that stood six feet high. A fountain underneath the cake flowed with pink champagne. He used real white roses for decorations. A picture of that cake still hung on the wall at Amadeo's. In the picture, Tina's father is standing under the cake, holding a big wooden spoon and smiling.

The day he got sick, he came home with a cake, trimmed in navy blue icing and candied violets.

"How do you like this?" he'd said. "They called the wedding off yesterday."

In thin blue writing across the top it said: Congratulations Dora and Chuckie. He cut a piece of cake for Tina and Bernie. It was white with lemon-rum filling.

"It's pretty cold in here," he'd said.

Tina remembered looking out the open window. It had been so hot, the air rippled with waves of heat.

"Better get me a sweater," her father had said, shivering.

His temperature reached 103. For three weeks it rose and fell. The doctors told them he had picked up a parasite in a foreign country. Probably Mexico. "But he's never been to Mexico," Bernie told them. They made her make graphs of his fever. The graphs lined the walls of the apartment, thin red lines climbing and dropping across the tiny blue squares on the paper.

Her father was never quite right after that. He talked all the time about ships carrying tea and spices. His hair hung down his back in a wispy white braid. All he ate was Chinese food—pork buns, fried rice, sweet-and-sour spareribs. He stayed in bed all day and made everyone call him Luck.

"How are you tonight?" Bernie asked him when they got home.

"Tired," he said. "The water was rough going into Melbourne. Almost lost the cargo."

"What cargo?" Tina demanded.

"Why, the tea," he said. "Orange pekoe."

"Do you know what I did today, Luck?" Bernie asked him. "I filled fourteen cannolis in under forty seconds."

"You weren't on a ship today," Tina said. "You were right here. In this bed."

Luck laughed.

"What an imagination," he said.

"I wonder if there's some kind of world record," Bernie said. "I'm sure I could break it if there is one."

Tina went into the living room and opened up the sofa where she slept. She turned on the TV but kept the sound off. There was an old "Mary Tyler Moore Show" on, and she watched as Mary, Rhoda, and Phyllis moved around Mary's apartment. Tina thought about Spanky's Bar and Grill. She was sure that the people who worked there made a lot of money. She pictured the girl with the long ponytail doing that headstand. Then she closed her eyes and tried to count how many cannolis she'd served that day. From her parents' room she heard her father's voice. "I'll take the night watch," he was saying. "You get some sleep."

"Pop," Tina said, "it's my birthday today."

"Aren't you lucky," he said. "Your birthday."

"Remember that time we went out to Shea for my birthday? Just you and me? The Cubs against the Mets? You let me drink an entire beer and I threw up on the number seven train."

Her father smiled.

"You have beautiful hazel eyes," he said. "In them I see brown and green and gold. I'll bring you emerald-colored silk back from China. What about that for a birthday present. Fit for an empress."

"Thanks," Tina said. And she left for work.

A bus full of tourists from Pennsylvania stopped at Amadeo's. The tour guide stood in the middle of the bakery. He was a fat man with very small hands and feet.

"This is a typical Italian bakery," he said. "The specialty here is cannolis. Go over and look at all the delicious pastries in the case. But I personally recommend the cannolis."

"Excuse me," a woman said to Tina. "I can't eat cream. It makes me sick." The woman's hair was white with a faint pink rinse. She grabbed Tina's arm. "It gives me the runs," she whispered.

Tina pulled her arm free.

Her mother was lining up empty pastry shells.

"You've never seen anything like this before," Bernie said to the group of tourists at the counter. "Nobody in Pennsylvania can do this as fast as I can."

"All I'm asking is for you to recommend something else," the woman with the pinkish hair said. "Isn't there something I can have besides a cannoli?"

Tina focused on the beauty mark on her mother's face. Every morning, Bernie put a fake beauty mark someplace on her face. She took a red pencil with a black point and pressed hard on her chin or near her mouth. Today it was on her cheekbone, under her right eye.

"Somebody time me now," Bernie said. She massaged the pastry bag, twisting it one way, then the other.

Some of the tourists got their cameras out.

"I saw this last year," one of them said. "It's amazing."

"I don't think I can watch," the woman said to Tina. "Can't you bring me something else?"

"Some people like pignoli tarts better than cannolis," Tina said.

"Fine," the woman said. "I'm just telling you I can't eat that cream."

As Bernie filled the shells she heard cameras clicking. Tina brought the woman the pignoli tart. She sniffed it, then poked it with her finger.

"Thank you," she said. The strap of her purse was fastened to her sweater with a big yellow diaper pin.

"Who's got the time here?" Bernie shouted, waving the pastry bag.

"Forty seconds," the tour guide said.

"Sixteen in forty," Bernie said. "That's got to be a record."

Tina started to fill a round tray with cannolis for the tourists.

"Do you think that's a record?" Bernie asked her.

"Maybe," Tina said. "I guess so."

"I've got a surprise for you," Bernie said. "After you serve all those cannolis we can go. Amadeo said it was okay since it was your birthday and all."

Tina looked at her mother. She was wearing a button that said Elephanatic over a purple elephant.

"You didn't have to ask for time off, Ma."

Her mother waved her away.

"Hurry up now," she said, "so we can get out of here."

It was after ten when they finally left. Bernie brought a bag of anisette biscuits with her. "For the ride," she said.

"What ride?" Tina asked her.

Her mother winked. "You'll see."

The streets were wet from a shower earlier that night. The buildings seemed to sparkle in the damp moonlight and there was a faint pink glow in the sky.

"Where are we going, Ma?" Tina asked, her voice almost a whisper.

"Right now to the E train, uptown."

They got off at Port Authority and her mother opened her bag, a deep pink one with a purple silhouette of a ballet dancer on it. Someone had left it at Amadeo's a few weeks before. In big white letters it said Omaha Ballet Company 1981. Bernie took out several rolls of quarters wrapped in off-red paper.

"They dance the ballet in Omaha," Bernie said. "What do you think of that?"

"Are we going to Omaha?" Tina said. She tried to think of where Omaha was. She imagined the country stretching to the west, flat and dry. Somewhere out there was Omaha.

"No," Bernie said. "Not Omaha. Atlantic City. We're taking the eleven-thirty Lucky Streak." She pulled a bus schedule from the bag. Tina smelled the anisette biscuits.

"We'll be back by seven A.M.," Bernie said. "I left Luck a whole carton of spareribs."

Tina's heart raced as they got on the bus. She couldn't sit still. Her legs swung back and forth and she kept pinching the skin on her left hand. A sign above the front window said Your Driver. Friendly. Safe. Courteous.

"What are you two supposed to be?" a man said, stopping beside Tina and Bernie. He swayed slightly. His breath was like old beer. "The Supremes?" he said. "The Pink Ladies?"

"Ma," Tina said, "we should have changed. We look dumb." She looked down at her uniform from Amadeo's Bakery. There was a small coffee stain on the sleeve.

"We don't look dumb," Bernie said. "We look like sisters."

The bus driver got on and slid a nameplate under the Your Driver sign. Byron Braithwaite.

"Lucky Streak," he said in a thick Jamaican accent. "Atlantic City. Bus number forty-four. Pickup five A.M." He didn't turn around when he spoke. "Lucky Streak," he said again. "Atlantic City."

"Bus driver," the woman in front of Tina said. Her hair was an unnatural black and teased very high. An ivory chopstick was stuck through it. "The man in seat three won't move. That's my lucky seat. I always sit in seat three and win big. If he doesn't move and let me sit there I'll lose all my money."

The driver backed the bus out.

"No smoking, no spitting, no radio playing," he said.

The woman turned around in her seat.

"These drivers," she said. "You think he'd make the guy move." Her eyes were lined with thick black eyeliner. "It's not his money, right?"

"It's my birthday," Tina said. "My mother's taking me to Atlantic City."

"No kidding. You ever been before?"

Bernie nodded. "Yes," she said. "Of course."

"No," Tina said.

The woman put some Chiclets in her mouth. "Me and Steve Winn are like this," she said, crossing two fingers. "But between you, me, and the lamppost, Caesar's Palace has it way over the Golden Nugget. Easy."

When they got to Atlantic City no one was allowed off the bus until a welcome hostess came on. She gave everyone a bright pink coupon that could be redeemed for ten dollars' worth of quarters.

"A welcome gift from me to you," she said to each person as she handed them a coupon. Her name tag was shaped like a slot machine and the letters spilled out of the bottom. Tina couldn't put them together into any recognizable name.

When Tina finally stepped off the bus, she was met by a burst of humid air. But almost immediately, the cool air from the ocean hit her and she soon felt cold. The air outside the bus was thick with fog and she could hear waves and see lights in the distance. For the first time in a long while, she didn't smell cannolis. Tina inhaled, and her head filled with salty air and the odor of fried foods.

The woman with the chopstick in her hair pointed through the fog. "Caesar's Palace is over there," she said.

Tina looked down the boardwalk. A jitney with a red-and-white-striped umbrella on it passed, honking its horn. She couldn't see anything very clearly, just vague shapes and hazy lights.

"It's not like the one in Vegas," the woman continued. She wore pink-and-black zebra-striped tights and shiny silver high heels. "But this is New Jersey, right?"

"We're going in there," Bernie said, pointing to the flashing lights of a casino.

"That's fine by me," the woman said. "Suit yourself."

When they walked into the casino, Tina gasped. There was noise and lights and people shouting. They passed a giant roulette wheel, men shooting dice, people crowded at felt-covered tables playing cards. They came to a stop in front of row after row of slot machines. The air smelled metallic, like Tina's hands after she counted her tips.

"Slots," Bernie said. "Do you feel lucky?"

They positioned themselves at adjacent machines. Tina read the winning combinations out loud. Cherries. Sevens. Bars. Then, side by side in their pink bakery uniforms they began to feed quarters into the machines. Tina caressed the knob on the tip of her handle slowly before she pulled it down. She felt, suddenly, powerful and alive.

Sometimes one of them hit, and quarters would clang down noisily. The first time Tina won, she shrieked and stepped back, still clutching the handle of the slot machine. With her other hand, she scooped up the quarters and pressed them against her face.

Finally, as if waking from a dream, Bernie stopped playing. Her hands were blackened from the money, and her eyes were red. She had all of her quarters in a big plastic cup.

"How much do you think we won?" she said.

Tina stopped feeding her machine, but she didn't let go of the handle. She pulled down on it until it stuck in place. Bernie jingled the quarters in the cup.

"This is better than bingo," she said. "No kidding."

Bernie and Tina walked outside. They each bought a corn dog and a Coke and sat beneath the boardwalk on the damp sand. The fog was thick, and in the early dawn light the air around them was tinged a yellowish gray. Tina breathed in the heavy salted air.

"Ma," she said.

But that was all.

Bernie took off her white shoes with the thick rubber soles and rubbed her feet in the sand. Her big toe hit a beer bottle, a crumpled cigarette pack.

Tina's arm tingled from clutching and pulling the handle of the slot machine. She shook it gently.

"What's on the other side of this ocean?" she asked.

"I don't know," Bernie said. "England?"

"I could sit here forever," Tina said.

"Maybe this is where they'd hold the cannoli-filling contest. They have Miss America here, right? Why not the cannoli-filling contest? Maybe I'd win."

"You would," Tina said.

As the sun came out, the fog began to burn off and the air looked like a layer cake, tiers of blue-green ocean, gray fog, reflected casino lights, and distant blue sky.

"Maybe I could get a job at Spanky's Bar and Grill," Tina said.

"I know," Bernie said. And her empty hand kneaded the air as if it were holding the pastry bag, filling the space around them.

# FINDING

# NATASHA

O

*Madison Smartt Bell*

"Hey, captain," Stuart said. He'd seen the dog as soon as he turned the corner, stretched over the doorsill of the bar in a wide amber beam of the afternoon sun. "Hey, babe, you still remember me?" He hesitated, just outside the doorway, in case the big German shepherd did not remember him after all. No doubt that Captain was a lot older now, shrunken into his bagging skin, the hair along the ridge of his back turning white. A yellow eye opened briefly on Stuart and then drowsed slowly back shut. Stuart took a long step over the dog and was inside the shadowy space of the bar.

He had expected Henry to be behind the counter and he felt a pulse of disappointment when he saw it was Arthur instead. On Saturday nights Arthur would often cover the bar while Henry and Isabel went out to dinner, but ordinarily they wouldn't have left so early, not at midafternoon. Stuart sat down at the outside corner of the bar. When Arthur got over to him Stuart could see he didn't remember who he was.

"Short beer," Stuart said, not especially wanting to get into it just yet. There were two people sitting at the far end of the counter, he couldn't quite make out their faces in the shadows, and nobody else in the place. He swiveled his stool back toward the door and as his eyes adjusted to the dim he saw the new paint, new paneling. It had all been done over, the broken booths and tables all replaced, a new jukebox right where the payphone used to be. The opposite wall was practically papered with portrait sketches of the Mets.

"Hey, what's going on?" Stuart said. Arthur had put down the glass of beer and picked up the dollar Stuart had laid on the bar. "Hey, you even got new glasses too? Henry and Isabel do all this work?"

"They retired," Arthur said, staring at Stuart, like he knew he ought to recognize him now. "What, you haven't been around in a while, right? You move in Manhattan?"

"Further than that," Stuart said. He pushed the beer glass a little away from him. A weird little bell-shaped thing, nothing like the straight tumblers Henry had used.

"Who would it be but Stuart?" said one of the men at the far end of the bar. Stuart peered back into the dim. "Give him a shot on me, Arthur."

"Clifton," Stuart said. Arthur was reaching behind him for a bottle of Jack, he'd remembered that much now, at least.

"Nah," Stuart said. "No thanks."

"What, you don't drink anymore either?" Clifton said.

"I drink," Stuart said. "It's a little early." Clifton was on his feet, walking up into the light toward him now. He looked like he'd had little sleep and there was reddish stubble on his face. Stuart shifted to the edge of his stool and put one foot on the floor.

"You're back, hey?" Clifton said.

"Righto," Stuart said.

Clifton parted T-shirt from jeans to scratch at his shriveled belly.

"Miss your old friends?"

"Some of them," Stuart said. "Any of them still around?"

"Like the song goes," Clifton said. "They're all dead or in prison."

"Ah, but I see you're still here, though."

"Yeah. Partially."

"What about Ricky?"

"He's around, sometimes. Moved over to Greenpoint, though."

"And Rita?"

"I don't know, I heard she went to LA."

"Thought I saw Tombo over around Tompkins Square . . ."

"Probably you did. He's still around there as far as I know."

"What about Natasha, then?"

"Ah," Clifton said. "You know I can't remember when I last saw Natasha."

"She still doing business with Uncle Bill, you think?"

"Uncle Bill got sick and died," Clifton said, and glanced up at the clock. "Speaking of which, I got to make a little run . . ."

"Yeah, well," Stuart said. "Great to see you and everything."

"Yeah," Clifton said. "What do you need?"

"Man," Stuart said. "You can't talk about that in Henry's place."

"You been away quite a while, babe," Clifton said. "It's not Henry's place anymore. So, you know. I can be back in a hour."

"Not to see me," Stuart said. "No more."

"Yeah? We'll see you," Clifton said. "Dig you later, babe." He stepped over the dog and went out through the bar of sunlight reddening in the doorway.

Stuart raised his hand and let it drop on the counter. "They moved too?" he said. "They moved out of upstairs?"

"Yeah," Arthur said. "Out to Starratt City."

"Man," Stuart said. "Can't quite get used to it."

"The new guy opens the kitchen back up," Arthur said, "that should really make a difference."

"What now?" Stuart got up and went toward the back. A half partition had been raised in front of the area where Henry and Isabel had used to have their own meals and now there were four small tables set up as for a restaurant. Stuart turned back to Arthur.

"Captain lets people go back in there now?" He walked back to his stool and sat. "Man, used to be if you just stepped over that line he was right there ready to take your leg off for you."

"I think he'll have to get over that," Arthur said. "He's old for all that, anyhow." The dog heaved himself up from the doorsill, walked back into the room and lay stiffly down again.

"Yeah, Captain, getting cold, you're right," Arthur said. Then to Stuart, "Want to shut that door?"

Stuart got up. It had been a mild fall day but now the air had a winter bite. He pushed the door shut and stayed for a minute, squinting through the window at the dropping sun, across the VFW decal on the pane.

"Can't believe they'd of left the dog here," he said, turning back toward the counter.

"Henry comes by to see him," Arthur said. "You couldn't take him out of this place, though. He would just die."

Upstate it had turned cold early, and alongside the railroad track the river was choked with ice. Stuart had bought papers at the station, the *News,* the *Post,* but he couldn't seem to focus on the print. From the far shore of the Hudson, chilly brown bluffs frowned over at him, sliding back and back. The train ran so low on the east bank it seemed that one long step could have carried him onto the surface of the river, though solid as the ice appeared it could hardly have held anybody's weight so early in the season. He stared through the smutty window of his car, the view infrequently broken up by a tree jolting by, or a building, or the long low sheds at the stations: New Hamburg, Beacon, Cold Spring. Opposite West Point the ice vanished and the river's surface turned steel smooth and gray.

If he'd been a fish, Stuart caught himself wondering, how much further down could he have swum without dissolving? Chemicals warmed the water down here, as much and more than any freaks of weather. What fish would swim into that kind of trouble? He'd slept little the night before, his last night in Millbrook, so maybe that and too much coffee accounted for the jitters that worsened as Tarrytown and Yonkers fell back by, and rose toward actual nausea when the George Washington Bridge, almost a mirage downriver, floated into clearer view. If he'd been a fish he could have breathed water, though the water here might kill or change him. He was headed into a hostile element, a diver for what pearl he couldn't say. The train dragged toward 125th Street like a weight pulling him under. The couple of years he'd been away were long enough he should have stayed forever. No point in coming back now, so late, unless to recover something, what? The train dropped along the dark vector of the tunnel to Grand Central, and Stuart, like a hooded hawk, grew calm.

An hour or two and he'd remembered how to swim again, or glide. A thermal carried him up into a Times Square hotel, one of the kind where they did a take when he said he wanted the room all night, but by the week it turned out to be a bargain. Suspended in some other current, Stuart lazed back out onto the street and drifted, from a bar to a street-corner stand to one of the old needle parks to another bar, and so on. *Don't go where you used to go,* they'd told him at the center, *don't see those same old people, or you'll fall.* No doubt that bigger, meaner fish still eyed him from its neighbor eddies, but he wasn't bleeding anymore, and a flick of tail or fin shot all of them away.

The weather was still bland down here, much milder than upstate, though it began to have its bitter aftertaste of cold. Stuart cruised up into the chill of the evening, watching whores and dealers check him over before they swirled away, always wondering if he might run into Natasha. He was not exactly looking yet, but developing a ghost of an intention. If he had asked himself, *Why her?* he would have had no answer. Just . . . Natasha. He had written her a time or two from Millbrook, hadn't had anything back, not that he'd expected it. Why Natasha? Others had been as close, or closer, and he didn't want to look for them. He wasn't looking for Natasha either, it was spontaneous, at first, this feeling that she was about to appear.

Clifton had been wrong about Rita, Stuart eventually found out. She wasn't in LA after all, she was in Bellevue getting over hepatitis B. They made him take a shot of gamma globulin when he went in to see her, even though he tried to tell them how long he'd been upstate. He also tried a joke about needles, but the nurses didn't laugh. When Rita invited him to sit down he had to tell her no.

"Funny, almost everybody seems to say that," Rita said. Her smile was not particularly bright. She was on a big ward, but curtains ran on tracks between the beds, and there were a couple of chairs pulled up to her nightstand, with magazines piled on the seats. The whites of her eyes were still a funny color and she was so thin that Stuart had trouble telling what were the lines of her body and what were only wrinkles in the sheet.

"Well, now," Stuart said. "You look good."

"Don't give me that," Rita said. "I look like I'm gonna die."

"You're not," Stuart said.

"Not this time," Rita said.

Stuart groped for a commonplace.

"Clifton told me you went west."

"No way," Rita said, patting the mattress with a bony hand. "I been right here."

"When do you get out?" Stuart said.

"I don't know. Two weeks more maybe. They don't want to give me a date."

Rita's folding alarm clock ticked loudly across the next patch of silence.

"You need anything?" Stuart said.

"Not that I can get."

"Well, let me know, okay?" Stuart pulled the curtain back and paused in the gap. "Hey. I been kind of trying to get hold of Natasha, you wouldn't know what she's been up to, would you?"

"I know she hasn't been up here," Rita said. "Not a whole lot else. Last I heard she was tricking for Uncle Bill."

"My God," Stuart said. "That sounds like a losing proposition."

"You know how it is," Rita said. "She's got a nice big nut to make every day."

"I guess," Stuart said. "Hey, but Clifton told me Uncle Bill was dead."

"Is that right," Rita said. "Clifton seems to be kind of full of bad information these days."


Bars and coffee shops, coffee shops and bars. Stuart circled the island from end to end of the old boundaries: the Marlin, McCarthy's, Three Roses, the Chinatown spots, anywhere she might have come in for any reason, rest her feet, get out of the weather, kill time waiting to score. Some places they remembered what he drank, but mostly not, and every now and then he'd meet somebody else who hadn't seen Natasha.

"Nah, man, she ain't been around *here.*"

"Didn't I hear she went to Chicago? I can't think if it was her or somebody else. Memory slips a little on the fourth one . . ."

"Haven't seen her in about eight months. Maybe not since last summer . . ."

"Hey Stuart, whatever happened to that snippy little black-haired girl you used to hang around with?"

*Wish I knew . . .* On sleepless nights, he'd eat small-hour breakfasts at the Golden Corner or someplace just about like it, hunched down behind a newspaper, eavesdropping on the booths around him full of hookers on break, waiting for the voice or the name. By the time winter set hard in the city he'd started on the false alarms, recognizing Natasha in just about any middle-sized dark-haired white girl. It happened more than once a night sometimes, he'd have to walk right up to whoever he'd spotted and then at the last minute veer away. He did that so many times that the hookers started calling him Mr. No-Money Man.


Uncle Bill's place was up at 125th Street near the Chinese restaurant, just past the train trestle. A black kid with his hair done up in tight cornrows was waiting by the entry when Stuart arrived, one leg cocked up on the railing, the loose foot swinging to its limit like the pendulum of a clock. Stuart stood sideways to keep one eye on him while he studied the row of bells. The third one now said "Childress" instead of "B.B." like it should have, but he reached to ring it anyway.

"Man done gone," the black kid said. Stuart turned all the way toward him.

"What man is that?"

"Billbro, who else?"

"Know where he went?"

The kid spat over the railing.

"You got a cigarette on you, man?"

Stuart passed him a single Marlboro.

"He in the trench," the kid said. "There's a place just about ten blocks up can fix what it is you need."

Stuart laughed briefly.

"You think I'm the right color to be going about ten blocks up from here?"

The kid grinned and blew some smoke.

"Long's you go with *me* you are."

"Thanks anyway," Stuart said. "It was a personal visit, kind of thing. What was this trench you were talking about?"

"Out on one of them islands, I forget." The kid's tennis shoe, fat with thick lacing and white as new bones, beat back and forth on the hinge of his knee. "You know, when you die without no money, then they shove you in the trench."

"Oh," Stuart said. "That trench. Do you get a box at least?"

"I don't think so, bro," the kid said. "Maybe you might get a bag."


Up at Millbrook, Stuart's image of Natasha had been clear as a photograph tacked to the wall, but once he was back in the city it began to blur and fade and run together in a swamp of other faces: magazine covers, or actresses on posters outside the movies, and always and especially the dozens of near misses that kept on slipping past him. Now her memory was less a face and figure than just a group of gestures, and these too began to dissipate and dissolve, until when he thought of Natasha he often thought of a painting he'd once seen by Manet: a full-length portrait of a woman in a gray dustcoat down to her feet, one hand lightly extended toward what? a birdcage? He couldn't even remember the painting all that well. The woman in the portrait was nothing like Natasha, she had a totally different face, was taller, heavier, had red hair. Yet the cool repose of her expression also managed to suggest that she was poised at the edge of something. Stuart began to doubt if he would recognize Natasha when he found her, and what if he'd already passed her by? He recognized people that *weren't* her frequently enough, that much was for sure.

Stuart was trying to outlast a drunk with a three A.M. breakfast at the Golden Corner when a hooker slid into the booth across from him.

"I been thinking about you, Mr. No-Money Man," she said. "I been thinking, if you ate a little bit less breakfast, you might have a little bit more money." When she laughed, her eyes half disappeared into warm crinkles at their corners. Stuart saw she was a lot older than she wanted to appear, but not bad-looking still, in a stringy kind of way. He sort of liked her face, under all the makeup. She was wearing white lipstick and white eye shadow, on skin the shade of tan kid leather. The wig she had on was a color no hair had ever been.

"I bet you got fifty cent right now," she said, "buy me a cup of coffee."

"Get the number ten breakfast if you want it," Stuart said. "Or anything else they got." He was in a slightly reckless condition and a lot of his concentration was being spent on keeping her from splitting into twos and fours.

"*Hell*, yes," she said, and shouted an order toward the counter. "I knew you had that money all along."

"Not that much," Stuart said, laying down his fork.

"Enough," she said, aiming a long fingernail at his nose. "Your trouble is you think you can't find what you need. You know I seen you looking. Up and down and up and down—" She slapped the table. "You might not think it but I can do it all myself, do it real well too."

"Breakfast only," Stuart said, and as if those were the magic words an oblong plate of hash and eggs came skidding into the space between her elbows.

"I got it now," she said, biting into a triangle of damp toast. "You not looking for some *thing*. You looking for some *body*, right?"

"Yeah," Stuart said. "Right."

"Have to be a girl friend."

"As a matter of fact, no," Stuart said. "Just somebody I used to know."

"What for, then?"

"I don't know," Stuart said. "I think I got survivor syndrome."

"Say what?"

"I feel responsible," Stuart said, hearing his words begin to slur. "For like . . . for everybody. Don't ask me why but I always felt like she'd be the only one I could do anything about." He elbowed his plate out of the way and clasped his hands in front of him. "It's got to be like a long chain of people, see? I take hold of her and she takes hold of somebody else and finally somebody takes hold of you maybe, and then if everybody holds on tight we all get out of here."

The hooker shoveled in a large amount of hash and eggs with a few rapid movements and then looked back up.

"Out of where?"

"Ah, I can't explain it," Stuart said, fumbling out a cigarette. "Whose idea was this, anyway?"

The hooker stared at him, not smiling so much now.

"You be knee-walking drunk once you stand up, won't you?" she said after a while. "Man, where you coming from with this kind of talk?"

"Straight out of hell," Stuart said, trying to get his cigarette together with his match. "You familiar with the place?"

. . .

Over the winter he started going to the kung fu movies, across Forty-second Street and around Times Square. It was a better time killer than drinking for him now; he'd tried getting drunk a few more times but he didn't much like where it took him. He went to the movies at night or sometimes in the afternoons, wearing a knit cap pulled down to his eye sockets so others couldn't tell much about him in the dark. It would take him a while, sometimes, to find a seat. Often whole sections had been ripped out, and also he liked to get one that put his back to a post or some other barrier. In the half-light reflected back from the screen, the rest of the audience milled through clouds of dope smoke, dealing for sensé or street ludes or dust, each cluster playing a different boom box, usually louder than the soundtrack. They only turned to the screen when there was fighting, but the fight scenes always got their whole attention, bringing screams of approval from every cranny of the huge decaying theaters.

Stuart, on the other hand, always watched all the way through, even the tedious love scenes. He was not very discriminating, could watch the same picture again and again, often staying so long he would have forgotten whether it was day or night by the time he returned to the street. The movies were all so similar that there was not much to choose between them, if you were going to bother to watch them at all. He observed that the theme of *return* was prevalent. What the returning person usually did was kill people, keeping it up until there was no one left or he was killed himself.

Twisted among the lumps and rickets of his moldy ricket of a bed, Stuart falls into a dream so deep and profoundly revealing that at every juncture of it he posts his waking self a message: you *must* remember this. The dream is room within room within room, each suppressing its breathless secret, and on every threshold, Stuart swears he will remember. Each revelation has sufficient power to make him almost weep. When he sits up suddenly awake, the message is still thinly wrapped around him, bound up in a single word, a name.

*Clifton.* Stuart stared at a gleaming crack in the gritty windowpane, an arm's reach across the space between the bedstead and the wall. *Clifton,* that was nothing but nothing, and the dream was entirely gone. He flopped back over onto his side, eyes falling back shut, fingers begin to twitch, and a shard of the dream returns to him. The self of his dream comes hurrying from a building and in passing glances at a peddler on the sidewalk, a concrete-colored man propping up a dismal scrap of a tree. Its branches are hung with little figurines carved in wood and stone, and Stuart, hastening on his way, takes in as a matter of course that each of them astonishingly lives, is animate, moving toward the others, or away. In the dream he rushes past as though it were completely ordinary, but now he was transfixed by the gemlike movement of the tree, this nonsense miracle, a mere wonder outside the context of the dream, and uninterpretable. Stuart sat back up in the knot of his grimy blanket, muttering, *Clifton.* Surely, somewhere in all of this there must be something to extract.


Back in Brooklyn, Stuart checked in Henry's old bar to see if anyone knew where Clifton was living now and found that no one did. He tried the old place up on Broadway and the super sent him back around the corner to a half-renovated building between two shells on South Eighth Street. It was a sunny day, though cold, and even the well to the basement door was full of light. Stuart rolled his newspaper tighter in his right hand and rapped on the door with his left. It took five or ten minutes of off-and-on knocking before the door pulled back on the chain, then reclosed and opened all the way.

"You been a long time coming," Clifton said. Inside, the light that leaked down from the street level was thin and watery. Clifton shimmered vaguely as he yawned and stretched; it looked like he'd been caught asleep, though it was well past noon. There was something that smelled to Stuart a little like old blood. He followed Clifton into the room and kicked the door shut behind him with his heel.

"The worried man," Clifton said, bending away from Stuart to get a T-shirt from the bed. "Well, babe, you ready for me to make your troubles go away?"

"Can you?" Stuart said. "Clifton?" When Clifton began to turn toward him, Stuart lashed at him with the rolled news-paper, and the heavy elbow of pipe he'd furled inside it knocked Clifton all the way over and sent him sliding into the rear wall.

"What in hell is the matter with you?" Clifton said. He sat up against the wall and stroked at the side of his mouth, his finger coming away red from a little cut. "Have you gone crazy or what?" Stuart looked down at him, trying to feel something, anything, but could not. He thought for no reason of the trench, bags jumbled into it, barely covered with a damp film of dirt.

"Just curious," he said haltingly.

"Yeah, well, are you satisfied now?"

"Not really," Stuart said. The newspaper hung at the full length of his arm, pointed at the floor. "I was thinking I might beat your face out the back of your head, but I don't really feel like it now."

"That's real good, Stuart," Clifton said. "I'm glad you don't feel like it now. You don't maybe want to tell me why you felt like it a minute ago?"

"I don't know why," Stuart said. "What happened to Natasha?"

"Man, are you kidding me, man?" Clifton said. "I'm going to tell you the truth now, okay, *I don't freaking know.*"

Stuart took a step forward, hefting the newspaper. Clif-ton raised one hand more or less in front of his face and pushed up into a crouch with the other.

"Hey, I would tell you now if I knew, man," he said.

"You got the edge on me, okay? Besides, what would I want to hide it for? I don't know any more than you do, man."

"Okay," Stuart said, and let the newspaper fall back to rest against his thigh. Clifton reached into the side of his mouth and took something out and looked at it.

"This is my tooth I got here, man," he said. "I cannot believe you did this over that dumb freaking chick."

"I had a dream," Stuart said, "but maybe this wasn't what it was supposed to be about."

Clifton pushed himself up off the floor and stood, pressing the T-shirt over the bleeding edge of his mouth.

"Yeah, well, thanks for stopping by," he said, words a little slurred by the cloth. "Next time I see you I'm going to kill you, you do know that, I hope."

"No you won't," Stuart said.

"Maybe, maybe not," Clifton said. "Don't turn your back."

Almost every day he bought a paper and almost every day he didn't read much of it. He'd glance through quickly and then roll it and carry it all day, till the front pages began to curl and tatter and the ink started to bleed off on his fingers. After a while the feel of the rolled newspapers stopped reminding him directly of Clifton and only made him uncomfortable in a dull way he couldn't identify.

There was always too much news about missing people, and too many of the ones that weren't missing were dead. Every time he heard about someone else missing he wondered how many just vanished without being missed. Every third person he passed on the street was probably missing from somewhere.

*Missing* was no more than a whitewash, a better word would be *gone*. *Gone people*. Whenever Stuart looked at the faces on the milk cartons, he had a deep feeling the children were dead. He didn't own a picture of Natasha, but all the same he was convinced that if she'd died he would have known that too.

When it got warm enough to sit outside again Stuart sat in Tompkins Square with one more unread newspaper flattened on the bench beside him and watched Tombo coming across from the east side. He would have let him go on by, but Tombo saw him before he could get the paper up, came over and sat down.

"Long time," Tombo said. "I wasn't even sure you were still around."

"I'm here," Stuart said. Tombo leaned back on the bench, shooting his long legs out before him. He had on a nice pair of gray pleated pants, expensive-looking. None of it ever seemed to age or even touch him. He still had his dark and vaguely foreign prettiness, perfect skin, red pouty mouth, long eyelashes like a girl's. Stuart watched him blink his eyes and sniffle.

"Hey, you know Clifton's been talking you down a lot," Tombo said, shifting around in Stuart's direction. "He keeps on telling everybody he's gonna fix your business."

"Good," Stuart said. "If he's talking about it then he won't do anything."

"You think?"

"Clifton's got a temper," Stuart said. "But he'll never let it take him all the way to jail."

"Maybe not," Tombo said. He snorted, pulled out a handkerchief and blew his nose.

"Allergies, man," he said. "It always gets to me around this time of year."

"What are you giving me that line for?" Stuart said. "I'm not a cop."

"Right, I forgot," Tombo said, glancing over at him under his eyelashes. "You still clean?"

"Yeah," Stuart said.

"They do a pretty good job on you up at Millbrook, huh? It sticks?"

"So far," Stuart said. "One day at a time and all that kind of thing."

Tombo shifted around on the bench.

"I'd been thinking maybe I might go up there sometime myself," he said.

"Well," Stuart said. "When you decide to go, then you'll go."

"People tell me you're looking for Natasha," Tombo said.

"Do they," Stuart said. "Everybody likes to talk to you about my business, seems. Why, you haven't seen her, have you?"

"Not in a year at least, nope. Sorry, bud . . . What are you looking for her for?"

"I quit looking for her," Stuart said. "You can't look for somebody around here, it's ridiculous. I'm just . . . I'm just waiting to find her, that's all."

"Interesting strategy," Tombo said, standing up. "Well, good luck."

Stuart started making trips to Brooklyn, back to what had been Henry's place, though he didn't much like the feel of it, not after the remodeling. Why he kept going out there he didn't really know, maybe just for the inconvenience of it, for the journey. Clifton had stopped coming in, the new bartender was a stranger, there was seldom anyone he knew there except the dog. They still hadn't opened up the restaurant section. Sometimes Stuart's visit would coincide with Henry's, who tended to drop in most Thursday and Friday afternoons. He'd take Captain out around the block and then come back and sit at the bar, drinking white wine on ice from one of the old straight glasses they'd apparently saved just to serve him with. It pleased Stuart that this one little thing was still the same, and he felt happier in the place when Henry was in there too, though they didn't have much to say to each other past *hello,* and though the old man looked all wrong, sitting on the outside of the bar.

Whenever the weather was good enough he walked back across the bridge and caught the subway at Delancey Street on the Manhattan side. He was in a lot better shape than he'd been in the old days, but it was still enough of an effort that doing it fast set his heart slamming. That sense of an urge out in front of him was familiar, though now he wasn't going for a fix; the energy he set out ahead of him had become its own point. The walkway was a little more run-down than he remembered it. A lot of the tiles had come loose and blown away and now he could look through cracks in the steel plating and see all the way down to the place far below the roadway where the water slowly turned and moiled. But the rise of excitement was the same as it always had been, as he pushed himself up to the crux of the span, where the howling of the traffic stopped being a scream and became a sigh. Arrived just there, with the afternoon barely past its daily crisis, he stopped and looked farther across at the tall buildings limned explosively with light, exultant, thinking, *This is what you always will forget, this is what you never can remember, this is what you have to be here for.*


It's not the first but the fifth or sixth day of spring when Stuart finally finds Natasha. All winter he's felt old and moribund, frozen half through, but now a new green shoot of youth begins to uncurl inside of him. It's a fresh and tingling day, the weather so very fine that it alone would be enough to make you fall in love. Everybody in Washington Square has bloomed into their summer clothes and they all look almost beautiful. Stuart walks around the rim of the fountain, hands in his pockets, a cigarette guttering at the corner of his mouth, smiling a little as the fair breeze ruffles his hair. He's headed straight for Natasha before he's even seen her, and then he does: she's tapped out there on one of the benches just at the bottom edge of the circle, head lolled back, mouth a little open, hands stretched palms-up on her knees. When he gets a little closer, he can even see her eyes darting under the closed lids, looking at the things she's dreaming of. Man, she's way too thin, she's got bad-looking tracks, infected, and it's a fifty-fifty chance she's dying, but Stuart won't think about any of that right now, just keeps on walking, up into the moment he's believed in for so long.

—For Wyn Looper

# MURDER

O

*Amy Hempel*

"SOMETHING SOMETHING something never/
Love for an hour is love forever."

If that's true, I thought, then we're in business.

I showed the inscription to Jean, there in the used books
store and she said, "Maybe we should have married Jim."

Jean had five boyfriends, all named Jim. Aren't two of
the Jims best friends? I asked. No, she said, this is a whole new
crop of Jims. Isn't one of the Jims a scientist? I asked. She
said I must be thinking of the Jim who had a Ph.D.

The Jim she thought we should have married was the Jim
that got away.

Jean said, "Here," and handed me a newer used book, a
book that, in its day, had been a best-seller.

She said, "This book gave me the will to live and have
fun." She said, "I read this book and went right out and got

myself asked out by a man—a man who liked me," she said, "and who didn't even have another girl friend."

Jean and I are bridesmaids. At last night's rehearsal dinner, the bride spoke to us in the plural. She said, "You've been going ninety in a locked garage." She said, "We've got to get you out on the open road."

By "the open road," the bride did not mean the Stretchmark. The Stretchmark is more of a locked garage.

In a biker bar called the Stretchmark Café, the tables of loudly muscled men ignore the strippers and leer at slides of choppers projected on the café walls. A chair in front of the stage is where the gals lob their T-shirts, bought in Laguna at Big Wave Dave's. The house cat wears a turquoise metal-flake collar and runs from the strippers' children, who are, quite naturally, back in the dressing room, playing slash fighting.

The Stretchmark is across from the used books store. Every time Jean and I make our entrance, the bartender sings in a Bugs Bunny voice, "I dream of Jeannie, she's a light brown hare."

Jean, the flutter of every male heart.

The bartender also has a crush on Sister Marianne, the former nun who moved to Phoenix for her health, then moved right back when she heard that the tarantulas there can jump eight feet, that some of them have landed on the saddle of a horse.

Sister Marianne, when her mind is someplace else, is not aware of the sound she makes there sitting at the bar—like a sprinkler kicker head going kk-kk-kk-kk-shooshooshooshoo.

Sister has her eye on the fellow from the post office. When you buy a sheet of stamps from him, he rubs the gluey side of the sheet across his hair. He says that the oil from human hair will keep the stamps from sticking to each other in your purse. It's a handy tip, and a gesture you want to remember when you go to lick a stamp.

The fellow from the post office wants to fix Jean up with

his friend from downtown. I have met the friend from downtown. He tried to sell me some sort of coin that he said was owned by Alexander the Great and Genghis Khan and Bobby Kennedy—"Only twenty dollars—okay, make it eighteen-fifty."

I warned Jean that the postal worker's friend was arrested one time for whipping taxicabs with a child's jump rope, the wooden handles rapping the windows and chipping paint off the hoods.

"Dust him," I said.

Jean could take him or leave him, she said, and I say it is a good way to be.


The day of the wedding, before a SWAT team of beauticians arrived to do the bride, the young son from the groom's first marriage gave his new stepmother a picture he had drawn of a scowling Green Beret with a sword through his flaming head.

The bride fitted the drawing into her vanity mirror. She looked beyond it, and made a wedding face.

For her second time around, the bride chose ivory tea-length lace, better flowers and better food, better music and a better man. In the wedding suite, a.k.a. the bride's parents' bedroom, the bride reached for her earrings; Jean reminded her to put her jewelry on last so she wouldn't snag the weightless Belgian lace.

The bride's first husband divided his time between Davis, San Pedro, and Encinitas. Say the word *home* and he could not stop talking about his rent, about the place he had for $37.50 when it was twenty years ago, and then, when the new owner raised his rent to sixty, there at the top of Emerald Bay, he could not stop himself from telling us that he had said, "Fuck this," and moved out.

Say the word *home* and you can watch the bride's heart drop through the floor.

The new groom is like a Force-o-Nature. But the bride plays down his looks, his size. "It's about trust," she says.

"And—yeah," she says, "it's about—who *knows* what it's about. We just go for these damn walks and listen to coyotes."

I dipped a finger in the pre-nup champagne and dabbed the cold fizz behind my ears, back of where Jean pierced them with a kilt pin back in school.

Jean said, "Men." She said, "They hate you at first. But all you have to do is be funny and sad and tall and thin and short and fat and wear them down, wear them down."

"You can look on the bright side," I said, "but think of the men who have unexplainably fled after they got to know us a little."

The bride's parents' dog came in just then and offered a frantic display of devotion, leaping about our legs.

"I used to think I wanted to be loved like that," I said. "But I don't want to be loved like that."

Pushing the dog from her skirt, Jean said, "Would it help if you thought it was insincere?"

The bride, gowned, was called away for pictures.

Jean let a strap of her pink dress fall. "Oh, Jim—please don't," she said in a breathy voice.

"Oh, Jim—please," I said, all in my throat.

"Oh, Jim—" Jean said.

"Oh," we all said together.


Jean recalled the time she asked the bartender about Sister Marianne, if he had ever considered the "M" word, and the bartender had said back, "Murder?"

"Imagine that it's you," Jean said to me. "Imagine it's you who is getting married today."

I do.

I imagine myself waking in some Jim's bed.

His telephone rings. I imagine it is a woman calling, and because I am the wife, I answer in the voice that says, I've had it ten times today and *I live here.*

This is what marriage means to me.

# "GORDON PENN IS

# A WINNER!"

O

*Michael J. Rosen*

I N  A  D R A W E R  beneath Penn's files "to pay" and "paid,"
an old fruit basket, a mourning gift, fills
with all the pending, unsolicited mail,
the pleas, campaigns, funds and drives, the letters
addressed *Parents of Cynthia Penn,*
*Concerned Citizen in 4C,*
and the least likely of his mistaken mail-
merged names, *Congratulations Gordon!*

A Saturday, bright and early and overdue,
Penn's mission is determining his tithe
for the injuries and infamies
that he and his own have yet been spared, a task
that Penn endures like a minor affliction,
postpones like visits to the physician.
This time the basket holds more months

than Penn has ever allowed himself before—
will ever allow himself again. The problem,
in part, is travel: the galling pile a week
can accumulate to spite him; the other part
is apprehension: shuffling the deliveries
from shelf to desk to counter—if only arrangement
alone could satisfy them!—until Penn tables
each in the fruit basket as if decision,
too, were a ripening (like starch's conversion
to sugar), something Time does blindfolded,
hands behind the back, but Penn can't.

Penn fans the postcard coupons from Jiffy Lube
with missing children who ask "Have you seen me?"
Penn has. He's seen them everywhere . . . once.
Auditioning each face outside the newsstand,
inside the mall, he shuffles through the face cards
and each one disappears again, drops
to the floor along with an important message
about the drought-afflicted trees of Israel.
Mothers Against Drunk Driving . . . the arthritic . . .
bulimic . . . UNICEF . . . will have to go it
alone this month. At best, Penn's feeling fair.
Is the basket half-empty or half-full?
Pessimist, optimist, what difference does it make
if money draws the limits in Penn's account book?
He needs a system, a form for sorting things.

For starters—restarters—Penn inverts the basket,
pulls three dining room chairs into a row,
a panel of jurors, and deals the stack of requests:
*unlikely, likely, never-in-a-million-years.*

### Never-in-a-Million-Years
The least he could have done, all along,
was pitch these envelopes. They take no time.

(Yet, Penn remembers doing just this.)
To build momentum, ensure that a likelier cause
hasn't slipped in, Penn double-checks the pile.
Though flattered to be nationally recognized
as one discriminating connoisseur,
Penn rips a once-in-a-lifetime chance to own
a twenty-piece Nativity of jade,
a chunk of undeveloped land in Maine,
the slipcased volume *Battles for the Ages*
("to teach your children the lessons of history").
Platinum credit cards, instant loans,
preferred, preapproved car and home
and life insurance for privileged customers
like Penn—these he tears in rapid succession,
embarrassed to be singled out like royalty
in a kingdom of the cheated, lost, and deposed.

Likely
Penn writes a check to save the harp seals.
Subtracting the sum from his savings, Penn hears
for the first time, the word's full meaning:
"from my savings to the saving of a seal."
Is there a correspondence, one-to-one,
between the stroke of a man's pen in Ohio
and the stroke of a hunter's club on an infant seal?

A man not really given over to paying
visits to the house of God, Penn wonders if each
check he writes is a prayer in God's eyes—
or in his own, and if so, a prayer
Penn answers—too godlike—or a prayer he makes.
In so many words, or numbers, Penn offers
a personal prayer for the Anne Frank House,
the Red Cross, and the victims of Alzheimer's
he saw portrayed in a miniseries (although

the misprint in the guide read "miseries"),
and seals each one inside an envelope
that by tomorrow will be out of his hands.

"Give until it hurts," Penn hears replaying
in his mind like the slogan from the local spa,
as though charity were exercise
for the soul, as though the phrase "No Pain, No Gain"
applied to the spirit of giving as well.
Compared to the perfected physiques of men
in the commercials, Penn's flesh is weak, or soft.
So what's that say about his soul? It says—
It doesn't. Penn doesn't know about his soul.

It's a gut feeling, Penn reasons, that if you give
more so it hurts more, then the hurt will ward off
further harm, will balance the scales of justice
so angels of death, of hunger, of burning houses
hovering above the neighborhood,
will witness the pain of giving, see the wince
of charity like a smear of blood by the door,
and spare the homes of the generous, be they
rich or poor. Like lightning, each must strike
a target: better the lightning rod of giving
than all the loved and lucky ones inside.

Unlikely
At least for today—today there's no excuse
or escape—it does appear Penn can't befriend
an ex-offender, an Ethiopian Jew,
American sons who fled an unthinkable war,
the specific number of children born each hour
with birth defects. Despite what Penn would like
to say on his behalf, to note for the record—
"I never decided, I hope to be a friend"—

the empty envelope is evidence,
all he needs to prove himself guilty,
guilt-ridden, as charged. Penn pleads himself:
"But isn't there a limit to the number of causes
to which a person can give?" Six cents a day
times an infinite number exceeds his holdings,
his small, pretend-hold on the ungraspable.

*Objection overruled.* There's nothing new
in Penn's defense. And yet what chooses hunger
over the homeless? Native American youth
above Cambodian orphans? Unwed mothers
instead of the urchins in Penn's own neighborhood?
Penn stares at his three newly recovered chairs,
a print that dwarfs the room. *Your answer please?*
Is there a granting center in the cerebellum
awarding on the basis of photos, eloquence,
a respectable racial, geographic mix?
Or would the arbitrary, inert as the gas
that lights the ceiling fixture, fill his conscience
with a cool, overall, and steady glow,
effecting the same result without the ordeal?

Never-in-a-Million-Years, Probably
Sometimes he uses the package of notecards
with watercolor landscapes an armless woman
creates with her toes and sends on Mother's Day
to "Mrs. Penn or Current Resident."
Although Penn never donates to her fund,
each year the set arrives and he debates
whether it's worse to pitch the cards or to use them.
His wife had always saved the cards, slipped them
among the tabs of an expandable file
that read: "Boy/Girl," "Get Well," "With Sympathy,"
"Happy—" and so on through life's fixed occasions.

Once Penn wrote a card to his daughter-in-law
who had lost a close aunt. He tried to say
the little he felt entitled to say, never
having met the woman, but midway through
Penn was telling about the paraplegic
in some displaced sense of mixed compassion.
Instead, he donated to the children's hospital
the aunt had designated in her will,
and sent a brief note, in one of the artist's
"Thinking of You" cards, to the artist herself,
wishing her well, and requesting his deceased
wife's name be dropped, for all the good it did.

## Time-Out
Penn changes from his bathrobe to walking shorts,
opens the blinds, and with his finger, starts
the coffee grounds landsliding from a tin.
Penn often gives to the row of the crippled or crazed
and unseasonably clothed who sway against
the department store displays of mannequins
disporting cruise wear and fun furs.
There's no prose, no distance, no time-lapse
to interfere with Penn's response, even
though he's read how much some beggars
*earn* from the loose change of passersby.
But Penn resists the contradictory
ideas that if you give to one, therefore,
you must give—or you *have* given—
to them all, just as he resists the idea
that fortune finds appreciation once
ill-fortune follows, or sight only by blindness,
speech by silence, riches (comparative)
by some impoverishment: Penn can feel
each loss intrinsically. Yet he doesn't,
much, given the other things he sets

himself to do. But he *can* feel, forcing
himself through the morning news, assuming each
of the aforementioned and possible fates.

The percolating ends. Penn takes his seat,
the father's seat, remembering the vacation
when his eldest urged a fast of water and rice
upon his siblings and parents, insisting they send
the difference in the week's grocery bills
to some sort of mission in Salt Lake City.
"You have to experience a problem to care about it,"
he pleaded as Penn's refusal was served up,
rote as leftovers, at every meal.
With autumn's return, his sophomore's attention
blew toward Vietnam, the students killed
at another Ohio college, and *e-pis-te-mol-*
*og-y,* which Penn had tried to understand
before his son declared a different major.
It wasn't that Penn ranked famine lower than rape,
higher than prisons, equal to equal rights.
But no one can tell you what you hope to feel
about your feelings, especially when you don't know
yourself—and especially when you *do* know.
It's daunting to Penn, knowing what he knows.
Penn gave to his children as if example
were precedent, prevention, palliative—
putting *epistemology* into practice.

### Likely

Penn orders a sweatshirt depicting an airborne hawk
in a catalog from the Raptor Rehab Fund,
whose cover is a picture of an owl
dangling from a post by one leg-trapped foot.
Since a previous mailing, its sequence of stills
has hung in Penn's remembered gallery
(a curator, he's not) of images

he can't get rid of: the owl struggling to free,
to right, but managing only to kill, itself.
He'll send the sweatshirt to his grandson, Tad,
along with a candid statement about . . . the threat
of owls to fisheries? the cruelty of traps?
Penn's exceptional fondness for birds of prey?
—no, with love for Tad. What more can he write?
His check's made out to the Tad Foundation, to spare him
from a world where raptors, and other creatures, are hanged.

Perhaps if everything but man did not depend
on man's protection (an unfit, unadaptive
strategy), Penn might resist their plights.
But testing cleanser in rabbits' eyes, grafting,
depriving, injecting, force-feeding, inflicting—
the mere idea is more than Penn can bear,
and he is not, and never will be, a subject.
He writes a pitiful check to several, unwillingly
subscribing to newsletters and updates
he'll pitch with the genuine hope to avoid even
a glimpse of a headline or photograph.

Penn balances his checkbook, facing the fact
that these last checks are less than those he wrote
to human causes, a fact that must contribute
to just such inhumanities. He turns
the "ones" to "twos" on his checks, forces the letters
into a hybrid handwriting that,
on second glance, no one would cash, rips
the checks and voids them all with the words "I'm sorry,"
trying to leave it at that until the next
season of letters, the next generation.

### Unlikely
Marian, his late wife, and Penn had saved
a Korean child for four years, their children

rotating the writing of the family's letter
that wrapped their monthly check for Woon Pil.
They took an interest in the child and her village
and when her replies spread weeks, then months, apart,
until, finally they stopped for over a year,
the Penns admitted they had forgotten the child—
Had Woon Pil grown, fled the village, died?—
until a renewal notice arrived requesting
the Penns redouble their life-giving support.
Penn has the crayoned pictures Woon Pil returned
in thanks, saved among the albums upstairs.
Penn makes a mental note to write—no,
he writes a note on a discarded card
to write the foundation about Woon Pil.
Penn sees her as the child in her own drawing
of her family, and not the mother of three.

### Never-in-a-Million-Years

Although it distresses Penn to know of advocates
of censorship, prayer in school, people
who want to lock America's doors to aliens
(as though citizenship was not a man-
made, made-up thing at all, but something
biological abiding nature's laws),
Penn's glad for any cause he can truly refuse.
The fine print, the actual sponsor, the slant
of graphed statistics, the cant of propaganda—
Penn wades through it all in good conscience
in hopes of flushing out a fact as suspect
as the mock telegrams with the fake red
rubber stamp of "POSTMAN, EXPEDITE!"
that *morally* Penn can't support, sparing him
the financial altogether. He plucks the penny,
"a shiny new one sent to you for caring,"
denying the Friends (With-Friends-Like-That-Who
Needs-Enemies!) of Unborn Lives, destroys

a postcard urging Congress to legalize
the sale of submachine guns, removes
the sticklet of a pencil before he shreds
a letter that begins, "Our hope is thin
and fragile as this pencil lead, and yet
it can inscribe the numbers on a pledge card."
Penn pledges to weigh each envelope in the future
to keep from hefting the world's weight at once.

Another error: Once Penn did order
the veterans' address labels for all
his grandchildren—a small enough donation.
But Penn had not predicted how he'd mind
their frequent letters' continual reminder:
the tiny American flag beside their names
as if each child were slated for the draft,
identified as would-be veterans
of future wars that Penn would never see.

Penn's feet are covered with the cast-out requests.
He stands to make more coffee, pulls free
of the houndings, tuggings, and beseechings. Penn knows
there's nothing he can cure or conquer with coffee.

Unlikely
Penn doodles his full name inside a circle
his mug has made on fancy stationery
from a famous actress he knows but can't quite place.
She's writing Penn from the bottom of her heart,
in red and blue, bold and italic types:
"Remember Francis the talking mule?" she asks.
(Vaguely. Mister Ed, the talking horse,
is more familiar.) "Remember how you gathered
in the family room—" (No, not the family room.
There was only the living room then, with the black-and-white
that served all year except for *The Wizard of Oz.*)

"Remember how Francis's funny lips would move?
Did your children ever ask you how
a mule could move his lips like human lips?"
Penn takes a slug of coffee, uses his hand
like calipers to feel how much the pile yet holds.
"And did your children ever ask you why?"
Penn can't see where this movie star is going.
(Had she ever gone anywhere at all?)
Agreed, his kids asked *how* much more than *why* . . .
*what* more than *when* . . . *who* more
than *where*. They weren't angels, his three monsters,
or monsters, after the age of, what? . . . twenty?
but Penn fell short when it came to reasoning.
*Why?* Things were what they were, weren't they?
But when it came to *how?*—mechanics, instructions—
Dad was handy. But *how* a mule can talk?
"It's a good thing they didn't ask," the actress
continues in red. "The answer to how is shocking.
I mean that exactly. By shocking Francis
with electrical currents that triggered sentences
of spasms through the animal's sensitive lips.
The answer to WHY I couldn't tell you or
my own four children. They'd never understand.
Won't you join us?" she asks in handwriting
that must have been her own originally.

Penn refolds the letter before it's clear
what he can do—about the inhuman ways
of elevating an animal to the human,
about the sick feeling inside his stomach,
about the resentment, too: her putting words
in the horse's mouth again—the mule's, he means,
although he can't imagine Mister Ed
was coached with other currents, for instance, kindness.
Resolving never to watch the reruns on cable
(no real concession; he never watched the show)

won't censor his memory: a blurry reel
of horses among the roadside pastures, charging
a silent Penn with their disquietude.

                    Likely
"A mind is a terrible thing to waste" is next
on top of the chair, a contribution Penn
has hoped to make so many times, returning
the envelope to the bottom of the pile, that now
he finds another *FINAL NOTICE* from the Fund,
and several other mailings he has ignored.
They make an inch-thick stack, with postmarks
ranging two full years. "Do I harbor
some selfish naïveté," Penn asks himself
as he writes a sizable check. "Do I hope the problem
is solved in the meantime and that my check
will then be stamped: RETURN TO SENDER, WITH
    THANKS."
"Not now" translates into a simple "no."
"Not now," Penn says, again, the word
testifying against him like the truth.
What's worse, the envelopes continue their claim:
"Not now," Penn says to the Nuclear Freeze Campaign—
but if not to them, then who survives to use
whatever else Penn thought his checks would aid?
"Not now," Penn says to the Special Olympics.
The two words beat against his breast like a fist,
like a heart, as though to symbolize the suffering
each of his repeated denials will cause.

          Likely, Unlikely, Never-in-a-Million-Years
Still, Penn feels like a good person, considers
his conduct moral, charitable, decent, kind.
"Aren't I entitled? Aren't there any boundaries
to cross—if not into safety perhaps
into the sector of having given, having tithed?"

No matter. As Penn confronts the causes—
the threatened, fearful, needy, distraught warp
of human history in which he must include
himself—Penn wishes he could send them all,
blessed and abandoned, down the trickling stream
behind his building. But who would find them,
who, care for them—for all the foundling,
the foundering requests—more and better
than Penn? "I'd like to know," Penn says aloud.
"I'd like to send him these."

### Penn's Condition

    Penn takes the basket,
refills it with the false prophecies
of sweepstakes mailers, the trial memberships,
as well as the pleas unfavorably judged,
and swaddles it, fruit basket and all,
inside a plastic bag that he ties and drops
beside the trash cans that border the elevator.
Tonight, the maintenance crew will gather it
and feed it to the basement incinerator,
a hellish room adjoining their office/lounge.

Penn's not immortal. For now, for the time being,
he can live with this decision as with a chronic
condition, something he can monitor
with diet, conscientiousness, and luck,
until the day he dies of some disease
he probably never heard of, let alone
contributed to. But others will have, thank God.
Penn's not alone in this: his bag of trash
fit among the others beside the cans;
his mailbox is but one of forty-some
along the lobby wall. There is some comfort
in shared responsibility—take
the condominium, for instance. On Monday

Penn pledges to start his new routine,
to exercise his measure of hopefulness
afresh with each thing as it arrives
in slot *4C, Penn, Gordon,*
a man who is, by today's standards, a winner,
or at the very least, a good loser.

# SHELTER

o

*Charles Baxter*

Cooper had stopped at a red light on his
way to work and was adjusting the dial on his radio when he
looked up and saw a man in a filthy brown corduroy suit and a
three-day growth of beard staring in through the front windshield and picking with his fingernails at Cooper's windshield
wiper. Cooper had seen this man before on various Ann Arbor
street corners. He always inspired in Cooper a feeling of un-
easiness and unpleasant compassion. Rolling down the window
and leaning out, Cooper said, "Wait a minute there. Just wait
a minute. If you get out of this intersection and over to that
sidewalk, I'll be with you in a minute." The man stared at
Cooper. *"I'll have something for you,"* he said emphatically.
Cooper parked his car at a meter two blocks up, and when he
returned, the man in the corduroy suit was standing under a
silver maple tree, rubbing his back against the bark.

"Didn't think you'd come back," the man said, glancing at

Cooper. His hair fell over the top of his head in every direction. "How do you do?" Cooper said. He held his hand out, but the man—who seemed rather old, close up—didn't take it. "I'm Cooper." The man smelled of everything, a bit like a municipal dump, and Cooper tried not to notice it.

"It doesn't matter who I am," the man said, standing unsteadily. "I don't care who I am. It's not worth anybody thinking about it." He looked up at the sky and began to pick at his coat sleeve.

"What's your name?" Cooper asked softly. "Tell me your name, please."

The old man's expression changed. He stared at the blue sky, perfectly empty of clouds, and after a moment said, "My mother used to call me James."

"Good. Well, then, how do you do, James?" The man looked dubiously at his own hand, then reached over and shook. "Would you like something to eat?"

"I like sandwiches," the man said.

"Well, then," Cooper said, "that's what we'll get you."

As they went down the sidewalk, the man stumbled into the side of a bench at a bus stop and almost tripped over a fire hydrant. He had a splay-footed walk, as if one of his legs had once been broken. Cooper began to pilot him by touching him on his back.

"Would you like to hear a bit of the Gospels?" the man asked.

"All right. Sure."

He stopped and held on to a light pole. "This is the fourth book of the Gospels. Jesus is speaking. He says, 'I will not leave you desolate; I will come to you. Yet a little while, and the world will see me no more, but you will see me; because I live, you will live also.' That's from John," the man said. They were outside the Ann Arbor Diner, a neon-and-chrome Art Deco hamburger joint three blocks down from the university campus. "There's more," the old man said, "but I don't remember it."

"Wait here," Cooper said. "I'm going to get you a sand-wich."

The man was looking uncertainly at his lapel, fingering a funguslike spot.

"James!" Cooper said loudly. "Promise me you won't go away!"

The man nodded.

When Cooper came out again with a bag of french fries, a carton of milk, and a hamburger, the man had moved down the street and was leaning against the plate-glass window of a sea-food restaurant with his hands covering his face. "James!" Cooper said. "Here's your meal." He held out the bag.

"Thank you." When the man removed his hands from his face, Cooper saw in his eyes a moment of completely clear lu-cidity and sanity, a glance that took in the street and himself, made a judgment about them all, and quickly withdrew from any engagement with them. He took the hamburger out of its wrapping, studied it for a moment, and then bit into it. As he ate, he gazed toward the horizon.

"I have to go to work now," Cooper said.

The man nodded again and turned his face away.

"What are we going to do?" Cooper said to his wife. They were lying in bed at sunrise, when they liked to talk. His hand was on her thigh and was caressing it absently and familiarly. "What are we going to do about these characters? They're on the street corners. Every month there are more of them. Kids, men, women, everybody. It's a horde. They're sleeping in the arcade and they're pushing those terrible grocery carts around with all their worldly belongings, and it makes me nuts to watch them. I don't know what I'm going to do, but whatever it is, I have to do it." With his other hand, he rubbed his eyes. "I dream about them."

"You're such a good person," she said sleepily. Her hand brushed over him. "I've noticed that about you."

"No, that's wrong," Cooper said. "This has nothing to do with good. Virtue doesn't interest me. What this is about is not feeling crazy when I see those people."

"So what's your plan?"

He rose halfway out of bed and looked out the back window at the treehouse he had started for Alexander, their seven-year-old. Dawn was breaking, and the light came in through the slats of the blinds and fell in strips over him. "Christine," he said, and his wife looked at him.

When he didn't say anything else, she said, "I was just thinking. When I first met you, before you dropped out of law school, you always used to have your shirts laundered, with starch, and I remember the neat creases in your trouser legs, from somebody ironing them. You smelled of aftershave in those days. Sexually, you were ambitious. You took notes slowly. Fastidious penmanship. I like you better now."

"I remember," he said. "It was a lecture on proximate cause."

"No," she said. "It was contribution and indemnification."

"Whatever."

He took her hand and led her to the bathroom. Every morning Cooper and his wife showered together. He called it soul-showering. He had picked up the phrase from a previous girl friend, though he had never told Christine that. Cooper had told his wife that by the time they were thirty they would probably not want to do this anymore, but they were both now twenty-eight, and she still seemed to like it.

Under the sputter of the water, Christine brushed some soap out of her eyes and said, "Cooper, were you ever a street person?"

"No."

"Smoke a lot of dope in high school?"

"No."

"I bet you drank a lot once." She was an assistant prosecutor in the district attorney's office and sometimes brought her professional habits home. "You tapped kegs and lay out on the lawns and howled at the sorority girls."

"Sometimes I did that," he said. He was soaping her back. She had wide flaring shoulders from all the swimming she had done, and the soap and water flowed down toward her waist in a pattern of V's. "I did all those things," he said, "but I never became that kind of person. What's your point?"

She turned around and faced him, the full display of her smile. "I think you're a latent vagrant," she said.

"But I'm not," he said. "I'm here. I have a job. *This* is where I am. I'm a father. How can you say that?"

"Do I love you?" she asked, water pouring over her face. "Stay with me."

"Well, sure," he said. "That's my plan."


The second one he decided to do something about was standing out of the hot summer sun in the shade of a large catalpa tree near a corner newsstand. This one was holding what seemed to be a laundry sack with the words *American Linen Supply* stenciled on it. She was wearing light summer clothes—a Hawaiian shirt showing a palm tree against a bloody splash of sunset, and a pair of light cotton trousers, and red Converse tennis shoes—and she stood reading a paperback, beads of sweat falling off her face onto the pages.

This time Cooper went first to a fast-food restaurant, bought the hamburger, french fries, and milk, and then came back.

"I brought something for you," Cooper said, walking to the reading woman. "I brought you some lunch." He held out a bag. "I've seen you out here on the streets many times."

"Thank you," the woman said, taking the bag. She opened it, looked inside, and sniffed appreciatively.

"Are you homeless?" Cooper asked.

"They have a place where you can go," the woman said.

She put down the bag and looked at Cooper. "My name's Estelle," she said. "But we don't have to talk."

"Oh, that's all right. If you want. Where's this shelter?"

"Over there." The woman gestured with a french fry she had picked out. She lifted the bag and began to eat. Cooper looked down at the book and saw that it was in a foreign language. The cover had fallen off. He asked her about it.

"Oh, that?" she said. She spoke with her mouth full of food, and Cooper felt a moment of superiority about her bad manners. "It's about women. It's about what happens to women in this world. It's in French. I used to be Canadian. My mother taught me French."

Cooper stood uncomfortably. He took a key ring out of his pocket and twirled it around his index finger. "So what happens to women in this world?"

"What *doesn't*?" the woman said. "Everything happens. It's terrible but sometimes it's all right, and, besides, you get used to it."

"You seem so normal," Cooper said. "How come you're out here?"

The woman straightened up and looked at him. "My mind's not quite right," she said, scratching an eyelid. "Mostly it is but sometimes it isn't. They messed up my medication and one thing led to another and here I am. I'm not complaining. I don't have a bad life."

Cooper wanted to say that she *did* have a bad life, but stopped himself.

"If you want to help people," the woman said, "you should go over to the shelter. They need volunteers over there. People to clean up. You could get rid of your guilt over there, mopping the floors."

"What guilt?" he asked.

"All men are guilty," she said. She was chewing but had put her bag of food on the ground and was staring hard and directly into Cooper's face. He turned toward the street. When he looked at the cars, everyone heading somewhere with a kind of fierce intentionality, braking hard at red lights and peeling rubber at the green, he felt as though he had been pushed out of his own life.

"You're still here," the woman said. "What do you want?"

"I was about to leave." He was surprised by how rude she was.

"I don't think you've ever seen the Rocky Mountains or even the Swiss Alps, for that matter," the woman said, bending down to inspect something close to the sidewalk.

"No, you're right. I haven't traveled much."

"We're not going to kiss, if that's what you think," the woman said, still bent over. Now she straightened up again, glanced at him, and looked away.

"No," Cooper said. "I just wanted to give you a meal."

"Yes, thank you," the woman said. "And now you have to go."

"I was . . . I *was* going to go."

"I don't want to talk to you anymore," the woman said. "It's nothing against you personally, but talking to men just tires me out terribly and drains me of all my strength. Thank you very much, and good-bye." She sat down again and opened up her paperback. She took some more french fries out of the sack and began to eat as she read.


"They're polite," Cooper said, lying next to his wife. "They're polite, but they aren't nice."

"Nice? Nice? Jesus, Cooper, I prosecute rapists! Why should they be nice? They'd be crazy to be nice. Who cares about nice except you? This is the 1980s, Cooper. Get real."

He rolled over in bed and put his hand on her hip. "All right," he said.

They lay together for a while. The moon shone in through

the slats of the bedroom blinds, and, together, they heard Alexander snoring in his bedroom across the hall.

"I can't sleep, Cooper," she said. "Tell me a story."

"Which one tonight?" Cooper was a good improviser of stories to help his wife relax and doze off. "Hannah, the snoopy cleaning woman?"

"No," Christine said. "I'm tired of Hannah."

"The adventures of Roderick, insurance adjuster?"

"I'm sick of him, too."

"How about another boring day in Paradise?"

"Yeah. Do that."

For the next twenty minutes, Cooper described the beauty and tedium of Paradise—the perfect rainfalls, the parks with roped-off grassy areas, the sideshows and hot air balloon rides, the soufflés that never fell—and in twenty minutes, Christine was asleep, her fingers touching him. He was aroused. "Christine?" he whispered. But she was sleeping.

The next morning, as Cooper worked at his baker's bench, rolling chocolate almond croissants, he decided that he would check out the shelter in the afternoon to see if they needed any help. He looked up from his hands, with a trace of dough and sugar under the fingernails, over toward his boss, Gilbert, who was brewing coffee and humming along to some Coltrane coming out of his old radio perched on top of the mixer. Cooper loved the bakery where he worked. He loved the smell and everything they made there. He had noticed that bread made people unusually happy. Customers closed their eyes when they ate Cooper's doughnuts and croissants and Danishes. He looked up toward the skylight and saw that the color of the sky had turned from pale blue to dark blue, what the sixty-four Crayola box called blue-indigo. He could tell from the tint of the sky that it was seven o'clock, and time to unlock the front doors to let the first of the customers in. After Gilbert turned the key and the Firestone mechanics from down the street shuffled in to get their morning doughnuts and coffee in Styrofoam cups, Cooper stood behind the counter in his whites and watched their faces, the slow private smiles that always registered when they first caught the scent of the baked dough and the sugared fruit.

The shelter was in a downtown furniture store that had gone out of business during the recession of '79. In order to provide some privacy, the first volunteers had covered over the front plate-glass window with long strips of paper from giant rolls, with the result that during the daytime the light inside was colored an unusual tint, somewhere between orange and off-white. As soon as he volunteered, he was asked to do odd jobs. He first went to work in the evening ladling out food—stew, usually, with ice cream scoop mounds of mashed potatoes.

The director of the shelter was a brisk and slightly over-weight woman named Marilyn Adams, who, though tough and efficient, seemed vaguely annoyed about everything. Cooper liked her officious irritability. He didn't want any baths of feeling in this place.

From night to night, depending on the weather, the shelter's population varied from a dozen or so to just under thirty. Battered wives came in and were directed to the women's shelter on the other side of town. The homeless women, and those with children, were given beds on the north side of the building and separated from the rest with partitions installed on ceiling tracks. In this building, everyone had some kind of makeshift partition to give some small sense of privacy. One of Cooper's jobs was to warn the male guests against trying anything weird with the women. "Tell them to take their social lives elsewhere," Marilyn Adams told him. "I don't want any funny stuff here. Any funny stuff and the town of Ann Arbor will close us like that." She snapped her pudgy fingers.

"Marilyn," Cooper said. "This is a shelter, not a party after a sock hop."

She peered at him over her reading glasses. She sagged a bit down in her chair. "No funny stuff," she repeated. "We've got to keep our luckless friends on the straight and narrow." She smiled her glacial smile.

Around five o'clock on a Thursday afternoon—the bakery closed at four—Cooper was making beds near the front window when he heard a voice from behind him. "Hey," the voice said. "I want to get in here."

Cooper turned around. He saw the reddest person he had ever laid eyes on: the young man's hair was red, his face flamed with sunburn and freckles, and, as if to accentuate his skin and hair tone, he was wearing a bright pink Roxy Music T-shirt. He was standing near the window, with the light behind him, and all Cooper could see of him was a still, flat expression and deeply watchful eyes. When he turned, he had the concentrated otherworldliness of figures in religious paintings.

Cooper told the young man about the shelter's regulations and told him which bed he could have. The young man—he seemed almost a boy—stood listening, his right foot thumping against the floor and his right hand shaking in the air as if he were trying to get water out of it. When the young man nodded, his head went up and down too fast, and Cooper thought he was being ironic. "Who are you?" he finally asked. "My name's Cooper."

"Billy Bell," the young man said. "That's a real weird name, isn't it?" He shook his head but didn't look at Cooper or wait for him to agree or disagree. "My mother threw me out last week. Why shouldn't she? I'm twenty-three. She thought I was doing drugs. I wasn't doing drugs. Drugs are so fucking boring. Look at those awful capitalist lizards using them and you'll know what I mean. But I *was* a problem. She was right. She had to get on my case. She decided to throw me away for a while. Trash trash. So I've been sleeping in alleys and benches and I slept for a couple of nights in the Arboretum, but there are too many mosquitoes this time of year for that and I've got bites. I was living with a girl but all my desires left me. You live here, Cooper, you homeless yourself, or what?"

"I'm a volunteer," he said. "I just work here. I've got a home."

"I don't," Billy Bell said. "People should have homes. I don't work now. I lost my job. I'm full of energy but I'm apathetic. Very little appeals to me. I guess I'm going to start some of those greasy minimum wage things if I can stand them. I'm smart. I'm not a loser. I'm definitely not one of these messed-up ghouls who call this place home."

Cooper stood up and walked toward the kitchen, knowing that the young man would follow him. "They aren't ghouls," he said. "Look around. They're more normal than you are, probably. They're down on their luck."

"Of course they are, of course they are," Billy said, his voice floating a few inches behind Cooper's head. Cooper began to wipe off the kitchen counter, and Billy Bell watched him as he worked. He began waving his right hand again. "My problem, Cooper, my problem is the problem of the month, which is pointlessness and the point of doing anything, which I can't see most of the time. I want to heal people but I can't do that. I'm stalled. What happened was, about a year ago, there was this day, I remember it was sunny, I mean the sun was out, and I heard these wings flapping over my head because I was out in the park with my girl friend feeding Cheerios to the pigeons. Then this noise: flap flap flap. Wings, Cooper, *big* wings, taking my soul away. I didn't want to look behind me because I was afraid they'd taken my shadow, too. It could happen, Cooper, it could happen to anybody. Anyhow, after that, what I knew was, I didn't want what everybody else did, I mean I don't have any desires for anything, and at some time of day I *don't* cast a shadow. My desires just went away, like that, poof, poor desires. I'm a saint now but I'm not enjoying it one bit. I can bless people but not heal them. Anybody could lose his soul the way I did. Now all I got is that sad robot feeling. You know, that five o'clock feeling? But all day, with me."

"You mentioned your mother," Cooper said. He dropped some cleanser into the sink and began to scour it. "What about your father?"

"Let me do that." Billy nudged Cooper aside and started to clean the sink with agitated, almost frantic hand motions. "I've done a *lot* of this. My father died last year. I did a lot of housecleaning. I'm a man-maid. My father was in the hospital, but we took him out, and I was trying to be, I don't know, a sophomore in college, which is a pretty dumb thing to aspire to, if you think about it. But I was also sitting by my father's bed and taking care of him—he had pancreatic cancer—and I was reading *Popular Mechanics* to him, the home improvement section, and feeding him when he could eat, and then when he died, the wings flew over me, though that was later, and there wasn't much I wanted to do. What a sink."

As he talked, Billy's hand accelerated in its motions around the drain.

"Come on," Cooper said. "I'm going to take you somewhere."


His idea was to lift the young man's spirits, but he didn't know quite how to proceed. He took him to his car and drove him down the river road to a metropark, where Billy got out of the car, took his shoes off, and waded into the water. He bent down, and, as Cooper watched, cupped his hands in the river before splashing it over his face. Cooper thought his face had a strange expression, something between ecstasy and despair. He couldn't think of a word in English for this expression but thought there might be a word in another language for it. German, for example. When Billy was finished washing his face, he looked up into the sky. Pigeons and killdeer were flying overhead. After he had settled back into the front seat of Cooper's car, his face dripping down onto the front seat, Billy said, "That's a good feeling, Cooper. You should try it. You wash your face in the flowing water and then you hear the cries of the birds. I'd like to think it makes me a new man but I know it doesn't. How old are you, Cooper?"

"I'm twenty-eight."

"Five years older than me. And what did you say you did?"

"I'll show you."

He drove Billy to the bakery and parked in the back alley. It was getting close to twilight. After Cooper had unlocked the back door, Billy walked into the dark bakery kitchen and began to sniff. "I like this place," he said. "I like it very much." He shook some invisible water out of his hand, then ran his finger along the bench. "What's this made of?"

"Hardrock maple. It's like the wood they use in bowling alleys. Hardest wood there is. You can't dent it or break it. Look up."

Billy twisted backward. "A skylight," he said. "Cooper, your life is on the very top of the eggshell. You have grain from the earth and you have the sky overhead. Ever been broken into?"

"No."

Cooper looked at Billy and saw, returning to him, a steady gaze made out of the watchful and flat expression he had first seen on the young man's face when he had met him a few hours before. "No," he repeated, "never have." He felt, suddenly, that he had embarked all at once on a series of misjudgments. "What did your father do, Billy?"

"He was a surgeon," Billy said. "He did surgery on people."

They stood and studied each other in the dark bakery for a moment.

"We'll go one more place," Cooper said. "I'll get you a beer. Then I have to take you back to the shelter."

. . .

Cooper's dog, Hugo, came out through the backyard and jumped up on him as he got out of his car. A load of wash, mostly Alexander's shirts, flapped on the clothesline in the evening breeze. Cooper heard children calling from down the street.

"Here we are," Cooper said. "We'll go in through this door."

Inside the house, Christine was sitting at the dining room table with two legal pads set up in front of her and a briefcase down by the floor. Behind her, in the living room, Alexander was lying on the floor in front of the TV set, his chin cupped in his hands. He was watching a Detroit Tigers game. They both looked up when Cooper knocked on the kitchen doorframe and came into the hallway, followed by Billy, whose hands were in his pockets and who nodded as he walked.

"Christine," Cooper said. "This is Billy. I met him at the shelter." Billy walked quickly around the table and shook Christine's hand. "I brought him here for a beer."

Christine did not change her posture. Behind a smile, she gave Billy a hard look. "Hello," she said. "And welcome, I guess."

"Thank you," Billy said. Cooper went out to the kitchen, opened a beer, and brought it back to him. Billy looked at the bottle, then took a long swig from it. After wiping his mouth, he said, "Well, my goodness. I certainly never expected to be here in your home tonight."

"Well, we didn't expect you either, Mr.—?"

"Bell," Billy said. "Billy Bell."

"We didn't expect you either, Mr. Bell. You're lucky. My husband never does this." She looked now at Cooper. "He never *never* does this."

Cooper pointed toward the living room. "Billy, that's Alexander over there. He's in the Alan Trammell Fan Club. I guess you can tell."

Alexander turned around, looked at Billy, and said, "Hi," waving quickly. Billy returned the greeting, but Alexander had already returned to the TV set, now showing a commercial for shaving cream.

"So, Mr. Bell," Christine said. "What brings you to Ann Arbor?"

"Oh, I've always lived here," Billy said. "Graduated from Pioneer High and everything." He began a little jumping motion, then quelled it. "How about you?"

"Oh, not me," Christine said. "I'm from Dayton, Ohio. I came here to law school. That's where I met Cooper."

"I thought he was a baker."

"He is now. He dropped out of law school."

"You didn't drop out?" Billy glanced at Christine's legal pads. "You became a lawyer?"

"I became a prosecutor, yes, that's right. In the district attorney's office. That's what I do."

"Do you like it?" Cooper thought Billy was about to explode in some way; he was getting redder and redder.

"Oh yes," Christine said. "I like it very much."

"Why?"

"Why?" She touched her face and her smile faded. "I came from a family of bullies, Mr. Bell. Three brothers. They tied me up and played tricks on me, and they did this for years. Little boy criminals. Every promise they made to me, they broke. Then I discovered the law, when I grew up. It's about limits and enforced regulation and binding agreements. It's a net of words, Mr. Bell. Legal formulas for proscribing behavior. That's what the law is. Now I have a career of putting promise breakers behind bars. That makes me happy. What makes you happy, Mr. Bell?"

Billy hopped once, then leaned against the counter. "I didn't have any dreams until today," Billy said, "but now I do, seeing your cute house and your cute family. Here's what I'd like to do. I want to be *just like all of you.* I'd put on a chef's hat and stand outside in my apron like one of those assholes you see in the Sunday magazine section with a spatula in his hand, and, like, I'll be flipping hamburgers and telling my kids to keep their hands out of the chive dip and go run in the sprinkler or do some shit like that. I'll belong to do-good groups like Save the Rainforests and I'll ask my wife how she likes her meat, rare or well done, and she'll say well done with that pretty smile she has, and that's how I'll do it. A wonderful fucking barbecue, this is, with folding aluminum chairs and paper plates and ketchup all over the goddamn place. Oceans of vodka and floods of beer. Oh, and we've sprayed the yard with that big spray that kills anything that moves, and all the flies and mosquitoes and bunnies are dead at our feet. Talk about the good life. That has got to be it."

Alexander had turned around and was staring at Billy, and Christine's face had become masklike and rigid. "Finish your beer, Mr. Bell," she said. "I think you absolutely have to go now. Don't let's waste another minute. Finish the beer and back you go."

"Yes," he said, nodding and grinning.

"I suppose you think what you just said was funny," Cooper said, from where he was standing in the back of the kitchen.

"No," Billy said. "I can't be funny. I've tried often. It doesn't work. No gift for that."

"Have you been in prison, Mr. Bell?" Christine asked, looking down at her legal pad and writing something there.

"No," Billy said. "I have not."

"Oh good," Christine said. "I was afraid maybe you had been."

"Do you think that's what will become of me?" Billy asked. His voice had lowered from its previous manic delivery and become soft.

"Oh, who knows?" Christine said, running her hand through her hair. "It could happen, or maybe not."

"Because I think my life is out of my hands," Billy said. "I just don't think I have control over it any longer."

"Back you go," Christine said. "Good-bye. Fare thee well."

"Thank you," Billy said. "That was a nice blessing. And thank you for the beer. Good-bye, Alexander. It was nice meeting you."

"Nice to meet you," the boy said from the floor.

"Let's go," Cooper said, picking at Billy's elbow.

"Back I go," Billy said. "Fare thee well, Billy, good-bye and godspeed. So long, Mr. Human Garbage. Okay, all right, yes, now I'm gone." He did a quick walk through the kitchen and let the screen door slam behind him. Christine gave Cooper a look, which he knew meant that she was preparing a speech for him, and then he followed Billy out to the car.


On the way to the shelter, Billy slouched down on the passenger side. He said nothing for five minutes. Then he said, "I noticed something about your house, Cooper. I noticed that in the kitchen there were all these glasses and cups and jars out on the counter, and the jars weren't labeled, not the way they usually label them, and so I looked inside one of them, one of those jars, and you know what I saw? I suppose you must know, because it's your kitchen."

"What?" Cooper asked.

"Pain," Billy said, looking straight ahead and nodding. "That jar was full of pain. I had to close the lid over it immediately. Now tell me something, because I don't have the answer to it. Why does a man like you, a baker, have a jar full of pain in his kitchen? Can you explain that?"

Out through the front windows, Cooper saw the reassuring lights of the city, the lamplights shining out through the front windows, and the streetlights beginning to go on. A few children were playing on the sidewalks, hopscotch and tag, and in the sky a vapor trail from a jet was beginning to dissolve into orange wisps. What was the price one paid for loving one's own life? He felt a tenderness toward existence and toward his own life, and felt guilty for that.

At the shelter, he let Billy out without saying good-night.

He watched the young man do his hop-and-skip walk toward the front door; then he put the car into gear and drove home. As he expected, Christine was waiting up for him and gave him a lecture, in bed, about guilty liberalism and bringing the slime element into your own home.

"That's an exaggeration," Cooper said. He was lying on his side of the bed, his hip touching hers. "That's not what he was. I'm not wrong. I'm not." He felt her lips descending over him and remembered how she always thought that his failures in judgment made him sensual.

Two days later he arrived at work before dawn and found Gilbert standing motionless in front of Cooper's own baker's bench. Cooper closed the door behind him and said, "Hey, Gilbert."

"It's all right," Gilbert said. "I already called the cops."

"What?"

Gilbert pointed. On the wood table were hundreds of pieces of broken glass from the scattered skylight in a slice-of-pie pattern, and, over the glass, a circle of dried blood the width of a teacup. Smaller dots of blood, like afterthoughts, were scattered around the bench and led across the floor to the cash register, which had been jimmied open. Cooper felt himself looking up. A bird of a type he couldn't identify was perched on the broken skylight.

"Two hundred dollars," Gilbert said, overpronouncing the words. "Somewhere somebody's all cut up for a lousy two hundred dollars. I'd give the son of a bitch a hundred not to break in, if he'd asked. But you know what I really mind?"

"The blood," Cooper said.

"Bingo," Gilbert nodded, as he coughed. "I hate the idea of this fucker's blood in my kitchen, on the floor, on the table, and over there in the mixing pans. I really hate it. A bakery. What a fucking stupid place to break into."

. . .

"I told you so," Christine said, washing Cooper's face. Then she turned him around and ran the soapy washcloth down his back and over his buttocks.

August. Three days before Christine's birthday. Cooper and his son are walking down Main Street toward a store called The Peaceable Kingdom to get Christine a present, a small stuffed pheasant that Alexander has had his eye on for many months. Alexander's hand is in Cooper's as they cross at the corner, after waiting for the Walk sign to go on. Alexander has been asking Cooper for an exact definition of trolls, and how they differ from ghouls. And what, he wants to know, what exactly is a goblin, and how are they born? In forests? Can they be born anywhere, like trolls?

Up ahead, squatting against the window of a sporting goods store, is the man perpetually dressed in the filthy brown corduroy suit. James. His hands are woven together at his forehead, thumbs at temples, to shade his eyes against the sun. As Cooper and his son pass by, James speaks up. He does not ask for money. He says, "Hello, Cooper."

"Hello, James," Cooper says.

"Is this your boy?" He pulls his hands apart and points at Alexander.

"Yes."

"Daddy," Alexander says. He tugs at his father's hand.

"A fine boy," James says, squinting. "Looks a bit like you." The old man smells as he always has: like a city dump, like everything.

"Thank you," Cooper says, beaming. "He's a handsome boy, isn't he?"

"Indeed," James says. "Would you like to hear a bit of the Gospels?"

"No, thank you, James," Cooper says. "We're on our way to get this young man's mother a birthday present."

"Well, I won't keep you," the old man says.

Cooper reaches for his wallet.

"Daddy, don't," Alexander says.

"What?"

"Don't give him any money," the boy says.

"Why not?"

Alexander can't say. He begins to shake his head, looking at James, then at his father. He backs away, down the sidewalk, his lower lip beginning to stick out and his eyes starting to grow wet.

"Here, James," Cooper says, watching his son, who has retreated down the block to get away from his father and is now hiding in the doorway of a hardware store. He hands the old man five dollars.

"Bless you," James says. "And bless Jesus." He puts the money in his pocket, then places his hands together in front of his chest, lowers himself to his knees, and begins to pray.

"Good-bye, James," Cooper says. With his eyes closed, James nods. Cooper runs down the block to catch up with his son. After Alexander has finished crying, he tells his father that he was afraid that he was going to bring that dirty man home, the way he did with that red-haired guy, and let him stay, maybe in the basement, in the extra room.

"I wouldn't do that," Cooper says. "Really. I wouldn't do that."

"Wouldn't you?" his wife asked, that night, in bed. "Wouldn't you? I think you might."

"No. Not home. Not again."

But he had been accused, and he rose up and walked down the hall to his son's room. The house was theirs and no one else's; his footsteps were the only audible ones. In Alexander's room, in the dim illumination spread by the Swiss chalet nightlight, Cooper saw his son's model airplanes and the posters of his baseball heroes, but in looking around the room, he knew that something was missing. He glanced again at his son's dresser. The piggy bank, stuffed with pennies, was gone. He had hidden it. He had hidden it from his father.

He's frightened of my charity, Cooper thought, looking under the bed and seeing the piggy bank there, next to Alexander's favorite softball.

Cooper returned to bed. "He's hidden his money from me," he said.

"They do that, you know," Christine said. "And they go on doing that."

"You can't sleep," Cooper said, touching his wife.

"No," she said. "But it's all right."

"I can't tell you about Paradise," Cooper told her. "I gave you all the stories I knew."

"Well, what *do* you want?" she asked.

He put his hands over hers. "Shelter me," he said.

"Oh, Cooper," she said. "Which way this time? Which way?" To answer her, he rolled over, and, as quietly as he could, so as not to wake their son in the next room, he took her into his arms and held her there.

# WORKERS TO

# ATTENTION PLEASE

O

*Jay Neugeboren*

H<small>E WAS A SMALL</small> man standing on a large box.
One percent of the population owned forty-five percent of the
nation's wealth, he cried. I held my father's hand and we
moved forward through the falling snow. Did we know about
the six hundred families? The six hundred families controlled
everything that controlled us: railroads, coal, gas, electrical
power, movies, newspapers, radio, banks.

Below us subway trains thundered through warm tun-
nels. In the Soviet Union, the man proclaimed, a new world
was dawning, where men and women were not wage slaves—
where men and women worked side by side and owned the
means of production! The man's hands moved through the
snow as if he were already dismembered—as if pieces of him
were flying here and there like clumsy pigeons.

I have seen the future, my father said, and it is bloody.

Come, darling. We moved closer, to the outer edge of the circle of listeners.

Evening to you, Mr. Krinsky, Officer Kelly said.

Good evening, Mike, my father said, and he tipped his hat.

My father lifted me onto his shoulders. I could see the sign for S. Klein on the Square blinking faintly through the snow.

The man turned to the side and I saw half his face, his eye glowing blue like the pilot light on our gas stove at home. The workers of America had to be educated to the fact that their true enemy lived in Washington! I thought of trains rumbling high above us in the heavens, knocking loose huge pieces of snow from the sky as if they were chunks of ceiling plaster. The man looked directly at me and spoke about children of nine and ten years old who worked in subhuman conditions at subhuman pay—in coal mines and paper mills, in factories and sweatshops right here in New York City.

My father set me down and kissed me. Watch this, he said.

Even though he walked through snow, below the level of the man's box, my father was taller than the man. My father was taller than everyone, including Officer Kelly. My father was so large he could carry small pianos on his back. Six days a week he worked for the Santini Brothers Moving and Storage Company. On the Sabbath he rested. When I visited him, after school and on holidays, to watch him load trucks and move furniture in and out of storage, the Italians bragged that my father was the strongest man in New York.

Sir, my father said.

The man stopped talking.

Your Mr. Stalin is a gangster worse than Mussolini. Your Mr. Stalin cleans out Hitler's ass with the undergarments of poor Jews like you and me.

The man gaped. My father smiled. Officer Kelly moved forward, slapping his billy club against his black-gloved hand.

I moved with him. We had seen my father like this before. The man reached to one side and grabbed a pole that held the American flag. He lifted the flag high above his head, but the flag did not stop the terror in his eyes. My father took the pole from the man's hand, and set it upright. Then my father drove his fist into the middle of the man's face so that blood spurted and spread, like a rose flowering in snow.

My father turned, lifted me in his arms. Come, darling.

The man screamed for help, but people moved away quickly. The man shouted for Officer Kelly to arrest my father, to do something. He had a right to give speeches! He had a right not to be abused by capitalist thugs.

Yes, my father said. Because this is a free country. But since you don't like it here I want to help you. Since it is better in Russia, I want to help you to get there. I want to help you fly.

My father set me down and lifted the man bodily, one hand between the man's legs, the other around the man's chest. The man thrashed in the air like a small boy trying to swim.

That's enough for now, don't you think, Mr. Krinsky?

My father threw the man forward as if tossing a log into a fire. The man's head cracked against a lamppost. The man rolled over and lay on his back.

An old woman slapped at my father with a large paper bag. The bag split open and the leaflets tumbled into the air. On the top of each page were the words WORKERS TO ATTENTION PLEASE. My father tipped his hat and smiled at the woman.

Is he your son? my father asked.

The woman cursed my father. She said that someday men like him would be lined up in front of firing squads.

I already been, my father said. So what I am trying to do now is to knock some sense into people's heads when I am given the chance. This is a wonderful country we live in, with abundant opportunities. This country has been very good to people like you and me. Here we can pray without being arrested.

Here if you work hard, people pay you enough so you can feed your family.

The woman dropped to her knees and packed snow onto the small man's face.


I couldn't sleep because of how loud my mother was yelling at my father for what he had done. No, she wasn't proud of him. No, she did not believe that might made right. I got out of bed and opened the door, to see. The angrier my mother became, the happier my father seemed.

I love you, he declared. I love you when you yell at me.

My father grabbed my mother and pulled her to him, so that she sat on his lap. He lifted her hair from the back of her neck and kissed her there.

She shivered, then pounded against his chest. You're a child, she said. You're such a child.

I'm sorry I hit the man. But he was saying very stupid things.

Will you promise you won't do it again?

I promise.

She rested her head against his chest.

I worry about you, she said. All day I worry.

Don't.

I closed the door. My brother was snoring. I lifted the board from the side of his bed and kissed his cheek. He woke up and bellowed like a cow, then rolled over and fell onto the floor. My mother rushed into the room. I moved back. My brother was as tall and strong as my father, except that he did not understand how to read or to work. Sometimes my father brought him to the warehouse, to try to teach him to use his size and strength, but my mother always ended by bringing my brother home early. Then she put my brother in his bed and sat in my room and cursed my father for making her love him.

Get the rope, my mother said. Quickly.

I brought the rope and while my mother talked to my brother, my father tied up his hands and legs.

In Russia and in Germany they would have killed him, my father said. In many nations of the globe he would already be dead. Here they let him live.

When my brother snapped his teeth sideways, so he could chew the skin from his own shoulder, my father took out his handkerchief and began to bind my brother's mouth.

Then blood spurted from my brother's mouth in a quick stream, like red tobacco juice. My brother stopped howling. Between his teeth, he held onto two of my father's fingers.

My father closed his eyes but he didn't scream.

I told you, my mother said. Someday. I warned you.

Do something, my father said. Please.

Because you don't want to hurt him?

Please.

I stared at my brother's teeth, and listened to a sound that came from them, like wind trying to move through water.

My mother left the room and returned with a hammer.

She looked at my father and again he said please. She banged my brother on the head, between his eyes. My brother's eyes closed. My father's eyes opened.

I'll get the police, my mother said. God willing, maybe this time he's dead.

My father tried, but he could not open my brother's jaw. My mother told me to leave the room, but I held on to my father's arm, and when my mother pulled she could not break me loose.

# A WEDGE OF

# SHADE

O

*Louise Erdrich*

EVERY PLACE THAT I could name you, in the
whole world around us, has better things about it than Argus.
I just happened to grow up there for eighteen years and the
soil got to be part of me, the air has something in it that I
breathed. Argus water, fluoridated by an order of the state,
doesn't taste as good as water in the Cities. Still, the first thing
I do, walking back into my mother's house, is stand at the
kitchen sink and toss down glass after glass.

"Are you filled up?" My mother stands behind me. "Sit
down if you are."

She's tall and board square, with long arms and big
knuckles. Her face is rawboned, fierce and almost masculine in
its edges and planes. Several months ago, a beauty operator
convinced her that she should feminize her look with curls.
Now the permanent, grown out in grizzled streaks, bristles like

the coat of a terrier. I don't look like her. Not just the hair, since hers is salt and pepper, mine is a reddish brown, but my build. I'm short, boxy, more like my Aunt Mary, although there's not much about me that corresponds even to her, except it's true that I can't seem to shake this town. I keep coming back here.

"There's jobs at the beet plant."

This rumor, probably false as the plant is in a slump, drops into the dim close air of the kitchen. We have the shades drawn because it's a hot June, over a hundred degrees, and we're trying to stay cool. Outside, the water has been sucked from everything. The veins in the leaves are hollow, the ditch grass is crackling. The sky has absorbed every drop. It's a thin whitish blue veil stretched from end to end over us, a flat gauze tarp. From the depot, I've walked here beneath it, dragging my suitcase.

We're sweating like we're in an oven, a big messy one. For a week, it's been too hot to move much or even clean, and the crops are stunted, failing. The farmer next to us just sold his field for a subdivision, but the workers aren't doing much. They're wearing wet rags on their heads, sitting near the house sites in the brilliance of noon. The studs of wood stand uselessly upright, over them. Nothing casts a shadow. The sun has dried them up too.

"The beet plant," my mother says again.

"Maybe so," I say, and then, because I've got something bigger on my mind, "maybe I'll go out there and apply."

"Oh?" She is intrigued now.

"God, this is terrible!" I take the glass of water in my hand and tip some on my head. I don't feel cooler though, I just feel the steam rising off me.

"The fan broke down," she states. "Both of them are kaput now. The motors or something. If Mary would get the damn tax refund we'd run out to Pamida, buy a couple more, set up a breeze. Then we'd be cool out here."

"Your garden must be dead," I say, lifting the edge of the pull shade.

"It's sick, but I watered. And I won't mulch, that draws the damn slugs."

"Nothing could live out there, no bug." My eyes smart from even looking at the yard, cleared on the north, almost incandescent.

"You'd be surprised."

I wish I could blurt it out, just tell her. Even now, the words swell in my mouth, the one sentence, but I'm scared and with good reason. There is this about my mother: it is awful to see her angry. Her lips press together and she stiffens herself within, growing wooden, silent. Her features become fixed and remote, she will not speak. It takes a long time, and until she does you are held in suspense. Nothing that she ever says, in the end, is as bad as that feeling of dread. So I wait, half believing that she'll figure out my secret for herself, or drag it out of me, not that she ever tries. If I'm silent, she hardly notices. She's not like Aunt Mary, who forces me to say more than I know is on my mind.

My mother sighs, "It's too hot to bake. It's too hot to cook. But it's too hot to eat, anyway." She's talking to herself, which makes me reckless. Perhaps she is so preoccupied by the heat that I can slip my announcement past her. I should just say it, but I lose nerve, make an introduction that alerts her.

"I have something to tell you."

I've cast my lot, there's no going back unless I think quickly. My thoughts hum.

But she waits, forgetting the heat for a moment.

"Ice," I say, "we have to have ice." I speak intensely, leaning toward her, almost glaring, but she is not fooled.

"Don't make me laugh," she says, "there's not a cube in town. The refrigerators can't keep cold enough."

She eyes me as if I'm an animal about to pop from its den and run.

"Okay." I break down. "I really do have something." I

stand, turn my back. In this lightless warmth I'm dizzy, almost sick. Now I've gotten to her and she's frightened to hear, breathless.

"Tell me," she urges. "Go on, get it over with."

And so I say it. "I got married." There is a surge of relief, as if a wind blows through the room, but then it's gone. The curtain flaps and we're caught again, stunned in an even denser heat. It's now my turn to wait, and I whirl around and sit right across from her. But I can't bear the picture she makes, the shock that parts her lips, the stunned shade of hurt in her eyes. I have to convince her, somehow, that it's all right.

"You hate weddings! Just think, just picture it. Me, white net. On a day like this. You, stuffed in your summer wool, and Aunt Mary, God knows . . . and the tux, the rental, the groom . . ."

Her head lowered as my words fell on her, but now her forehead tips up and her eyes come into view, already hardening. My tongue flies back into my mouth.

She mimics, making it a question, "The groom . . ."

I'm caught, my lips half open, a stuttering noise in my throat. How to begin? I have rehearsed this but my lines melt away, my opening, my casual introductions. I can think of nothing that would, even in a small way, convey any part of who he is. There is no picture adequate, no representation that captures him. So I just put my hand across the table, and I touch her hand.

"Mother," I say, like we're in a staged drama, "he'll arrive here shortly."

There is something forming in her, some reaction. I am afraid to let it take complete shape.

"Let's go out and wait on the steps, Mom. Then you'll see him."

"I do not understand," she says in a frighteningly neutral voice. This is what I mean. Everything is suddenly forced, unnatural, as though we're reading lines.

"He'll approach from a distance." I can't help speaking

like a bad actor. "I told him to give me an hour. He'll wait, then he'll come walking down the road."

We rise and unstick our blouses from our stomachs, our skirts from the backs of our legs. Then we walk out front in single file, me behind, and settle ourselves on the middle step. A scrubby box elder tree on one side casts a light shade, and the dusty lilacs seem to catch a little breeze on the other. It's not so bad out here, still hot, but not so dim, contained. It is worse past the trees. The heat shimmers in a band, rising off the fields, out of the spars and bones of houses that will wreck our view. The horizon and the edge of town show through the spacing now, and as we sit we watch the workers move, slowly, almost in a practiced recital, back and forth. Their headcloths hang to their shoulders, their hard hats are dabs of yellow, their white T-shirts blend into the fierce air and sky. They don't seem to be doing anything, although we hear faint thuds from their hammers. Otherwise, except for the whistles of a few birds, there is silence. We certainly don't speak.

It is a longer wait than I anticipated, maybe because he wants to give me time. At last the shadows creep out, hard, hot, charred, and the heat begins to lengthen and settle. We are going into the worst of the afternoon, when a dot at the end of the road begins to form.

Mom and I are both watching. We have not moved our eyes around much, and we blink and squint to try and focus. The dot doesn't change, not for a long while. And then it suddenly springs clear in relief, a silhouette, lost a moment in the shimmer, reappearing. In that shining expanse he is a little wedge of moving shade. He continues, growing imperceptibly, until there are variations in the outline, and it can be seen that he is large. As he passes the construction workers, they turn and stop, all alike in their hats, stock-still.

Growing larger yet as if he has absorbed their stares, he nears us. Now we can see the details. He is dark, the first thing. I have not told my mother, but he's a Chippewa, from the same tribe as she. His arms are thick, his chest is huge and the features of his face are wide and open. He carries nothing in his hands. He wears a black T-shirt, the opposite of the construction workers, and soft jogging shoes. His jeans are held under his stomach by a belt with a star beaded on the buckle. His hair is long, in a tail. I am the wrong woman for him. I am paler, shorter, unmagnificent. But I stand up. Mom joins me, and I answer proudly when she asks, "His name?"

"His name is Gerry."

We descend one step, and stop again. It is here we will receive him. Our hands are folded at our waists. We're balanced, composed. He continues to stroll toward us, his white smile widening, his eyes filling with the sight of me as mine are filling with him. At the end of the road, behind him, another dot has appeared. It is fast-moving and the sun flares off it twice, a vehicle. Now there are two figures. One approaching in a spume of dust from the rear, and Gerry, unmindful, not slackening or quickening his pace, continuing on. It is like a choreography design. They move at parallel speeds, in front of our eyes. At the same moment, at the end of our yard, as if we have concluded a performance now, both of them halt.

Gerry stands, looking toward us, his thumbs in his belt. He nods respectfully to Mom, looks calmly at me, and half smiles. He raises his brows, and we're suspended. Officer Lovchik emerges from the police car, stooped and tired. He walks up behind Gerry and I hear the snap of handcuffs, then I jump. I'm stopped by Gerry's gaze though, as he backs away from me, still smiling tenderly. I am paralyzed halfway down the walk. He kisses the air while Lovchik cautiously prods at him, fitting his prize into the car. And then the doors slam, the engine roars and they back out and turn around. As they move away there is no siren. I think I've heard Lovchik mention questioning. I'm sure it is lots of fuss for nothing, a mistake, but it cannot be denied, this is terrible timing.

I shake my shoulders, smooth my skirt and turn to Mother with a look of outrage.

"How do you like that?" I try.

She's got her purse in one hand, her car keys out.

"Let's go," she says.

"Okay," I answer. "Fine. Where?"

"Aunt Mary's."

"I'd rather go and bail him out, Mom."

"Bail," she says, *"bail?"*

She gives me such a look of cold and furious surprise that I sink immediately into the front seat, lean back against the vinyl. I almost welcome the sting of the heated plastic on my back, thighs, shoulders.

Aunt Mary's dogs are rugs in the dirt, flattened by the heat of the day. Not one of them barks at us to warn her. We step over them and get no more reaction than a whine, the slow beat of a tail. Inside, we get no answers either, although we call Aunt Mary up and down the hall. We enter the kitchen and sit at the table which contains a half-ruined watermelon. By the sink, in a tin box, are cigarettes. My mother takes one and carefully puts the match to it, frowning.

"I know what," she says. "Go check the lockers."

There are two, a big freezer full of labeled meats and rental space, and another, smaller one that is just a side cooler. I notice, walking past the display counter, that the red beacon beside the outside switch of the cooler is glowing. That tells you when the light is on inside.

I pull the long metal handle toward me and the thick door swishes open. I step into the cool, spicy air. She is there, too proud to ever register a hint of surprise. Aunt Mary simply nods and looks away, as though I've just gone out for a minute, although we've not seen one another in six months or more. She is relaxing, reading a scientific magazine article. I sit down on a barrel of alum labeled Zanzibar and drop my bomb with no warning. "I'm married." It doesn't matter how I tell it to Aunt Mary, because she won't be, refuses to be, surprised.

"What's he do?" she simply asks, putting aside the sheaf of paper. I thought the first thing she'd do is scold me for fooling my mother. But it's odd. For two women who have lived through boring times and disasters, how rarely one comes to the other's defense, and how often they are willing to take advantage of the other's absence. But I'm benefiting here. It seems/ that Aunt Mary is truly interested in Gerry. So I'm honest.

"He's something like a political activist. I mean he's been in jail and all. But not for any crime, you see, it's just because of his convictions."

She gives me a long, shrewd stare. Her skin is too tough to wrinkle, but she doesn't look young. All around us hang loops of sausages, every kind you can imagine, every color from the purple-black of blutwurst to the pale whitish links that my mother likes best. Blocks of butter and headcheese, a can of raw milk, wrapped parcels and cured bacons are stuffed onto the shelves around us. My heart has gone still and cool inside of me, and I can't stop talking.

"He's the kind of guy it's hard to describe, very different. People call him a free spirit, but that doesn't say it either because he's very disciplined in some ways. He learned to be neat in jail." I pause, she says nothing, so I go on. "I know it's sudden, but who likes weddings? I hate them, all that mess with the bridesmaids' gowns, getting material to match. I don't have girl friends, I mean, how embarrassing, right? Who would sing 'Oh Perfect Love?' Carry the ring?"

She isn't really listening.

"What's he do?" she asks again.

Maybe she won't let go of it until I discover the right answer, like a game with nouns and synonyms.

"He, well he agitates," I tell her.

"Is that some kind of factory work?"

"Not exactly, no, it's not a nine-to-five job or anything . . ."

She lets the pages fall, now, cocks her head to the side and stares at me without blinking her cold yellow eyes. She has the

look of a hawk, of a person who can see into the future but
won't tell you about it. She's lost business for staring at customers, but she doesn't care.

"Are you telling me that he doesn't"—here she shakes her
head twice, slowly, from one side to the other without removing
me from her stare—"that he doesn't have regular work?"

"Oh, what's the matter anyway," I say roughly. "I'll
work. This is the nineteen seventies."

She jumps to her feet, stands over me, a stocky woman
with terse features and short, thin points of gray hair. Her
earrings tremble and flash, small fiery opals. Her brown plastic
glasses hang crooked on a cord around her neck. I have never
seen her become quite so instantaneously furious, so disturbed.

"We're going to fix that," she says.

The cooler instantly feels smaller, the sausages knock at
my shoulder and the harsh light makes me blink. I am as stubborn as Aunt Mary, however, and she knows that I can go
head-to-head with her.

"We're married and that's final." I manage to stamp my
foot.

Aunt Mary throws an arm back, blows air through her
cheeks and waves away my statement vigorously.

"You're a little girl. How old is *he?*"

I frown at my lap, trace the threads in my blue cotton
skirt and tell her that age is irrelevant.

"Big word," she says sarcastically. "Let me ask you this.
He's old enough to get a job?"

"Of course he is, what do you think. Okay, he's older
than me. He's in his thirties."

"Aha, I knew it."

"Geez! So what? I mean, haven't you ever been in love,
hasn't someone ever gotten you *right here?*" I smash my fist on
my chest. We lock our eyes, but she doesn't waste a second in
feeling hurt.

"Sure, sure I've been in love. You think I haven't? I
know what it feels like, you smartass. You'd be surprised. But

he was no lazy sonofabitch. Now listen . . ." She stops, draws breath, and I let her. "Here's what I mean by 'fix.' I'll teach the sausage-making trade to him, you too, and the grocery business. I've about had it anyway, and so's your mother. We'll do the same as my aunt and uncle—leave the shop to you and move to Arizona. I like this place." She looks up at the burning safety bulb, down to me again. Her face drags in the light. "But what the hell. I always wanted to travel."

I'm kind of stunned, a little flattened out, maybe ashamed of myself.

"You hate going anywhere," I say, which is true.

The doors swings open and Mom comes in with us. She finds a can and balances herself, sighing at the delicious feeling of the air, absorbing from the silence the fact we have talked. She hasn't anything to add, I guess, and as the coolness hits her eyes fall shut. Aunt Mary too. I can't help it either, and my eyelids drop although my brain is alert and conscious. From the darkness, I can see us in the brilliance. The light rains down on us. We sit the way we have been sitting, on our cans of milk and flour, upright and still. Our hands are curled loosely in our laps. Our faces are blank as the gods. We could be statues in a tomb sunk into the side of a mountain. We could be dreaming the world up in our brains.


It is later and the weather has no mercy. We are drained of everything but simple thoughts. It's too hot for feelings. Driving home, we see how field after field of beets has gone into shock, and even some of the soybeans. The plants splay, limp, burned into the ground. Only the sunflowers continue to struggle upright, bristling but small.

What drew me in the first place to Gerry was the unexpected. I went to hear him talk just after I enrolled at the U of M and then I demonstrated when they came and got him off the stage. He always went so willingly, accommodating everyone. I began to visit him. I sold lunar calendars and posters to raise his bail and eventually free him. One thing led to another and one night we found ourselves alone in a Howard Johnson's where they put him up when his speech was finished. There were more beautiful women after him, he could have had his pick of Swedes or Yankton Sioux girls, who are the best-looking of all. But I was different, he says. He liked my slant on life. And then there was no going back once it started, no turning, as though it were meant. We had no choice.

I have this intuition as we near the house, in the fateful quality of light, as in the turn of the day the heat continues to press and the blackness, into which the warmth usually lifts, lowers steadily. We must come to the end of something. There must be a close to this day.

As we turn into the yard we see that Gerry is sitting on the stairs. Now it is our turn to be received. I throw the car door open and stumble out before the motor even cuts. I run to him and hold him, as my mother, pursuing the order of events, parks carefully. Then she walks over too, holding her purse by the strap. She stands before him and says no word but simply looks into his face, staring as if he's cardboard, a man behind glass who cannot see her. I think she's rude, but then I realize that he is staring back, that they are the same height. Their eyes are level. He puts his hand out.

"My name is Gerry."

"Gerry what?"

"Nanapush."

She nods, shifts her weight. "You're from that line, the old strain, the ones . . ." She does not finish.

"And my father," Gerry says, "was Old Man Pillager." He has said this before but I never heard any special meaning in it.

"Kashpaws," she says, "are my branch of course. We're probably related through my mother's brother." They do not move. They are like two opponents from the same divided country, staring across the border. They do not shift or blink and I see that they are more alike than I am like either one of them, so tall, solid, dark-haired. She could be the mother, he the son.

"Well, I guess you should come in," she offers, "you are a distant relative after all." She looks at me. "Distant enough."

Whole swarms of mosquitoes are whining down, discovering us now, so there is no question of staying where we are. And so we walk into the house, much hotter than outside with the gathered heat. Instantly the sweat springs from our skin and I can think of nothing else but cooling off. I try to force the windows higher in their sashes, but there's no breeze anyway, nothing stirs, no air.

"Are you sure," I gasp, "about those fans?"

"Oh, they're broke," my mother says, distressed. I rarely hear this in her voice. She switches on the lights, which makes the room seem hotter, and we lower ourselves into the easy chairs. Our words echo, as though the walls have baked and dried hollow.

"Show me those fans," says Gerry.

My mother points toward the kitchen. "They're sitting on the table. I've already tinkered with them. See what you can do."

And so he does. After a while she hoists herself and walks out back with him. Their voices close together now, absorbed, and their tools clank frantically as if they are fighting a duel. But it is a race with the bell of darkness and their waning energy. I think of ice. I get ice on the brain.

"Be right back," I call out, taking the keys from my mother's purse, "do you need anything?"

There is no answer from the kitchen but a furious sputter of metal, the clatter of nuts and bolts spilling to the floor.

I drive out to the Super Pumper, a big new gas-station complex on the edge of town where my mother most likely has never been. She doesn't know about convenience stores, has no credit cards for groceries, gas, pays only with small bills and change. She never has used an ice machine. It would grate on her that a bag of frozen water costs eighty cents, but it doesn't bother me. I take the Styrofoam cooler and I fill it for a couple dollars. I buy two six-packs of Shasta sodas and I plunge them into the uniform coins of ice. I drink two myself, on the way home, and I manage to lift the whole heavy cooler out of the trunk, carry it to the door.

The fans are whirring, beating the air.

I hear them going in the living room the minute I come in. The only light shines from the kitchen. Gerry and my mother have thrown the pillows from the couch onto the living room floor, and they are sitting in the rippling currents of air. I bring the cooler in and put it near us. I have chosen all dark flavors—black cherry, grape, black raspberry, so as we drink it almost seems the darkness swirls inside us with the night air, sweet and sharp, driven by small motors.

I drag more pillows down from the other rooms upstairs. There is no question of attempting the bedrooms, the stifling beds. And so, in the dark, I hold hands with Gerry as he settles down between my mother and me. He is huge as a hill between the two of us, solid in the beating wind.

# GROOM

# SERVICE

O

*Michael Dorris*

"SHE'S A PIECE OF pure agate," Bernard's mother Martha said to Marie's mother Blanche. "A one in a million that you find after walking the beach for half your life with your eyes on the ground. If I had a child like that I would keep her in a safe place."

Blanche paused, her blade midway down the side of the fish she was scaling. Her face betrayed no expression except exertion, and even in this intermission her teeth remained set against each other, flexing her jaw. The trader steel reflected what little light filtered through the planks of the smokehouse, and the confined air still smelled green. Blanche had hewn the boards with a mallet and chisel in May, as soon as the ground firmed from the spring runoff, and it took a while before the scent of fire crowded that of drying wood. With her broad thumb she flicked a piece of fin off the carved knife handle, then continued her motion.

Martha waited. She had all the time it took.

"You don't know," said Blanche. She shook her head as if its secrets rolled like line weights from side to side. She drew a heavy breath. "You can't imagine. You with such a boy."

Martha sat straighter, all ears, while her hands continued to explore, repairing the tears on the net that lay across her lap and hid her pants and boots. Her fingers moved automatically, finding holes, locating the ends of broken cord and twisting them into bow knots. She kept her nails sharp and jagged, and when they weren't enough she bowed her head and bit off any useless pieces. This was mindless work, the labor of ten thousand days, and could be done as easily in the dark as in the light. It required no involvement. Her thoughts were elsewhere.

"You mean Bernard?" Her voice was wary. She had three sons and needed to be sure she knew the one Blanche had in mind.

"Ber-*nard,*" Blanche nodded, giving the knife a last run, then inspecting the fish closely before tossing it into the large basket at her feet. The water slopped onto the floor and, from there, leaked to the shale ground inches below. Blanche arched her back and massaged her spine with her fist. With her other hand she reached for the cup of cooled tea that she had nursed for the past half hour. Martha let the net rest and joined her.

"People talk about him, you know," Blanche said. "His looks, that goes without saying, but the other things too. The respect he pays the old folks. His singing. His calmness. His hunting skill. You must be proud."

Martha closed her eyes as if in great pain. "He is my punishment," she confessed, "but I don't know what I could have done so terrible as to deserve him. He stays out till all hours. His hair is always tangled. I sometimes think that the game he brings home has died before he found it, the meat is so tough. You must have him confused with another boy. Or perhaps, with a girl like Marie, you find it hard to think ill of any child."

"Now you make fun of me," Blanche said. "It is well known that Marie has turned out badly. She is lazy and disrespectful, conceited and stubborn. I try my best to teach her, and so do my sisters and even my mother, but she folds her arms and stares at nothing. Hopeless. And she will never find a husband. A boy's mother would have to be desperate to send her son courting at my house."

"But not as desperate as the mother who could tolerate the thought of Bernard as a son-in-law," Martha said. "That would be true desperation. I will never be free of him. I will grow old with him at my side, and with no granddaughters or grandsons to comfort me."

"If only someone like your Bernard would find an interest in Marie," Blanche said as if she had not heard Martha. "If only some young man exactly like him would consent to live in my house, how I would welcome him. I would treat him as my own blood."

The two women met each other's gaze at last. Each raised a cup to her lips, and after a few seconds, each drank. Each replaced her cup on the table between them. Each held her mouth firm. Blanche found her knife and reached for a new fish, cool and slippery as a stone over which much water has rushed. Martha shifted the net in her lap, moving a new section to the center. The smell of salt rose like steam as her hands went to work.

"I will speak to him," Martha said.

"And I to her," Blanche replied. "But I know her answer already. I have seen how she regards him."

"She will not be disappointed." Martha allowed one wave of pride to crest. "He's not so bad."

Blanche glanced at Martha, then looked quickly back to her work. Bernard must be good indeed, she thought, if Martha could not better contain herself.

## II.

Bernard was drawing with charcoal on a piece of driftwood when his mother returned home. He was twenty-two, lean, and had large teeth. His eyes were dark beneath unusually thick brows, and his hands were long and broad. At the sound of Martha's step, he jumped to his feet and assumed the air of a person about to do something important. His fingers curved as if to hold a tool or a weapon and his eyes narrowed as if to see something far away. He was busy at nothing, his energy humming, ready for a focus. But for once she made no comment about his sloth. She did not despair at the time he wasted scratching on any smooth surface. She did not inspect his sketch and then toss it into the cooking fire. In fact, this afternoon she regarded him rather mildly.

"Well, it's arranged," she announced. "I spent an endless morning with your future mother-in-law and before I left she had agreed to let you come to see Marie. Don't think it was easy."

Bernard's eyes followed his mother's movements as she crossed the floor and sat in exhaustion on the bed. She pushed off her boots, still caked with beach mud, and rubbed her feet together. She wore no socks.

"Marie?" he said at last. "She's too young. You should have asked me first."

Martha's glare clapped a hand over his mouth. In a moment, Bernard tried again.

"I know they're a good family. I know you want to do right for me. But you could . . . we could have discussed this. I mean, I think of her as a little girl, not a *wife.*" The word, a stranger to Bernard's vocabulary, vibrated in the air.

"Stop whining," Martha said, losing patience. "Who do you 'think of' as a wife? *Doris?*"

Bernard blushed. He wasn't surprised that his mother knew about him and Doris, but it did not seem fair for her to mention it. Doris was a widow whose name brought nervous laughs to teen-age boys and frowns of disapproval to everyone else. She was a woman almost twice Bernard's age with a missing front tooth and eyes that sparked in his memory, a woman who had summoned him for an errand six months ago and whom he now loved better than he would have thought possible, and not just for the way she moved. But it was true: he had never thought of Doris as a wife.

"You should see yourself," Martha said. "Keep that face and you won't have to worry about marrying anyone. But don't expect me to support you forever." She noticed the driftwood, still on the floor, and nudged it with her toe to get a better look. Bernard had outlined the mountain across the bay from the village, and tucked a large sun behind its peak. When he drew it he thought it was his best work, but now its lines looked smudged and shaky. Martha leaned forward to pick it up and turn it over, as if expecting another illustration on the back. Finding none, she held it out for Bernard to take.

"Give this to your Doris," she said. "It looks like her under the blanket where she spends her time."

Bernard didn't move, but he watched the wood until his mother let it fall to the floor. He was angry at the shame he felt. He was angry that he knew it was just a matter of time until he would have to call on Marie. He was angry that his mother was right: his mountain *did* look like Doris, turned on her side.

### I I I.

When Blanche went into the house and told Marie that their problems were over, that Bernard, the catch of the village, would be courting, she expected some reaction, but her daughter simply folded her arms and stared at nothing.

"Don't you hear me?" Blanche demanded. "Bernard. Coming to see you. Can't you be happy? Can't you say something?"

Marie, however, only rolled her eyes and drummed her fingers against the bench upon which she sat. She wore a close-knit woven cap that, in combination with her unfortunately weak chin, made her head resemble an acorn. She was fifteen, just out of her confinement, trained for adulthood to the limits of Blanche and her sisters' abilities, but still a sulking child. At length she drew up her knees, circled them with her arms, and watched her mother from the corner of her eye.

Blanche was across the long room, talking to her older sister Bonnie. She was not hard to overhear.

"Does she say 'thank you'? Does she appreciate what it means to her, to all of us, to get that damn Martha to agree? Does she care that Bernard could have any girl, from any family?"

Bonnie shook her head sadly. Her surviving children had all been boys and had long since moved to the houses of their wives' families, so she had no experience with reluctant girls, unless, she thought, she counted her memories of Blanche. But that would not do to say, especially not in earshot of Marie, who sat with her head cocked in their direction. Blanche's daughter was the hope of the next generation, the one who had to bring in a husband and produce more daughters than her mother or aunt, if the family was to regain its position. For a moment Bonnie thought of suggesting to Blanche that they present that information to Marie directly, to drop the shadows and point out both her responsibility and her power, but then she rejected the idea. The girl was impressed enough with herself as it was. Instead, Bonnie sympathized with her sister and cast occasional looks at her niece in hopes of catching on Marie's face a secret, fleeting expression of pleasure.

## I V .

"What am I supposed to do?" Bernard asked the next time his uncle visited. Bernard had waited for a private moment, and it

came when, just before sleep, Theodore had stepped outside to
relieve himself.

From the darkness came rattling sounds of strangulation
that Bernard eventually identified as the older man's yawn.
When it, and the noise of splashing water, had abated, Theodore spoke. It was clear that he understood Bernard's problem.

"You do whatever they tell you and you hope they're not
as bad as they could be," Theodore said. "You don't complain.
You don't assume anything. You stay out of the way, because
you never know what they're going to find to dislike. You be
what they want."

"It's not fair." Bernard leaned against the side of the
house and searched the sky. Thin clouds, silver as wet spider
webs, passed in the night wind.

"That's true, but there are other things in the world besides owning real estate. Your true home will remain here in
your mother's house, just as it has been for me, but you can't
*live* here forever. You need independence, distance, the chance
to be a man in a place where you were never a boy. Once you
get yourself established, once you pay your dues, you'll understand what I mean. Your life is not all indoors. You'll hang
around with your brothers-in-law, your uncles, your friends.
Spend time at the men's club. Go to the sweat bath and gripe,
or listen to the complaints of others and make jokes. In a year
all your wife's family will care about is whether or not you
bring in your share. By then you'll know what's what."

"But what if I don't get along with Marie?"

"*Do* get along with her. Get along with her mother. Get
along with her auntie. But on your own time do what you
want. It's not a big price to pay. It's a daughter-poor clan and
the one they've picked out for you is going to control everything someday: fabulous fishing sights, a big house. Behave
yourself now and you'll get your reward. It's not like you're
marrying a youngest sister with no prospects."

Which was, Bernard knew, what had happened to Theodore. No wonder he was not more sympathetic.

"How do I tell Doris?" Bernard asked. This was something he had struggled with for days.

"Doris! She could have told you. It's good news to her. She gets a younger guy, fresh the way she likes them, and no hard feelings between you." Theodore laughed, not unkindly, and put an arm around Bernard's shoulders. "Listen to some advice, from your great-uncle through me to you," he said. "The groom service is the worst part, so make it as short as possible by winning over her family. Convince them you won't be a pain in the ass to live with. And to do that, rule number one is, whatever you do, be appreciative. Fall all over yourself."

"Did you do that?" Bernard asked. "Did my mother's husband do that?"

"Do fish swim underwater? But don't take my word for it. Ask Pete. He's your father."

"I'd be embarrassed," Bernard said. "He and I never talk about serious matters, and this is not the kind of thing you can easily ask a person who's not of the clan."

"It's every man for himself, when it comes right down to it," Theodore said. "Let's go in. You're going to need sleep."

## V.

"This is what you do," Martha instructed.

It was not yet light and she had awakened Bernard from a sound sleep. He blew into a cup of hot tea as he listened, letting the darkness hide the resentment in his face.

"You go hunting and you catch something *good,* I don't care what. Something a little unusual. A beaver, maybe, or a goose. *Not* something small and easy. *Not* a squirrel. *Not* fish. You bring it home and I'll help you clean it. You leave a portion for me as if that's what you always do, to help provide for your family, but you take the best part with you and you park yourself in front of Blanche's door. You only speak if you're spoken to. You wait for *them* to ask *you*. And if they don't, which they won't right away, you act unconcerned. You do this every day until they invite you in, and then I'll tell you what to do next. This is your chance, so don't ruin it. Now move."

Bernard stepped out into the chill morning grayness, thought briefly of visiting Doris before he went hunting, but then abandoned the idea. He had heard through his mother's husband that Doris had made friends with a seventeen-year-old boy named James.

The dew from high grass had soaked through to Bernard's feet before he reached the edge of the woods. He realized his mother had forgotten to feed him breakfast, forgotten to make him a lunch. He heard a duck call from the lake and paused, but then continued on. He could hear his mother in his mind, and she said a duck wouldn't do.

## VI.

"He's *there!*" Bonnie dropped the firewood she was carrying and rushed to Blanche's side.

Her sister was stirring a pot on the fire, a study in indifference. "I have eyes," Blanche said. "Keep your voice down. He'll hear you."

"Did you see what he had?" Bonnie asked. "I got a glimpse of something brown but I didn't want him to catch me looking."

"I think it was a beaver. Or an otter. Would you believe, he had the nerve to hold it up to me and smile the first time I passed."

"No!"

"I thought he was better trained. It simply means he'll have to wait longer."

"Did Marie see him yet?"

"She won't go out the door." Both sisters turned to the gloom in the rear of the room where Marie crouched, her head lowered over a stick game. Her long hair was loose and covered her shoulders like a shawl.

"She *could* try to fix herself up a bit," Blanche said, loud enough to be heard.

"Give her time," Bonnie whispered. "She's young."

## V I I .

"Well, what happened?" Martha demanded when Bernard returned home late in the evening.

"Nothing happened," Bernard said, and threw himself down on his blankets. He raised an arm to cover his eyes, then turned to face the wall.

Martha spotted the sack her son had dropped on the floor and looked inside. The beaver tail and quarters were exactly as she had cleaned them that afternoon, and she took them out to add to the broth she had prepared.

"At least we'll eat well for a while," she said.

"I'm not hungry," Bernard replied, but his mother ignored him.

"Tell me everything."

"There's nothing to tell. I walked over there, dressed like I was going to a party, carrying that beaver. I never caught such a one. I surprised it so there wasn't even adrenaline in its blood. I thought they'd see it and invite me to supper, but they walked by me like I wasn't there, their noses in the air."

"Whose noses?" Martha wanted to know.

"The mother and the aunt."

"Not the girl?"

"I saw no girl. I heard no girl."

"Ah," said Martha. "So she's shy. Good."

"Why good?"

"Because then she won't bully you at first, stupid boy. I've seen what happens to the husbands of the bold ones."

The smell of stewing meat filled the room, warm, rich,

brown. Martha's husband Pete came into the house at the scent, tipped his head in his son's direction, and asked, "Hard day?"

## VIII.

For a week, then two weeks, the same pattern was repeated. Only the animals changed: they ranged from a porcupine to a hind quarter of caribou, from a fat grouse on a bad day to a string of matched silver salmon on a good one. Once Bernard thought he saw a black bear dive into the brush at the side of a stream, but he was momentarily afraid to investigate, and later berated himself. With a bearskin, he thought too late, he would have been irresistible and his long afternoons and evenings at Blanche's closed door would have been over.

As a month passed, Bernard lost hope. He lost the alertness he had once felt when Blanche or Bonnie or Marie, the most unsympathetic of them all, approached, and he soon tired of the commiseration that Blanche's and Bonnie's husbands cast in his direction as they went about their business. They could remember, their expressions said, what it was like to wait outside this house, but there was nothing they could do. A word from them might slow the process rather than speed it up, might do more harm than good. If boredom was patience, Bernard achieved patience. If learning to exist without expectation of fulfillment was maturity, Bernard matured. At first he used his time to remember Doris, to wonder what she was doing and to regret not doing it with her. Later he thought about hunting, how he could have succeeded the times he had failed, how the animals behaved, how they smelled and sounded. Finally he found himself thinking about Pete, his father, in different ways than he ever had before. In Bernard's mind Pete became more than just his father, more than just his mother's husband; he became another man, an earlier version of Bernard, a fellow sufferer. It had not previously oc-

curred to Bernard how hard it was to be forever a stranger in
the house where you lived, to be always a half visitor. He wondered how Pete stayed so cheerful, and wondered if Martha's
mother had kept his father waiting long at her door before inviting him inside. On an afternoon late in the second week,
Bernard had a thought so profound, so unprecedented, that it
startled him into erect posture. What if, he wondered, his
grandmother had not let Pete in at all? What if Pete had been
judged inadequate? Where would that have left Bernard?

The next morning when he went hunting Bernard returned to the place where he had seen the bear, hid himself
behind a log, and waited.

## I X .

"Did you hear?" Pete asked Theodore as they walked the trail
from the steam bath to their wives' houses.

"About Bernard's bear?"

"It must have weighed three hundred pounds. I didn't
know Bernard had it in him."

"Have you forgotten what sitting in front of a house will
drive you to? What did you catch to get inside Martha's?"

"Nothing," Pete said. "It was me she couldn't resist."

"You forget," Theodore replied. "I was still a boy in that
house. I recall their words of you. Let me see . . . I seem to
remember some mention of the small size of certain of your
parts."

"Poor brother-in-law," Pete said. "You still don't realize
the lengths to which they went to avoid hurting your feelings!
And how *is* your wife? How is the health of her many elder
sisters? Is it true that they become stronger and more robust
with every year?"

# X .

On the second day of the fifth week, just as she passed through the door, Blanche reached down her right hand and snagged one of the bear claws that rested in the basket by Bernard's leg. So quick was her movement, so apparently disconnected to the business on her mind, so complete her distraction, that Bernard had to look twice to make sure it was gone. All the same, he felt a warm flush spread beneath the skin of his neck, and a feeling of inordinate pride suffused him so thoroughly that he had difficulty remaining still. He had been found worthy, and now it was only a matter of time.

Every day now, and each time with more pause and deliberation, Blanche browsed through his offerings and always selected some prize. Her expression betrayed no gratitude, yet Bernard was sure that occasionally she was pleasantly surprised. Afraid to unbalance their precarious arrangement, he sat still as a listening hare in her presence, not even a bystander at her shopping. He kept his eyes lowered and held his breath until she had departed, but remained ever watchful for any cue that the situation had progressed to another stage. At last it came.

"Bernard!" Blanche said one day, looking out the door. "Is that you crouching there so quietly? Please, come in and share our supper, poor as it is. What a pleasure to see you."

Bernard rose slowly, stiff in his joints and half skeptical that this was some joke, some new test, but when he entered the house Blanche's hospitality continued and was joined by that of Bonnie, who sat by the fire trimming her husband's hair with a squeaking scissors. "Sit, sit." She motioned to a bench near the door. "What a shy boy you are. Luckily we have some nice moose to feed you."

Indeed they did. Bernard recognized the remains of the foreleg he had offered yesterday. Bonnie passed him a plate with a small portion of tough gristle, gray and cooled. He knew what to say.

"This is wonderful," he exclaimed. "The best I've ever tasted. What cooks you are. But you are too generous. Let me put some back in the pot."

When they refused, politely and with many denials of his compliments, Bernard made a great show of eating. The act of digestion absorbed his total concentration. He rubbed his stomach and cast his eyes to the ceiling in delight. With great subtlety he periodically raised his hand to his mouth, as if to wipe some grease, and used that motion to conceal the small bits of undigestible food he removed from his cheeks and tucked secretly into his pockets.

When he finished, Bernard sat nervously, breathless with anxiety. From the corner of his eye he detected a space so devoid of movement that it attracted his attention. He looked, then quickly looked away. Yet his eyes still registered the image of Marie, her hair oiled and braided, wearing a new dress and a necklace made of bear claws, sitting composed and shaded as a perfect charcoal sketch. He thought she was truly beautiful.

## XI.

"You know, Pete," Martha said as she lay by her husband's side under a blanket, "watching Bernard lately brings back memories."

"To me too. Your mother was a terror."

"I notice you still whisper such words, even though she's more than four years gone."

Pete shifted his position and propped on an elbow. In the moonlight Martha's face looked seamless and young. A beam like the hottest part of a coal danced off her dark eye. He ran his fingers along her cheek and she turned her head in comfort. "You look the same as then," he said.

Martha caught his hand and brought it to her mouth, let it feel the smile.

"I pestered her, you know, to let you in," she said.

"You didn't know I was alive."

"I didn't know the day you found the eagle feathers? I didn't know the day you came an hour later than always?"

"It was raining," Pete said. "The ground was soft and I kept sinking to my knees. I couldn't arrive at your door covered in mud."

"I thought you weren't coming. I confronted my mother and told her that her slowness had cost me . . ."

"Cost you what?" Pete asked, when Martha's silence persisted.

"Enough talk."

## XII.

Marie watched the back of Bernard's head and admired the dark sheen of his long hair, the play of muscles in his arms at his every movement. During the last month she had studied every part of him so completely that she could create him in her imagination whenever she chose, and lately, she chose often. She had to fight not to laugh when they gave him the worst meat and he had to spit into his hand and act as though it were delicious. She watched the way his fingers held the plate, the way he sat so compact and attentive. She waited for the sound of his soft voice and wondered what he would say when he could speak in private. She made a game of observing his eyes until just the second before they turned to her, and believed she had been discovered only once.

## XIII.

Bernard ate almost all of his meals at Blanche's house now, and gradually had become more relaxed. For one thing, his distribution increased in both quality and quantity, and he could now expect a reasonably digestible piece of meat or salmon. For another, Blanche and Bonnie's husbands had begun to join him on his hunts, to show him places to fish that only the members of this household knew. He found he liked these men and began to call them "uncle."

Blanche herself still frightened him, but not all the time. There were moments when he found approval in her gaze, times when some word of hers sounded almost like a joke. Bonnie was warmer, more solicitous of his needs, more complimentary of the food he brought, and Bernard thought of her as an ally.

As far as Marie was concerned, he still had no clue to her feelings. Even Pete and Theodore observed that this game was lasting longer than the usual and debated whether something might be wrong. They were full of advice for Bernard, full of ideas of how to please Marie, full of reminders that it was her agreement, in the last analysis, which was necessary. But no matter what Bernard did, Marie would not look at him or give him any sign of encouragement. He grew despondent, lost his appetite, found himself thinking once again of Doris and the ease of their association. Marie seemed totally beyond his reach, the focus of mystery and impossible desire. And so he was unprepared on the night, just before the first frost of winter, when, with shaking hands, Marie herself passed him a plate of food.

"This is for you," she said so softly he could barely hear, and she sat beside him while, slowly and with great emotion, he ate.

## XIV.

A year later, while waiting for the birth of Marie's first child, Blanche and Martha passed the time by nibbling strips of dried eel. Martha, who had no love for the oily skin, threw hers into the fire, where it sizzled briefly.

"The midwife predicts a girl," Blanche said. "When she

spun the charm above Marie's stomach, it revolved to the left."

"A girl is most rewarding," Martha nodded. "But there is a special satisfaction in raising boys. So often I think of times when Bernard was young, so often I miss him around the house."

Blanche reached for another stick of *baleek* and did not answer. Her silence was immediately noticed, as she knew it would be.

"How is he doing?" Martha asked at last.

"He will learn," Blanche said. "He has potential. It is clear he cares greatly for Marie, and she is patient."

"That is one word for it." Martha tossed a handful of scraps into the flame and watched the light flare and dance. "Of course Bernard was used to . . . He had such a *happy* home that I'm sure it has taken some adjusting on his part in new surroundings."

"Yes, he was somewhat spoiled. But I think he has a good heart."

"As well he must, to remain loyal to such a chinless girl."

"One only hopes their child will inherit the mother's disposition and not be sulky and resentful of every request."

"One can but pray it will have the father's looks and personality."

A single rope of eel remained on the plate. Both women extended a hand toward it, hesitated, and withdrew. It rested between them as they cleaned their teeth with fine bone picks and slowly wiped the grease from their fingers, and when, at the sound of Marie's first muffled protest, they rose together and rushed to her side, it remained behind.

# ANGEL OF MERCY,

# ANGEL OF WRATH

O

### *Ethan Canin*

O**N ELEANOR BLACK'S** seventy-first birthday a flock of birds flew into her kitchen through a window that she had opened every morning for forty years. They flew in all at once, without warning or reason, from the gingko tree at the corner of Velden Street, where they had sat every day since President Roosevelt's time. They were huge and dirty and black, the size of cats practically, much larger than she had ever imagined birds. Birds were so small in the sky. In the air, even in the clipped gingko ten yards from the window, they were nothing more than faint dots of color. Now they were in her kitchen, though, batting against the ceiling and the yellow walls she had just washed a couple of months ago, and their stink and their cries and their frantic knocking wings made it hard for her to breathe.

She sat down and took a water pill. They were screaming

like wounded animals, flapping in tight circles around the light fixture, so that she got dizzy looking at them. She reached for the phone and pushed the button that automatically dialed her son, who was a doctor.

"Bernard," she said, "there's a flock of crows in the flat."

"It's five in the morning, Mom."

"It is? Excuse me, because it's seven out here. I forgot. But the crows are flying in my kitchen."

"Mother?"

"Yes?"

"Have you been taking all your medicines?"

"Yes, I have."

"Has Dr. Gluck put you on any new ones?"

"No."

"What did you say was the matter?"

"There's a whole flock of crows in the flat."

Bernard didn't say anything.

"I know what you're thinking," she said.

"I'm just making the point that sometimes new medicines can change people's perceptions."

"Do you want to hear them?"

"Yes," he said, "that would be fine. Let me hear them."

She held the receiver up toward the ceiling. The cries were so loud she knew he would pick them up, even long-distance.

"Okay?" she said.

"I'll be damned."

"What am I supposed to do?"

"How many are there?"

"I don't know."

"What do you mean, you don't know?"

"They're flying like crazy around the room. How can I count them?"

"Are they attacking you?"

"No, but I want them out anyway."

"How can I get them out from Denver?"

She thought for a second. "I'm not the one who went to Denver."

He breathed out on the phone, loud, like a child. He was chief of the department at Denver General. "I'm just making the point," he said, "that I can't grab a broom in Colorado and get the birds out of your place in New York."

"Whose fault is that?"

"Mom," he said.

"Yes?"

"Call the SPCA. Tell them what happened. They have a department that's for things like this. They'll come out and get rid of them."

"They're big."

"I know," he said. "Don't call 911. That's for emergencies. Call the regular SPCA. Okay?"

"Okay," she said.

He paused. "You can call back later to let us know what happened."

"Okay."

"Okay?"

"Okay." She waited a moment. "Do you want to say anything else?"

"No," he said.


She hung up, and a few seconds later all the birds flew back out the window except for two of them, which flew the other way, through the swinging door that she had left open and into the living room. She followed them in there. One of them was hopping on the bookshelf, but while Eleanor watched, the other one flew straight at the window from the center of the room and collided with the glass. The pane shook and the bird fell several feet before it righted itself and did the same thing again. For a few moments Eleanor stood watching, and then she went to the kitchen, took out the bottle of cream soda, and poured herself a glass. Yesterday it had been a hundred degrees out. When she finished she put the bottle back, sat down again, and dialed 911.

"Emergency," said a woman.

Eleanor didn't say anything.

"Nine-one-one Emergency."

"There's a flock of crows in my apartment."

"Birds?"

"Yes."

"You have to call the SPCA."

"They're going to break the window."

"Listen," she said, "we're not supposed to give this kind of advice, but all you have to do is move up quietly behind a bird and pick it up. They won't hurt you. I grew up on a farm."

"I grew up here."

"You can do that," she said, "or you can call the SPCA."

She hung up and went back to the living room. One still perched itself on the edge of her bookshelf and sat there, opening and closing its wings, while the other one, the berserk one, flew straight at the front window, smashed into it, fell to the sill, and then took to the air again. Again and again it flew straight at the window, hitting it with a sound like a walnut in a nutcracker, falling to the sill, then flapping crookedly back toward the center of the room to make another run. Already the window had small blotches of bluish feather oil on it. The bird hit it again, fell flapping to the sill, and this time stayed there, perched. Through the window Eleanor noticed that the house across the street from her had been painted green.

"Stay there," she said. "I'm going to open the window."

She took two steps toward the bird, keeping the rest of her body as still as she could, like a hunting dog, moving one leg, pausing, then moving the other. Next to her on the bookshelf the calm bird cocked its head in little jerks—down, up, sideways, down. She advanced toward the window until the berserk one suddenly flew up, smashed against the glass, fell to the sill, flew up again, smashed, and perched once more. She stopped. It stood there. To her horror Eleanor could see its grotesque pulse through its skin, beating frantically along the wings and the torso as if the whole bird were nothing but a speeding heart. She stood perfectly still for several minutes, watching.

"Hello," she said.

It lifted its wings as though it were going to fly against the window again, but then lowered them.

"My husband was a friend of Franklin Roosevelt's," she said.

The bird didn't move.

"Why can't you be like your friend?" She pointed her chin at the one on the bookshelf, which opened its beak. Inside it the throat was black. She took another step toward the window. Now she was so close to the berserk one she could see the ruffled, purplish chest feathers and the yellow ring around its black irises. Its heart still pulsated but it didn't raise its wings, just cocked its head the way the other one had. She reached her two hands halfway toward it and stopped. "It's my birthday today," she whispered. She waited like that, her hands extended, until she had counted to forty. The bird cocked and retracted its head, then stood still. When it had been still for a while she reached the rest of the way and touched her hands to both sides of its quivering body.

For a moment, for an extended, odd moment in which the laws of nature didn't seem to hold, for a moment in which she herself felt just the least bit confused, the bird stood still. It was oily and cool, and its askew feathers poked her palms. What she thought about at that second, of all things, was the day her husband Charles had come into the living room to announce to her that President Kennedy was going to launch missiles against the Cubans. She had felt the same way when he told her that, as if something had gone slightly wrong with nature but that she couldn't quite comprehend it, the way right now she couldn't quite comprehend the bird's stillness until suddenly it shrieked and twisted in her hands and flew up into the air.

She stepped back. It circled through the room and smashed into the glass again, this time on the other window next to the bookshelf. The calm bird lighted from its perch, went straight down the hall, and flew into her bedroom. The berserk one righted itself and flew into the glass again, then flapped up and down against it, pocking the wide pane with its wings like a moth. Eleanor went to the front window, but she couldn't open it because the Mexican boy who had painted the apartments last year had broken the latch. She crossed into the kitchen and looked up the number of the SPCA.

A child answered the phone. Eleanor had to think for a second. "I'd like to report two crows in my house," she said.

The child put down the phone and a moment later a woman came on the line. "I'd like to report two crows in my house," said Eleanor. The woman hung up. Eleanor looked up the number again. This time a man answered. "Society," he said.

"There are two crows in my house," said Eleanor.

"Did they come in a window?"

"I always have that window opened," she answered. "I've had it opened for years with nothing happening."

"Then it's open now?"

"Yes."

"Have you tried getting them out?"

"Yes, I grabbed one the way the police said but it bit me."

"It bit you?"

"Yes. The police gave me that advice over the phone."

"Did it puncture the skin?"

"It's bleeding a little."

"Where are they now?"

"They're in the living room," she said. "One's in another room."

"All right," he said. "Tell me your address."

When they had finished Eleanor hung up and went into the living room. The berserk one was perched on the sill, looking into the street. She went into the bedroom and had to look around a while before she found the calm one sitting on top of her lamp.

She had lived a long enough life to know there was nothing to be lost from waiting out situations, so she turned out the light in the bedroom, went back into the living room, took the plastic seatcover off the chair President Roosevelt had sat on, and, crossing her arms, sat down on it herself. By now the berserk bird was calm. It stood on the windowsill, and every once in a while it strutted three or four jerky steps up the length of the wood, turned toward her, and bobbed its head. She nodded at it.

The last time the plastic had been off that chair was the day Richard Nixon resigned. Charles had said that Franklin Roosevelt would have liked it that way, so they took the plastic off and sat on it that day and for a few days after, until Charles let some peanuts fall between the cushion and the arm and she got worried and covered it again. After all those years the chair was still firm.

The bird eyed her. Its feet had four claws and were scaly, like the feet on a butcher's chicken. "Get out of here," she said. "Go! Go through the window you came from." She flung her hand out at it, flapped it in front of the chair, but the bird didn't move. She sat back.

When the doorbell rang she got up and answered on the building intercom. It was the SPCA, though when she opened the door to the apartment she found a young Negro woman standing there. She was fat, with short, braided hair. After the woman had introduced herself and stepped into the apartment Eleanor was surprised to see that the hair on the other side of her head was long. She wore overalls and a pink turtleneck.

"Now," she said, "where are those crows you indicated?"

"In the living room," said Eleanor. "He was going to break the glass soon if you didn't get here."

"I got here as soon as I received the call."

"I didn't mean *that.*"

The woman stepped into the living room, swaying slightly on her right leg, which looked partly crippled. The bird hopped from the sill to the sash, then back to the sill. The woman stood motionless with her hands together in front of her, watching it. "That's no crow," she said finally. "That's a grackle. That's a rare species here."

"I grew up in New York," said Eleanor.

"So did I." The woman stepped back, turned away from the bird, and began looking at Eleanor's living room. "A crow's a rare species here too, you know. Some of that particular species gets confused and comes in here from Long Island."

"Poor things."

"Say," said the woman. "Do you have a little soda or something? It's hot out."

"I'll look," said Eleanor. "I heard it was a hundred degrees out yesterday."

"I can believe it."

Eleanor went into the kitchen. She opened the refrigerator door, stood there, then closed it. "I'm out of everything," she called.

"That's all right."

She filled a glass with water and brought it out to the woman. "There you go," she said.

The woman drank it. "Well," she said then, "I think I'll make the capture now."

"It's my birthday today."

"Is that right?"

"Yes, it is."

"How old are you?"

"Eighty-one."

The woman reached behind her, picked up the water glass, and made the gesture of a toast. "Well, happy eighty-first," she said. She put down the glass and walked over and opened the front window, which still had smudges on it. Then she crouched and approached the bird on the other sill. She stepped slowly, her head tilted to the side and her large arms held in front of her, and when she was a few feet before the window she bent forward and took the bird into her hands. It flapped a couple of times and then sat still in her grasp while she turned and walked it to the open window, where she let it go and it flew away into the air.

When the woman had left Eleanor put the plastic back on the chair and called her son again. The hospital had to page him, and when he came on the phone he sounded annoyed.

"It was difficult," she said. "The fellow from SPCA had to come out."

"Did he do a decent job?"

"Yes."

"Good," he said. "I'm very pleased."

"It was a rare species. He had to use a metal-handled capturing device. It was a long set of tongs with hinges."

"Good. I'm very pleased."

"Are you at work?"

"Yes, I am."

"Okay, then."

"Okay."

"Is there anything else?"

"No," he said. "That's it."

A while after they hung up, the doorbell rang. It was the SPCA woman again, and when Eleanor let her upstairs she found her standing in the hall with a bunch of carnations wrapped in newspaper. "Here," she said. "Happy birthday from the SPCA."

"Oh my," said Eleanor. For a moment she thought she was going to cry. "They're very elegant."

The woman stepped into the apartment. "I just thought you were a nice lady."

"Why, thank you very much." She took them and laid them down on the hall vanity. "Would you like a cup of tea?"

"No, thanks. I just wanted to bring them up. I've got more calls to take care of."

"Would you like some more water?"

"That's all right," said the woman. She smiled and touched Eleanor on the shoulder, then turned and went back downstairs. Eleanor closed the door and unwrapped the flowers. She looked closely at their lengths for signs that they were a few days old, but could find none. The stalks were unswollen and cleanly clipped at an angle. She brought them into the kitchen, washed out the vase, and set them up in it. Then she poured herself a half glass of cream soda. When she was finished she went into the bedroom to the bedside table, where she took a sheet of paper from the drawer and began a letter.

> Dear President Bush,
> I am a friend of President Roosevelt's writing you on my eightieth birthday on the subject of a rare species that came into my life without warning today, and that needs help from a man such as yourself

She leaned up straight and examined the letter. The handwriting got smaller at the end of each line, so she put the paper aside and took out a new sheet. At that moment the calm bird flew down and perched on the end of the table. Eleanor jerked back and stood from the chair. "Oh," she said, and touched her heart. "Of course."

Then she patted her hair with both hands and sat down again. The bird tilted its head to look at her. Eleanor looked back. Its coat was black but she could see an iridescent rainbow in the chest feathers. It strutted a couple of steps toward her, flicking its head left, right, forward. Its eyes were dark. She put out her hand, leaned a little bit, and moving it steadily and slowly, touched the feathers once and withdrew. The bird hopped and opened its wings. She sat back and watched it. Sitting there, she knew that it probably didn't mean anything. She was just a woman in an apartment, and it was just a bird that had wandered in. It was too bad they couldn't talk to each other. She would have liked to know how old the bird was, and what it was like to have lived in the sky.

# CREDIT

O

*Scott Spencer*

JACK MITCHELL WAS A beautiful man. His eyes were a shade of tan usually seen only in animals and they were large, wounded eyes that at once shoved you against a wall and begged you for mercy. He had a sleek, powerful body, with something gentle woven into it and he came to the movies with respectable stage credentials. He was touted as the next James Dean and given a small part in a picture called *Hill Folk,* in which he tried to stab the hero with a pitchfork and was shot ten times in the chest. It was a pretty good role; he made the most of it and then he was hired to star in that remake of *The Petrified Forest.*

It was during rehearsals for *Petrified Forest* that Jack was caught in the undertow off the beach near his producer's house. He was swept out to sea and surely would have been lost forever had it not been for a few early morning surfers who were out there riding the cold, inky waves, casting their broken

shadows over the troubled surface of the water. The surfers
saw Jack trying to claw his way back toward shore and then
saw him go down. They risked their own lives to save him and
finally got him back to the shore, where they stretched him out
on the cold sand, blew into his lungs, pounded his chest, and
brought him back from his own internal undertow that seemed
to have wanted to swallow him up forever.

He was saved but he had been so long without a decent
breath of air that damage had been done to his brain and when
he came to on the beach—gagging, spitting salt water—he was
paralyzed on his left side and could not speak intelligibly. The
California newspapers were full of Jack's tragedy for a week
and when he was released from Cedars Sinai eleven weeks later
there were a few photographers on hand to record the nurses
wheeling a rigid, not quite handsome Jack Mitchell to the limo
the studio had provided as a final gesture of goodwill.

*The Petrified Forest* never did get made and Jack Mitchell
went home with a brain that seemed empty of everything but
the capacity for silent anguish. He couldn't speak, write, or
read; it was more than he could do to take off his slippers. He
was looked after by a swing shift of nurses while the money
held out and when that was over his mother appeared with a
plaid suitcase and a cocker spaniel named Grumpy. She was a
small, good-natured woman from St. Louis who liked to paint
landscapes; she threw herself into the task of not only caring
for Jack but rehabilitating him, too. Mrs. Mitchell made Jack a
project and made a chart of their progress. She raised him
from infancy again, teaching him to eat and speak, to keep
himself clean, and even to read. Jack struggled. Life had never
been terribly difficult for him. He had always been handsome,
reasonably bright; the world had thrown open its doors to him.
But he found the mettle to make the fight and he pushed the
stone of his stunned and empty mind up the hill again, like
Sisyphus.

In a couple of years, Jack was leaving the house on his
own. He was up to six hours of exercise and he read out loud to

his mother from noon till two. There was a singsong quality to his voice but he didn't let it discourage him and it only improved, though very slowly.

Five years after the accident, and after uncountable hours of lonely struggle, Jack felt he was well enough to go back to work. He was very poor and he wasn't too proud to work an ordinary job, but it was hard after having heard applause to think about working behind the desk at a rent-a-car agency. Jack very much wanted to live the life that had been taken away from him—fame is not something that comes from within but is bestowed and then taken away and given to somebody else. Jack didn't want to hurt anyone nor did he want to live the rest of his life longing for what might have been. He didn't want to be one of those guys working on LaBrea with a couple of yellowed clippings in his wallet.

The woman who had been his agent was no longer in the movie business; Jack needed to find someone to represent him. He and his mother sent his picture to fifty agents and after a week began to meet with those who responded, but the meetings didn't go well. He still had his compelling tan eyes and his handsome face and his body was still sleek, but there was something in the way he spoke that seemed a little strange. It was as if English were a language he had memorized without being entirely certain what the words meant and there were times when he sounded as if he were terribly, incurably tired.

Jack knew it was the trouble with his speech that prevented his getting representation and he worked day and night to improve it. He went to a speech therapist and he continued to read aloud to his mother, who by now had remarried and worked with her husband in his dry-cleaning business and could only spend two or three hours a day with her son. Before bed, Jack listened to his voice played back on his tape recorder and tried to be absolutely honest with himself about his own deficiencies. He was frightened and he was lonely, but he was too determined to quit.

Before the accident, Jack had been friends with Paul

Slattery, who had been a well thought of writer and would have been given a shared credit on the remake of *Petrified Forest,* if it had been made. Jack and Slattery had once been a part of a Thursday night basketball game in a funky West Los Angeles gym and they had also both courted the same junior vice-president at Warner Bros., who surprised them both by marrying a doctor and moving to Vancouver.

Like many screenwriters, Slattery's dream was to one day direct pictures. And at the time Jack was working to reconstitute himself, Slattery had sold a screenplay called *Send for Me* and had made it a condition that he himself be hired to direct it. Now he was working in a small Quonset hut on the studio lot and he was working day and night, making certain every detail was as perfect as he could make it. He wasn't given a large enough budget to hire stars for his first picture—but he didn't want any stars, really. He wanted this picture to be *his.*

While casting, Slattery heard that Jack Mitchell was trying to get back into the business and not meeting any success. It was sickening to Paul how forgetful and disloyal people were. Paul was raised in a household that put a high premium on conscience—his father was a civil liberties lawyer and though he was rich it all seemed the right sort of money, and Paul's mother had collected signatures for peace petitions on the very coldest Westchester mornings.

Paul remembered Jack's touching and mysterious talent, his beautiful face, the excitement he created, and Paul told himself he would at least give Jack a chance to read for *Send for Me.*

It is here that Eric Sands enters the story. Eric was also a writer, though few people knew that about him. He had worked in the technical end of filmmaking and made a living. He was clever, efficient, and inscrutable and this made him a valuable ally. Slattery had hired Eric as a personal assistant when preproduction work on *Send for Me* began and when Paul came up with the idea of hiring Jack Mitchell it was Eric who was first to say it was a great idea.

"I don't want the offer to come from me," Paul said. "I know Jack and he'll think it's charity."

"Then it'll come from me," Eric answered, quickly, a little before Paul had completely formed his own thoughts. "What'd you have in mind for him? The reporter?"

Paul was silent for a moment. From the window over his desk, he could see three extras dressed as Victorian beggars walking toward Sound Stage #2. Ah, this was the life. "Yeah," he finally said. "The reporter."

The reporter was a small but pivotal role and it did Eric's heart good to offer it to Jack. Eric's experiences in the movie business had convinced him that those who succeeded always did so at the expense of whatever moral fiber they had once had. Eric hadn't thought much of Paul Slattery, but now he was willing to believe that perhaps he had been wrong. True, Slattery gave the impression of being ambitious and timid and not quite trusting in the luck that had brought him this far. Yet he was willing to give an old friend a second chance. Granted, Jack's appearance in *Send for Me* would be newsworthy and likely to garner publicity and goodwill for the movie, but then nothing is pure. Nothing is all one way and not the other.

When Jack showed up at Slattery's offices, the two men threw their arms around each other. It was a real embrace and Eric, who was talking on the phone at the time, was taken aback by its sincerity. They did not even cut it down to size by slapping each other on the back.

Jack was nervous and Paul worked to make him feel at ease. He apologized for asking an actor of Jack's stature to read for a part. "It's the studio," Slattery explained, with a conspiratorial grimace. "They're nervous about giving a guy like me so much responsibility so I have to do everything just so."

Eric, listening in, wondered what Paul meant by a guy like me. As far as Eric could see, Paul wasn't very different from any of the directors who were routinely given large budgets or even from the studio executives who granted them. But, still, it was good of Paul to make an excuse for the screen test.

Paul asked Eric to run the test. "He'll drown in flop sweat if I'm there," Paul had said. Eric fed Jack lines while someone videotaped. Jack played the reporter in the scene in which he barges into the district attorney's office and accuses him of being part of a cover-up. Eric felt a cold knot in his stomach as Jack went through the test. The first two takes were so awkward and poorly timed that even the techie running the videocamera was rolling his eyes and after the third Jack was beginning to tire.

"You're being very nice," Jack told Eric. "And it's appreciated."

"No. You were fine. Really good."

"It's a good role," said Jack. He made a fist and then thoughtfully covered it with his other hand.

"It's well written," said Eric. "There's a lot of warmed-over crap in this script but the reporter's a good part."

"Are you a writer?" asked Jack.

"Me? I'm Paul's assistant. I answer the phones and say 'Paul's office.'"

Jack smiled his beautiful smile. "Everyone does something else out here."

"Oh, I write," said Eric, shrugging. "When I can."

"I knew it. I could tell from how you talked about the script."

They were walking across the studio lot as they conversed. Eric was thinking about three film scripts he had at home, all of them uncompleted. Across the broad, sunstruck boulevard was a character actress who had been in Jack's first film. When Jack saw her, he waved. But she didn't recognize him and Jack tried to hide his embarrassment by pretending to stretch his arm. He made the gesture five or six times.

. . .

As it happened, Jack was hired to play the reporter. Paul was proud of how he'd handled the hiring of his old friend. He hadn't showed the studio executives Jack's test. Paul had heard from a few people that Jack's speech problems were so bad that he could barely be understood. The speech was not perfect, but it wasn't that bad. It seemed to Paul that Jack's pronunciation was somehow *personalized* by the shadow of affliction. The studio was naturally nervous about hiring an actor with brain damage, but Paul also made them aware of how much free publicity the move would bring them.

Besides everything else, changing the decision might have meant wasting a lot of costly time because Paul had delayed telling the studio about Jack until the last possible moment.

"That was the brilliance of my strategy," Paul said to Eric. "I tell you, half this business is knowing when to talk and when to remain silent because anything you say can and will be used against you. There should be a Miranda decision for directors, you know?" He was delighted with himself and there seemed, to Eric, something puerile in Paul's pride. It just got on Eric's nerves.

Eric's animosity deepened once filming began on *Send for Me.* The production moved to a small town in Oregon, where the weather was worse than expected. They all lived in a shitty Days Inn. Separated from his fiancée, whom he did not really intend to marry, but whom he clung to anyhow, and separated as well from what he considered his real work, Eric became moody, irritated. He found his every moment dominated by Slattery's increasingly ill-considered demands. Slattery was hysterical about the rain and the movie going overbudget. He had seemed as if he were going to burst into tears a few times. He was forever sending Eric on errands—to find Los Angeles and New York papers in a small town where you were lucky to find an old issue of *Newsweek,* to get pages retyped, to find a back brace, to get hold of a videocassette of *Sweet Smell of Success,* which Paul thought was a precursor of *Send for Me*—a pitiful inflation of the project at hand, in Eric's view. Worst of all, Slattery was venting his own terror and confusion on Eric, speaking to him in coarse, brutal tones and once going so far as to smack Eric on the back of the head, barking, "Anybody home?"

Eric often wondered why he didn't walk off the picture. But no one in the business would fail to see it all from Slattery's point of view and Eric would only be spoiling his own chances to work on another picture.

Slattery knew how miserable he was making Eric, but he couldn't help himself. He tried to acknowledge the problem by speaking sarcastically. "Uh, Eric, I know this is beneath an important writer such as yourself, but I wonder if you could make a fresh pot of coffee and then call my service and take any important messages."

As for Jack Mitchell, he was thankful to be working again. The delays, the boring little town, the jittery director, didn't faze Jack. His problem was a constant high hum of nerves; his subconscious was like a vacuum cleaner being run in the next room. He was terrified of failing.

Jack wanted to spend more time with Paul, hoping to engage his goodwill. But everyone on the set wanted Paul for something or other. It was inevitable: grown people became like children around a director, currying favor, acting out crises— even with a first-time director.

Paul Slattery felt the strain of the enterprise and after the second week of shooting he moved out of the Days Inn and into a nicer hotel, a mile away. Slattery lived in this new hotel with a woman production assistant named Daphne—Daphne was not attractive but there nevertheless was an assumption that she had managed to begin an affair with Paul. Eric was kept at the Days Inn as Paul's factotum; he was expected to report to Paul everything that was being said at the Days Inn.

Eric worked day and night and could barely even think about his own writing. When he wasn't answering the phone— "Paul's office"—or retyping pages, or picking up someone at the airport forty-eight miles away, or filling in the daily log, or reporting to Paul what people were saying in the Days Inn cocktail lounge, then he was in bed, trying desperately to sleep.

In the midst of this, Eric found himself suddenly cast in the role of Jack Mitchell's best friend. Jack needed a best friend and Eric just let it happen.

Jack prevailed upon Eric to rehearse scenes with him and then insisted upon frank evaluations.

"To be perfectly honest with you Jack, there's still a little slowness now and then."

Tears came to Jack's eyes, but he nodded, encouraging Eric to continue.

"It's not terrible or anything," said Eric. "But it's there, a little slowness."

Slattery was far too consumed with the mechanics of getting *Send for Me* on film to notice any problems in Jack's performance and the other actors were too kind to mention anything, even to each other.

Jack's main scene, in which he avoids questions put to him by the film's hero but does so in a way that suggests an additional layer of conspiracy in the town, was shot over the course of three days. Slattery and Daphne seemed suddenly and extravagantly in love, in the way peculiar to ambitious energetic people far from home, and they watched Jack's scenes together at night and then sent the unedited film back to Los Angeles, where it could be seen by the studio executives.

"I can't help resenting sending the dailies back to the studio," Slattery said to Eric the next day. "They don't know what the fuck they're looking at." The word *fuck* seemed to have become prominent in Slattery's patter since the ascendancy of Daphne. "If they knew how to make fucking movies then they'd make fucking movies, you know?"

Eric, however, recognized the true cause of Slattery's complaint: Paul was afraid to have his work judged, worried that the Los Angeles people would find such alarming deficiencies in the work that they'd want a new director. After all, Slattery was still new to the game. No one owed him a thing.

"Well," said Eric, with a quick shrug. "It's their dough. Spending millions makes anyone a little nervous."

Slattery glared at Eric. It wasn't an explicitly disloyal statement but Slattery resented it nevertheless. He also resented the cleverly oblique way Eric framed his snotty little remark—it seemed to suggest he had taken the time to find exactly the right words.

"Those fucks are going to make a lot of fucking money on this picture and they fucking know it," said Slattery. "Give me a break, Eric. You have no idea what it's like on this end of the business. It may be a drag answering phones and all but at least you don't have to put up with all this fucking tension."

The next day, Eric took a call from a man named Joel Walters, who was the new head of production at the studio. "Where's Slattery?" said Walters. "He needs to talk to me right now."

Slattery was on location and Eric brought him the message. Slattery rolled his eyes and said he would call LA when he was good and ready, but Eric could see that Paul was worried.

Late that evening, Slattery showed up at the office, where Eric was still working. Slattery was ashen.

"They want me to fire Jack Mitchell," he said, sitting down and putting his feet on the desk. "They hate him in the dailies. They say he sounds crazy or something. They want me to hire Cody Jones. Christ. Cody Jones is a TV star. He's terrible. I really hate him. How am I going to tell poor Jack? It's painful."

Eric shook his head. He noted that the *fuck*s had left Slattery's speech pattern, as if this bad news had a kind of sexually sobering effect. Eric was very much afraid that Slattery was going to ask him to fire Jack.

But Slattery got up, stretched, dusted off his trousers, and said, "I better do it right now. Poor Jack."

In the middle of that night, the phone next to Eric's bed began to ring. Automatically, Eric grabbed it and said, "Paul's office."

"I'm having a heart attack," said the voice on the phone. It was Jack and his voice was gasping, shrill.

Eric rubbed his eyes, sat up in bed. "Where are you?"

"My room. Eric. Please."

Eric called the front desk and in a few minutes there was an ambulance at the motel. In the meantime, Eric got dressed and ran to Jack's room, where he found the stricken actor holding his chest and staggering erratically around the small blue-and-orange room. "Oh God, oh God," Jack was saying. Eric tried to hold him up but he slipped through his arms and fell to the floor.

When they got Jack to the hospital they found he wasn't having a heart attack after all. It was a great relief, even though it was slightly annoying, too. The doctor said it was anxiety and he gave Jack a little oxygen and some sedatives. Jack didn't seem at all embarrassed by the doctor's diagnosis and he elected to spend the night in the hospital. He looked solemn, as if the diagnosis of anxiety were as grave as cardiac arrest.

Eric was driven back to the motel by a policeman and because he was so tired and the policeman so friendly, Eric told the cop what had happened to Jack, his accident, ruined career, years of struggle, his being hired and fired.

"Heartless bastards," said the cop, shaking his large head. "All they care about is money."

Eric realized this was the logical response to the story as he'd told it. But hearing the cop go on about the unfairness of it all made that point of view seem rather oversimplified and naïve. After all, thought Eric, did Slattery really have a choice? Should he have walked off the picture, or fought to have Jack remain and risk ruining the whole movie? Eric couldn't honestly say what he would have done had the decision been his.

The next afternoon, Eric went to the hospital to look in on Jack. He was dressed and ready to go back to the motel, where he would have to pack his bags and return to LA. When they got into Eric's car Jack asked him if they could take a slightly longer route, one that would bring them past a large farm where they raised horses.

"I love those horses," Jack said, in a soft, terrifyingly melancholy voice.

It was odd. Eric had always loved horses, too. He had wanted a horse as a child and his parents, great kidders, had promised him one year after year, though they lived in a small house in Toledo, with a tiny backyard.

"I've always wanted to own a few horses," Jack said, rapturously depressed.

Well, Eric had only wanted one horse, not a few, but that was the only difference. He felt something long dormant in his heart suddenly awaken, something unreasonable and loyal, even passionate. He loved Jack Mitchell at that moment and by loving Jack he was beginning to love himself in a way he had forgotten. It gave him a ferocious hope for the future to feel these things for Jack.

"I'm going to kill myself," Jack softly announced, when they passed the three-plank fencing of the horse ranch.

"What are you talking about?" said Eric. "You can't kill yourself."

"I've worked five years to get myself in shape and I still can't cut it. I don't want to live like this."

"If everyone who wasn't in the movies killed themselves it would be a pretty empty world," Eric said.

Jack smiled. "Thanks," he said, sinking lower in his seat.

Eric drove on and then realized there actually was a good chance Jack would carry out his threat. He felt his own heart race. "Jack! Look. You can't take it like this. Paul didn't want to replace you. It was very complicated."

"I know. He told me it was the studio. That makes it worse."

Eric was struck with an idea, a solution, a radical reshaping of reality he would have been incapable of before remembering the horses, before his heart had awakened to Jack.

"You know that character Evans?" He waited for Jack to nod. "Well how about you playing his sidekick? Gangsters always have a sidekick."

"But it's not in the script."

"And what a mistake that is," said Eric. A feeling of almost lunatic well-being went through him. "What a fucking mistake. Here's what. We'll write it up, just a few scenes. Then you can give them to Paul. He feels fucking lousy about your being off the picture and this will give him the perfect way of putting you back on."

Back in Jack's room, Eric was able to write out the sidekick's scenes in less than half an hour. He had never been so fluent in his life and though he didn't think his work was brilliant it suddenly achieved something else, something that had been even more elusive to Eric—a professional slickness that approached perfection.

Jack read the new scenes and his eyes filled with tears. His posture improved, he regained his full height. He put his hand on Eric's shoulder and squeezed. "You're terrific, man. I'd like you to write all my stuff." Jack walked happily around the motel room, reading the new lines to himself. Suddenly, he stopped, looked pensive. "You think Paul will go for it?"

"He will, if you tell him you wrote the scenes," said Eric, his heart sinking. "He doesn't like to think I can write. I'm supposed to say 'Paul's office,' and that's all. If you tell him I wrote this stuff he'll hate it."

Jack nodded. "Good idea," he said. Then he stopped again. "But wait . . ." Eric was preparing to tell Jack not to feel guilty, but what Jack said was, "You better type this up, Paul might recognize your handwriting."

That evening, Jack gave Slattery the new pages and asked if he could play the sidekick. "It won't matter if my speech is off," said Jack. "In fact, it'll work better that way."

Paul was pleased to get Jack working again; it was too awful to see the actor sink, it would be a curse on the film. And the truth was Slattery loved the new scenes.

He didn't feel he could give an immediate yes, however. The studio was nervous about Paul's ability to make the picture without close supervision and they were sending one of their executives up to oversee the rest of the shoot. Slattery realized this was a defeat but since the defeat was his he figured he might as well wait for the morning before giving Jack the new role.

When Slattery showed the new pages to the studio executive the man was immediately enthusiastic. He was a lanky, soft-spoken man named Gregory Green and he said, "These are superb. This could really make the picture."

Slattery didn't tell Gregory Green that Jack had written the scenes, though he had meant to. But hearing the pages praised made Slattery hesitate. It would be better for the project, overall, if the studio thought Paul himself had written the new scenes. It would restore their confidence in him and that would be best, in the long run.

When Paul put Jack back in the picture, Jack was thrilled, reprieved. Eric, for his part, drove by himself to the horse farm and pulled off to the side of the road and wept into his hands, overcome with happiness and a sense of private virtue.

When the dailies of Jack's scenes were sent back to the studio, Joel Walters himself called Paul and said, "We think you're finally hitting your stride now," Walters said.

Jack's scenes were over and he went back to LA. Word was already circulating about how well he'd done in *Send for Me* and Jack was anxious to return and wait for new offers. He called Eric from the airport to say good-bye and to thank him for his help, though he did fail to specify exactly what that meant.

The evening of Jack's departure, Eric was sitting around with Slattery and Daphne. The director and his production assistant seemed to be deliberately giving off postcoital vibrations, while Eric totaled up the week's room-service receipts for the entire cast and crew. (Slattery had been warned that incidental expenses were running inexcusably out of control.)

"You know," Paul said, beating out a drum rhythm on Daphne's leg, "maybe I shouldn't have let Jack Mitchell go home. He might have come in fucking handy."

"Oh?" said Eric. He felt his own annoyance, coiled within.

"The guy's a fucking talented writer," Slattery said, with an Isn't that amazing? turn of the hand.

Eric nodded. I am never going to say *fuck* again, he thought. Then the phone began to ring and Eric failed to answer it. It rang and rang. Slattery and Daphne looked at Eric and he looked back at them and then the phone stopped ringing.

"What's that about?" asked Slattery. "You just let it ring?"

"I'm a writer, too," said Eric. His lips felt hard and cold.

"You just let the phone ring and didn't pick it up," said Slattery.

"In fact," said Eric, looking away, out the small office window, out toward the highway, where eventually his line of sight, if it had had wings, would have come to the horse farm, "I'm the one who wrote Jack's scenes. I made up the idea of the sidekick. It was all my work. We told you Jack wrote it because if it had come from me you wouldn't have gone for it."

The phone started up again. Slattery sprang up and grabbed it. "Hello?" he said, in a hoarse, unstable voice. It turned out to be a call from the studio and Slattery laughed, talked, listened, and laughed some more. After he was finished, he turned to Daphne, and said, "Let's go to my room."

Eric understood he wouldn't be fired as long as the picture was in production. But he knew he had better line something up beginning the day after production because he wouldn't be getting any high recommendations from Slattery, who was no longer speaking to him.

What Eric wanted to do was finish and sell a script. Whatever doubts he had had were dispelled by the scenes he had written for the sidekick, but what he wasn't prepared for was that writing lines on the set for a picture already being photographed had spoiled him for the solitude and languor of writing alone in his room. It was like playing with toy soldiers after having been in a real war.

Eric kept at it but he was professional enough to know it wasn't amounting to much. He didn't dare ask Slattery for a recommendation and that made it difficult getting any more production work. There seemed to be some kind of "word" out on him.

Financially speaking, all Eric had going for him was his relationship with Jack Mitchell and so he became the actor's manager. Then he convinced Jack to fire his agent and he became the out-of-work actor's agent, too.

Slattery in the meantime was having postproduction problems and for a while it seemed as if *Send for Me* might never be released. No one was going to make a firm offer to Jack Mitchell until they had a look at Slattery's movie. Eric got a call from a TV talk show inviting Jack to be on a panel with other people who had fought their way back from crippling disabilities but it seemed to Eric that it wouldn't be smart to emphasize that aspect of Jack's life without some solid accomplishments under their belts. Maybe after *Send for Me* was out they could get a little extra bounce from the brain damage—but not before.

Eric still knew a few people at the studio and he managed to find out, a few months later, that Paul had finally cut the picture and was going to be showing it to the cast and core crew in a screening room on the Burbank lot. Eric didn't expect he'd be invited but on the day of the screening he showed up—with Jack.

Jack had just gotten a haircut that hadn't quite worked out and he had knocked back a few Coors to take the edge off his nervousness. "You know," he said, as they drove through the studio gates, "this town is full of people who act like friends. But when you come down to it, you're the only one who's been there for me."

"You can thank me after you thank the members of the Academy," Eric said. Jack was silent for a few moments and then laughed slowly, with spaces of nearly a full second between the ha's. It was the first time in a long while that Eric noticed his friend's persistent disability.

Eric didn't want to tell Jack they hadn't been invited to the screening and that they were, in effect, gate-crashing Jack's comeback. They slipped into the screening room after the lights had gone out and found a couple of seats in the back. They could feel the high spirits in the air; the audience loved every frame of the picture. But Eric and Jack just sat there in rigid disbelief as the story unfolded. Jack's performance was completely edited out of the picture. The character of the sidekick was gone. No one in the picture or the room missed him.

"I'm on the cutting room floor, man," Jack whispered to Eric. His breath was beery. It mixed with the smell of the Santa Monica haircut.

"That lowlife coward," Eric said and he reached over and clasped Jack's forearm in solidarity.

When the lights came up there was applause, cheers, handshakes, hugs, victory whoops. It seemed the people in the screening room were a pack of dingoes and the movie was the smell of meat. Jack and Eric stayed in their seats and except for a few well-meaning, embarrassed hellos directed toward Jack, they were left alone. Jack was pale; his eyes were sparkling with pain, like a teen-ager who has been slapped in the face.

Slattery was surrounded by production assistants, happy cast and crew members, who were all relieved the picture was finally cut and who, for the time being, were convinced *Send for Me* was going to be a hit and help their careers.

"Eric," Jack said.

"Shh," said Eric. "I'm thinking."

"You're thinking? I'm out of the picture and you're thinking?"

194 • SCOTT SPENCER

"I know you're out of the picture, Jack," Eric said with exaggerated patience. "And it means just as much to me as it does to you."

"I'm sure," said Jack, looking away.

Finally, the room started to clear. Slattery was talking to the film editor and Greg Green, who was still the studio's point man on the project. The room was empty enough by now for Slattery to notice Jack and Eric sitting in the back. He made a small, quick smile in their general direction. Was it shyness? Nerves? Satisfaction? Slattery quickly returned to the conversation he was having with his film cutter and Green. Daphne was with him, not even pretending to listen. She was staring at her fingernails and jiggling her leg to a rapid beat. As for Slattery himself he seemed expansive, fit; he laughed a rich amber imperial laugh.

"Aren't you going to say something?" Jack asked Eric.

"I think the best thing we can do right now is just try and get what he took out and use it for your sample reel," Eric said, nodding.

"Sample reel? I'm out of the picture."

"I know, Jack, I know."

"I'm out of the picture!"

"Jack, we have already established that."

Jack tugged at the center of his shirt, pulling it away from him as if he needed more room to breathe.

"Maybe I was just no good," he said.

Eric looked at him and wondered if it would be the right thing, or even useful in any way, to tell Jack the reason the sidekick was cut was that Slattery had found out it was he, Eric, who had written those scenes. This isn't about you, he could say. This is about some sick jealousy Slattery has toward me.

But then he thought: Am I sure that's what's happening here? To look at Slattery now, it was hard to understand how he could feel competitive with someone on Eric's level. Wasn't there something a little arrogant and pitiful in thinking someone with as much success as Paul could be threatened by some-one as fringe as Eric?

"You told me he loved the scenes and he thought I was good," Jack said.

"He did, Jack, he did."

"Then why did he do this to me? He knows how much I need this break." Suddenly, Jack's face was bathed in sweat and he pulled so hard at his shirt one of the buttons popped. His chest was moist, slack.

"You want to know why?" Eric said, stalling for time. He had to tell Jack something; the man was having a break-down right here and now. And it was then that a wave of beneficence went through Eric: he was going to tell Jack some-thing very close to the truth, even though it would endanger and perhaps even destroy their relationship. He would do this to make the man feel better.

"All right," Eric said. "You may as well know. Paul found out I wrote those scenes for you. And it really pissed him off. He hates me, for some reason." As he said this, Slat-tery looked at him from across the theater. Eric felt his heart leap.

"He found out?" said Jack. "How?"

"I have no idea. Maybe you told him?"

"I didn't tell him. You think I would do that to you?" He wiped the sweat off his upper lip with his fingers and then looked at them, as if they might be bloody.

"Well, I didn't either." There was no point confessing to that part, that part was really beside the point.

Jack stood up and when Eric tugged at his hand he tore it away. "Hey, Slattery, you shit-for-brains."

"Hello, Jack," Paul said, fixing him with a stare and then nodding very slowly.

"You just stabbed me in the balls," Jack said. He walked out into the downward-sloping aisle but he hadn't yet begun stalking toward Paul.

"Sorry about that, Jack," Paul said, his voice reasonable,

friendly. "I had a three-hour movie I had to cut down to a hundred and six minutes. A lot of wonderful stuff went."

"I know why you did it, man," Jack said.

"But I'll tell you what," Paul said. "We'll loop it for you, put it into great shape, and you can use it on your sample reel."

Jack had by then started moving toward Paul but that suggestion stopped him, as if the plug that gave him power had been kicked out of the wall. He turned toward Eric and his eyes suggested that he had just discovered the conspiracy against him. It was all so clear just then.

He opened his mouth to say something to Eric but was suddenly overcome by a sharp bright terrifying pain in his chest. He grabbed his shirt and tore at it, gasping for breath.

"Oh-oh," said Greg Green, bouncing up. There was something about him that radiated competence. "Take it easy there," he called out to Jack.

"I'm going to kill you," Jack said, pointing his finger at Paul.

Eric reached to touch Jack, just a cautionary hand on the elbow. "Take it easy, Jack. This is nuts."

But Jack jerked his arm away from Eric, as if he was no better than Slattery. Then Jack staggered forward and held on to the armrest on an aisle seat. And then he fell forward, onto his knees. He held his chest but kept his eyes open wide.

"You're going to be all right, Jack," Greg said, very loudly, as if the pain had transported Jack to a distant country. "The infirmary is less than six hundred feet from here. Think you can make it?" He already had his hands under Jack's arms. He gently helped the actor to his feet.

Jack nodded weakly.

"Good, Jack, that's good," said Greg. "Let's go."

"I'll give you a hand," Eric said. But as soon as he touched Jack, Jack used up precious strength jerking away from Eric.

"I'll be able to handle this OK," Greg said, in a neutral

way. He didn't want to appear to be blaming Eric for Jack's reaction to him.

Greg led Jack out of the screening room. Jack's steps were not particularly unsteady, after the first few. Eric just stood there, looking at the doorway through which they had left. He could hear their feet on the concrete steps outside. When he turned around again, Paul Slattery was looking at him with a vague, bemused expression.

"Sorry about that," Eric said.

"All actors are Marilyn Monroe," Slattery pronounced. "All of them." He waited for Eric to nod and smile and then he said, "You know, there's something I've been meaning to say. Those lines you wrote for Jack. They were pretty good."

Eric took a deep breath. There was a vast invisible justice at work here. Somehow this long-overdue praise was coming to him because he had done the right thing, he had told Jack the basic truth about why his scenes had been cut. And now this was the reward. What goes around comes around, he thought. He was glad he had done the right thing. He had the same warm sense of well-being he had had when he and Jack had looked at the horses, back then, on location.

"Thanks, Paul. Coming from you, those words mean a lot."

Slattery nodded, incorporating in the gesture a brief bow of humility.

"You realize, of course," Slattery said, "we'd all behave better if there wasn't so much goddamned money involved."

"I better get over to the infirmary and see how Marilyn Monroe is doing," Eric said.

"He's fine," Slattery said. "Just another anxiety attack. Why don't you stick around?"

# JACK

O

*Michael Downing*

THE ROMANTIC VIEW of Jack is that he's ageless, a slipshod accounting for powerfulness in a man of seventy-two. He is big, his long limbs and heavy head tribute to generations of farming Yankee forebears. And as New England gentlemen are meant to do, he keeps his twenty acres north of Boston trim and unproductive.

Jack scythes. His rhythmic slashing back and forth along the slight embankment at the bottom of his sloping land leaves the grass to roll like waves behind a wind, activity that far exceeds the movement of the meager Ipswich River.

He makes a similar impression on a woman when he presses his bare hand against the small of her back and leads her through the thrill of potent promises to one of his chairs with a sprung seat cushion. The woman has the look of *something happened here,* while Jack moves slowly to his place beside the mantel, circumventing painting, drinking, younger women. In terms of unexpended passions he is very well preserved.

Jack lives alone and does not issue social invitations. Every visit is, per se, an imposition. Making matters worse, he hates the telephone and has never learned the simplest tricks of disembodied conversation. "It's not *machines* I mind," he told me once, unprompted, as his explanations often are, "it is unsuitable. Talking to a telephone. You enroll in a life drawing class and the instructor hands you a typewriter?"

The last time I imposed myself on Jack began with maybe thirty rings. As is his unaccommodating habit, he lifted the receiver and coughed.

"It's me, Jack. Thought I might come up for dinner. Maybe spend the night." His coughing never fails to incite bad manners; I refused to declare myself directly.

"You intend to *stay?* You'll . . . eat here as well?" His elevated diction raised this to the level of accusation. "Come. If you think you might *enjoy* being here."

"I have some reading I'd like to get done."

"Yes, that. Mann. Broch. All that."

Without effect I said, "I couldn't order a meal in German. Never mind read it."

He sputtered a Latin epigram and then said, "Modesty is always a virtue. So long as it is false." Then he dropped the receiver to the floor, as if he'd forgotten it was up to him to hang on. I heard him pick it up, and before I spoke again he laid it back into its cradle.

From a distance you are forced to take Jack at his word, in this case, "Come." Face-to-face his voice is something else again. The classical strains and the individual beats and rests are a music he's invented to resolve the countervailing forces he exerts. Two wives, several lovers, six children, a dozen self-appointed best friends, and unnumbered admirers orbit around him, each one of us several times drawn in—as if the very thought of him creates a vortex.

No one's ever managed to spend time with Jack; you rebound off the point of contact, propelled away again. His voice is compensatory, guiding and informing your descent. And fleeting as it is, his touch seems true.

Every word he's ever spoken (with approximations of his tone and tenor), the progress of decay along the open seams and sagging walls, even just the way he holds himself at dinner—all is data for the archive. Jackography. The probing and reporting are sanctioned by the scientific aspect.

Attractive, static Jack: How did he come to be?

The evolutionary premise makes a fossil of a fragment. Events are scrambled into sequence. Time as the comprehensive fiber of our prepositional existence: we live through it, in it, on borrowed stretches of it, from time to time. It never had occurred to me that time might prove unequal to its task.

You enter Jack's house from the back, through an unupholstered hall. The walls are frescoes of neglect. The tiny kitchen once was painted white; the bits and streams of meat and soup might be regarded as at least a couple decades' worth of dietary evidence. The downstairs otherwise is just one giant room with ancestral chairs and standing lamps, two horsehair divans, and anywhere from four to seven tables. An obsessive rearranger, Jack has never hit upon a grouping that is leastways practical. A few years back, with all the best intentions, a short-term girl friend bought him six extension cords. That was the final blow to friendly navigation.

Any one of four might be Jack's bedroom on a given day. You know which he has chosen; he'll have shoved his leather trunk of clothes beneath the bed. The dresser drawers in every room are filled with letters, canned goods, soap and towels, china plates, and photographs. A choice of bathrobes for his guests hangs in every closet.

In a corner of his one, huge bathroom (as Jack would say, "a proper *salle de bain*") is a three-panel screen. Folded in on itself, the canvas passes as a relic of Victorian discretion, a dressing shade. Pressed into service, the hinges scream, so it is best to run a bath.

Apparently unfinished, the unfurled panels form a triptych, though the middle one is just unsteady shades of gray. Close inspection (and, admittedly, a touch or two) brings you nearer to the truth. The center has been painted and rejected more than once, each failure calling forth a darker shroud. Still, the wings deliver you to Jack at twenty-eight or twenty-nine, made ancient by the war but believing he had time to paint.

On the right you see a man in standard ballet garb against a barnboard wall. He might be just another skinny dancer in Position One too long except for two details. A mottled sky shines through a window just below his knees. And his feet are noosed together and raised a length of rope above what ought to be the floor. The whole thing's upside down.

The left is painted on the horizontal; a lady at her piano. Her hands and forearms are deep inside the eviscerated instrument. But it is her silly, desperate smile (her teeth are elongated, too, and yellowed; a couple of the missing octaves?) that leads you to the little bloodstains underneath the rococo legs and chassis. She's got to play it like a harp, pluck the wires with her fingers.

In forty years, he's made some illustrations for the covers of books written by friends, sent etchings of his land in lieu of Christmas cards for three years running, delighted his children with sketches on demand until they were old enough to satisfy their longings with the color photographs in catalogs and magazines. This meager output often meets with a kind of philanthropic scorn. A hasty sketch on loose-leaf of a garden he is planning will be saved and framed and later spoken of with reverence, as if encouragement is what he's lacking.

The truth is, all the shows he gave before the war were attended by acclaim. At twenty-one, escaped from home and

Harvard, he was prominent in Paris, nicknamed "Jack American" as Giacometti's handpicked protégé. "Prolific days
those," he told me, "and perfumed nights. It's an indictment
of either me or the powers that inhere in people. But my rise—
*to power?*—coincided with Mr. Hitler's rather more spectacular
ascension."

Jack's peculiar admixture of cultures and breeding im-
pelled him to join the war before his countrymen, with a regiment of the Canadian Air Force. In his chauvinistic estimation
of the British might, he left everything he'd ever painted in his
Paris studio. On the evening of his third day at the front, half
his regiment was incinerated in an air strike. The survivors
were collected and marched to German prison camps, where
Jack spent the better part of the next four years.

This is the celebrated, secret center of Jack's life. No less
than four escapes, and intervening weeks in a solitary hut
hanging by his feet while planning yet another route to free-
dom, won him a second nickname, "Jack Who Comes and
Goes." "More epithet than sobriquet. One who comes and goes
incites the captors of those left behind to *rhapsodic* cruelty. I
seem to remember dreading the recaptures most because I
knew I would be marched several times around the camp to the
rhythm of the *English* hissing."

It seems clear that wedged between the torment and adventure is the rest of what he might have been. You always
have the urge to lead him toward it, as if together you could
reach it and release it. That's really why I went to Ipswich late
last August.

I heard the tractor when I got there, let myself in, and
chose a bedroom. The contents of the living room had been
dragged into a circular arrangement just off center; the lamp
cords stretched like spokes from every wall. I moved cautiously
to the porch with my books, which Jack would insist were
printed in German or another language I don't have.

Jack gives a person too much credit. This overzealous at-
tribution problem is more than odd. It's a window on to what

in him is humbled by his oddball status, a window I would like
to shutter tight.

I didn't hear his approach because he left the tractor
idling a couple hundred yards away. "Yes." He said this
softly, sort of slid it down a scale. "Before you start all *that?* I
don't want not to tell you. I read a most extraordinary book."
He held his gloved hands, palms up, above the table, as if to
ask permission to be seated. "Yes. I'll even put my hands on it
later. But this other man who lives in—of *all* places—Wolverhampton? That would be in England. A pilot in the RAF. He
has written my life story." He forced his eyes to open wider,
his way of sanctioning my confusion and surprise. *"You* know
in advance," he pointed to my books, "as a book it was a failure."

"A pilot in the war?" I was hoping to attach myself to a
single, simple fact.

"He *means* to tell what it was like. How it *felt."* He
turned toward his tractor marooned between the flag of new-
mown stripes and the ragged riverbank, to let me know he had
time only for a story, not for a discussion. "In 1963 he was
flying in an air show in the Midlands. He was performing
spins." He spun his index finger in the air above his head. "A
thousand English eyes upon him. He popped out of the cockpit,
made a kind of loop, and fell back *inside* the tumbling plane."

"He fell out? Unattached?"

"And *in.* As if nothing had happened." He stood up from
his seat clumsily, affected the posture of an earthbound specta-
tor. "From below? The man looks to be a hero, at least. Or was
that a miracle? *You* can imagine the years of reporters' questions, television interviews, appearances with the local MP."

"And the book is *How I Lived to Tell My Story?"*

"And why, and why me. Well, you can imagine." Jack
took his seat again. "He *can't.* It was he all right. And he can
re-create the sequence. But he'll always not have time to think
*midair.* If he'd had the time to think he surely would have
fallen." Jack was up again, smiling. "The problem is, anyone
who hears of it can feel and think his way through that little

loop. You feel a perfect fool for never finding time there for *emotion,* never mind a *thought.*"

"I'd like to see it later, if you find it."

Jack said, "I wouldn't bother with the book," then headed to his fields.

Of course, I didn't need the book. One's imagination is compliant. I returned several times to Wolverhampton circa 1963, put myself through many loops.

As he always does, Jack got dinner started without a word, sat staring at the river, and jumped up to rescue two barely discolored steaks from his stone grave of a barbecue pit. Each steak was laid on a handful of Ipswich watercress. Those two plates and two blue plastic tumblers of tap water are what he means by dinner April through October.

But you never really share a meal with Jack. He feeds. This momentary activity may be followed by a conversation, or a story, or his odd, attentive silence. Summer evenings always end with his cursory inspection of the largely incidental fire.

Only while he's eating is Jack free of his elaborate truss of manners, as if he hopes to satisfy his hunger by indulging a voracious appetite. When the solids were dispensed with, he raised the painted china plate and drained the tepid pool of herbed blood. Then he pushed the plate aside, disappointed. No meal would ever be enough.

"The fourth time was with Jeremy, a *lawyer's* son from Ottawa." He leaned back in his chair, slowly lowered himself back toward the table, to make a clean break from dinner. "For weeks we saved our cubes of oleo, impacting them with sugar."

"This was your fourth escape?"

Jack received this as an accusation of incompetence. "I *did* keep the Germans busy, which is the *duty* of the taken man."

"It's remarkable is what I meant."

He can't abide a compliment. Like a jostled needle on a record, he skipped ahead. "The fifth night running brings us to a river." He traced his finger in an arc along the table. "We

were cold enough without *this.* Will it make a degree of difference, being colder than we are already? Besides, the very notion of the river raises the question of which side is the right
side. If fording *is* going forward, do we *want* to go that way?"
He swung his face away from mine, as if an unseen third had
asked these questions. He whispered, "Juris imprudence."

Without attributions, he pantomimed the forty-year-old
conversation. He punctuated every question with his turning,
tilting head.

"Forward *is* to France?"

"France is just a detour. Aren't we just headed back to
the front?"

"If that is *forward.*"

"Suppose we didn't cross?"

*"Backwards?* To the camp?"

"Quicker than this route through that river, into France,
out to one front or another, back to camp."

"Surely, we *would* have to leave the camp again?"

"We're crossing then?"

"If we went *barefoot,* saved our shoes the crossing?"

Jack was up and kicking off his shoes, frantic. He made a
few elaborate gestures for my benefit, theatrical asides to keep
the audience in tow. It was clear enough that having got
through the freezing water Jeremy and Jack had left their
shoes behind, but Jack added, "So the question of direction
would arise again." He forded back to his chair. "And then
again."

I had a feeling that he thought he'd brought the drama to
an end. "Did someone see you at the river?" I didn't want to be
abandoned at this juncture.

"We slept inside a hedge above the river and woke when
the sun slanted in against us, like a stranger in the bed. Up
above *us* is a portico, *occupied.* I can't move or they will hear
me. But I have a frame." He held his hands above his head and
looked only at the space between them. "A pleated greatcoat on
a soldier's sloping back. Over this, the yellow hair and ample

forearms of his fräulein, who is moaning with delight. *He's got her in his hands.* He can't see that she is tracing crosses on his back, blessing him."

Jack brought his hands down to the table, turned his palms up in surrender. "Jeremy and Jack are not *in* life. They've been killing living men who belong to pretty girls, crossing rivers back *and* forth. Where they get to is *here?* Just this close to life?" His hands shot up again, framing what was happening above him. "In Paris three years later I won't find the paintings I remember. In *my* studio I'll only find three un-posted letters from a German officer to his sister. *I* can't read German."

As if his silence was a cue that had been worked out in advance, I heard the squeaking crickets all at once. I was sure he'd let them take the night away. Impatiently, I said, "But you could paint the portico, the forearms," as if this might dislodge him.

"*You* can imagine such a painting. But if the fräulein raised her head and lifted up her blessing finger, and she screamed? *Well.* She did. I hadn't time to figure out the *angle.* I was in the picture. I seem to see that now.

"Because I've come and gone before, I am taken to a new camp, with a tennis court surrounded by a fence. Two soldiers keep the barrels of their guns deep inside my pockets until they leave me at the service line. Sixteen soldiers line up against the net."

Jack composed this picture with his framing hands, then adjusted his angle slightly. He was squaring faulty memory with the unstable contours of this picture. He was taking up the through line tethering a hungry gentleman in Ipswich to a young man with no time to see. "An officer is seated at the side, *straddling* the painted edge." He curled his hand to show me that the seated man's back offended the picture's proper frame. Then Jack screamed, *"Zieg heil,"* slammed his hands down on the table as sixteen guns slammed into sixteen shoulders. And I heard the English soldiers hissing and the crackle of his canvas

in a fireplace on St-Germain, where a German soldier drops his
pen midsentence to his sister, pulls another painting from the
wall because its heavy frame will warm the studio.

But all Jack said was, "Did he cough or was he *laughing?*
I walked off the court, pockets full of guns again."

"I don't know how you lived through that." I was thinking of his entire loop.

Jack was back on the service line. "I didn't live *through*
that. *Did* I? Like a million other unsuspecting men I was not
shot by a firing squad."

This struck me as a simpleton's conclusion. "That begs
the point. Of having been so close to death."

"You can't *be* close to death." This was a pronouncement.
It was given with full weight, the counterbalance to the futility
of thinking you could stand outside the frame of life and see it
all.

He ambled over to his fire and kicked the coals, teasing
flames high above the piled stones. In that shot of light I saw
the sky was milky gray and starless. It was no bigger than
Jack's famous triptych.

And it seemed to me that maybe none of us had ever
touched him. Descending toward his lovely, grizzled patch of
sky we see the inverted, hanging soldier and the sideways,
grinning artist who has to bleed to play. We see both sides but
we are drawn in to the center. It is not Jack we touch and
bound away from. It's just the frame he's built to keep himself
from falling off the twenty acres that he keeps in Ipswich.

# THE ROAD

# AGENT

○

*Robert Olmstead*

Mike's the road agent. He drives the roads, replacing guardrails, laying down cold patch, cutting brush and running culvert. In the winter he plows snow, sometimes around the clock. He knows at which temperature to salt and when it's too cold to do any good.

Often, as he rides the roads, he pulls over to talk to people. He tells them the whole country is shutting down. More cops, more criminals, fewer outlaws, he says. The old-timers nod in a way that says they've known it for a long time. For them, it becomes the word of the road agent, something they can bank on.

Mike drives an orange GMC pickup with the New Hampshire state seal on the door. The windshield wipers slap at the rain, sweeping it off, sluicing it to the side. The number plate says *Live Free or Die,* the state motto. Prisoners make the number plates in Concord and most people think it's a good job for

them to have. It keeps them busy. Mike says the words are
strong words for people who don't know much about either
living or dying. It's the kind of thinking that can get you in
trouble.

*"Come on, Mike. Getcha ears on."*

It's Flambeau, the retired road agent. He comes on the
radio in Mike's truck, trying to raise him up. The crew is in
Chesterfield opening a beaver dam that has caused a quarter
mile of road to be flooded.

"Mike here. Back to you."

*"Yeah. We got beaucoup problems with this beaver dam,
given the rain and all."*

"You there now?"

*"Roger."*

"I just turned into the hollow. I'll be right along."

The game warden has been trying to trap the beavers all
summer so he can relocate them. Until he does, the road crew
has to go at the dam with axes and shovels. Mike won't let them
use the chain saws because the beavers pack clay in amongst
the wood. The boys bitch about it, but they know he's right,
and besides, until the rain started, they'd been able to keep up
with the beavers. It becomes a day-long job that a stick of dy-
namite could take care of in less than a second. Much less. But
the game warden won't let them. He tells the road crew it isn't
up to him. It's up to Fish and Game. If he had his druthers,
he'd let them blow the goddamn thing to kingdom come, what
with his busy schedule of being up all night and day contend-
ing with poachers, jacklights, mad dogs and rabid coon.

The road crew laughs at him. They offer to stay off the
back roads at night, keep their spotlights under the seat, if
he'll promise to catch the goddamn beavers. Winter's coming
soon enough and they've yet to get in their salt and paint the
plows, not to mention making one last attempt to catch the pervert who draws filthy pictures in the outhouse at the Route 12
rest stop. The pervert leaves his phone number so other per-
verts can call him up and they can talk about the dirty things

they'd like to do to each other. He leaves little sketches too, a kind of pervert hieroglyphics. They know who he is, but they have to catch him in the act. They offer to give the warden the pervert's number, seeing how he is that good at trapping beaver. Maybe he'd like to try some muskrat, they say. He calls them bastards, leading them to think he didn't find their joke funny.

Mike winds his way down into the hollow. He's on a road the high school kids call the seven curves. They race it in their trucks and cars. Four-wheel drives with roll bars and GTOs with headers and glass pack pipes. Sometimes they don't make it to number three, sometimes they don't make it past number one. Mike and Star used to race the seven curves when they were young. Now she lives there. She and her girls live up the other side on welfare.

Mike yawns and then sips at the coffee he has perched on the dash. He's been away to St-Pamphile in Quebec to hunt spring bear. It's the last town on the map for a long ways. He stayed at the Manoir Tangueray with ten other hunters, plus the guides. By chance there were three men on the trip named Everett. Most people talked about this because it was such a rarity to have three men named Everett in the same place at once. One of the Everetts was best friends with the man who murdered the Boston Strangler, Albert DeSalvo, in prison.

It's been raining for three days now and according to the sky-scan radar, more is on the way. Mike knows this. The weather is important to road agents. He cracks the window so he can get a little air circulating in the cab to help keep the windshield clear. The air stirs up the faint stink of bear bait from his clothes. Rainwater whips in at his cheek so he pulls up his collar. A mile downstream there are summer homes where the hollow opens up and the brook meets the river. If the rain keeps on as predicted there'll be trouble, because the beavers have loaded quite a wallop behind their forty-foot dam of poplar, birch and maple.

He comes through the last curve. The rain is slow and

steady. He clicks back the wipers. Ahead of him he sees the
patrol truck parked beside the flooded road. Flambeau is inside
reading the *Sentinel* and drinking coffee. One time Mike caught
Flambeau playing with himself in the salt shed but didn't say
anything because Flambeau is an old man.

Star is there too. She's in the lake made by the beavers.
She stands up to her knees in the brown water crossing the
road, while her daughters swim between her legs. She has the
blue shadow of a four-pointed star tattooed on her forehead,
high and to the right of her widow's peak. You can't see it
unless she pulls back her bangs, which she never does. But
Mike's seen it. She's shown it to him and for that he loves her.
He loves her and her sisters and their babies, but he loves Star
the most. He tells her everything and she listens to what he has
to say. She hears it all and when her sisters ask her what he's
said, she only smiles.

The rain's coming down on her head. He watches her
standing where the yellow line must be and thinks about how
he likes to smell her after she's been rained on. She left a comb
in his truck once and he kept it for a long time, holding it in
the palm of his hand, using it to comb his beard and mustache,
breathing deeply as he pulled it through the hair on his face
and thinking himself foolish for doing so, foolish for holding
the scent of a woman in his hand.

Flambeau gets in the orange GMC next to Mike. He was
Mike's boss and taught Mike everything he knew, which wasn't
much, so Mike has had to learn a lot on his own. Flambeau's
retired now, but he still likes to keep his hand in. Mike calls on
him whenever he goes on vacation or whenever he needs someone to ride wing on the snowplow. Flambeau works the crew a
little harder when Mike's away, but it's busywork. And they
don't mind. Some of their fathers worked for Flambeau.

"Mikey," Flambeau says, "did you get your bear?"

Mike doesn't answer. He's looking through the windshield
at Star, wading toward the truck, her sleek thighs rising and
falling in the brown water the beavers have backed up. He

reaches in his breast pocket and takes out a pack of Export A's, Flambeau watching the hand that holds them. Mike rolls down the window when Star gets to the truck. She rests her elbows in the opening, her chin on her hands.

"Long time no see," she says.

"It's only been a week," Mike tells her.

"Or four," she says.

They look at each other and smile. Star's bangs come to her eyebrows, where they shed rainwater onto her face. For a moment he considers booting Flambeau out the door and bringing Star and her girls inside the truck, wrapping them in blankets and holding them to him, but he knows she won't go for that.

He looks away to her daughters, bobbing in the shallows, slapping at the water with their open palms, making motorboat sounds. He thinks that one of them is his own and he'd like for Star to tell him which one, but he knows she won't go for that either.

"Come for supper," she says. "We haven't had company since the rain started. No one can get through unless they go all the way around the mountain. My sister brought groceries. If I didn't have the base unit, I'd have gone nuts by now."

"I'd like to come for supper," Mike says.

Star nods, then turns and wades back to the other side. She doesn't say anything, but the girls fall in line behind her, rising up from the water and stepping out onto the road. The littlest one wears a diaper. It's filled with water and hangs to her knees. Star stops so she can catch up and when she does, Star picks her up and carries her on her hip. Mike watches them make the turn and disappear behind the black spikes of pine that file up the hill and out of the hollow.

"Mikey," Flambeau says, tapping his watch crystal, "it's time to get these boys back to the garage. Whatcha got there anyways?"

"Export A's. For you. I brought them back from Canada."

Flambeau takes the box. He studies it from all angles,

looks around and then stashes them inside his shirt. Mike gives two blasts on the horn and Flambeau hangs out the window, waving the crew in. Then they both get out in the rain to wait for them.

The crew comes along the near bank, traversing the hill to stay on good footing. At times they get on their hands and knees to keep from sliding into the brown water that rides full over rotted stumps and the tangle of young poplar, bent under its weight. They scale boulders and wind their way through skeletons of trees that totter on the brink. One tree crashes down at the touch of a hand but the others grab the boy before he follows it in. They keep walking until they make it to the truck, where they shake their arms and stamp their feet, liking the feel of the black tar between them and the earth. They are happy to see Mike on the job. They slap him on the back, making loud claps in the air when they hit his rain gear.

"How does she look, William?" Mike says.

"We've breached her down by the lodge. That should help, but I doubt it will."

Mike reaches into the truck and takes a carton of Export A's from the glove box. He passes them out until they're gone. William takes his last and then asks if there's any word from Fish and Game.

"Not yet," Mike says. Then he tells Flambeau to give each one a smoke and a light because their fingers are all wet. Flambeau goes around the circle, doling out his cigarettes and then lighting them. "Now boys. These are Canadian smokes from Canada," Flambeau says.

William laughs and says they're more like sucking a blowtorch from Benny's Auto Body.

"You boys get home and if I get authorization tonight, I'll call you out. Me and Flambeau will finish up here."

"Good to have you back," William says. He shakes Mike's hand and then tells the others to load up the tools and get in the patrol truck. He turns to Mike and says, "Now you call me. I'll be waiting."

Mike nods and waves him off. William climbs in the driver's seat and starts the engine. A yellow beam of light sweeps out from the roof, scanning the trees and bending in the rain. Flambeau and Mike watch him drive up out of the hollow. Then they set barriers with flashers secured to the top.

"I'm going to be at her house," Mike says, pointing across the water with his thumb. "You take my truck back to the garage and wait for the call. If you get tired, there's another carton of those cigarettes in my desk. Make *damn* sure you close this road off at the other end when you turn out. And stay off the sauce."

Flambeau smiles and makes a quick move as if he's going to grab Mike by the crotch, but Mike ignores him. Flambeau dances around on the balls of his feet, snapping punches in the air. "Hot time in the old town tonight," he says.

"Would you *go,*" Mike says.

"Damn straight, Mikey," Flambeau says, taking the wrong meaning out of the words. "I sure would if I were you," he says, getting in the orange GMC pickup, waving his hand and then leaving up the road.

Mike listens to the last sounds of the pickup disappearing by the third curve. When it's gone, he still listens, trying to find it in the air but he can't. The only sound is made by the weight of the water coming from the sky, shedding off the hills and traveling the land. He lets it get loud inside his head, so loud he thinks for an instant it might blow him over. He looks about and feels alone without the crew or the trucks or the equipment. He knows it to be the feeling he had in St-Pamphile, hiking out at night with an empty gun because by law it had to be unloaded at sunset. Upstream he hears the sound of an undercut tree slamming into the water.

Mike sits down on the highway and takes off his boots and socks, then cinches the drawstring at the bottom of his rain pants. Holding a boot in each hand, he wades the rising brown water, leaning to his left to keep from being swept under. He feels the cold coming through his pants and working toward his chest.

On the other side, he gets his socks and boots on and begins the hike out of the hollow. He gets to where Star disappeared. Knowing she's at the house, he still looks for her. He turns around to see where he's been, wondering what she would have seen if she'd done the same. He makes himself see Flambeau and the orange GMC. He sees the patrol truck and off to the left, the crew breaching the dam. Mike looks for himself but he's not there, so he puts himself in where he wants and thinks it's good enough, but knows it isn't. At least the rain is beginning to let up.

Star's house is wrapped in plastic. Batten strips hold it in place. It's the beginning of a siding job her last man started. He tore out part of the foundation too and now that corner of the house sits on wooden posts.

The girls are in the yard when Mike gets there. They're trying to drink from the garden hose, but the water comes too fast. At first it's in a fine cone-shaped spray, but then it closes down into a tight shot that comes like a fist. It fills their cheeks and gets up their noses.

"You must be thirsty," he says, "to want a drink with all this rain."

The girls don't say anything, they only laugh and try to squirt him with the hose. Mike opens his arms and lets the water spray against his yellow rain suit. They take turns blasting him with the hose until one of them goes for his face and knocks his cap off. He yells at them and they drop the hose, hightailing it for the far corner of the yard, the hose snaking about their feet, shooting plumes of muddy water into the air.

Mike gets his hands on it and waves them back. They come to him slowly, ready to take off again if he should try to get them. He unclips the handle and the water stops, stiffening the hose all the way back to the spigot.

"Now," Mike says showing them, "you can't go like this and get a drink because the spray is too wide and you can't go like this because it's too much force." The girls laugh at him as he first sprays himself in the face and then as he makes his cheeks bulge. "But you can fold a kink into the hose with one hand and squeeze the handle with the other and it comes out like a bubbler."

Mike takes a drink and then holds it for the girls. They line up and one after another they drink from the nozzle. They drink until their bellies ache and are hard. He then hands the hose to the last one. She tries to do what he did but she can't, so they go back to spraying each other and laughing. Mike laughs too and then he goes inside.

The house is warm and dry. He peels off his slicker and rain pants. He holds down the heel of his boot with his toe and pulls his foot out. Then he does the other one. He lays them down in front of the refrigerator, where the hot air coming off the compressor can dry them out.

Star sits at the table shucking peas. She throws the pods into a paper bag at her feet. Her base station crackles from a shelf next to the cereal boxes. The Dixie Belle comes in on the skip from North Carolina. She's trying to raise the Big Red Rooster. His rig's two days overdue and she hasn't heard a goddamn word. Star keeps the base station on the same channel the road crews use so she can know the whereabouts of Mike, but when the conditions in the atmosphere are right, she receives North Carolina.

"The Big Red Rooster late again?" Mike says.

"It's that damn skip."

Mike takes a handful of peas and pops them in his mouth, one at a time. He likes the feel of eating fresh peas more than the taste. When he finishes that handful, he takes another.

"What's up this time?"

"It's their anniversary. He missed their goddamn anniversary. He's supposed to be hauling steel out of Auburn, New York, and somebody spotted him in Waco. She's mucho pissed. This could be the last roundup for the Big Red Rooster."

Mike begins to shuck peas too. He pleasures in their satin feel as they ride out of the pod on the end of his thumb. Every other one he does, he pops in his mouth.

"What's for supper?"

"Lettuce sandwiches," she says, slapping his hand when he goes into the bowl for ones she's already shucked. He laughs and looks out the window at her girls.

"My father showed me that trick with the hose," he tells her. "It was the day he took me and my brother to Fort Ticonderoga. We went to a restaurant and had baked chicken. That was the day he showed me how to drink out of a hose."

"I wouldn't know," she says, "I've never been to Fort Ticonderoga."


After the girls are asleep, Mike and Star sit out on the porch. The rain comes harder now, drumming on the roof and slicing over the gutters, harder than it has in the past three days. Mike reaches over and takes Star's hand inside his own.

"Did you miss me while I was away?"

"No more or less than usual," she says, but then she squeezes his hand and says, "I'm sorry. I didn't mean it to come out that way."

"There were three Everetts on the trip. It was quite something."

"What do you mean, three Everetts?"

"There were three men named Everett. Out of a dozen people from all over. That's something."

The kettle on the stove begins to whistle. Star goes in to make them each a cup of instant. Mike watches her through the screen door. He watches her move inside the light. It's as a sleepwalker would, tired and comfortable, with a concern for the small details of making a good cup of instant. She goes to the door of the room where the girls sleep. She gets close to it and listens. Mike thinks he would like to try and do that, just the way she did. The thought gives him courage. Tonight he'll ask her to marry him, so she might begin to think of life as something brand-new.

Star comes out with the coffee in blue steel cups. She hands one to him and then sits down and sighs, letting the air leave her chest of its own accord.

"Is everything all right?" Mike says.

"Everything's fine. It's just that sometimes I get so tired, I forget to breathe."

"That happened to me in Quebec. Twice when I heard crashes in the woods. They sent chills through me. I forgot to breathe. Crashes like that scared off the three Everetts. They left before breakfast, one by one. Don't tell anyone I told you that."

"Was it nice up there?"

"We were in a boardinghouse north of St-Camille. After dark we went to town. They had dancers in the bar who took off their clothes. They were beautiful girls. *La femme petite.* For ten dollars American they'd take you behind a curtain, but none of us went. They were too beautiful to touch."

Mike stares straight ahead, thinking about the dancers. He tries to think if what he just said is a lie and if it is, whether she believes it. He looks to the night. It's black with rain. He tries to find something to see, but he can't.

"So how are the roads up there? Do they go in two directions like down here?" she says.

He knows she's making fun of him. It's her way of loving him, he tells himself and then wonders if that's a lie too.

"After my father showed me how to drink from the hose, he let go of the kink and sent a spray of water up my nose. You know how much that hurts." Mike reaches out to take her hand again. Star has to switch her cup over to the right. The hand that held the cup is warm and soft.

"I had time to think when I was up there. I decided that I want to marry you. I would like to have a child."

Star listens to what he has said. Mike tries to get a sign from her but he can't, so he waits for what seems like a long time, until she speaks.

"You shouldn't talk that way, Mike. You shouldn't talk about what's in your heart. Unless it's a lie and if it is, it's mean."

Mike knows she's looking at him. He still stares into the night trying to find something to see.

"These aren't lies at all. I want to be with you."

"I believe you," she says, "but that doesn't mean anything."

"You could get off welfare. The girls could have more."

Mike turns to look at her as he says these things. She closes her eyes and shakes her head.

"But I like welfare," she says. "It's the last hope there is in this world for women and children."

Mike remembers they are holding hands. He tightens his grip and she does the same.

"I hope to be working soon, anyways. I want to buy my girls a horse so they won't need men, like I need you."

Mike can feel in his face the pain that comes when tears are first there and then they do come, like a seep in the ground.

"But I know I would like to have a child," he says.

"You can't though, only I can," she tells him, pulling his hand against her stomach and holding it there. Then she says, "What would it be if you could, a boy or a girl?"

"It doesn't matter. Maybe it's just not in the cards."

Mike puts his cup down and then holds his hand across his eyes. He makes them stop what they're doing, but it tires him out to give up so much strength for such a small thing. His body aches more than it has all day.

Inside the house they can hear the littlest one start to cry. At first it's a whimper and then it becomes more urgent. Mike waits for Star to do something. After ten minutes he says he'll go get her, but Star hangs on to his hand.

"No," she says. "She knows she's all right. She has to learn to sleep through the night."

Mike listens to the cries turn to anger. Star's grip on his hand doesn't lessen and after another ten minutes, the littlest one is quiet.

She squeezes his hand to her stomach again. She holds it like that until he turns to look at her. She's smiling and nodding her head. She opens her mouth to say something, but then she doesn't. Instead, she stands and leads him into the house.

Mike wakes up when he hears his name being called on the base unit. The room is dark and he's alone. He finds his trousers and goes into the kitchen. A small red light, smaller than an eye, flashes next to the cereal boxes.

*"Come on, Mike. Flambeau here. Come on Mike. Flambeau here. Getcha ears on."*

He keys the mike and says, "Come on, Flambeau."

*"We got beaucoup trouble. There's big water headed your way. When it funnels into the hollow it's going to take the dam and the lake with it and we're going to have some pissed-off hombres downstream."*

Mike stops to think, but all he can hear is the sound of rain. It comes in a roar, a big engine driving rain.

*"Back to you, Mike. You there?"*

"Yeah. Bring on the satchel and I'll meet you in the hollow."

*"Where are you keeping the stuff these days? Back to you."*

"The closet in the office. The key's in the door."

*"Be right out. Ten-four."*

Mike gets dressed and goes out on the porch. Star is wrapped in a quilt, drinking instant. Without looking at him she says, "Some rain, isn't it. The kind you'd be better off sleeping through."

"We have to blow the dam," he tells her.

"Don't worry about us. We're just fine," she says.

He touches her face with the back of his hand. She tilts her head toward him until his hand is pressed between her cheek and shoulder. With his other hand, he brushes back her bangs and traces her forehead with his fingers.

"You go on," she says. "You're a big man. You have to keep loving those girls of mine. They dream about you."

"Think about what I said and call me," he tells her. Then he leaves.

When Mike crosses back to the other side, the water is over his belt. It runs down his pants, soaking him through to the skin. Branches and limbs bump against him, almost knocking him over, but he makes it and Flambeau arrives shortly after. The two men have to yell to be heard over the sound of rain that takes their words like a strong wind.

"This is bad, Mikey. Division six called in just before I talked to you. We've got to get up on it or we're royally screwed."

Mike opens the door to the pickup. On the seat is a spool of wire, a satchel and the rack bar. He throws the switch for the flood lamp and directs its beam over the water, lighting up the dam and both banks. Through the sheets of rain sparkling as if in sunlight, he can see a fir caught sideways, its roots still full of earth, raised up into the sky. Black and twisted, its limbs catch and hold everything that washes its way to make the dam that much bigger.

Mike pushes the rack bar toward Flambeau and then gives him the end of wire coming off the spool. He sheds his rain gear, because it doesn't help anymore.

"Keep your hands off the friggin' radio," he says.

"Don't worry about me, Mikey. I know that love's a hurtin' thing."

Mike looks at him and shakes his head. Then, shouldering the satchel, he leaves for the dam, trailing the firing line out behind him. The bank is slick with rivulets, now running as full brooks into the hollow. He has to cross the bank on a path higher than the one the boys took, earlier in the day.

At the dam he stops. He shakes his head again and smiles. It makes him feel better to think how quickly he's gotten here. He looks about, scanning the high black mountain until he finds the spot where Star's house must be. The rain slows and the light of the flood lamp seems warm on his skin. He hears Flambeau yelling for him to get a move on. He's saying, "Get your ass in gear. We haven't got all night."

Mike laughs and waves. He remembers William saying once that if Flambeau had another brain, it'd be lonesome. Then he drops down onto the fir, makes his way to the crown and onto the dam. He walks the white branches and limbs the beavers have stripped for the cambrium under the bark to secure their feed bed for the winter. He ties off the firing line and goes to the center where it curves out to meet the current, jumping from one bolt of wood to another. Working his way back, he punches the sticks, sets the detonators and wires in the legs. Back at the place he started, he strips off the shunts and wires them in too.

It's now quiet, the scent of castoreum in the air. The rain has moved up the hollow. He knows before long the water will begin to rise, slowly at first and then swell in a rush and the dam will give before its weight.

The mobile unit in his truck crackles and off in the distance he hears her voice calling his name. From where he stands inside the configuration of wires, he hears her say, *"Come on, Mike. Come on, Mike."*

He starts to laugh because he knows it's her. He knows she wants to talk to him.

"No. Don't," he yells, laughing and running for the bank as Flambeau keys the mike, making the connection with Star that induces current in the wires under Mike's feet. "No. Don't," he yells and then he's on his way so fast he doesn't even have time to spread his arms like angel wings, or lift up on his toes for takeoff.

He's still laughing as he's lofted into the lights of the wet night sky toward her house on the hill. Her faint sweet smell is rising in his head and he's laughing at death in the last moment he'll ever remember.

*"It ain't right. It just ain't right. Back to you."*
*"I know,"* she says. *"I just wanted to tell him something."*

# PIX TK

## O

### *Frederick Busch*

Y ES, SHE WAS CAREFUL. Yes, I'm being
careful, she lied. Penelope drifted in morning traffic on Canal
Street and drove one-handed, carelessly, crossing to New Jersey through the Holland Tunnel. As if Bob were nagging her
as he had when he taught her how to drive the year after college, she lied about safety, but this time to the man who gave
out Turnpike tickets. She reached for hers while her car still
rocked on its brakes, and he said, "Jesus, lady! Take it easy!"
And she told him, "Yes, I will."

Driving to the widow's house near Bethlehem, Pennsylvania, Penelope looked past the road and registered only the
trucks before her, or cars she passed too close and too quickly.
Where she really looked was beyond the Jersey Turnpike at
the glowing grids of computer graphics, or penciled shapes on
paper. The road she drove she saw as a thick blue line on a
map. The line became thinner and black, the border of a layout

she composed for a future issue of the magazine. She shifted columns of type, she specified characters per line and ems of space, selected picture-caption face.

It wasn't strange or interesting to her that while she drove the public highways she reduced them to private measurements. Her cubicle at work was posted with her photographs of where they'd traveled to, and whom they'd met—her capturings. The children's growth, from elementary school to college, was on display in colored prints, and not pinned there for visitors so much as for herself. When she saw something, she knew it; everything else had to be taken on faith, and Penelope hadn't much confidence. That was why, after a year of intensifying searches—she had finally whimpered as she moved cartons in their building's damp storage bins: she had actually heard herself *mew*—she was here, in Pennsylvania, at this isolated farmhouse, calling on the dead minister's wife, and lying to herself that she remembered flashbulbs going off on a Saturday morning in 1963.

Maybe it's a wish. Maybe it's a memory, she thought, and not a lie, though "farmhouse" surely was, she knew, ringing the bell, telling herself she remembered the chime of the bell, the aluminum siding and plastic mullions clipped to the windows' aluminum frames, the colored, pebbled plastic of the metal front door. It was farmy because it was rural, but there wasn't a barn, or a dog, or a cat that sharpened its claws on the dooryard sycamore. It was prettier than a trailer or a residential hotel, and it was the only place left to look.

Mrs. Haasen, in a dark dress and a white apron that said in red serif characters *The Rib Doctor Is In,* was staring at her. "Yes? Hello? Yes?"

She said, "I'm Penelope Chasen. I wrote to you. After your husband's death. Do you remember me?"

Mrs. Haasen's face was round, its skin milky and soft. Its flesh was like a baby's, she thought, looking at the mild, young eyes, very light blue, surrounded by devastated sockets—dark, almost brown-black, pulpy-looking; they were the eyes of someone in pain; they were eyes unused to sleep. Her lovely round head, with its gray-yellow hair on a short neck, bobbed without hesitation. Mrs. Haasen's low, soft voice said, "Yes, of course. You were kind to write. He spoke of you often."

"He did?"

"And thank you for calling. But I don't—I am not up to visitors yet."

"No," Penelope said. "Of course. He *remembered* me?"

The bright eyes stared at her, and Penelope was ashamed for troubling this woman as much as she was embarrassed by the lies they'd both been wrapped in so promptly.

"I cannot remember for certain," Mrs. Haasen said, stepping back from the door as if to close it. "But."

"But," Penelope said. "Exactly. I wrote a condolence letter. I reminded you that your—Dr. Haasen married us. He married my husband and me."

"I didn't read any of the letters," Mrs. Haasen said at last. "I couldn't. My children did, but they've gone home. I don't remember. No."

"Oh, Mrs. Haasen, my husband's dead, too!"

The eyes didn't change. The mouth did, though, working as someone's lip and tongue cooperate to dislodge something stuck between teeth. "Are you in great pain?" Mrs. Haasen asked.

Penelope's throat swelled, and she felt her eyes grow wet. She looked away, back at the sycamore, and she insisted to herself that she would not weep at this stranger in these cool and apple-scented breezes (not an apple tree in sight). She said, "I'm forty-eight years old. I was married to him more than half the time I've been alive. I knew him better than my mother and my father. Yes," she said. And then: "I'm sorry. You're suffering, too, and I'm sorry."

"I did my suffering."

"Already?" The little woman, not quite stout, with her baby's face, lifted her chin defiantly. Penelope couldn't control her thinking that this woman seemed like a maid, a refined and witty maid, or superior shopgirl, and not the longtime wife of a college professor who also was a minister. Understanding nothing, now, and angry at herself for her incomprehension, for coming here at all, she grew angry at Mrs. Haasen. "Look," she said, "I wrote you a letter. I wish you had read it. I drove here from New York."

"Is that a long drive these days?"

"An hour and a half, once you get out of town."

"Would you like to drink a cup of coffee?"

"Would you mind giving me one?"

Mrs. Haasen regarded her, and Penelope was certain that she was about to say yes, and close the door. Instead, she turned and walked toward the back of the house. Penelope followed her, wiping her feet on a mat made of sisal and decorated with the silhouettes of ducks in flight instead of the cross Penelope had expected. She'd assumed that there were mail-order houses for clerical gadgets and housewares. She wiped as though she had stood in mud, telling at least the secular mat how grateful she was.

On the floors and on the walls Penelope saw much of what she'd reviled inside furniture, wallpaper or carpeting stores. Dark, curved, spindly furniture with caramel-colored slipcovers stood on make-believe oriental carpets of muddy reds—the Orient-after-the-floodwaters-recede motif, Penelope thought, looking for pit vipers and ox droppings. The walls were papered in a champagne color that almost matched the slipcovers. She saw no sculpted cruciform wall hangings, no tinted prints of Jesus among babes. All the lamps in the living room were converted—from lanterns, sconces, jugs—and each occasional table bore an empty glass dish it seemed too frail to support. The kitchen, a little brighter, was small and crowded with appliances plugged into an electric outlet strip that ran the length of the counter. Penelope wondered why an electric knife was kept plugged in near the Waring blender and the fake French food processor. The paper here was a repeated motif of barnyard animals of blue and pink being fed by a pink little lady in a dark skirt and white apron. A large fluorescent ceiling fixture hummed. Mrs. Haasen measured coffee from a can into a giant electric coffee maker, and she poured water into its top. She asked about cream and sugar, and Penelope shook her head. She offered cookies and Penelope shook her head again.

"Then what?" Mrs. Haasen said, standing at the counter to watch her while the coffee machine huffed.

"Your husband taught Bob. My husband's name was Bob. Robert Chasen. Dr. Haasen taught philosophy of the Old and New Testaments, a course along those lines. Bob took it in around 1961 or '62, I guess. He was a political science major, but he took the course because your husband was so popular with the kids. He was a great teacher, wasn't he?"

Mrs. Haasen said, "That was his reputation. That's what everyone said. Women loved him, I know this for certain."

"I never studied with him," Penelope said. "I went to Skidmore. In New York State?"

"Yes."

"Mrs. Haasen, am I difficult for you? Being here, so soon after his death?"

"No."

"But you're, I don't know, angry."

The blue eyes were naked. It was as though a mist that had lain over them now blew away. The little blue eyes were wet. Penelope saw how often she must have wept onto the dark, tortured skin above her round cheeks.

Mrs. Haasen shook her head, twice, and then she turned to the coffee machine. She poured the coffee into mugs with handles too small for the fingers of an adult, and she held one toward Penelope, who took it without speaking.

"No," Mrs. Haasen said, "I am not angry. I am struggling."

"Struggling," Penelope said. "Oh, yes."

"Struggling."

Penelope said, "I'm sorry. I know how you feel. Oh, I don't know exactly how you feel, but I must know a lot of it, or

something similar, don't you think? I've been—it's been nearly
a year. It's why I'm here, Mrs. Haasen. Your husband married
us here! I always talked about this sweet little farmhouse in
Pennsylvania when I told people how we got married. On account of Bob's being Jewish and me not, and the families being
a little silly about it. We thought the best thing was a civil
ceremony. Reverend Haasen did the service here—is there a
room that's like a study? With a big pine desk, and books, and
fossils, I think it was, in wooden frames on the walls?" Mrs.
Haasen nodded into the steam of her coffee, and Penelope
thought to sip hers. It was weak, boiled-tasting. "And your
husband and you were here, of course, and Bob's parents and
mine, and his brother. They had an argument, would you remember? Bob's mother insisted on giving flowers to everyone
to wear during the ceremony, and he was angry—well, we were
so young! twenty-three!—because Bob thought it should be, I
don't know, austere. Plain, I suppose. And your husband did
the wedding ceremony and at the last second, just before he
pronounced us husband and wife, he smiled and winked, he
made the sign of the cross. He whispered, 'It wouldn't hurt.' "
Penelope felt herself smiling broadly. She wanted to talk and
talk and talk about their wedding day. She wanted to weep and
lean her head on this woman's round breast. She looked at it
again: *The Rib Doctor Is In.*

Mrs. Haasen whispered, over her coffee mug, "So you
went on to be happy with your Jewish boy. You didn't fight
about faith, or churches."

Penelope suddenly couldn't talk. She nodded.

"You were busy and faithful to each other."

Penelope nodded again. "Yes," she finally croaked. Then
she cleared her throat and said, "You couldn't possibly remember, could you?"

Mrs. Haasen shrugged.

"You're being kind," Penelope said.

Mrs. Haasen said, "I am being jealous." She offered the
coffeepot, but Penelope smiled and covered the top of her cup

with her hand. "My husband was famous for sleeping with students and other men's wives from the faculty. I cannot believe that he had his faith anymore. You knew this?"

Penelope wanted to cover her eyes so that Mrs. Haasen could be invisible, but she wrapped her hands around the coffee mug for its heat. She wished that they'd been married by a preacher who believed, and she thought herself ridiculous. She said, "No. I never heard of it."

"Your husband never spoke of it?"

"He never heard of it either."

"You knew each other so well, you could say he never heard of it? Instead of saying he never *told* you, but *maybe* he heard of it?"

"That's right," Penelope said.

"Lucky."

That was when Penelope began to weep, an oozing kind of awful leak she couldn't staunch. She felt her lip tremble, and she bit it.

Mrs. Haasen's lip moved, too, as if it worked with her hidden tongue to remove the piece of food. "I didn't hear of it, too," Mrs. Haasen said. "After he was so sick, and in the hospital, and they were giving him so much morphine he was always sleeping, *then* I heard of it. A friend wrote me a letter. She told me it was all right, because he didn't do it anymore since he was sixty. *Sixty!* I had him to myself twelve years. Yours never—"

Penelope shook her head. She wondered why she did it with such certainty. You never ever really knew, did you? Was she boasting instead of believing? She said, "Bob died while he was running. Forty-seven years old, slim, he never even had *headaches*. He was running in Central Park and he just sat down to rest, somebody said, in the middle of his run. He sat, and he died. When he fell over on the bench, they called the police. Is this a non sequitur?"

"I wouldn't know," Mrs. Haasen said.

Penelope started to giggle. She clamped her hand on her mouth. At least, she thought, her eyes had stopped leaking.

"What do you want, Mrs. Chasen?"

"Oh."

"You said you wrote to me. I'm sorry I didn't read any letters. You said you drove here all the way from New York City. You want something. I don't have anything for you. So: what?"

"Nowadays, the people I know, when they plan a wedding for their kids, depending on the size, they budget three or four thousand dollars for the photographs. Did you ever hear of anything like that? All that money? And you wind up with an album. I would pay that much money, right now, if somebody would sell me one sticky, bent picture of Bob and me inside of your house, or outside, or anyplace, really, as long as it was on our wedding day. But I wish it could be here. I had this white wool suit with a tailored skirt. He wore a blue suit they sold him at Broadstreet's." She giggled. "They convinced him that bold stripes and tiny little lapel notches were coming in." She giggled harder. "He kept waiting, he said, but they never did arrive." She was beginning to laugh too hard, she knew, and she rubbed her fingers back and forth on her lips. "Nobody took a picture," she said. "Not my parents. Not his. Not his brother. It's the only regret I have from our marriage."

Mrs. Haasen said, very softly, "Oh!"

"I was hoping—I'm in magazine journalism. Production. We put out a bimonthly controlled circulation magazine for people who own or manage apartment houses, not that it matters. But when we send a layout up, a, you know, a projection of what the pages of the magazine will look like, where the words of the articles will be, where the pictures will be, we leave a space for the pictures we'll add in later. Photos, drawings, graphs, whatever. We call it a hole, that space. It's really rectangular. In the hole, someone will write *Art TK*. The art's to come later. TK means 'to come.' All right? If we know it'll be a drawing, we say *LD/TK*—line drawing to come. Photographs, halftone etchings we make from photographs, we call pix. We write *Pix TK*. All the years that I wanted a photo of us, because we were so silly and stupid and hopeful and *young*. Even after Bob died, I'd think of there being no photo. A hole. And I would tell myself, Pix TK."

"Tee Kay," Mrs. Haasen said.

"Yes. And what I wrote about, why I came, is I was wondering: did you ever take pictures at weddings? When your husband did the service, did anybody ever ask you to take a picture of them?"

"Oh, yes."

"Did you *always* take pictures?"

"Whether people asked me to or not?"

"Yes."

"I don't think that would be right. I didn't do that."

"But *sometimes* you took pictures."

"Yes."

"Do you remember me now?"

The sweet blue eyes, the ancient sockets, the milk-white infant's face, said no. Then her voice did. "I wish I would have."

"Do you have family albums?" Penelope asked. "You probably do. Don't most people? Boxes of pictures? Doesn't everyone have those?"

"I cannot look at them. How many of them would be my husband and me at picnics, socials, university functions? We would be smiling at each other. We would be perhaps holding hands. We would be dancing. We would be at hotels in foreign countries together, wearing silly clothes for travel. In all of the pictures, he would be lying, I would be stupid. I could not look."

"No. Of course. *I* would," Penelope said. "Would that be all right? Oh, my God, did you burn them? Did you throw them away? Maybe your children have some of them. Were any of your children there when we were married? Maybe *they* took pictures."

Mrs. Haasen only looked at her, and in the stillness of the kitchen Penelope heard the echoes of her clattering voice.

"Someday, before I die, I will look at them," Mrs. Haasen said.

"Do you know when?"

Again, Mrs. Haasen only looked.

"I have to wait," Penelope said. "Is that right?"

"I promise you, if I can look, and if I find it, I will send you the picture."

"Couldn't I look through them for you, Mrs. Haasen?"

"That would not be right. Those are my memories. That is my life."

"But you don't *want* it!"

"Oh, no," Mrs. Haasen said, in a voice as gentle as her eyes. "It is that I cannot bear it."

This time Penelope could only stare.

Finally Mrs. Haasen said, "Write down, please, your address. You see. I am earnest." She took a small lined yellow pad and a pencil from a wrought-iron shelf above the appliances and handed them to Penelope.

"Do you think it might be soon? God. Mrs. Haasen." Penelope saw that she had written only her name. She thought to remind the old woman of whom she was to search for in the pictures of her life, so she crossed it out, and she rewrote: *Bob and Penny Chasen.* Then she put parentheses in so that it was *(Bob and) Penny Chasen.* She looked up, and then she looked down at the page and she drew brackets: *[(Bob and)] Penny Chasen.* And then she drew a line through Bob's name and the *and.* With first the point, and then the edge, she crossed out his name, so that in the midst of the scratched, smudged page there was only her name and address. She heard herself breathing raggedly, an out-of-shape runner. "I'll put my phone number down," she said. "Would you call me if you find it?"

"A couple of widows in a kitchen," Mrs. Haasen said.

"I'd be happy to run up here and get it, if you'd rather not bother with mailing it."

"Drinking coffee and talking."

"Call collect!"

"It would be hard to tell, just seeing us, what we were talking about, wouldn't it? People who left us? Men?"

"So, will you?"

"What? Look for the picture?"

Penelope said, "I never knew your husband before he married us. I never spoke to him. I never even *saw* him."

Mrs. Haasen's eyes were narrowed, furious, and her skin for an instant looked purple. Then it ebbed, and she was pale, though her lips remained dark. She said, "What do I think you mean by this?"

"I thought it was important to tell you."

Mrs. Haasen closed her eyes and held a finger up. She was thinking, and she needed silence. Penelope saw that the finger, where it had been curved around the cup, was still flattened, white. As its pinkness returned, Mrs. Haasen opened her eyes and said, "It was generous? A gift—what you just said?"

Penelope opened her mouth and then closed it. She shook her head. "Please forgive me," she said.

"And what for, then?"

"For having no gift to give you. For saying that for me. So you wouldn't distrust me. So you would want to find the picture."

Mrs. Haasen smiled a smile that Penelope remembered from when her children were small and fragile and so trusted her that they asked about snow coming, or the mercies of teachers, or whether the phone would ring that night as they required it to. She remembered a patient, tired feeling on her face and especially about her eyes. She remembered assuring them and how, so peculiarly often, they believed what she said and greeted the next moments or hours of their lives with calmness, even tranquillity. Faith, she thought. They had it, and it's my turn now.

"I will try very, very hard," Mrs. Haasen said.

"Well, then, I'll wait to hear from you," Penelope said.

Standing in that awful kitchen with the minister's widow, Penelope thought of the drive home. She saw her car, as from above, on the road. She saw its route, as if her finger traced it, through the bold colors and intricate linework of a map. She saw then, as Mrs. Haasen walked her through the gloom and writhing furniture of the living room, a layout for an issue of the magazine. There were the strong, fine lines she loved, the certainties she oversaw—*here* columns of type would stand, their subject labeled in her angular writing, and *here,* like a window, the artless hole surrounded by the expectation of language. And *here,* in the hasty hand that had written Bob's name, and then crossed it out, were the words once prediction, that were now her prayer.

# CIMARRON

O

*Francine Prose*

CORAL WAS STEAMED WHEN it looked as if
Kenny might not be home for her due date. She felt personally
cheated; she couldn't turn on a talk show without having to
watch some soap opera actor's eyes fill with tears as he gave
you the whole play-by-play of his new baby's birth. She was
just getting used to it that her in-laws, Gene and Margo, would
come to the hospital with her. Really, that would be better:
Gene was a safer driver than Kenny, Margo more patient. That
was how she had started to think when Kenny got killed in
Beirut. She was lying down, mildly dizzy, watching the evening news. She stood and inched toward the television like a
child at the edge of the surf.

At the funeral, Kenny's minister read from Ecclesiastes:
a time for this and a time for that. How gradual it all sounded,
how stately, like the seasons. Coral's own experience was: Ka-

boom! Your whole life could suddenly hit the brakes and take a wide screeching turn for the worse. The right way to read that scripture was in a Daffy Duck voice, wacky and speeded-up. Everything was a cartoon. All through the service, Kenny's father kept his arm around her; she imagined his fingers shot Spiderman webs, gluing her in one piece.

Coral bought a *Newsweek* with pictures of Beirut. She kept stopping at a photo of bombed-out barracks, a ragged dark hole full of metal and concrete. She kept trying to see inside it. Where were the guys' rooms, the magazines stacked by their beds? A time to read magazines and a time to be in them. She'd stare at the picture, sometimes for a half hour, always a little shaky, as if someone might come in and catch her, though this, she knew, was unlikely; right after Kenny's death, her apartment was full of people, but soon it emptied out. Now no one came but Gene and Margo, and they always called first. Even when she was alone in the house, she hid the magazine in a drawer. Several times a day these words ran through her head: this is my current life-style.

She knew that this life was unhealthy and probably bad for the baby. She hardly got any exercise or went any farther than the supermarket freezer section, where she shopped for one meal at a time: shrimp cocktail, egg rolls, enchiladas. Everyone knew that the chemicals in these foods were bad for an unborn child. Coral lay awake whole nights, picturing the delivery room, seeing in the nurse's eyes that something was terribly wrong. She tried reading, she'd always liked science fiction; but now every book she picked up turned out to be about mutants.

Coral was so relieved when Gene and Margo took charge and came and got her that she willingly did what they said— put her feet up and took it easy while they packed up her apartment. First she sneaked the *Newsweek* outside and threw it in someone else's garbage. Then she lay down and thought how her in-laws were like those machines that mash cars to shoebox size. It took them four hours to fit her and Kenny's whole life onto Gene's pickup and into the prefab metal shed in their yard.

Coral felt like Dorothy in *The Wizard of Oz,* plucked out of Oneonta and dropped in a trailer park twenty minutes away. Her girlish-voiced, cheery mother-in-law reminded her of Glenda, the good witch, except that Margo was three times Glenda's size. And this wasn't Oz, or Kansas or even Oneonta, this was Cimarron Acres with its one frozen-solid brown road, rutted and covered with dog turds, its junk machinery everywhere and, behind it the mountain Kenny used to call Godzilla Hill because it grew like a monster; dump trucks came in every day. Coral marveled that people could live like this, a mountain of poisonous garbage outside their kitchen window. But when Coral mentioned it, Gene and Margo said, "Oh, the landfill." Coral hoped the baby would be all right if she drank orange juice instead of water. Basically, she was grateful to be here, away from the apartment in Oneonta, where the noise outside on the street at night had begun to scare her, grateful for Margo's solid presence when Coral buried her face in Margo's pillowy shoulder and cried. "Cry all you want," Margo said. "Just try to keep up, for the baby."

What comforted Coral most was that Margo had gone through what she was going through, Margo had been pregnant—not just once but six times. On top of the TV, the framed Christmas portrait of all six grown kids and *their* babies and spouses proved that having a child had been done. Though Coral had always liked Margo, she used to tune out when Margo got onto her favorite subject—home canning advice. But now she took Margo's word on everything: when to take a nap, what to eat, how much exercise she needed.

Six children, said Margo, six different people. Some gave her trouble, some didn't, she wasn't going to say which. Some of the births were hard, some were easy, but none of them was very hard, and Kenny's was the easiest. There was a line Coral tried not to cross as she maneuvered the conversation toward the story of how three pushes sent Kenny flying into the world.

At first it cheered them both; then Margo would get weepy, and it was Coral's turn to comfort *her,* even as a small ungrateful voice chanted at the back of her head: Come on, you still have five.

But Margo ticked off on her fingers where they had gone: Syracuse, Rochester, Utica, Watertown, Cortland. And Margo and Gene seemed to like having Coral there. Soon Coral knew secrets Margo hadn't told Gene in thirty-one years of marriage. Most had to do with food, goodies Margo polished off in the car driving home from the market, but Margo's deepest secret was that she was terrified of elevators. She laughed a little when she admitted this. Gene was an elevator repairman.

Once Margo confessed this, she referred to it every day. She kept telling the story of how she and Gene had to go somewhere requiring an elevator ride and she pretended she'd left something in the car and ran upstairs to meet him. Coral knew she was getting advice here, deeper than how many minutes safely to process green beans. The point was that Margo had never told Gene. The point was some tact and good manners you were supposed to have regarding your husband's work. Was Margo saying it was okay for Coral to let Kenny go to Beirut? Coral couldn't have stopped him, no more than she could have kept him from jumping in the water after a drowning kid. Everyone knew that. At Kenny's going-away party, no one said a word about danger. They pretended his going to Lebanon was just business in another part of the world. The week Kenny left, Coral found, in the public library, a *National Geographic* on Beirut; in one photo, a boy weaved through city traffic with round flatbreads stacked in his arms.

Nights when Gene worked late or went out on call, Margo went through the trailer, turning on all the lights. Coral remembered noticing that Kenny used to trick her into walking into dark rooms first. How funny, to be scared of your own bathroom and not of those maniacs in Beirut. Sometimes, at night, someone would knock on the door, and Margo and Coral would stop and stare at each other, frozen, until they realized it was probably Don and Peggy from next door, or else Lee, the single mother who lived with her ten-year-old daughter Tracy on the other side.

Don and Peggy were close friends of Gene and Margo's; they'd lived near them in Endicott for thirty years and followed them here from there. They laughed a lot, fought a lot about Don's chain-smoking, laughed some more. Lee was a moody, high-strung woman with great cheekbones and narrow sulky eyes whose fashion style veered between hippie (work boots, long paisley dresses) and country (tight jeans and cowboy shirts). Though Lee was probably thirty, she looked about fifty, and drained. Tracy and Lee reminded Coral of science fiction stories about bodies hooked up to live off a central brain or blood supply—little spacecraft fueled by the mother ship. Coral could almost imagine Tracy's curls unfurling from the rollers Lee wore on her "country" days.

Margo was a natural mimic who could do all the neighbors; she did a wicked Lee. As soon as Lee left, Margo's voice would turn shrill and she'd do frantic chicken pecks with her head as she imitated Lee telling how she'd got the school bus stop moved to their side of the road. Lee managed this with a story about a Binghamton girl run over crossing the street, a story that got gorier, organs and limbs flung everywhere, as Lee took it to the school board and announced: she didn't want that for her Tracy. Coral tried to see this as a good sign, as evidence of some diamond-hard flame of motherhood burning in Lee. If that was how Lee burned for Tracy, what would light up in Coral for *her* child?

At first Coral thought Margo should lighten up on Lee; at first she sort of liked Lee, and imagined they could be friends. At the very least, Lee seemed like the type who'd have all Tracy's baby clothes, washed and pressed, in boxes. Already, motherhood had changed Coral. Now when she looked at children, she thought: Outgrown clothes. This neighborhood was full of kids, but no one offered, and there was no one she knew well enough to ask. And though Lee came every few nights to drink cup after cup of instant coffee and light one Vantage from another, Coral never got around to asking. Perhaps it was that Lee looked not-quite-there and bored until she found a way to bring the conversation around to either of her two subjects.

The first of these topics was the hard lives of single moms. Each week, it seemed, Lee saw in the paper where single moms have three times as many ulcers and stress-related conditions and twice the chance of dying from cancer before age forty. Last month there was a story about a single mom with two sets of twins and her house caught on fire and one set of twins burnt up because there was no one around to help rescue them. She just didn't have enough arms. Coral guessed these stories were true. But why was Lee telling *her?* What did Lee think that *Coral* was going to be? Coral decided she had been wrong about Lee, had been giving the benefit of the doubt to anyone who didn't strap explosives onto themselves and drive a truck straight at her.

Lee's other subject was, of course, Tracy, her special daughter. Tracy had second sight. Lee had taken her down to Memphis for a convention of spiritual children. Once she had been on a Christian radio network out of Pittsburgh. Tracy, thought Coral, was perfect—perfectly like those creepy kids in films about children possessed by the devil. Magnified by thick lenses, Tracy's ice-blue eyes spun like pinwheels as, poising her chin on a fingertip, she swung her curls and stared at you as if you were an animal in the zoo.

Coral often watched the neighborhood children—in fact the school bus stop was directly outside Coral's window, and in the chilly mornings their voices often woke her—and she saw how other girls Tracy's age put on fingerless gloves and tied on tarty Madonna scarves the minute their mothers were out of sight. Only Tracy spun on her heel and turned her back on them, only Tracy wore printed corduroy pants, a lavender down coat, glasses with pearly harlequin frames. Her long sandy hair hung down in precise and elaborate Little Lulu corkscrews.

Coral was slightly scared of Tracy, though she couldn't have said quite why. Maybe it was being pregnant. Sometimes, when she was on the examining table, waiting for Dr. Weiss, Dr. Weiss's nurse talked to her, warning her about everything from mood changes to hemorrhoids, saying none of this should alarm her. But much here in Cimarron Acres alarmed her, and it all came together at the end of those March afternoons when Margo opened the door and said, "Go. Get some exercise. Take a hike."

Margo herself had so many fears—botulism, electric shocks from appliances, toddlers choking on balloons—that if she said something was safe, Coral did it, even when she was afraid. The minute Coral stepped outside, all the neighborhood dogs started barking. Everyone had a Doberman or a shepherd that followed her to its own piss-marked bounds, then dropped back, growling from the sidelines like tag team wrestlers. The children walking home from school quit hitting each other and stared as Coral walked quicker, trying not to run, faint and weak in the knees from fear and from wondering how the baby inside her was handling *this*. The small kids seemed upset, but the older ones watched and did nothing to call off their dogs. The kids played in T-shirts in forty-degree weather, and when Coral heard their mothers yelling at them to wear coats, she felt tied by a ribbon of barking and intimidation running from the ugly mothers to the ugly children and through the ugly children's ugly dogs to her.

Coral couldn't believe she could feel this way about a whole neighborhood full of kids. There wasn't a single cute one, or one she halfway liked. They were all either overweight or scrawny; their skin tones ranged from white-bread white to a mottled baloney-pink. When she worried about not liking kids—and being about to have one—she told herself it was the place. She sent messages down to her baby: Hey, I don't mean you. She wondered if what scared her about Tracy and the others was this: how weird your so-called normal child might turn out to be.

One morning, before work, Lee rushed over to tell them about her baby's beautiful dream of heaven. It took Lee a good ten minutes to describe Tracy's vision: clipped green lawns rolling down to ponds, miniature-golf windmills turning in the breeze. High in the trees, millions of birds all sang at the top of their lungs, and every bird was the living soul of someone who'd passed away. Scores of gophers and bunnies popped out of gopher holes, and these too were human spirits.

It was just as Lee said this that Coral felt the baby take a fluttery turn inside her. And only then did she let herself think how Kenny would have howled to hear about Tracy describing heaven like a production number from "The Muppet Show."


Slowly the weather got warmer. Gene had built a deck off the kitchen door, behind the trailer, shielded from the road and from Godzilla Hill. The land fell off beneath it, and on clear days, Coral sat on the steps going down to the yard and turned her face toward the sun. She poked around in the shed till she found her and Kenny's science fiction books, and began reading *The Left Hand of Darkness* for the third time. But reading in the sun gave her a headache, and, when Tracy and her friends came out to play on Tracy's swing set, Coral shut her eyes and listened.

Gleaming in the afternoon sun like some tubular city of the future, Tracy's swing set was nicer than Lee's whole trailer and often Tracy said as much to Denise and Michelle from across the street. Both girls were younger than Tracy—six or seven—and maybe that was why they put up with the monologues she kept up while they were there. Like Lee, Coral noticed, Tracy had a limited conversational range: how good and beautiful she was, and how much everyone loved her. Her tone never varied, and nothing—spelling-test scores, shopping trips to Kids 'Я' Us, visions of heaven—was any more important than anything else.

Coral began listening for the sound of the school bus and for the ritual yelling back and forth as Tracy, Denise and Michelle agreed—always as if for the first, thrilling time—to meet later in Tracy's yard. She began to appreciate Tracy, even the maddening things—her repetitiveness, for example. For if Coral missed something Tracy said, she knew it would come round again so she could memorize it and repeat the especially awful parts to Margo and Gene. Tracy was easy to mimic, both Coral and Margo had it down, but Coral's Tracy was funnier and meaner, and became a kind of currency she brought Gene and Margo in partial return for their kindness. They particularly liked Coral's imitation of Tracy lecturing her friends about what would happen right after they died: ice-cold hose baths in the chilly funeral home basement. But by the end of May, Coral caught herself telling Gene and Margo she hadn't heard anything good and saving the good parts for when Kenny's brother Paul came for dinner.

Paul lived in Syracuse, where he had a small business, contracting Formica counters. Coral could barely remember Paul's wife, who'd left him two years ago and gone back to her parents in Maine. Paul didn't talk about her, or about anything much, but in private Margo told Coral what a difficult person Paul's wife had been. Mostly Paul ate, heaping his plate with food. When he was done, he grinned appreciatively, and Gene and Margo smiled. The son come home for Mom's home cooking—what else was family for? Paul laughed when Coral mimicked Tracy; he laughed quietly, trying to keep his mouth shut because it was full of food.

Soon Coral found herself waiting for the end of the meal, when Paul balled up his paper napkin and tossed it overhand into the trash. Kenny used to do it just like that, and neither of them ever missed. Coral knew there used to be laws against people remarrying within families; now she understood why. It seemed somehow criminal to like someone because the way he threw out his napkin reminded you of someone else.

One Saturday afternoon, Coral was sitting on the back steps; she jumped when Paul sat down a few steps above her. The sun was very hot, and Coral longed to lean back against his knees and feel the soft weave of his faded blue jeans against her shoulders. Down below, Tracy was talking about how the souls of the blessed have canoe races on the River Jordan, like on Memorial Day in Bainbridge. Coral heard Paul snicker. When Margo called them in to dinner, Coral stood and saw spots in front of her eyes. Paul steadied her, and, to keep his arm around her longer, she acted dizzier than she was.

That night, over ham, potato salad and cole slaw, Margo told Gene that the Chevy would need a new muffler by Thursday if she was going to get Coral to Oneonta for her monthly appointment with Dr. Weiss.

Paul said, "I'll drive her. It's sort of on my way."

Coral stared down at her plate, thinking that if Paul came with her, everyone in the doctor's waiting room would think he was the father.

Margo said, "I'd worry. I would. The last thing Coral needs is to bounce around in Paul's pickup."

Coral was disappointed, but when Paul looked over at her, she shrugged; maybe Margo was right.

As Coral got bigger and bigger, time started moving more slowly. Now Coral spent the warm afternoons on her bed, staring at the ceiling, wondering if it could be true that the days and minutes moved slower the slower you walked. Sometimes, when she stood up, a twinge of sciatica shot down one leg: harmless, Dr. Weiss said, but Coral, with Margo's encouragement, gave up her afternoon walks. Suppose Coral fainted, said Margo.

One Saturday night, Paul was over for dinner when the

front door burst open and Lee leaned in, waving a cardboard ticket. She'd won five hundred dollars at Lotto playing a number Tracy picked. Gene opened a bottle of Lambrusco, and even Coral, who knew she shouldn't drink, let him pour her a quarter inch. They toasted Lee and Tracy's good luck, and though Lee raised her glass, she smiled knowingly—luck had nothing to do with it.

The next afternoon, Paul and Coral sat on the back steps and heard Tracy tell Denise and Michelle how last week she'd seen numbers whirling in the air above the counter in the Busy Bee. The numbers were on fire, 7-6-9-4-3 burning and spinning like Ezekiel's wheel, and she'd cried: Mama, buy a chance! According to Tracy, they'd already spent the money on party dresses for Tracy and Lee and on a deluxe aboveground pool for the summer.

Paul whispered to Coral, "You watch. There'll be a parking crunch outside Lee's house, fancy late-model American cars and guys chomping big cigars and reading OTB forms."

But nothing like that happened. Here was a walking, talking winning number, right on their block, and nobody crossed the street. Maybe no one believed Lee's story, or maybe it was their mind-your-own-business social code. In a way, thought Coral, Cimarron—with its pickups and Western shirts, its cowboys working the line at GE—*was* like your Wild West shoot-'em-up town where no one planned on hanging around very long. In a way they *were* pioneers; the frontier was Godzilla Hill.

But now something seemed to change. Perhaps it was summer, some thickening in the air. Perhaps it was Lee's pool—four feet wide, three feet deep, a blinding-turquoise plastic liner surrounded by a redwood ledge. But some focus of interest sharpened, some edge of attention formed, and now when Peggy and Don came over, all they talked about was the guest list for the pool party Lee was giving for Tracy's birthday in July. Several times a day, Lee popped in for advice on everything from toothpicks to ice cubes to the preferred brand of hot dog. Margo asked Lee why Tracy couldn't have a vision about something practical, like was Hebrew National better or worse than Hormel, but Lee didn't think it was funny.

On the night of the party Coral dressed with special care, in white maternity jeans and an oversized men's shirt. As she crossed the yard, the baby stirring inside her felt almost like the butterflies she used to get on her way to high school dances where she knew Kenny would be. But what did she think was in store for her now—eight months pregnant, big as a whale, socializing with these dirty-faced kids and their hard-luck moms and dads?

The pool was teeming with children, splashing each other and shrieking. The grown-ups drank beer and ate. Most of the women wore bathing suits, though none of them swam; their husbands were bare-chested above their jeans. Some men had bellies that swelled out from the breastbone and were shaped not unlike Coral's; on others, flaps of skin hung like pouches over their belts. Coral had never seen so much unhealthy flesh—even the children's thighs were slack and wobbly with cellulite—but then she had never seen her neighbors so undressed. It was as if they had taken off clothes for the party, and yet they looked oddly dressed up, conscious that this *was* a party, so transformed into their festive selves as to be practically unrecognizable. Lee and Tracy were nowhere around.

Coral looked for Paul, whom she spotted at the barbecue. She realized that this was the first time she'd seen him from far away; she was struck by how nice he looked. He picked out a burger with great care, and slid it onto Coral's plate. He said, "Go find a corner of this zoo where we can eat in peace. I'll join you when I can find someone to take over here at the grill."

At the edge of the yard, nearest their own trailer, Margo and Gene sat at an umbrella table with Peggy and Don, all four of them in the exact positions they would have taken at Margo's kitchen table; Coral knew that if she joined them, she'd never get up. Instead she sat at a picnic table with two

248 • FRANCINE PROSE

women and their kids—two little Madonnas from the bus stop.
Both girls were their mothers' clones; one pair was skinny,
curly haired, tough and giggly; the other two were heavier,
with tiny features stranded in the center of their large moon
faces. One of the women was saying, "We *went*. But we started
arguing in the car so bad, when we got there I wouldn't go in."

Coral looked up and saw Paul beckoning to her. She
hadn't touched her food, but she threw her paper plate in the
garbage and went and sat beside him on a bench. They didn't
say anything for a while; they watched the evening light fade.

Suddenly a floodlight flashed on, and, as the children
blinked grumpily, Lee and Tracy appeared in the spotlight,
both smiling, both wearing identical frilly white dresses, big
and little Loretta Lynns. It was really quite a performance,
and the whole party stopped. A few guests whistled and
clapped. Paul rolled his eyes at Coral.

Lee sashayed around, lighting candles in paper lanterns
with stagy, swooping gestures, like Cinderella's fairy god-
mother turning pumpkins into coaches. And yet when the lanterns were lit, it *was* a little magical: it could have been Mexico,
China, India, anyplace but this. Leaning her weight against
Paul, Coral closed her eyes for a second and had to make herself reopen them.

People walked by without giving Coral and Paul a second
glance. Most of them knew Coral by sight; they'd probably
heard about Kenny. Still, with all the partying and beer, many
would forget; they'd assume she and Paul were the zoned-out
parents-to-be, frightened and stupefied by what was about to
befall them. Even if people remembered the truth, it was only a
story to them, a story they would have gladly rewritten so that
what happened to Kenny never happened, and it was always
Coral and Paul.

When Coral saw Tracy moving from group to group, it
took her a while to figure out that Tracy was collecting birthday presents. Tracy unwrapped each gift, kissed whoever gave
it to her, then bore it, arms outstretched, to a table. In the soft

lantern glow, it was all very ceremonial. Tracy was thanking
Denise and Michelle for a satin stuffed unicorn when Coral
realized she hadn't bought Tracy a thing. Coral felt awful.
Whether or not she liked Tracy or Lee, the fact was, this was a
child's birthday, one of the last few birthdays that Tracy
would have as child. All at once Coral's guilt over not buying
Tracy a present seemed to spread in her mind like a stain, like
a blot of something spilled, taking in all her angry, evil
thoughts about Tracy and Lee and her neighbors in Cimarron
Acres. Who was Coral to call Tracy a creep when she had been
ten times as creepy? *She* was the one who stared at the picture
of the barracks where Kenny was killed, all charged-up and
trembly and scared to get caught like some kid reading *Playboy*
at the rack. Poor Tracy, Coral thought. This was the only
childhood Tracy would ever have, and she was spending it in
Cimarron.

But when Tracy looked at Coral, this rush of sympathy
seemed to miss her, seemed to whiz right by her curly head; all
that Tracy registered was that Coral had no gift. She marched
up to Coral and cocked her head and said, in a lilting voice, "I
saw your baby last night. In heaven. Laying on a soft white
blanket on a beautiful green lawn. It was waving its tiny arms
and legs and petting the Doberman that killed it. And the dog
was just laying there like a lamb." Then Tracy stalked off with
the spin on her heel that Coral had watched her do every morning when the other girls put on their Madonna gear.

It took Coral a minute to catch her breath, and then she
felt as if she'd been in a car accident and had to check herself
for damage. She knew what Tracy had said and that Tracy was
supposed to have second sight. She thought about the baby,
haltingly, testing: How scared am I now? But she wasn't
frightened at all. She was, if anything, *less* scared. She
thought: Tracy is out of her mind. And this was the strangest
thing: Now for the first time since Kenny got killed, she felt
almost certain that her child would be fine. Hearing Tracy say
the opposite had somehow made it seem *logical* that the baby

would be born and grow up and not get eaten by a Doberman.

But what Coral couldn't get past was that someone could say such a thing in the first place. Even a child—with no sense at all of how a pregnant woman might feel—even a child should know better. Coral considered the possibility that Tracy's prophecy was just a junior version of Lee rattling on about the poor single mom without enough arms to save both sets of twins from a burning house. And suddenly Coral thought: There is no limit to how evil people can be. Everywhere they are just waiting for you to nod off so they can drive into you and blow you up.

Coral leaned forward and wrapped her arms around herself, as if these thoughts were flowing from her to the baby—as if, by squeezing hard enough, she could stop them. She felt how round her stomach was, how much like a separate planet as she hung on to it and spun out into orbit, spinning billions of miles per second past wherever Paul's voice was coming from, so that only very distantly, very faintly could she hear him saying, "Hey, are you all right?"

# THE POLITICS OF

# PARADISE

O

*Lisa Alther*

AS THE FERRY PULLED into the sagging
wooden dock, Ryan knew he was about to disembark on Eden.
The wide deserted Conch Cay beaches, pink from ground-up
shells, were the most spectacular in the Caribbean. Worthy of
a back cover on *The New Yorker.* Sea gulls swept down, mewing
and fighting over scraps discarded by two men cleaning bone-
fish on the pier. Half-wild tiger cats darted in and out, dodging
the flying knives and vying with the gulls for their share. Ryan
grabbed his two suitcases and clambered onto the dock.

The village was as he remembered it: several dozen pink
and light green and bare weathered wood houses in various
stages of collapse, huddled around the cove seeking shelter
from the hurricanes that pounded the ocean side of the island.
Beached motorboats. Sidewalks of packed sand. Rustling palm
trees that dwarfed all these puny works of man. The drone and
clatter of electric generators. The Primitive Baptist church

with its eternally burning light bulb over the doorway—a fitting tribute to Christ on this island where electricity was almost as precious as fresh water. And over everything, the vast blue sky and searing sun.

Eight hours ago in New York City icy winds howled down narrow streets. Snow swirled around the tall glass-and-steel buildings on Park Avenue as Ryan's taxi carried him to the East Side Terminal, an appropriate name for a place that was witnessing his final departure from the rotting Big Apple. A jet to Miami, a DC-7 to Orono Island, a ferry twelve miles across Orono Bay to Conch Cay. Like a snake shedding a tattered skin, he'd fled the collapsing civilization that had spawned him. No longer would he go in a pin-striped suit to an office in an Art Deco building on Madison Avenue to write copy for new improved Stir 'n Serve Pudding. No longer would he jockey for recognition from R. L. Marsh, senior copy chief. No longer would he pick up the phone at his East Sixty-sixth Street apartment, to hear Elaine in Connecticut itemizing the ways he'd failed her and the children. Instead of looking out his office window to a flashing sign to learn the temperature, he need only look at the sky now, and feel the sun on his bare forearms. Instead of trying to convince housewives to buy a carcinogenic mix of chemicals, he'd supply people with fresh food and comfortable shelter at his newly purchased inn. His entire life would take on an uncharacteristic integrity.

Ryan had made one unbreachable rule: He must keep to himself on Conch Cay. Human interaction in the past had led only to disappointment and disillusion. Once he had been young and in love—with a Cornell coed in a camel cashmere sweater set and pearls, a Tri Delt met while making Kleenex carnations for the Easter Seals float in the Spring Fling parade. Their marriage had accomplished little but saddling Ryan with responsibilities, the fulfillment of which had systemically robbed him of his credibility by requiring him to do and say things he didn't really believe. Just as he'd pared down his belongings to the contents of these two suitcases, so had he pared down his involvement with other people. Elaine would get her money every month, but he wouldn't have to listen to her litany of complaints every night. And he would not become entangled again. He felt like a pioneer on the Oregon Trail casting aside household possessions for passage over the Rockies.

During the divorce he couldn't sleep, couldn't eat. His wife of twenty-six years loved some balding investment banker. Jessica and Kevin were grown, off to Vassar and Yale. Ryan himself was graying, impotent, bypassed for promotion to copy chief. Burnt out. Self-respect was gone, but so were the wife and children for whom he'd sacrificed it. He descended into a pit of self-loathing. But then one day he impulsively cashed in his Keogh to buy the Conch Cay Inn from Ed Norton. And here he was, reborn, a new improved life ahead of him.

Ryan strode up the sand sidewalk past a gaggle of small children, naked, blond, sunburnt, grinning shyly and whispering. His inn was soon before him—two buildings, one a long low line of bedrooms, the other a bar and dining room. Listing palms swayed over both.

Three years ago he and Elaine and the Achesons, after a day of nude sunbathing at the far end of the island, had anchored their rented sailboat in Conch Cay harbor and rowed the dinghy ashore for dinner at this inn. The food was simple and fresh—native lobster, conch chowder, turtle steak, fresh vegetables, papayas, coconut pie. They sat drinking gin under the palms until dawn, talking loudly and laughing and pretending that Elaine didn't wish Ryan were a balding banker named Stan.

Ryan stood behind the massive wooden bar polishing glasses and watching Ida set the dining tables on the screened porch. He'd read in a history book left behind by Ed Norton that Ida's four-times-great-grandparents had owned vast stretches of South Carolina. They'd fled to Conch Cay with their herds and slaves during the American Revolution. The thin topsoil

soon becoming depleted, crops began to fail. The slaves moved
to their own cay. Ida's forebears began a numb struggle for
subsistence. They fished. They hunted wild boar, descendants
of pigs left to propagate as a meat supply by passing pirates.
They went to sea in homemade boats to dive for sponges. They
walked mules with lanterns around their necks up and down
the dunes at night, luring ships onto the shoals. Then they exe-
cuted the survivors and plundered the wreckage.

Their scion was setting tables for a New York Irishman.
Ida's father raised vegetables in a patch in the mangrove
swamps, hidden where passing boats couldn't raid it. He
trapped lobsters for sale to Ryan and to a Miami restaurateur
who flew in on a seaplane once a week. Ida's brother Sandy
dove for turtles, sold the meat to Ryan, and shellacked the
huge patterned shells for sale to visiting yachtsmen. He also
did repairs around the inn in his soiled Harley-Davidson T-
shirt and baggy Levi's. Like the other cay inhabitants, he was
almost albino, with pale blue eyes and hair bleached white by
the sun.

Ryan felt a bond with these simple people. Their life,
pared down by necessity to the essentials, possessed inherent
dignity. He was proud to have cast his lot with them. He found
himself gazing at Ida's hips as she leaned across a table, maid's
white dress stretched taut. Stooping, he rearranged bottles beneath the bar.

"Mr. Ryan, you want the tables in here set, too?"

Ryan stood up. Ida rarely spoke. When she did, he was
startled by her cockney accent. It was harsh, in contrast to
Ida's languid mannerisms. She strolled rather than walked,
lolled rather than sat, had a slow lazy smile. Like Henry Hig-
gins in *My Fair Lady,* he felt he should correct her vowel
sounds.

"I don't think we'll need them tonight."

All evening Ryan mixed daiquiris and planter's punches
for yachtsmen from New York and Connecticut. The men wore
pressed white trousers, deck shoes or Reeboks, striped T-shirts,

white captain's hats. They had clipped mustaches and styled hair. The women wore caftans or pants suits. Long painted nails, eye makeup, careful coiffures. Bronzed by the sun. The beautiful people. They shrieked with laughter and clinked the ice cubes in their glasses and ordered many refills, just as he and Elaine and the Achesons had done three years earlier. This former self seemed foreign to Ryan now. He answered their friendly questions curtly, feeling like a reformed alcoholic who must avoid all contact with his poison.

A Connecticut captain shouldered his way to the bar and leaned on it. "Some place, this Conch Cay. Just like Hemingway, huh?"

Ryan nodded, not looking up.

"How'd you find this place anyhow?"

"Same as you," muttered Ryan, shaking a margarita in a silver container. "Sailing around on vacation." Every yachtsman who stopped here regarded the cay as his private discovery.

"Where you from? I can hear you're not native."

"Manhattan," snapped Ryan, wishing the guy would go back to his boat and stick his head in his chemical toilet.

"Threw it all up for the simple life, huh?"

"Something like that."

"Jesus, I envy you. To turn your back on the rat race. Just pack it in. Man oh man. How'd you do it?"

Ryan shrugged. "I just did it."

"Christ, you must have a pair and a half!" whistled the florid-faced captain, moving away.

Ryan smiled grimly, since he hadn't been able to get it up for the last year. He could hear this man at a Westport cocktail party: "Lillian and I discovered this great little island. Gorgeous pink beaches. Mile after mile with nobody around. And right in the middle of nowhere, an inn with this fabulous native cooking, run by this ballsy guy from Manhattan . . ." And next year half of Westport would arrive on Conch for dinner. Ryan's living depended on these people, but he didn't

want them to come here. He didn't like the way the men's eyes
moved down Ida's body, the way they tossed coins to Sandy for
carrying their bags from the ferry. He should be protecting
the islanders from people like this, instead of making his living
off them.

Ryan's gaze sought out Ida—languidly serving these impossible people in her white uniform. A woman had just sent
something back to the kitchen. Ryan felt sure from Ida's toler-
ant smile that she could see through all their blustery preten-
sion.

Ida was excited as she carried a turtle steak back to the
kitchen for more cooking. She loved these well-dressed, attractive continental people, the way they demanded that everything
be done exactly right—requesting a clean glass if there were
water spots, a clean fork if theirs were flecked with food. At
her own house it was a miracle if there was even an official
meal, never mind how it was cooked. Her mother washed
clothes all morning in cold water from the cistern, then sat
around all afternoon munching Cracker Jacks and watching
soap operas on the Miami station. Each of them would fix a
bowl of Captain Crunch, or go to the store for a Dolly Madison
cake and a Coke.

Ida studied the woman whose turtle steak she was returning. A floral caftan, gold filigree on her wrists, emerald pen-
dants hanging from her ears. A high black hairdo. Just like the
models in the *Vogue*s guests sometimes left behind in their
rooms. Ida sighed. They came and they went, these people, but
she was stuck forever on this boring little island. Her life was
all mapped out for her. Day after day, year after year, she'd
do the exact same things—change sheets, wait on tables, go for
a ride after supper in Ben's boat, go into Orono for a movie,
watch the soaps on TV. She'd probably marry Ben, have babies, wash diapers all morning in cold water.

Once Ida had taken the ferry to Orono and the plane to

Miami, to visit an aunt who'd managed to escape. Fancy cars,
tall glass buildings, hotels with huge trees growing inside them.
Men in suits and ties, something she'd never seen except on TV
and in the *Gentlemen's Quarterlys* guests left behind. What she
couldn't figure out was why people like that voluntarily came
to Conch Cay when they could go anywhere in the world—
Paris or Rio or Disney World. And why they paid more money
than she earned in an entire day to eat conch and turtle when
they could be eating hamburgers.

There had to be a way out of this place. Once four men
invited her onto their thirty-foot yacht. All day long she did
everything they wanted. Some of it hurt, but she thought if she
could please them, they'd take her to Miami as they promised.
Instead they dumped her at the far end of the island. She
walked home barefoot over the coral. Her feet got all cut up.
Sandy went looking for them. He washed ashore in his boat the
next day, unconscious, ribs broken and face bruised.

Looking up, Ida caught Mr. Ryan staring at her again.
He'd come to Conch Cay and meant to stay. From New York
City. All by himself. On purpose. Said he liked it here. He was
always staring at her, then looking away when she caught him.
But he never did more than look. He seemed like a nice man.
He never pinched her as she walked by. She liked his auburn
hair streaked with gray, liked his sad green eyes, liked to pic-
ture him in his New York City suit and tie.

Ryan spent his days buying fish and vegetables from the islanders, answering mail about rates and dates, dealing with the
perpetual water shortage, going to Orono in his boat to pick up
guests and supplies. At night he ran the bar. He was busier
than he'd ever been on Madison Avenue. But he was healthy
and happy. His hair was bleaching in the sun, and he was
tanned a reddish brown. He'd stopped smoking and drinking.
His eyes, always bloodshot in New York, were clear now.

The only source of agitation was Ida. Ryan watched her

from his office window one morning as she moved slowly from
room to room in the long low building across the yard, uniform
dress stretching tight across hips or breasts as she bent and
stooped and shook out rugs in the white sunlight. Unable to
stop himself, Ryan pictured her naked beneath him on a deserted pink sand beach, tongues of frothy surf licking away
their sweat. He smiled sadly. His lechery was strictly pro
forma. That phase of his life in which his stiff penis propelled
him into all kinds of delicious disasters was over. He might as
well resign himself to a dignified old age. He'd become wise
instead. Ida would come to him for advice. He'd be a refuge
from all the other men who wanted only sex. She was so innocent. He wouldn't want to contaminate her with lusts learned
from a dying civilization, even if he could.

"Mr. Ryan, *sir.*" Ryan discovered Sandy disdainfully
watching him watch Ida. "Would you radio Orono, get me half
a dozen two-by-fours for the porch roof on the next ferry?"

"Uh, certainly, Sandy."


Arlene Dominique had been coming to the inn for years, she
told Ryan as he dined at her table that night. He nodded as he
sipped his turtle soup. He disliked this woman, as an individual and as a type. She was like Elaine, like all the pampered
spoiled women he'd ever known, in her low-cut sundress, gold
sandals, jade eye shadow, Opium perfume, with strategic
chunks of gold and diamond at ears, neck, and wrists. But she
was an old-timer, belonged on Conch Cay more than he. He had
to be polite.

". . . and then my husband died. That was two years ago.
I've come back to Conch alone both years. It's therapeutic.
Herb and I were so happy here. I talk to the natives about him.
It's balm on my wounds to hear the wonderful things these
simple souls have to say about my poor Herbie."

Ryan nodded with what he hoped was a sympathetic expression.

"But I'm a man's woman, Mr. Ryan." She looked at him through lowered eyelashes, heavy with crumbs of mascara. "I feel only half alive without a man."

It hadn't occurred to Ryan that sex was a service he was expected to provide, along with fresh linens. Ida's hip brushed his arm. She had been silently bringing new dishes and taking away soiled ones. Ryan looked up with a long-suffering smile and was met by an icy glare. She stalked to the kitchen with the soup plates.

"She's lovely, isn't she?" Mrs. Dominique noted his eyes following Ida's hips. "So innocent. A child really. I've known her since she was five. A darling little girl. And such a nice family. A real comfort to me after Herb's death."

Ryan nodded, grimly flaking yellowfish from its bones.

"But of course sympathy doesn't remedy certain needs associated with widowhood, Mr. Ryan. After eighteen years of constant physical contact with a man, a woman can't just suddenly turn it off at the funeral . . ."

A plate of soup flipped off Ida's tray into Mrs. Dominique's lap. The dining room erupted—Mrs. Dominique shrieking, Ida mopping at her lap with a napkin, Ryan stuttering apologies. Mrs. Dominique retired to her room, scalded and outraged.

Ryan found Ida hiding in the pantry. "You have to be more careful, Ida," he began. "Mrs. Dominique has been coming here a long time and sending her friends here. I know it was an accident, but it's one we can't afford."

She looked up, eyes red and puffy. "I'm sorry."

"It's all right. Please don't cry about it."

"I'm not."

"Not what?"

"Crying about the soup."

"What's wrong then?"

"Nothing," she said sullenly.

Ida guessed she was in love with Ryan. It was hard to say since she'd never been in love. She had had boyfriends, but

they were just that—boys who were special friends. Ben, the
current one, drove his boat every day to a nearby cay to build
condominiums. She'd known him from infancy; knew his parents, grandparents, brothers and sisters; was some kind of
cousin to him; knew exactly what their marriage would be like
before it even began. She liked Ben fine, but there was no mystery. She didn't feel about him the way Laura did about Brad
on "The Young and the Restless," for instance, trembling
when he walked in the room.

Ryan, however, did give her tremors. She thought about
him a lot as she changed sheets and scoured toilet bowls, as
she set tables and wrote orders, as she walked along sand
sidewalks late at night to her parents' house on the far side
of the cove, as she lay in bed and listened to the wind drive
the palm fronds together like clashing swords. She pictured
him in New York City—tall, slim, sophisticated, dressed in a
business suit. She imagined meeting him for cocktails in a
New York hotel, riding to the roof in an open glass elevator.
She would wear an Indian print caftan, jewels, mauve eye
shadow, and a high hairdo with a spit curl at each ear.
They'd gaze at each other without speaking, and toy with
their plastic swizzle sticks. Then he'd take her to a room with
wall-to-wall carpeting, thick drapes, and a marble sink, where
you could run water day and night without the cistern ever
going dry. On a huge bed with a quilted spread she'd do all
the things she'd learned from the passing yachtsmen. And
Ryan would insist she never leave.

Ida buried her face in her hands and wept. How was she
to get to a bed in a fancy New York hotel, from a barrel in a
pantry on Conch Cay? How could she compete with someone
like Arlene Dominique? She couldn't. Ryan would go tonight to
Aunt Arlene (as Ida had been instructed by her parents to call
the bitch years ago so the Christmas checks would keep coming), and Aunt Arlene would do those things to him, and he'd
love her and go away with her, leaving Ida to rot on Conch Cay.

Ida sat sniffling in the bushes to one side of Ryan's door,

waiting to watch him sneak to Aunt Arlene's room, while the generators clanked and the palm fronds clashed, and mating wild cats yowled in the swamp. But dawn eventually streaked the night sky with gray and pink, and still Ryan hadn't appeared. Aunt Arlene's door opened. Dressed in a long brown satin dressing gown, she strode back and forth along the porch smoking a cigarette. Finally she threw it down and marched to Ryan's door. She paused there, then whirled around and stalked back to her own room. Ida wiped away her tears with her dingy white uniform skirt.

As she served Ryan breakfast, she said, "Mr. Ryan, you work too hard. I bet you've never even seen Coral Cove."

"I've never even heard of it."

"We could go there this afternoon. After I finish the rooms."

Ryan hesitated. She was right of course. He was working harder than was really necessary. He swam in the ocean every day for relaxation, but he hadn't yet toured his new island home. He studied Ida's eager face. She was Jessica's age. Was he a father figure? Ida was a devoted employee trying to ingratiate herself with the boss? She was lonely too, wanted a new friend? Or was she propositioning him? He smiled, realizing he was flattering himself to think an attractive young woman would be interested sexually in a graying old man. He had spotted her around the village with various young studs—the white-haired, red-faced, blue-eyed youth whom it was impossible to tell apart. She probably had a boyfriend. She was just being hospitable.

"I'd like to. That sounds like fun."

They walked under the white-hot sun along the pink sand for several miles. Ryan wore tennis shorts and carried their picnic hamper. Ida wore a two-piece bathing suit and a large straw hat with a gingham band. The surf swirled around their ankles. Periodically they squatted to inspect some object washed up by the waves—slimy convoluted green noodle lasagnas, a Portuguese man-of-war like a limp blue condom.

"How come there are never any village people on the beaches?"

"When you grow up here, you don't think about the beach. My mother hasn't been over here in years."

"But do you all realize how unbelievably beautiful it is?"

Ida shrugged.

They were passing a ruined house, roof missing, walls crumbling, lush tropical bushes pushing up through the tile floor. Vines wound in and out the window openings like boa constrictors.

"Someone's house?" asked Ryan.

"Mr. Norton's. The continental who owned the inn before you."

"What happened?"

"Burnt down."

"Fires must be a real problem here once they get going," mused Ryan. "No rain, no roads, no fire-fighting equipment, no water except the ocean."

Ida nodded.

Coral Cove was pink sand on one side. Along the far side coral formations in shades of black, purple, and deep red shimmered in the heat. They spread a blanket, ate sandwiches, ran in and out of the water, and baked in the hot sun. Despite himself Ryan watched Ida's breasts bouncing as she leapt into the waves. And her long brown legs stretched along the olive army blanket. He concentrated on thinking of her as his daughter, an innocent young woman entrusted to his protection. Not that Jessica had been innocent since she was two years old. But it was pointless to think of Ida any other way. If he did, and if she responded with anything other than horror, he'd only disappoint them both.

Handing Ryan a mango from the hamper, Ida felt confused. This man was unlike any other male she'd ever met. It had always been a question of fighting them off. But now she found herself wanting one who apparently wasn't interested. Maybe he was shy. What if she reached over and took his hand? But what if he really wasn't interested in her that way? What about her job? She thought men couldn't manage for very long without shoving themselves into some woman. That's what passing sailors and the boys on the cay always told her. Did Ryan have someone else? But he never left the island except to pick up arriving guests, and he hadn't gone to Aunt Arlene last night. She'd heard there were men who wanted other men instead of women. Maybe he was one of those? She bit into her orange-fleshed mango, juice coursing down her chin.

"Mr. Ryan?"

He turned to look at her, mouth and hands mango-wet.

"Mr. Ryan, do you like me?"

"I like you very much, Ida."

"Do you like me—that way?"

"Which way?" he asked nervously.

Tossing her mauled mango into the surf, Ida rolled over and pressed her body against his. Ryan drew a sharp breath. They began to entangle juice-coated limbs and to kiss stickily, stirring up sand that clung to their moist skin.

Abruptly Ryan rolled on his back and stared at the blue sky. This young woman whose innocence he'd pledged himself to protect had been writhing against him like a lady wrestler. She seemed to know exactly what she was doing. And his hands had taken on a life of their own, running up and down her curves with abandon. He felt ashamed of himself, and betrayed by her. Some of her moves involved gymnastics described in the sex manuals Elaine had taken to leaving on his bedside table before they split up. Perverse gimmicks dreamed up by a sick civilization to flog response out of zombies in whom all spontaneity was dead. The more demands Elaine made, the more she chronicled his failures, the more she outlined techniques for "satisfying" her, the less he was able to sustain an erection. How did a young girl on a remote island know about such repulsive behavior? If his role weren't to be her guardian, at least *he* should be the one to instruct *her* in lovemaking.

"You don't want to—love me?" asked Ida, bewildered.

"It's not that simple."

Ida felt panic. She wasn't pleasing Ryan. She didn't know how the sophisticated women he was used to behaved. With Ben it was enough simply to lie down and open her legs and think about "The Young and the Restless" until he was finished. But the men on the boats expected more exotic things. She recalled a scene from a late movie on TV. Climbing atop Ryan, she ran her tongue around and into his ear, and sucked his lobe. "But it *is* simple, my darling," she whispered. "So simple."

Ryan shoved her off, leaped up, grabbed the blanket and basket, and stalked off toward the village.

"But I only want to please you, Mr. Ryan," she wailed, trotting alongside. "Just tell me how."

He stomped along wordlessly, past the ruined house of his predecessor.

"Please, Mr. Ryan. God, I love you so much."

He stopped and whirled around, glaring at her with outrage. Love? The only time he had ever said, "I love you" to someone, he ended up with two spoiled children, a mortgaged house in Darien, loans on a Volvo station wagon and a Honda Accord, a wife who was a compulsive shopper, a job writing lies, and a limp prick. He could tell this child of nature a thing or two about "love"! But when he noticed her tearstained face, he remembered she was hardly more than a teen-ager.

"You love me?" he rasped.

"So much."

"You don't know what love means."

"It means I want to be close to you."

"That's not all it means. And you're too young to know about the rest."

"I don't care. Please," she said, holding out her arms. They embraced gingerly and walked to the village in silence, sand fleas feasting on their ankles.

For several days Ryan avoided Ida. He didn't know

how to behave anymore. On the one hand, she was an innocent who had to be protected from himself. On the other
hand, with her abandoned writhings on the beach, she repre-
sented some sort of primal sinkhole against which he had to
protect *himself.* And yet he'd experienced no physical warmth
in a long time. He craved it. Here was an attractive young
woman who claimed she loved him. Was it possible his notion
of love was askew, shaped as it had been in the molds of a
corrupt civilization?

Late one night after the last sailor returned to his yacht,
Ida slipped into Ryan's room, out of her white uniform, and
into his bed. He moaned and held her close. They lay without
talking in each other's arms until dawn.

Ida was startled. She hadn't known how to act, had
known only that her behavior at Coral Cove had not been a hit.
So she decided to make herself available to him to do with as he
wanted. What he apparently wanted was just to lie with her,
occasionally brushing back her hair and kissing her forehead.
What an odd man. Was this really how New Yorkers had sex?
All the stuff the men on the boats made her do must have been
saved for vacations.

This went on for several weeks. Ryan became more and
more reassured. They'd just gotten off to a bad start. He had
misinterpreted a healthy young girl's innate enthusiasm for
sex as corruption. She merely happened to be still in touch
with the natural tides of her own body. He had projected his
own sickness onto her, the contagion that had led him to regard
sex as an exchange—the woman consenting in return for material support from the man. The sun, the sea, the wind, the
preparation of food and shelter—might there be a place in this
natural cycle for a kind of lovemaking he'd never imagined,
lovemaking that could salve the loneliness without dragging
PTA meetings in its wake, a melding and merging rather than
a commercial transaction?

In the course of such musings one night, Ida snuggled
naked against him playing with the springy red hairs on his

chest, Ryan felt a swelling in his groin. He lay still, waiting for it to subside, but it didn't.

In the ensuing months, Ryan experienced things he hadn't known were possible between two people. He felt both resentful and apologetic toward Elaine. Resentful because she had been content for so many years with a tepid counterfeit of lovemaking, despite her self-portrayal as a slighted courtesan. Apologetic because he hadn't given her this kind of pleasure, hadn't even known it existed. Possibly it didn't exist in Darien. He suspected it required the stripping off of material obsession and cultural conditioning he'd undergone on Conch. Perhaps it required a partner in a similar state of simplicity.

Whatever, every minute Ryan and Ida weren't working, they were in bed together, discovering and inventing new ways to give each other pleasure. Never had he felt more virile. Ida was constantly praising his revived cock. In between demanding to be told about New York City, block by block, building by building.

"You must look so handsome in a suit," she kept insisting.

"I promise you I look better without one."

"No, Ryan, I can just picture you," she sighed, closing her eyes.

One afternoon as they lay in each other's arms on the deserted pink beach, the warm salt surf licking their legs and the shell of the burnt-out house keeping watch behind them, Ida whispered, "Ryan, I have something to tell you." She paused, not knowing how he'd react. "I'm going to have your baby."

Ryan said nothing. He felt strangely proud. He, a graying old man, had impregnated this gorgeous young woman. And after all, it was right that a union as simple and natural as theirs should come to this. But he'd been through it all before—diapers, toilet training, teething, braces, piano recitals. He'd done the parenting trip for all time. He wanted nothing more to do with it. No, it was out of the question. Ida would have an abortion. He'd take her to Miami.

"That's wonderful," he said faintly.

"Do you really think so?" She snuggled against him, taking his hand and running it over her swelling belly. He'd marry her, take her away from this awful place.

"Sure. Great." He could climb in his boat in the morning, be in Miami before noon, sell the inn by proxy, send Ida money.

"Ryan, I'm so happy to have your baby growing inside me."

That night Ryan sat in the yard under the rattling palms and downed half a bottle of brandy. Time after time he ran through his options—abortion, flight, suicide, marriage. In that order of desirability. Abortion made the most sense. He'd take Ida to Miami, have it over with before anyone on the island even knew about it. Take her to a fancy hotel for a few days to cheer her up. But she was so pleased to be pregnant. She had no children, hadn't experienced the drudgery of rearing them. The abortion, if she agreed to it, would be a trauma. How could he have been so stupid not to think about birth control? Elaine and the other women he'd been with had always taken care of it. But how could he expect an innocent like Ida to know about, much less have access to, all that stuff? Besides, it would have seemed a sacrilege to impose a rubber shield or a plunger of foam between them.

Sandy staggered out of the bushes, already drunk. The spotlights illuminating the palms bathed his body in white and reduced his face to eerie shadows. "Got summin I wanna tell ya, Ryan."

"What, Sandy?" he asked wearily.

"You do right by my sister, mon."

Ryan stared at him, horrified. Ida had already told her family? "Why don't you mind your own goddamn business?"

"Fuck you, Ryan! You been balling my sister all over this bloody island and everybody knows it! You do right by her or I'll cut your goddamn balls off!"

Ryan leapt to his feet and swung at Sandy, missing.

"Shut up, you maniac! You're going to wake up the whole damn place!"

Sandy swung at him and missed, and they ended up lying on the ground passing the brandy bottle and exchanging life histories. Sandy's voice oozed hatred as he described how the visiting yachtsmen came on shore and acted as if they owned the cay, stealing vegetables from his father's garden and knocking up the local girls and beating up the local boys and taking lobsters from their traps.

"And some of them even come back here to live," said Sandy, apparently forgetting whom he was talking to. "They think the island's so fucking beautiful. And they act like we're just turds who happen to have washed ashore. But they don't last long."

"What do you mean?" Ryan felt himself sobering up quickly.

"Quality control, mon."

"Norton's burnt house," Ryan realized.

Sandy grinned slyly. "Ain't saying nothing 'bout no burnt house, Ryan." He thrust the bottle at him, and Ryan took a long gulp.

Early the next morning Ryan climbed in his boat. He had errands on Orono. But he might be on the afternoon flight to Miami, watching from the air as his abandoned inn went up in flames. Abortion was probably out. Ida's family was Primitive Baptist. They'd never allow it. If Ida were dumb enough to tell them, she could cope with the consequences alone. Steering his Boston whaler out of the harbor, he turned to follow the shoreline. It wasn't that he didn't love Ida, insofar as he knew what that word meant. It was just that he'd been through all this before with Elaine, knew how devotion turned into duty, and duty into dislike. It was better to end it while it was still perfect. He was doing them both a favor.

As he passed the shoals, a large speedboat swept up, nosed toward him, and forced him sharply shoreward.

"What the fuck?" he screamed. His boat lurched, throwing him into the dashboard. He heard a sickening crunch as his keel ran aground on the coral. There was a sharp pain in his chest.

Looking up, he saw Sandy, idling his boat in the nearby water. "Remember what I said, Ryan. Do right by my sister, mon, or you'll wish you had." His boat roared away.

Ryan shut off his grinding engine, climbed onto the reef, and inspected the damage. A hole in the hull. The boat was done for. The motor could maybe be saved. He waded and swam to shore over the shoals where Ida's ancestors had looted wrecked ships. Then he hiked back to the village along the pink sand beach where he and Ida had first kissed, past the vine-wrapped ruins. The physical pain in his chest began to subside, only to be replaced by despair. There was no way to get off this island alive without Ida. Everyone on the whole fucking place was related to her. Maybe a passing yacht would rescue him?

As he reached the wooden stairs over the dunes to the village, he came upon the Baptist minister, who wore a handkerchief, knotted at each corner, on his balding head. A Canadian, he'd come to Conch as a missionary forty years earlier and never left. He held a dried palm frond in one hand, with which he had printed in the sand, "The Lord Has a Plan for Your Life." The rising tide was eating its edge. He started as Ryan greeted him. Ryan pointed to the eroding message. "Do you really think so, Reverend?"

"I know so," replied the old man, gazing at Ryan through crazed blue eyes.

That night in bed Ida whispered, "Ryan, our baby is moving!" She placed his hand over her abdomen, and he felt the tiny shiftings. But he'd done this with Elaine twice already. The experience had lost its power to enchant. He was instead calculating that it had to be about four months old, too late for a simple suction abortion. A saline abortion would be necessary. Ida would miscarry a dead fetus.

"Ida. I don't want a baby. I've had two already. I thought we could go to Miami. You could have an abortion.

Then we could stay in a fancy hotel for a few days. Order from room service. The works. We'll tell your parents you miscarried."

Ida said nothing for a long time. Finally she replied, "Abortion is a sin."

"Oh come on. Don't be ridiculous. Millions of women have abortions every year."

"That doesn't make it right."

"But Ida, I liked things the way they were."

He realized that perhaps abortion *was* a sin. In any case, it was to her. She was an innocent he'd pledged to protect from the barbarities of modern civilization, and here he was asking her to murder her fetus. The whole situation seemed unreal. He was playing in a different league on Conch Cay and hadn't even realized it.

Ida wept and called him godless. As he held her, patted her, and felt awful, he wondered if, just as sex with Ida had been a totally new experience, rearing a child on Conch Cay might not be different from rearing them in Darien. What was one more kid on this island? He'd marry Ida and move her in with him, hire a new waitress. Ida would have the baby, tend it. The little kid would run free in the sun and the sea. It might be beautiful. He shouldn't impose his warped view. All right, he finally concluded, he'd become a father again.

The next morning as Ida and Ryan walked on the sand sidewalk around the cove to announce to her parents their impending marriage, they passed the one-room schoolhouse. Ryan took a close look. This was where his child would be educated. Baby Ruth wrappers swirled around their feet. They waded through Cracker Jack boxes and Coke bottles. Most of the children screaming in the playground were cousins to his incubating child. Their teeth were black. Several had crossed eyes. He walked on, feeling uneasy. It was different from how Jessica and Kevin had grown up, with their Montessori nursery school and piano lessons, but that didn't make it worse.

Ida smiled. Ryan wouldn't allow his child to grow up on

Conch Cay with privies and cisterns, no phones, and mail boats
once a week, no high school. It was merely a matter of time
until he'd take her and the child away. She was sure of it.

Ida and Ryan looked at each other and smiled warily.


Ryan sat in the cocktail lounge of their Miami honeymoon
hotel absently clinking the ice in his scotch. Ida stood in the
doorway watching him. A frown creased her forehead. Ryan
looked uncomfortable in his suit, kept stretching his neck
against his tight collar and tie. His hair was bleached almost
white, and his face was dark red. He looked like the Conch Cay
men, instead of the *GQ* models. Ida struggled to put on her
brightest smile.

Ryan looked up and saw Ida sweeping toward him in a
floral print caftan, swelling belly breaking up the flowing lines.
She'd had her hair done—piled high on her head with spit curls
at each ear. Bracelets clanked on her wrists.

"Well?" she demanded, demurely lowering mauve eyelids.

"You look lovely," Ryan assured her with a bemused
smile.

# VICTORY

# MILLS

O

*Mona Simpson*

### *Katy:* CONFIDENCE

I HAVE DRIVEN A CAR on acid, carried my mother
drunk upstairs and slept with numerous men and one woman
to no consequence. I am comfortable in airports. There are
things I don't tell, small things of my own. I collect: snowball
paperweights from all the cities I've been, buttons, books about
birds. I am twenty-five years old and I only left home once and
that was a long time ago.

I was, believe it or not, the librarian type. All I really
loved to do was sleep. I couldn't get enough of it. Nine, ten
hours, and I'd wake up on my belly, lift my arm off the pillow
and it would drag a sleeve of dream, green, sequiny, dripping.

That was when I lived a life of trying. I scrubbed floors
for money, did homework, checking it over, staying in from the

sun. Every step I took seemed dire. Doing things that might be
good for me later. I learned things the hard way. I believed in
it—the value of work, earning everything, nothing free.

All that changed and came crashing down. I began to hate
people for talking, dealing, making bargains, for getting what
they wanted from each other.

There were three of us smart in the high school, home in
Victory Mills. I'd busted ass all through, trying for college in
New York City. Then, April 15, 1979, comes around and I
didn't get in. Grades were supposed to be money we could
spend; I had the money and they wouldn't let me buy. I still
don't know why for sure. I only applied two places. I suppose I
should have done more.

This was still that period when I wouldn't go out in the
sun to tan because I'd read about skin cancer and I wanted to
keep my skin pure. I wanted to save my whole self, preserve me
as if I were a fruit to be eaten sugared in winter, instead of
now, summer, ripe, fresh from the tree.

I only mean my body. The outside. I don't mean sex. That
went well with work. Other people reward themselves with
cookies. I was trampy, but hardworking too. Some prune guid-
ance counselor maybe wrote me down as slut. The two boys—
the black boy I loved and the faggot—they both got in. I'd been
waiting all my life. To get in. To get out. It all came raining
down around me, touching my ears. It was the outside but it
felt like the inside, the way when you run and stop it rushes to
your ears like warm velvet.

I had been saving myself for some Kennedy at college. I
figured out from the old *Life* magazines in the cellar, one of
those red-haired freckle-faced kids would be about my age.
They all went to college. They got in. My life's motto had been:
later.

Don't get me wrong. I wasn't saving myself inside. A girl
gets horny too. I just didn't want to sunburn or get lines or
hurt myself somewhere that would show. Sex I considered exercise.

Not that I made myself pretty. I was a tomboy bad. I
didn't want to end up a slave to pretty, like my mamma whose
biggest problem in life was keeping her nails long working the
second assembly, swing shift at the mill.

It began to change the night I smoked my first cigarette,
a Marlboro. I let go. It has to do with dancing. I had no future
anymore. I was at the Holiday Inn late, hearing Tray jam with
the band. Tray was my boy and he was going. Alex, the faggot,
sat there too. Alex asked me to go along to New York City. I
figured it would be random from now on. Anyway, I wouldn't
stay here. And maybe you could get things other ways than
trying.

That night I thought of something I'd always wanted.
Victory Mills elects a beauty queen every May. I decided to be
it. I started the next morning campaigning. I watched the
pretty girls in their ribbon-bonded matching sweaters, sticking
to themselves on the top tier of the lawn—they all wanted to be
beauty queen too. Betsy, the black Betty Crocker, she was the
meanest snob. And I kicked the gravel down by the parking lot
smiling at how stupid they were. I talked to everyone, every
nerd, every baldy, all the weirdos nobody else would have. It
didn't cost to say good morning. Those pretty birdy girls
didn't think. Everyone gets a vote, the rejects too.

## *Alex:* MEMORY

There is something I'll never forget, the day we took the bus
down to New York from Victory Mills. Tray and me. Katy
came later. Didn't seem to matter who was going to college anymore. We three were going. We passed outside town, through
Schuylerville and on a hill in the country, from an old gray
house, sagging above a little makeshift farm, Betsy comes running in her homemade skirt and Peter Pan collar, arms and

legs pell-mell, beating hard as an eggbeater, her chest leading, she runs up to the bus and screams.

I looked hard at Tray, leaving her. She was his sweet girl, they did everything the straight way, the date, the pictures, prom.

"I got things to do," he said, that day on the bus, stern, spitting into his hand.

He didn't end up in school long. He started a band in New York City. And it was going. We turned roommates, Katy and me. Back home in Victory Mills, Katy was a weird thing. No one knew what to make of her. She and her mom lived in an old house on the slow main street, looking right across into the mill, our beautiful brick mill, founded 1897 and still working. Once a paper mill, now they make cardboard containers. We've all been there once, punched our cards.

Back home in Victory Mills, she wore big blue gym shorts, a kind you can't get anymore, with elastic waist, a yellow border around the leg holes, a high school name on one leg. She lay on her couch with her hair ringed back and taught little boys to lick her after school. It was like lifting a wet baby up to breast and teaching it to nurse. They would sometimes gag and try to bob up but she pushed their heads down. This was in the afternoon, her momma working the second shift across the road at the mill.

I know because I was one of the boys. Alexander Sutter. Best boy in the fourth-grade class. I had a nine-year-old Catholic boy crew cut. She wrote on my hair with her finger. I remembered her fat belly, undulation, wetness, long after old man Whipple from the antique store made me his boy, dry and smelling of talcum, dry clothes on dry skin, layers, like old leaves patched on a long autumn road.

I only went to her that once and never back. It was a Friday and I threw up my mother's fish that night. The next morning I showed up at Whipple's door, asking for work as a scout. It was quiet in there, like backstage at church. They had

an old radio playing organ. There were two guys, Whipple
with his black plastic glasses, and the tall younger one you
never saw, who sat in a corner, needling a rug. He hand-hooked
rugs. I learned what you called it later.

While Whipple got me the keys to the car, the tall one
looked up and said, "Rouse."

So they sent me to Rouse, an old filthy broken-down place
on Rouse Road. I loved to drive, I'd always known how, driving this hilly, glowing road, like over a body. All that country,
a few barns—as far as you can see something warm inside
those hills, a ticking, grass and weeds like hair with a breeze in
it. All named Rouse.

Rouse must have owned it all once.

But I drove down the long gravel into a house held by
termites and a broken-down barn full of old things with no
grace, chipped dishes, years of filth, a prodigy of cobwebs, and
behind the decrepit desk in the basement a woman worthy of a
circus tent, a fat lady sitting under blue light in ruffles and
layers of pink makeup.

"Can I help you young man? What do you collect?"

My eye caught on the chips, the hairline cracks, damage.
I didn't buy anything and when I climbed out of that basement
back to the light, two yapping dogs came at my leg, biting
through the denim.

I returned to Whipple with a bloody patch of trouser. He
made me take them off to wash, he cleaned the tears with io-
dine, I got the job as scout, and in two months time the tall rug
hooker was gone, in an apartment of his own on Lake George,
near the amusement park.

I saw him years later, giving a hand-hooking demonstra-
tion in a tent at the Washington County Fair.

Katy kept the other boys coming, the neighborhood boys
from the fourth grade up through high school. She had them
afternoons, before she fixed her own supper and started on her
homework. I went over nights after dinner with Whipple.

Whipple turned out to be a brilliant cook. He is a very careful person; neat, he measures well. But I left at nine o'clock and walked to Katy.

She didn't like the boys to know she came. It took them years to learn to ask and then she told them no. In fourth and fifth and even tenth grade, she had them all believing it was for them they were doing it. That they were getting something off of her.

You left feeling a mouthful of dust, dust from that couch. You ate dust and a smell entered your clothes. With me that one time, it went on forever, I didn't know how it could stop, I heard the clatter of slow heels on the broken sidewalk, I had a vision of her body severing at the waist, all I had was her legs on either side of me, my fingers on her tummy actually told a ridge, an end of muscle and skin.

Then the five o'clock whistle blew and the shift came out at the mill. I was the only boy that never came back and that turned out for a good reason. I always blamed it a little on her, all of it. Whipple too. I didn't want him then, I was too young and owlish, I was still such a boy. It shouldn't have happened to me then. Maybe I could have been different.

We had something holding us together besides our need for and hatred of school. The faggot and the slut—those teachers hated giving us A's, it was like squeezing out pellets.

But we were in love with the same boy. It was a funny class. Three decent students and something wrong with every one of us. She's trampy in her high heels she falls off of, I'm an old man's queer and Tray—the best boy in our high school is black. He didn't look at either of us, except for talking. He wanted Betsy who made her own dresses with little flowers on them. He had a wild life, though. I think Betsy always dreamed she could straighten him out, like something under a dumb hot iron. By tenth grade he dealt dope and stayed out all night, learning piano and sax from the guys who traveled and played the Lucky Lounge in the Glenns Falls Holiday Inn, thirty miles north of Victory Mills.


## *Katy:* CONFIDENCE


There is a kind of woman, you've met her, she's real old, thirty-nine, forty, or something, fat, no makeup, legs like loose sausages, hair a flat piece of cloth, nothing to draw even a fly to her and she'll tell you a secret, the pride of her solitude— men are threatened by her intelligence.

I used to be the sort of person that believed looking good took lots of time. Shopping got a bad name with me. As if fingernails took hours. You eat protein, they grow like claws. But it is true. There are drawbacks.

Riding the Greyhound down to New York City I decided in the Albany bus station that this was the last day of my life for doing what I don't really want to do.

No more school. Didn't do me any good anyway. Even things I learned for myself and just liked before, remembered in my minutes off—how a bee flies even though it's physically impossible and all about Andrew Jackson's duel—those seemed tainted now and I was ashamed for what pleasure I took in any of it.

I looked like shit in the bus-station bathroom mirror. My hair was mush dead, there were zits around the corners of my mouth, pale skin, I was eating a candy bar, dirty fingers.

First and mostly I wanted all that to change. I wanted to carry myself like somebody. I wasn't garbage and I wasn't going to let anybody treat me that way. I felt a pang for my mother, back in Victory Mills, probably ironing right now, trying in her little ways to keep things up. I remember she told me once how when she went to the hospital to deliver me, she was taking out curlers in the car. She thought if she looked a little nice, people in the hospital would treat her better.

And then I wanted to act and sing. I knew I wasn't trained for singing. Old Man Whipple, the volunteer choir leader, had to admit I had a voice, but he didn't do anything to teach me. He always looked at me from the corner of his eye, like some horror. But I can act. I could act better than the people who got into college, who had never looked this bad in a cracked Greyhound mirror. I could act better than people who won things.

And I started that day.

Growing up with just a mom, I learned no morals the way other people did. She understood when I lied or cheated on a school test. She could feel for a person wanting a thing so bad. I used all that in acting. My mamma taught me pity. That's all you need. That's all you need. I said that once before and Tray used it as a refrain in his band. He didn't credit me either, the bum.

On the bus from Albany to New York I wrote my name on the window's steam with my finger, the way I used to on boys' crewcuts, when their hair was soft and short like an otter's.

I was all alone.

My old man was an old old man who sat in front of the fire all day in the woods, his hands hung down like severed claws, just down in front of him. Even when I went to see him, he couldn't take his eyes off the flames.

## *Alex:* MEMORY

I come into the Fifth Street apartment, my own and only home in New York, turn the key and walk into what should be a Balthus painting. Schubert songs ring off the walls, it's seven o'clock, softly dark outside and not a light on in the place. It's as if nothing works, time stopped, there's some quality of density in the air. The old record player moves over those sad songs. I flicked the hall light on and went into the living room. There she was: Katy. And a new guy, one I hadn't seen before. The windows were open and a breeze blowing in, lacy hialanthus leaves netted against the fire escape. Wind scattered papers—our bills—from the table onto the floor and I sat down in a chair, but they didn't acknowledge me.

Katy—aged twenty-four—lay stomach-down on the couch, wearing only gym shorts, face jammed into the end pillow.

He was kneeling behind her, hovering over her, alert as a cat. One of her knees was bent and her bare calf dallied in the air. He caught her foot, rubbed it, working it between his hands. Then he stopped, squeezed out oil, snuck between her toes, then down her legs, in the cup of her knee, down her thighs.

She seemed floppy to the point of dead, motionless. I didn't worry. I'd seen her like this plenty. It was her state with straight men, with her dates. Sleepy. They were always kneading her, rubbing her, licking her, jamming their tongues into ears, trying to surprise her to interest. She closed her eyes, sank, relapsed, curled down under their fingers. Not what would turn me on. But they massaged her, pummeled her, scratched her, petted her, dug into her neck, whatever she wanted.

And they all helped. Her career was inching up. She got parts. One, the one who braided her hair into a hundred tiny braids, he paid for her singing lessons. She got better. She knew the ones to know.

This is what the men she finds are like—their names are always Jeremy or Joshua or Eliot. She's never once brought home a Chuck or a Dave. They're usually short, no-shouldered—she likes that—and every one of them so far has worn wire-rimmed glasses.

There was a crack, a scratch in the record. The lights

were still out. I sat in my chair, my arms on the armrests thinking how we'd changed. A scratch on a record could make Katy hate her life. I almost found it soothing. I could still hear the music in music. I scouted weekends, I bought a car my sophomore year and drove up Saturday mornings, visited Whipple.

I put myself through college buying antique needlework and Limoges upstate, trotting it in to Sotheby's and selling. I was in graduate school now. As soon as I left for New York, I didn't want Whipple to touch me anymore. For a year or two, we had a weird thing when I visited. We'd sleep in the same bed but we never touched, not even accidentally, even an arm. We fell into deep sound sleeps. I began to understand Katy. Now, the tall man is back with Whipple. They're planting a Japanese garden. They still have the best house in Victory Mills.

Katy shifted on the couch with the scratch. Her eyelids open a little.

"Knobs," she said, her foot wiggling in the air near his face.

Knobs were the hip joints, those ball-bearinglike places in her back and this one knew that. He bent over, greedy, eager, with the silence of a vocation. In the position of a woman kneeling by a river with a washboard, he dug and pummeled her lower back.

She was already successful. She had a running part then, a record contract on an independent label. But still we couldn't imagine in our wildest dreams what she is now. Maybe she could. She had it in her secret and unfolding all the while.

The apartment was trashed that night. Her prosthetic-looking runner's bra hooked over a chair's arm, empty bottles of seltzer lay on the floor. That's right, this one was a runner. Eliot, I think his name was.

They got up and left it all, went to dinner, her head bent down, mumbling, him massaging one of her hands between his. As they walked, he rubbed her wrists and hands and neck, finally getting her in a taxi and then paying for her food in the end.

"Get your hands off her," I wanted to say.

I don't know what time she got in. I stayed up late reading *Varieties of Religious Experience*. A first edition I took from Whipple. It seemed to mean more, words on pages—the first of something. I didn't hear her come in, but the next morning when I woke I heard her humming "Pomp and Circumstance" and I find her sitting on the closed toilet seat, the bathroom door open, combing her hair. It's wet and the comb leaves carved ridges. I always think her hair looks best like that— wet, dark, combed straight back.

"I don't know what you see in him."

"You don't see it?"

"There's not much to see."

"Not everybody's a size queen."

"There are two kinds of people in the world. Size queens and liars."

"Nooooo. There are girls." She sighed, looking at her face in profile. "I've never seen one I couldn't see. It doesn't matter."

"Not if all you want to do is fall asleep."

She picked up the blow-dryer, blared it on.

"You're the one who always wants your life to look more like a magazine," I said. "So stop doing that to your hair. It looks like everybody else. A million cocker-spaniel girls."

"I want white tulips and marble tables and tarnished silver candlesticks. I don't mean my hair. My hair can be like everyone else. You're weird," she says.

"Why do you want to stamp out everything idiosyncratic?"

"It's only looks," she shrugs. "I know what works."

I'm sitting by the window and I hear her move through her closet, hangers jangling on the metal rod, drawers bang shut, the puff and clink of things.

Then I hear her dig through my coin can.

Is it my imagination or do people expect me to pay for

things? Me. The graduate student. I stand up and walk so she can hear me.

"The bus," she calls. "I'm seeing Tray and the guys jam today. You wanna come?"

"No." All these years later, I don't want Tray in the state of New York, not to mention in my life.

But sure enough, that's where he is, in my life, in my apartment, that night and many nights for a long, long time. Our walls are sheer plaster. I can hear and imagine everything. For the first time in years, she doesn't sleep.


It's rare that I get her alone now. But tonight we ate Chinese noodles ourselves on the floor. She was distracted. "He's home in Victory Mills," she says.

"And you're home here with me. So pay attention."

"I'm sorry. I'm just—it's hard to only be noticed for your looks," she says.

"The only thing worse than being wanted for your body is *not* being wanted for your body."

The saving element in Katy is her grin, it's as fast or slow as a thought—real time. "Yeah. You're right. I remember."

The thing about men is, we're not supposed to care about that stuff. We're not supposed to try. Women, they can be beautiful, they should be, we want them smooth. Women talk about buttons and shopping and dry cleaners. We're supposed to just perspire and be.

Have you ever seen a guy who does nothing? Let me tell you something about him. He doesn't look like Cary Grant. You don't remember him. You didn't like him. You hardly even saw him. He reads too many books. He smokes cigarettes. He's attached to black and white movies on TV, popcorn late at night with his roommate on the bed. His friendships mean everything to him. He's getting too old for all this, but he doesn't think so. This—this life—could go on forever. He doesn't understand why all the others want to get up and leave.

## *Katy:* CONFIDENCE

Have you noticed that when couples are just about to split forever, they buy big things? Houses. Cars. Even boats. If they're poor and they can't buy they make. That's when my parents got me, 1961, Victory Mills, New York, my father a Samsonite man.

I was with the same kids all my life from class to class, year to year, that's the way it was in Victory Mills. Once in a while a kid would move and he'd drop off the face of the earth. Once they were gone, they were forgotten. A girl named Linda wrote me a letter once from Michigan. It was really strange getting a letter. It was the first letter I ever got.

It said things like, "I quit smoking and making out," which was weird because she was my friend and I never knew she did those things. It opened up a world like the lid of a trunk.

That was Linda, I could show you her. My roommate Alex had a framed picture of our second-grade class; he can point to each one and tell you what they are doing now, which ones are dead. If he didn't have that, I wouldn't remember what any of them looked like. He's different.

"After the age of twenty-five, everyone you meet is a stranger." That is a direct quote from Alex. He believes it. Probably one reason he's with me. But I don't think that myself. I think the past is random, as random as anything that happens to you today on the street. You can pick what you want, leave the rest. I've abandoned most of my family. Not my mom. My old man just sits in front of the fire and ruins himself.

They weren't any good for me. I still send a present to my mom every Christmas. I remember her, when I was little, giving me blackjack gum. If there was only one stick left at the bottom of her purse, we'd split it.

The rich people, storybooks, the conventions—they had it

right all along. So that is the way I try to live now. That is
why my hair looks like everybody else's. But there are drawbacks. You're less dexterous with long moon-filed nails. Today
I spent twenty minutes with a knife trying to get the knots out
of my sneaker laces. Have you ever thought how knots get *in*to
sneaker laces?

It is a drawback. Being pretty. Doing it in a way like
everybody else. You might say, well, you can get someone else
to get your knots out. I've noticed, now, if you say you live in
downtown Chicago but you miss the country, people will tell
you the country is full of bugs, blackflies, yellow-jackets, blue-
whatevers, and that every bar closes at eleven.

People want to talk you out of regret. As if we can't bear
to know that there are other lives humming along, parallel.

## *Alex:* MEMORY

New York City is really two hundred people. The rest is done
with mirrors.

So come summer, we had to get out. We rented a place
upstate. The year had changed us, none more than Katy, who
had girls coming up to her even at the Saratoga Springs race-
track asking for her autograph.

Tray had a club he was playing downtown with his band,
and even I had a financial coup. After my orals, an eighteenth-
century creweled sampler I found in Rutland ("By the hand of
Rebecca Cole, in her Eight year") went for a hundred and
eleven times what I paid for it.

And Katy was in love with Tray. Most of the reason we
were back upstate was him. We were following him. But I
knew there was trouble, I don't know how I knew. One day I
was driving to Hudson to see some pillars and Tray said he'd
come along. He was like that with me. He didn't ask.

I had just a faint inkling because he wasn't talking as

much to Katy, and a long time ago I heard Betsy and her family had moved.

In Hudson, Tray told me where to drive and then we saw her—I didn't think I'd recognize her, but of course I did, right away. She stood there on the porch, looking out into nothing specific, into Hudson, her lower lip slung open from time, her body taller and fuller than I'd ever seen it, her breasts more subject to gravity. She looked what we used to call ample. She was more grown-up than we were, she had on a housedress, sturdy shoes.

One arm hung down by her side, her palm forward. Whipple once told me that was how you knew women from men, the carrier angle of their arms. And her long arm hung open, asking, her other hand clasped it at the wrist.

I remembered those fisted arms beating the morning air, at nineteen chasing the bus, angry, promising, saying, I can keep up, I'll show you.

And now it was all the humility of disappointment, she stood on the porch, not quite looking at us, staring out blank. "This is what I've become," she seemed to be saying. "Take it or leave it," she said, like a statue.

Rest of the summer, Katy was different. Pretty soon she found an admirer. He was a local caretaker who climbed over the hedge next door and drank tea with her. By August, he was coming through her room window at three o'clock afternoons, so I figured she'd be all right. He's married now, with three kids. The last time I was in Saratoga, I saw him in his green uniform pants, standing by the desk at the library. I walked up behind and heard him asking the librarian for Katy's new album. "It must be checked out," the librarian said.

## *Katy:* CONFIDENCE

There is no front door into acting. You can't do it a straight way. Regular practice, diligence, graduations from one right school to another, all that is nothing. What would the meant confession of a goody-good be, the jazz of a regular guy, a practicer? Acting is the way we all hurt ourselves and bad. It's not about good habits.

I went to NYU today to give a talk to a class. When I left I stood there at the square, watching the hundreds of students that I never was, carrying books. They came to hear what I said, took notes. Two will write me letters thanking me, at the same time asking for help in some obscure way, wanting to know how they can make it like I did and for sure.

If one of them could give a monologue on his own scheming, how he feels silly doing his exercises alone in a room, trying to scream, but the neighbors, from two to four every day, his terror that he doesn't have the thing, the thing without properties, the invisible, the amorphous dark which moves like a roving organ and I know is in me as sure as I have a hand. I like that: the confessions of a schemer. The go-getter's secret terror. But schemers are grudging. All show, no fall down. They'd never tell that.

Still I envy those students with their books. But not for acting.

I am not the first girl men notice. But once they know me, I have them for a long time. I used to say, my open legs are good to fall on. But now I've used that in acting, I've given it words.

When I moved out of the apartment with Alex, I didn't know where I was going. I packed to leave in one morning while he watched me. There was one thing of his I wanted to take and I lifted it off the nail in the wall from where it was hanging over his desk. It was that picture of our second-grade class. Alex is so organized. He keeps his things so nice and neat. He can see where to put a picture on the wall.

He was standing there and his face fell. I saw him go old in an instant, loose flesh from the sides of his cheeks fell around his mouth.

"I need that," he said.

## *Alex:* MEMORY

They all still come around the house. They want to tell me dirt about her. As if it's not perfectly clear where I stand. I've taken to wearing pedal pushers when I receive them.

There is much discussion of her hair, the issue of whether the waves, the mess, are real.

I remembered the bald man, Charlie, he'd sit on the toilet seat, she'd be naked on a towel over the floor, weaving braids.

The last one here was the professor, a married man, wearing wing tips.

"There was one afternoon in this apartment," he told me, "I thought, shit, she'd got this place in this funny neighborhood, it was all she could afford then, I suppose. A lot of girls," (you should have heard him say *girls,*) "would have taken a smaller place in a nice area, decorated, bought clothes . . ."

"Waited," I said.

He sputtered out, laughing. "It was completely empty and I came over to help her paint. We painted for hours, those tin ceilings were a bitch. I sweated. I did the kind of work I'd never done at home.

"There was one wooden chair in the middle of the room." (He pointed to where I was sitting.) "Her belt buckle, still in her jeans, knocked on the floor. She was wearing just an old thin blue T-shirt, paint on it, ripped at the neck, and nothing else.

"I was on that straight chair, just my fly open, she strad-

dled me, I rocked her from her bare waist, all that hair in front
of her face.

"I knew about the others, after me," he said, "Kreiser,
Bustello. I knew about it. They poured so much money into
her." He swallowed the last of his coffee and put the glass
down. "She did what she had to do. She came up here all alone.
Her parents were mill workers. She didn't have any help. She
did what she had to do."


They come here one by one. It's like I'm taking gentleman call-
ers. They tell their lewd stories, looking greedily around the
room, I serve them one cup of coffee and then they leave. And I
never tell them my story. How quiet she was last year after we
came back from the summer Tray married Betsy. I worked on
my dissertation, she was in rehearsal, we were like man and
wife. The house was running a way houses can sometimes—a
good factory, everything comes on time and when you need it.

We jogged together. We steamed vegetables. Her collection of snowball paperweights we lined up on top of a black
bookcase. Our secrets were things like two pints of strawberry
ice cream with our own spoons at midnight. Once, we went to
an old movie (*Easy Money* with Ray Milland at his peak) and
made out under the silver light and then when we came home,
we went to bed. It was my idea, Valentine's Day, and when I
told her I'd never been with a woman since her in fourth grade,
I think she felt she had to go through with it. It was easy, an
underwater feeling, her skin had a smell I was used to, we slept
cradled in each other's arms.

But the next morning, she was standing on a ladder, collecting her snowballs in a bag, leaving. "I feel like getting married," was her apology. "I'm old," she said.


I still live in this apartment. I've done the foyer in a teal blue
copied precisely from a Braque, but nothing in my life changes

fast. I still have her great-grandmother's arched slate grave-stone—Katy's one attempt at collecting. She came home with it after a weekend with Tray, exuberant, falling over from the weight. "You took it from the cemetery?" I asked. She nodded, proud. "Nobody uses it," she said. "And I'll look at it. We'll put it somewhere prominent. You figure out where." We set it on the mantelpiece over the fireplace, our apartment's best thing.

The pushers on our corner still hawk politely, then say, "Have a nice day, Sir," when I shake my head no. So the neighborhood hasn't gone yet. I go to Bergdorf's, the clerks hiss at me in my stretch pants, "Get out if you're not going to buy anything." I pick up a tie and want to whimper, "I can afford it, I just don't *like* it." But here, on Fifth and A, I feel like Mr. Man. "Have a nice day, Sir." *Sir.*

I'm smoking as I walk west, past the low lighted houses, looking up in the windows, the way people in New York always must, where you can partially see.

Katy lives in a house like this, behind solemn brick, she'll be in bed now, dusk, late afternoon, the time when it's still light outside but too dim to read or see clearly in rooms. The air outside turns blue, brighter blue, inside, shades of grey, the thick sheets around her in folds, the furniture still and large beyond her bed, she sinks down turning, her hair a weight, a tickle across her bare back. She hugs the baby, they mold to each other like that and begin turning in the grey, as the out-lines of buildings in the window soften and with a sound like pouring, sifting sand, they turn together, letting themselves loose, allowing footsteps below at the faint edge of hearing. And then there is a streak of pleasure through her breast down her thigh, the elastic push and pull, the exact gasping, they are falling, his feet curl under her hand, they are feeling them-selves fall asleep.

I put out my cigarette under my shoe, wipe my hand on my jeans. They are not thinking of me tonight. Tray is home

where we came from, Katy and her baby bob asleep somewhere
in the sky, and I am out again walking the night streets to-
wards a party, a thin man, eager, believing myself the same
boy who came here years ago, unchanged, still waiting.

A year later, I finally see her again. It's been that long. She
used to phone me, we'd meet at her house, at a restaurant, I'd
write back a postcard, something witty and old, and I wouldn't
hear from her again for about eight months. I'd leave messages. Letters. No answer. Then she calls and it's exactly the
same again. I began to feel guided, she runs the timetable, she
even moved the conversation. Aren't we cool talking about our
love lives last, long after careers and old friends. Moms and
Dads.

We never mention Tray. Not with the baby. Never. I have
no idea what the husband thinks. Barry.

I'd had it. I stopped calling, stopped postcards, this year
I even missed Valentine's Day, which is—for a certain kind of
swish-fag I've become—a national holiday. I had one picked
out too, Thirties' violets, brown letters. Forget it. I gave it to
the fat lady who runs the cheese shop downstairs.

Then her momma died. All those years of smoking. I
heard it from Whipple and went right home. She died on a leaf
weekend in New England, I couldn't get a car, I took the bus
up. It was a rainy day, misty rain, and we were all there in the
cemetery. Whipple, Brad-the-rug-hooker and me in good dark
suits. There were lots of people from the mill, neighbors. I
didn't know anymore who they all were. She came in from the
city carrying her baby through the cemetery, her good high
heels ruining in the grass.

I'd seen her in the city, years of winters, carrying her
shoes in little plastic grocery bags, wearing her sneakers into
fancy parties, hiding them in the lobby.

She'd driven up in a Mercedes, a car as big and dry as a

boat. She stood there, after, fastening the baby into the seat and Whipple bends over and asks her to tea. For my surprise, she says she'll come. She and Whipple were never fond.

"Where's your husband?" Brad says.

"Not here." She's still fussing with the belts on the baby-seat.

And then right there, at the edge of the cemetery, cars pull up, a line of headlights through the fine rain. Mothers wait, hands on steering wheels. Preteen girls run out and clamor at her with their open autograph books, vinyl-covered affairs with little gold locks the way diaries used to be when we were that age.

"I think I'm busy doing something," she said, not taking her eyes off Roy. Then she closed his door, locking it, and walked around to the other side, them tugging at her. "I've got a wet child," she said.

At Whipple's, they served us a real tea. They used everything they'd always had wrapped and hidden and behind glass. Tea and hot milk from the silver samovar with Russian eagles, Sèvres cups and saucers, perfect heavy Georgian spoons. Hot buttered scones, crème fraîche. Katy took her shoes off and set the baby on the floor. He was still a baby but just the end of it, becoming a little boy. She asked for a blanket and got a love-chain Amish quilt and took out her canteen of equipment and started changing him. We all stared. I'd never really seen a baby changed before.

Roy is a beautiful child, one eye blue, one eye green. I'd often daydreamed, walking alone down Manhattan blocks, her tragic death and my inheritance. I imagined the phone calls, the men knocking at my door. Husband and wife on the same plane—

I'd made myself cry when the truth was I wanted to steal him. But now, watching her patient quick fingers move with thoroughness, impersonal purpose, the shit, wiping more of the shit, so a smear streaked the edge of her hand, I turned away. My stomach flipped over once. I didn't want any of it anymore.

It was not for me. Not what I wanted. When I looked back, Whipple and Brad were still staring. Their manners slipped off them. We forgot the order, the tea, the food.

Katy and I were alone a little later when the men moved to the kitchen. All the finery had to be washed and wrapped and put back. The baby was clean now and a baby again, the boy I daydreamed of and Katy and I hung our heads over the carpet. We really hadn't seen each other much for a long time.

Of course, Tray wasn't here and I was, like always. Like the night ten years ago they crowned her beauty queen and Tray didn't come because Betsy was home crying. Tray could have made her safe today, rescued it by showing for one hour. Me, the whole day, gave only a consolation. I knew that, she knew that. I didn't like it. It felt an embarrassment. Why was I still here if I couldn't do more?

Her daddy wasn't there at the cemetery either. He was bad off. He'd been living out in the woods in a little cabin years now, hardly talked to anybody. I guess that's what people do after the big social events—the parties, the weddings, the funerals. They sit around counting who came and who didn't.

"You know what I found?" She showed me a letter in a yellowed envelope. Whipple sold old letters mixed in with the box of postcards.

"From my mom to my dad accepting his proposal."

"Proposal," I said. I scanned the letter. "If you want me, OK," she had written. "You know what you are getting. You understand that my heart is tired. I will try to help us to be happy. But please believe that a part of me is already given away, thrown away, gone forever."

I was stunned. I read on. I didn't want to but I smiled. Her heart had been broken by a man, she said, named Rudy. This had been seven years earlier.

"When was this?" Then I looked at the postmark. Victory Mills, 1949.

"Who is Rudy?"

She shook her head. "Some guy. Some guy in the world. I

don't know. I found it in the basement. I think of it as this trickle of green water, here" she motioned one hand over her chest.

I asked Whipple if there had ever been a guy named Rudy around here. Somehow, I pictured him in New York City. But I was wrong. Whipple and Brad were giving each other sliding, funny looks, Katy and me turned in bewilderment until Whipple said, "I was Rudy. That was me. Rudolph's my middle name. They called me Rudy till I was thirty."

"Did you know that?" Katy went at me like an accusation.

"I never knew till this minute." I looked at Whipple. "You never told me June was in love with you."

He shrugged and rustled, preened a hand through his thin hair. "She wanted to marry me and have children. I could have been your father. But it wouldn't have been you. That was June and your dad. It was a long time ago, I don't remember much. It was nothing that mattered. Just when we were kids."

Katy nodded. It was true. She folded her mother's letter up to save it.

"Were you actually lovers?" This wasn't for Katy anymore. She had her son in her arms, she was rocking, touching the bottoms of his feet so they pulled up back into him, a reflex. She looked ready to go.

This was for me. I was interested.

"Not really. She was, I guess, more than me. It was a one of those."

"But did you sleep together?" I had a photograph, a little snapshot of A. R. Whipple in his twenties. He was a pretty boy, the kind of boy a girl would fall for. Of course, he'd never looked like that since I knew him. I stole the picture once from Whipple long ago.

"Oh, yes. A year almost. She was my first and my last woman. I thought for a while—I don't know. I broke it off with

her and I did the right thing, I'm sure of it. I couldn't have.
Not like that."

And it was still raining outside, shining and dulling spots
of the Japanese garden.

I wanted to talk about it more, all night, I had a thousand
questions, but it was Katy's mother and Katy wanted to go
now. I helped her into her car. Inside she turned the heat on
and it hummed comfortable as a room. We strapped the baby
in, carefully, struggling on his socks. The others had the sense
to leave us alone.

"Don't you want to stay, Katy? Aren't you curious about
what really happened? It's your family."

She shook her head. "No one remembers right. We'll
never know." She lay her hands on the steering wheel and
pushed her shoulders up. Her head fell. The steering wheel was
bound in pale leather and she bit it, held it in her mouth. I slid
down next to her, rubbing her shoulders, rubbing both sides of
her neck. Her eyes closed, her lips loosened. That was all.

# OLD WEST

o

*Richard Bausch*

D ON ' T LET MY AGE or my clothes fool you. I've traveled the world. I've read all the books and tried all the counsels of the flesh, too. I've been up and I've been down and I've lived to see the story of my own coming of age in the Old West find its way into the general mind, if you will. In late middle age, for a while, I entertained on the vaudeville stage, telling that story. It's easy to look past an old man, now, I know. But in those days I was pretty good. The Old West was my subject. I had that one story I liked to tell, about Shane coming into our troubled mountain valley. You know the story. Well, I was the one, the witness. The little boy. I had come from there, from that big sky, those tremendous spaces, and I had seen it all. And yet the reason I could tell the story well enough to work in vaudeville with it is that I no longer quite believed it.

What I have to tell now is about that curious fact.

I've never revealed any of this before. Back then, I couldn't have, because it might've threatened my livelihood; and later I didn't because—well, just because. But the fact is, he came back to the valley twelve, thirteen years later. Joe Starrett was dead of the cholera, and though Mother and I were still living on the place, there really wasn't much to recommend it anymore. You couldn't get corn or much of anything green to grow. That part of the world was indeed cattle country and for all the bravery of the homesteaders, people had begun to see this at last.

We'd buried Joe Starrett out behind the barn, and Mother didn't want to leave him there, wouldn't move to town. Town, by the way, hadn't really changed, either: the center of it was still Grafton's one all-purpose building—though, because it was the site of the big gunfight, it had somewhat of the aspect of a museum about it now, Grafton having left the bullet hole in the wall, and marked out the stains of blood on the dusty floor. But it was still the center of activity, still served as the saloon and general store, and, lately, on Sundays, it had even become a place of worship.

I should explain this last, since it figures pretty prominently in what happened that autumn I turned twenty-three: One day late in the previous winter a short, squat old bird calling himself the Right Reverend Bagley rode into the valley on the back of a donkey, and within a week's time was a regular Sunday sight, preaching from the upstairs gallery of the saloon. What happened was, he walked into Grafton's, ordered a whiskey and drank it down, then turned and looked at the place: five or six cowhands, the cattle baron's old henchmen, and a whore that Grafton had brought back with him from the East that summer. (Nobody was really *with* anybody; it was early evening. The sun hadn't dropped below the mountains yet.) Anyway, Bagley turned at the bar and looked everybody over, and then he announced in a friendly but firm tone that he considered himself a man of the gospel, and it was his opinion that this town was in high need of some serious saviorizing. I wasn't there, but I understand that Grafton, from behind the bar, asked him what he meant, and that Bagley began to explain in terms that fairly mesmerized everyone in the place. (It is true that the whore went back east around this time, but nobody had the courage—or the meanness—to ask Grafton whether or not there was a connection.)

But as I was saying, the town wasn't much, and it wasn't going to *be* much. By now everybody had pretty well accepted this. We were going on with our lives, the children were growing up and leaving, and even some of the older ones, the original homesteaders who had stood and risked themselves for all of it alongside Joe Starrett, who had withstood the pressure of the cattlemen, had found reasons to move on. It's simple enough to say why: the winters were long and harsh; the ground, as I said, was stingy; there were better things beyond the valley (we had heard, for instance, that in San Francisco people were riding electric cars to the tops of buildings; Grafton claimed to have seen one in an exhibit in New York).

I was restless. It was just Mother and me in the cabin, and we weren't getting along too well. She'd gone a little crazy with Joe Starrett's death; she wasn't even fifty yet, but she looked at least fifteen years older than that. In the evenings she wanted me with her, and I wanted to be at Grafton's. Most of the men in the valley were spending the evenings there. We did a lot of heavy drinking back in those days. A lot of people stayed drunk most of the time during the week. Nobody felt very good in the mornings. And on Sundays we'd go aching and sick back to Grafton's, the place of our sinful pastimes, to hear old Bagley preach. Mother, too. The smell of that place on a Sunday—the mixture of perfume and sweat and whiskey, and the deep effluvium of the spittoons was enough to make your breathing stop at the bottom of your throat.

Life was getting harsher all the time, and we were not particularly deserving of anything different, and we knew it.

Sometimes, the only thing to talk about was the gunfight, though I'm willing to admit that I had contributed to this: I was, after all, the sole witness, and I did discover over the years that I liked to talk about it. It was history, I thought. A story—my story. I could see everything that I remembered with all the clarity of daytime sight, and I *believed* it. The principal actors, through my telling, were fixed forever in the town's lore. Several of them were still buried on the hill outside town, including Wilson, the gunfighter who was so fast on the draw, and who was shot in the blazing battle at Grafton's, by the quiet stranger who had ridden into our valley and changed it forever.

He came back that autumn, all those years later, and, as before, I was the first to see him coming, sitting atop that old paint of his, though of course it wasn't the same horse. Couldn't have been. Yet it was old. In cold fact, it was, as I was soon to find out, a slightly swaybacked mare with a mild case of lung congestion. I was mending a fence out past the creek, standing there in the warm sun muttering to myself, thinking about going to town for some whiskey, and I saw him far off, just a slow-moving speck at the foot of the mountains. Exactly like the first time. Except that I was older, and maybe half as curious. I had pretty much taken the attitude of the valley: I was reluctant to face anything new—suspicious of change, afraid of the unpredictable. I looked off at him as he approached, and thought of the other time, that first time. I couldn't see who it was, of course, and had no idea it would actually turn out to be him, and for a little aching moment I wanted it to *be* him—but as he was when I was seven; myself as *I* was then. The whole time back, and Joe Starrett chopping wood within my hearing, a steady man, good and strong, standing astride his own life, ready for anything. I stood there remembering this, some part of me yearning for it, and soon he was close enough to see. I could just make him out. Or, rather, I could just make out the pearl-handled six-shooter. Stepping away from the fence, I waited for him, aching, and then quite suddenly I wanted to signal him to turn around, find another valley. I wasn't even curious. I knew, before I could distinguish the changed shape of his body and the thickened features of his face, that he would be far different from my memory of him. And I knew we would be so much the same—so heartbreakingly like we were the last time he saw us. I thought of my meager town, and the years of idleness in Grafton's store. I wasn't straight or tall, particularly. I was just a dirt farmer with no hope of much and no gentleness or good wishes anymore, plagued with a weakness for whiskey.

Nothing could have prepared me for the sight of him.

The shock of it took my breath away. His buckskins were frayed and torn, besmirched with little maplike continents of salt stains and sweat. He was huge around the middle—his gunbelt had been stretched to a little homemade hole he'd made in it, so he could still wear it—and the flesh under his chin was swollen and heavy. His whole face seemed to have dropped and gathered around his jaws, and when he lifted his hat, I saw the bald crown of his head through his blowing hair. Oh, he'd gone very badly to seed.

"Are you—" he began.

"It's me," I said.

He shifted a little in the saddle. "Well."

"You look like you've come a long way," I said.

He didn't answer. For a moment, we simply stared at each other. Then he climbed laboriously down from the nag and stood there holding the reins.

"Where does the time go," he said, after what seemed a hopeless minute.

Now I didn't answer. I looked at his boots. The toes were worn away; it was all frayed, soiled cloth there. I felt for him. My heart went out to him. And yet as I looked at him I knew that more than anything, more than my oldest childhood dream and ambition, I didn't want him there.

"Is your father—" he hesitated.

"Buried over yonder," I said.

"And Marian?" He was holding his hat in his hands.

"Look," I said. "What did you come back for?"

He put the hat back on. "Marian's dead, too?"

"I don't think she'll be glad to see you," I said. "She's settled into a kind of life."

He looked toward the mountains, and a little breeze crossed toward us from the creek. It rippled the water there and made shadows on it, then reached us, moved the hair over his ears. "I'm not here altogether out of love," he said.

I thought I'd heard a trace of irony in his voice. "Love?" I said. "Really?"

"I mean love of the valley," he told me.

I didn't say anything. He took a white handkerchief out of his shirt—it was surprisingly clean—and wiped the back of his neck with it, then folded it and put it back.

"Can I stay here a few days?" he asked.

"Look," I said. "It's complicated."

"You don't want me to stay even a little while?"

I said nothing for a time. We were just looking at each other across the little distance between us. "You can come up to the cabin," I told him. "But I need some time to prepare my mother for this. I don't want you just riding in on her."

"I understand," he said.


Mother had some time ago taken to sitting in the window of the cabin with my old breech-loading rifle across her lap. When she'd done baking the bread and tending the garden, when she'd finished milking the two cows and churning the butter, when the eggs were put up, and the cabin was swept and clean, and the clothes were all hanging on the line in the yard, she'd place herself by the window, gun cocked and ready to shoot. Maybe two years earlier, some poor, lost, starved, lone Comanche had wandered down from the north, and stopped his horse at the edge of the creek, looking at us, his hands visored over his eyes. He was easily ninety years old, and when he turned to make his way west along the creek, on out of sight, Mother took my rifle off the wall, loaded it, and set herself up by the window.

"Marian," I said. "It was just an old brave looking for a good place to die."

"You let me worry about it, son."

Well, for a while that worked out all right, in fact, it kept her off me and my liquid pursuits down at Grafton's. She could sit there and take potshots at squirrels in the brush all day if she wanted to, I thought. But in the last few months it had begun to feel dangerous approaching the cabin at certain hours of the day or night. You had to remember that she was there, and sometimes, coming home from Grafton's, I'd had enough whiskey to forget. I had her testimony that I had nearly got my head blown off more than once, and once she had indeed fired upon me. This happened about a week before he came back into the valley, and I felt it, even then, as a kind of evil premonition of what was about to happen to us. There I was, ambling sleepily along, drunk, barely able to hold on to the pommel, and letting the horse take me. It crossed the creek, and headed up the path to the house, and the shot nicked me above the elbow—a little cut of flesh that the bullet took out as it went singing off into the blackness behind me. The explosion, the stinging crease of the bullet just missing bone, and the shriek of my horse all sent me flying into the water of the creek.

"I got you, you damn savage Injun," Marian yelled from the cabin.

I lay there in the water and reflected that my mother had grown odd. "Hey," I called, staying low, hearing her put another shell into the breech. "It's me, your little boy."

"I got a repeating rifle here," she lied. She'd reloaded and was aiming again. I could actually hear it in her voice. "I don't have any children on the place."

There is no sound as awful and startling as a bullet screaming off rock, when you know it is aimed earnestly at you.

"Wait," I yelled, "God dammit, Marian. It's me. For Christ's sake it's your own family."

"Who?"

"Your son," I said. "And you've wounded me."

"I don't care what he's done, you'll never get him," she said, and fired again. This time the bullet just buzzed overhead like a terribly fast and purposeful insect.

"Remember how you didn't want any more guns in the valley?" I shouted. "You remember that, Mother? Remember how much you hate them?"

She said, "Who is that down there?"

"It's me," I said. "Good Christ. I'm shot."

She fired again. This one hit the water behind me and went off skipping like a piece of slate somebody threw harder than a thing can be thrown. "Blaspheming savages," she yelled.

"Mom," I screamed. "It's me. I'm sick. I'm coming from Grafton's. I'm shot in the arm."

I heard her reload, and then there was a long silence.

"Marian?" I said, keeping low. "Would you shoot your own son dead?"

"How do I know it's you?"

"Well, who the hell else would it be at this hour?"

"You stay where you are until I come down and see, or I'll blow your head off," she said.

So I stayed right where I was, in the cold running creek, until she got up the nerve to approach me with her lantern and her cocked rifle. Only then did she give in and tend to me, her only son, nearly killed, hurting with a wound she herself had inflicted.

"You've been to Grafton's drinking that whiskey," she said, putting the lantern down.

"You hate guns," I told her. "Right?"

"I'm not letting you sleep it off in the morning, either."

"Just don't shoot at me," I said.

But she had already started up on something else. That

was the way her mind had gone over the years, and you never knew what she'd be into next.

And so that day when he rode up, I told him to stay out of sight, and then went carefully back up to the cabin. "Mother," I said. "Here I come."

"In here," she said from the barn. She was churning butter, and she simply waited for me to get to the window and peer over the sill. I did so, the same way I almost always did now; carefully, like a man in the middle of a gunfight. "What," she said. "What."

I had decided during my stealthy course up the path that my way of preparing her for his return would be to put her out of the way of it, if I could. Any way I could. She was sitting there in the middle of the straw-strewn floor, with a floppy straw hat on her head as though the sun were beating down on her. Her hands looked so old, gripping the butter churn. "Mother," I said. "The Reverend Bagley wants you to bring him some bread for Sunday's communion."

"Who's dead?"

On top of everything else, of course, she'd begun to lose her hearing. I repeated myself, fairly shrieking it at her.

"The Reverend Bagley always wants that," she said, looking away. "I take it on Saturdays. This isn't Saturday. You don't need to yell."

"It's a special request," I said. "He needs it early this week." If I could get her away from the cabin now, I could make some arrangements—I could find someplace else for our return visitor to stay. I could find out what he wanted, and then act on it in some way. But I wasn't really thinking very clearly. Marian and old Bagley had been seeing each other for occasional Saturday and Sunday afternoon picnics, and some evenings, too. There could have been no communication between Bagley and me without Marian knowing about it. I stood there trying to think up some other pretext, confused by the necessity of explaining the ridiculous excuse for a pretext I had just used, and she came slowly to her feet, sighing, touching her back, low, shaking her head, turning away from me.

"Hitch the team up," she said.

It took a moment for me to realize that she'd actually believed me. "I can't go with you," I told her.

"You don't expect me to go by myself." She wiped her hands on the front of her dress. "Go on. Hitch the team."

"All right," I said. I knew there would be no arguing with her. She'd set herself to my lie, and once her mind was set, you couldn't alter it or change it. Besides, I was leery of giving her too much time to think. I'd decided, without having to think about it, that I'd go along, and deal with everything as it came. There was a chance I could get away after we got to town; I could hightail it back here and make some adjustment or some arrangement. "I have to tie off what I'm doing with the fence," I told her. "You change and I'll be ready."

"You're going to change?"

"You change."

"You want *me* to change?"

"You've got dirt all over the front of you."

She shook her head, lifted the dress a little to keep it out of the dust, and made her slow way across to the cabin. When she was inside, I tore over to the fence, and found him sitting on his horse, nodding, half dozing, his hat hanging from the pommel of his saddle, his sparse hair standing up in the wind. He looked a little pathetic.

"Hey," I said.

And he tried to draw his pistol. The horse jumped, stepped back, coughing. His hand missed the pearl handle, and then the horse was turning in a tight circle, stomping his hat where it had fallen, and he sat there holding on to the pommel, saying, "Whoa. Hold it. Damn. Whoa, will you?" When he got the horse calmed, I bent down and retrieved his hat.

"Here," I said. "Jesus."

He slapped the hat against his thigh, sending off a small

white puff of dust, then put it on, and the horse turned again, so that now his back was to me.

"For God's sake," I said. "Why don't you get down off him?"

"Damn spooky old paint," he said, getting it turned. "Listen, boy, I've come a long way on him. I've slept on him and just let him wander where he wanted. I've been that hungry and that desperate." The paint seemed to want to put him down as he spoke. I thought it might even begin to buck.

"Look," I said. "We need to talk. And we don't have a lot of time, either."

"I was hoping I could ride up to the cabin," he said.

I shook my head. "Out of the question."

"No?"

"Not a chance," I said.

He got down. The paint coughed like an old sick man, stepped away from us, put its gray muzzle down in the saw grass by the edge of the water, and began to eat.

"A little congestion," he said.

The paint coughed hoarsely into the grass.

"I can't ride in?"

"On that?"

He looked down.

"Look," I said. "It would upset her. You might get your head shot off."

He stared at me. "Marian has a gun?"

"Marian shoots before she asks questions these days," I said.

"What happened?" he wanted to know.

"She got suspicious," I said. "How do I know?" And I couldn't keep the irritation out of my voice.

He said nothing.

"You can use the barn," I told him. "But you have to wait until we leave, and you can't let her see you. You're just going to have to take my word for it."

Again, he took the hat off, looking down. Seeing the freckles on his scalp, I wished he'd put it back on.

"Wait here and keep out of sight until you see us heading off toward town," I said. And I couldn't resist adding: "There's a preacher who likes her, and she likes him back." I watched his face, remembering with a kind of sad satisfaction the way—as I had so often told it—he'd leaned down to me, bleeding, from his horse, and said, "Tell your mother there's no guns in the valley now."

He put the hat back on.

I said, "I'm hoping she'll be tied up with him for a while, anyway, until I can figure something out."

"Who's the preacher?" he said, staring.

"There's nothing you can do about it," I said.

"I'd just like to know his name."

I said the name, and he nodded, repeating it almost to himself. "Bagley."

"Now will you do as I say?" I asked.

"I will," he said. "If you'll do something for me." And now I saw a little of the old fire in his eyes. It sent a thrill through me. This was, after all, the same man I remembered single-handedly killing the old cattle baron and his hired gun-fighter in the space of a half second. I had often talked about the fact that, while my shouted warning might have been what saved him from the backshooter aiming at him from the gallery, the shot he made—turning into the explosion and smoke of the ambush and firing from reflex, almost as if the Colt in his flashing hand had simply gone off by accident—was the most astonishing feat of gun-handling and shooting that anyone ever saw: one shot, straight through the backshooter's heart, and the man toppled from that gallery like a big sack of feed, dead before he even let go of his still-smoking rifle. That was how I had told the story; that was how I remembered everything.

"All right," I said.

He took a step away from me, and took the hat off again, stood there smoothing its brim, folding it, or trying to. "This Bagley," he said over his shoulder. "How long's he been here?"

"I don't know," I said, and I didn't, exactly. Nobody ever counted much time in those days, beyond looking for the end of winter, the cold that kills. "Sometime last winter, I guess."

"He's your preacher."

"He's one of them."

"Ordained?"

In those days, I didn't know the word.

"What church is he with?"

"No church," I said. "His own church."

"Set up for himself, then."

"He preaches at Grafton's every Sunday."

"Does he wear a holster?"

"Not that I know of."

"You ever see him shoot?"

"No," I said. Then: "Listen, shooting the preacher won't change anything."

He gave me a look of such forlorn unhappiness that I almost corrected myself. "Maybe I won't be staying very long at all," he said.

"Just wait here," I told him.

He nodded, but he wasn't looking at me.

On the way to town, I kept thinking of the hangdog way he'd stood watching me go back to the cabin for Marian—the beaten look of his face and the discouragement in his stance. I wasn't prepared to think I could've so defeated him with news, or with words. Certainly there was something else weighing him down. Marian rode along beside me, staring off at the mountains, her rough, red hands lying on her lap. To tell the truth, I didn't want to know what she might be thinking. Those days, if asked, she was likely to begin a tirade. There was always something working on her sense of well-being and symmetry. Entropy and decline were everywhere. She saw evil in every possible guise. Moral decay. Spiritual deprivation and chaos. Along with her window-sitting, armed to the teeth and waiting for marauders, I'm afraid she'd started building up some rather strange hostilities toward the facts of existence: There had even been times, over the years, when I could have said she wanted all the privileges and rights of manhood, and I might not have been far from wrong. In any case, way out there in the harsh, hard life of the valley, I had managed to keep these more bizarre aspects of her decline from general knowledge. And I'd watched with gladness her developing attachment to old Bagley, who had a way of agreeing with her without ever quite committing himself to the same folly.

"So," she said now. "Why'd you want to get me away from the house?"

For a moment, I couldn't speak.

"I can't believe you'd remember it's the anniversary of our coming here."

Now I was really dumbfounded. Things had worked into my hands, in a way, and I was too stupefied to take advantage of the fact.

"Well?" she said.

I stammered something about being found out in my effort to surprise her, then went on to make up a lie about taking her to Grafton's for a glass of the new bottled Coke soda. Grafton had tried some of it on his last trip to New York, and had been stocking it ever since. Now and then, Marian liked to be spoiled, driven in the wagon to some planned destination and treated like a lady. For all her crazy talk, she could be sweet sometimes; she could remember how things were when Joe Starrett was around and she was his good wife.

"We're not going to see Bagley?"

"We can stop by and see him," I said.

The team pulled us along the road. It was a sunny day, clear and a little chilly. She turned a little and looked behind us in that way she had sometimes of sensing things. "Look," she said.

It was the dust of a lone rider, a long way off, following,

gaining on us. I didn't allow myself to think anything about it.

"I thought I heard you talking to somebody down at the spring," she said. "Could this be him?"

"Who?" I said. It was amazing how often her difficulty hearing yielded up feats of overhearing, long distances bridged in some mysterious transmutation of her bad nerves and her suspicions.

"I don't know," she said. "Whoever you were talking to."

"I wasn't talking to anybody," I said, and I knew I sounded guilty.

"I thought I heard something," she mumbled, turning again to look behind us.

I had ahold of the reins, and without having to think about it I started flapping them a little against the hindquarters of the team. We sped up some.

"What're you doing," she said. "It's not Indians, is it?"

We were going at a pretty good gait now.

"It's Comanches," she said, breathless, reaching into her shawl and bringing out a big six-shot Colt. It was so heavy for her that she had to heft it with both hands.

"Where in God's name did you get that thing?" I said.

"Bagley gave it to me for just this purpose."

"It's not Indians," I said. "Jesus. All the Indians are peaceful anyway now."

She was gazing back, trying to get the pistol aimed that way, and managing only to aim it at me.

"Will you," I said, ducking, "Marian."

"Just let me get turned," she said.

When she had got it pointed behind us, she pulled the hammer back with both thumbs. It fired, and it was so unwieldy in her hands, going off toward the blue sky as she went awry on the seat, that it looked like something that had got hold of her.

"Marian!" I yelled.

The team was taking off with us; it was all I could do to

hold them. She was getting herself right in the seat again, trying to point the Colt.

"Give me that," I said.

"Faster!" she screamed, firing again. This time she knocked part of a scrub pine branch off at the rim of the sky. Under the best circumstances, if she'd been aiming for it and had had the time to draw a good bead on it, anyone would have said it was a brilliant shot. But it knocked her back again, and I got hold of the hot barrel of the damn thing and wrenched it from her.

"All right," she yelled, "God dammit, give me the reins, then."

I suppose she'd had the time to notice, during her attempts to kill him on the run, that he was quickly catching up to us. Now he came alongside me, and he had his own Colt drawn. I dropped Marion's into the well of the wagon seat, and pulled the team to a halt, somehow managing to keep Marian in her place at my side. She was looking at him now, but I don't think she recognized him. Her face was registering relief that he wasn't a Comanche.

He still had his gun drawn. "So," he said. "You were going to warn him."

"What the hell are you talking about?" I said. I was pretty mad now. "Will you put that Colt away, please?"

He kept it where it was, leveled at me.

"I know," I said. "I'm going to get shot. It must be God's plan. First her, and now you."

"You were shooting at me."

"No he wasn't," Marian said. "I was."

He looked at her, then smiled. It was a sad, tentative, disappointed smile. I don't think he could quite believe what time had done to her. She was staring back at him with those fierce, cold, pioneer-stubborn, unrecognizing eyes. "Marian?" he said.

"What."

"You were going to warn him, weren't you."

"Warn who?" I said.

"She knows." He looked past me at her. "Well, Marian?"

"I can't believe it," she said. "After all these years. Look at you. What happened to you?"

He said nothing to this.

"Will you please holster your Colt," I said to him.

"Marian," he said, doing as I asked with the Colt. "You were going to tell him I was here, right?"

"Will somebody tell me what's going on here?" I said.

Marian stared straight ahead, her hands folded on her lap. "My son was taking me to Grafton's for a bottle of Coke soda."

"That's the truth," I said to him. "I was trying to spare her the shock of seeing you. I told you I had to make some arrangements."

"I—I was sorry to hear about Joe," he said, looking past me again.

"Joe," she said. She had merely repeated the name.

He waited.

"She thought you were an Indian," I said.

"I'm here to get a man named Phegley—self-styled preacher. Squarish, small build. Clean-shaven. Rattlery voice. I was hired to chase him, and I think I chased him here."

"This one's name is Bagley," I said. "And he's got a beard."

"He's used other names. Maybe he's grown a beard. I'll know him on sight."

Through all this, Marian simply stared at him, her hands still knotted on her lap. "You're going to kill him," she said now.

"I'm going to take him back to Utah, if he'll come peacefully."

"Look at you," she said. "I just don't believe it."

"You haven't changed at all," he said. It was almost charming.

"I don't believe it," my mother said under her breath.

He got down off his horse and tied it to the back of the wagon, then climbed up on the back bench.

"I hope you don't mind," he said, nodding politely.

"We really are going to Grafton's," I said.

"That's fine."

"I don't think Bagley will be there."

"I'm sure I'll run into him sooner or later."

"If somebody doesn't warn the poor man," Marian said.

"Well," he said. "Bagley will use a pistol."

Then we were just going along toward town. In a way, we were as we had once been—or we were a shade of it. The wagon, raising its long column of dust, and the horse trotting along, tethered to the back. I held the reins as Joe Starrett had held them, and wondered what the woman seated to my right could be thinking about.

Bagley lived in a little shed out in back of the old stables. The smell of horses was on him all the time, though he never did any riding to speak of, and he never quite got himself clean enough for me to be able to stand him at close quarters for very long. Back then, of course, people could go through several seasons without feeling it necessary to be anywhere near the vicinity of a bath, and Bagley was one of them. On top of this, he was argumentative, and usually pretty grumpy and ill-tempered. And for some reason—some unknown reason fathomable only to her, and maybe, to give him the credit of some self-esteem, to Bagley, too—Marian liked him. He had a way of talking to her as if the two of them were in some sort of cahoots about things (I had heard him do this, and had marveled at it, wondered about it). And he'd done some reading. He'd been out in the world, and around some. He'd told Marian that when he was a younger man, he'd traveled to the farthest reaches of the north, and got three of his toes frozen off, one on one foot and two on the other. Marian said she'd seen the proof of this. I didn't care to know more.

What I found interesting was the fact that Bagley was usually available for our late-night rounds of whiskey drinking, and was often enough among the red-eyed and half sick the following morning—even, sometimes, Sunday morning. In fact, it was when he was hung over that he could be really frightening as an evangelist: the pains of hell, which he was always promising for all sinners, were visible in his face. He looked like one of those crazed, half-starved prophets come back from forty days and nights in the desert.

I hadn't had a lot to do with him in the time he'd been in town, but I had told him the story of the gunfight. It was on one of those nights we were all up drinking the whiskey and talking. We were sitting in Grafton's around the stove, passing a bottle back and forth. It was late. Just Grafton and Bagley and me were left. I went through the whole story: The cattle baron and his badmen trying to run us all off, and the stranger riding into the valley and siding with us, the man with the pearl-handled Colt, and the tense nervous hands, who seemed always on the lookout for something. The arrival of Wilson, a killer with the cold blood of a poisonous snake. And the inevitable gunfight itself, my memory of Wilson in black pants, with a black vest and white shirt, drawing his Colt, and the blazing speed of the hands that beat him to the draw. Bagley listened, staring at me, like consternation itself.

"Wilson was fast," I said to him. "Fast on the draw."

"Young man, you should tell stories of inspiration and good works. Do I detect a bit of exaggeration in your story?"

"Exaggeration," I said. I couldn't believe I was being challenged.

"A little stretching of things, maybe?"

"Like what?" I said. Angry now.

"I don't know. What about this Wilson? Was he really so cold-blooded?"

"He shot a man dead outside on that street. We buried him the day before the fight."

"And he wore black?"

I nodded. "Except for the white shirt."

"I knew a Wilson," he said. "Of course, that's a common name. But this one was a professional gunfighter, too. Sort of. Not at all like the one you describe. I heard he was shot somewhere out in the territories."

This had the effect of making me quite reasonlessly angry, as though Bagley was trying to cast some doubt on me. It also troubled something in my mind, which glimmered for a second and then went on its unsettling way. I was drunk. There were things I didn't want to talk about anymore. I was abruptly very depressed and unhappy.

"What is it, son?" he said.

"Nothing."

He leaned back in his chair and drank from a bottle we had all been passing around.

"I seem to remember Wilson as wearing buckskins," Grafton said.

"No," I said, "he was wearing black pants and a black vest over a white shirt. And he had a two-gun rig."

"Well," said Bagley. "The Wilson I knew carried this old heavy Colt. Carried it in his pants."

"I don't think I remember two guns," said Grafton.

"It was two guns," I said. "I saw them. I was there."

"Boy *was* there," Grafton said to Bagley.

"Must not be the same Wilson," Bagley said.

"You ever been in a gunfight, Reverend?" Grafton asked him.

"No, I usually run at the first sign of trouble."

"Do you own a gun?" I asked him.

He shook his head. "I had one once. Matter of fact, this Wilson fellow—the one I knew—he gave it to me. Come to think of it, he had three of them. And he carried them all on his person. But the one he used most was always stuck down in his belt."

"Why would he give you a Colt?" I asked him.

"I don't recall. Seems to me I won it from him, playing

draw poker. We were both a little drunk. He could be an amiable old boy, too. Give you the shirt off his back if he was in a good mood. Trouble was, he wasn't often disposed to be in a good mood."

"Was this Wilson fast on the draw?" I asked.

He made a sound in his throat, cleared it, looking at me. "When he was upset, he was quick to shoot people, if that's what you mean."

"Was he fast?"

"I don't think he thought in those terms. He usually had his Colt out and already cocked if he thought there would be any reason to use it. And as I said, he was quick enough to use it."

Grafton said, "You know quite a bit about this sort of thing, don't you, Reverend?"

Bagley nodded, folding his hands across his chest. He looked at me. "I guess I saw some things over the years of my enslavement to sin."

"But you were never in a gunfight?"

"I said I usually run."

"Did you ever find yourself in a circumstance where you couldn't run?"

"Once or twice," he said, reaching for the bottle.

"And?" I said.

He smiled, drank, wiped his whiskered mouth. "Why, I shot from ambush, of course." Then he laughed, loud, offering me the bottle. "There are several states of this union which I am not particularly anxious to see again."

"Do you mean you're wanted?" Grafton asked him.

"I don't really know," he said. "It's been a long time, and I've traveled so far."


When he wasn't preaching, he seemed fairly inactive. Marian had never had any trouble figuring where he'd be. His sole support was what he could collect on Sunday, and what he could make helping out with the work of keeping the stables. He was fond of saying that no task was too low for sinners. Sometimes when he preached, if he wasn't thumping the Old Testament and spitting fire, he was inclined to talk about the dignity provided by simple work. And sometimes, too, he talked about odd, unconnected things: Galileo and Napoleon; the new English queen; the tragic, early death of the English writer Dickens. Everything was a lesson. He'd fix you with his old, hooded eyes, and his thin lips would begin to move, as though he were chewing something unpalatable that was hurting his gums, and then he would begin to talk, the sentences lining up one after the other, perfectly symmetrical and organized as well as any written speech. We had all got to trusting him, not as the figure we would look to for succor, or solace, particularly; but as a predictable and consistent form of diversion, of entertainment.

At least that was how I felt about him.

And so some coloration of that feeling was rising in me as I drove the wagon into town and stopped in front of Grafton's, wondering if Bagley was there and what would happen if indeed he was. The street was empty. There weren't even any other horses around. Wind picked up dust and carried it in a drunken spiral across the way, where the dirt lane turned down toward the stables.

"Grafton," Marian called, getting down. "You open or not?"

The door was open. She went up on the wooden sidewalk and down to the end of it, looked up and down that part of the crossing street. She waited there, a minute. Then she came back and went into the saloon. In the wagon now it was just me and our returning visitor.

I said, "Tell me. What did Bagley—Phegley—do?"

"I can't say I know, for sure. His name was posted. There's a reward."

"How much?" I asked.

He shrugged. "Five hundred dollars dead."

"And alive?"

"Five hundred twenty-five."

I looked at him.

"It was a private post."

"And you don't even know what he did?"

"I could use the extra twenty-five dollars," he said. "I'm willing to take him back alive."

"You're—you're a peace officer, then?"

He shook his head, looking beyond me at the tall façade of Grafton's storefront.

"Is it personal?" I said.

"It's business," he mumbled. "Old business, too."

"You're just a bounty hunter," I said. "Is that it?"

He gave me a quizzical look, as if he hadn't understood the question. "What do you think?"

"And you wanted me to grow straight and tall," I said.

"You were a little boy. That's what you say to little boys. Some of them do, you know. Some of them grow straight and tall. Look at Joe Starrett."

"I don't want to think about that," I said. "I was thinking about you."

Now Marian came back toward us, and behind us Grafton opened the door to the saloon, looking worried. "Don't come in," he said. "I don't want any trouble here," He squinted, and peered at us.

"We're looking for Bagley," I said. By now, I simply wanted to see what would happen.

"I don't think you should come here."

"Is he in there?" I said.

"He's where he always is this time of day," Grafton said. "The stables, sleeping it off."

Marian had climbed back onto the wagon seat. "Take me to him," she said to me.

"Wait," Grafton said. "I want to see this, too." And he climbed up into the back of the wagon, arranging his besmirched white apron over his knees.

. . .

So it was the four of us who rode around to the stables, and pulled up at the shady, open entrance. We sat there for a moment. Then Marian got down and stood in the rising dust and looked at me. "I'm going to go tell him we're here."

"He's a man who will use a gun," Shane said.

"This isn't your man," said Marian.

And Bagley's voice came from one of the windows above the street, I couldn't see which one. "Who wants to see the preacher?"

Now Grafton got down, too. He and Marian were standing there next to the wagon.

"Bagley," I said. "There's a man here looking for somebody named—

But then Marian went running toward the open doorway. "Don't shoot!" she yelled. "Don't anybody shoot!"

Grafton had moved to take hold of her arms as she swept past him. She was dragging him with her toward the shade of the building.

From the nearest window, I saw Bagley's black gun barrel jutting out.

"Everybody just be calm," Marian was shouting. "Let's all just wait a little bit. Please."

But nobody waited for anything. Bagley fired from the window and the bullet hit the planks just below my foot. I have no idea what he could've been trying to hit, but I assumed he had through some mistake been aiming at me, so I dove into the back of the wagon—and there I collided painfully with the balding, deeply lined face of my childhood hero.

I had struck him in the bridge of his nose with my forehead, and instantly there was blood. It covered both of us. We looked at each other. I saw blind, dumb terror in his eyes. All around us was the roar of gunfire, explosions that seemed to come nearer, and we were crouching there, bloody and staring at each other. "Save me," I said, feeling all the more frightened for what I saw in his eyes—the scared little life there, wincing back from danger, sinking, showing pain and confusion and weakness, too.

I was a boy when the other thing happened. I had remembered it a certain way all those years, and had told the story a certain way, and now, here under the random explosive, struck-wood sound of ricocheting bullets, I was being given something truer than what I'd held in my mind all that time.

At least that is what I've been able to make of it. I know that everything seemed terribly familiar, and that something about it was almost derisively itself, as if I could never have experienced it in any fashion but like this, facedown in a wagon bed with my hands over my head.

"Everybody shut up," Marian was yelling. "Everybody stop."

From somewhere came the sound of Bagley reloading, counting aloud. "One, two, three." His voice was imbued with an eerie kind of music, like happiness.

"Bagley!" I yelled. "It's me!"

"I'm going to have to shoot all of you," Bagley said. "That's the way it's going to have to be. Unless you turn that wagon around and get out fast. And take him with you."

"John Bagley you listen to me," Marian said from somewhere in the dust.

But then everything was obliterated in the noise of the shooting, even her shrill and frantic cries. It seemed to go on and on, and to grow louder. I didn't know where anyone was. I lay there in the wagon bed and cried for my life, and then it was over and in the quiet that followed—the quiet that was like something muffled on the eardrums, a physical feeling, a woolly, prickly itch, coupled with the paralyzed sense of a terrible dumbfoundedness—I heard my own murmuring, and came to understand that I had survived. After a long wait, I stood up in the wagon bed and looked at Marian lying in the dust of the street, and at poor Grafton, sitting against one of the bales of hay by the stable door, his hands open on his thighs as though he had just paused there to get out of the brilliant autumn sun that was beating down out of the quiet sky. Bagley lay in the upstairs window, his head lolling down over the pocked sill. A little breeze stirred his hair. The man who had brought his gun back into the valley lay at the back wheel of the wagon, face up to the light, looking almost serene. The whole thing had taken about thirty seconds, if that.

I have come from there to here.

I buried Marian with Joe Starrett out behind the barn. Someone else, I don't know—someone from the town—took the others away. I traveled away from the valley, and never went back. I have grown old. My life draws back behind me like a long train. I never knew what it was Bagley had done to be posted, nor what Marian wanted to accomplish by throwing herself into the middle of everything, nor what poor Grafton must've thought when he dropped down in the street with the bullet in his lungs.

When I think of it, though, I find a little truth that means more to me than all my subsequent reading, all my late studies to puzzle out the nature of things: nothing could be simpler, but what I remember now, in great age, is that during the loudest and most terrifying part of the exchange of shots, when the catastrophe was going on all around me, and I was most certain that I was going to be killed, I lay shivering in the knowledge, the discovery, that the story I'd been telling all my life was in fact not true enough—was nothing more than a boy's exaggeration.

And this is what I have come to tell you.

That the clearest memory of my life is a thing I'd made up in my head. For that afternoon at the stables, in the middle of terror, with the guns going off, I saw it once again, without words, the story I'd been telling since I was seven years old, only this time it was just as it had actually been. I saw again the moment when the gunfighter Wilson went for his Colt, and he was indeed not all in black, not wearing two guns, nor any holster, but sloppily draped in some flannels of such faded color as to be not quite identifiable. I saw it like a searing vision: what it had *really* been—a man trying to get a long-barreled pistol out of the soiled tangle of his pants, catching the hammer of it on the tail of his shirt. And the other, the hero, struggling with his own weapon, raising it, taking aim, and firing—that shattering explosion, a blade of fire from the end of the pistol, and Wilson's body crashing down between a chair and table. The hero then turning to see the cattle baron on the other side of the room reach into his own tight coat, and a boy watching the hero raise his heavy Colt to fire upon the cattle baron, too—the cattle baron never even getting his weapon clear of the little shoulder holster he had.

And it was all over. Like murder, nothing more.

Do you see? No backshooter firing from the gallery. Just the awful moment when the cattle baron realized he would be shot. And the boy watching from under the saloon door saw the surprised, helpless, frightened look on the old, whiskered face, saw this and closed his eyes, hearing the second explosion, squeezing his eyes shut in horror, for fear of looking upon death anymore, but hearing the awful clattering fall, and the silence that followed, knowing what it was, what it meant, and hearing, too, now the little other sounds—the settling in of ragged breath, the sigh of relief. Beginning, even then, in spite of himself—in spite of what he knew and had just seen—to make it over in his mind, remembering it already like all the tales of the Old West, the story as he would tell it for more than seventy years, even as he could hear the shaken voice, almost garrulous, of the one who had managed to stay alive—the one who was Shane, and who, this time, hadn't been killed in the stupid, fumbling blur of gunfighting.

# DON'T EVER GET

# DAUNTED

O

*Carolyn See*

"I TOOK THE TRAIN from Dallas, caught it as the sky turned a pale and milky green. I rode it down to El Paso, then over to San Antone. I had murder on my mind. I had my father's pistol. He was once in a gunfight. He shot a man. Right there in the dust. This here's his watch."

The gold circle swung out from tweed vest, carefully buttoned. Gray light spun away from it. Lucinda put off turning on the lights. ("How *you* were raised is one thing, Bowlie. But pennies saved add up.")

"My daddy was one of the last of the slave owners. *His* daddy gave him his own boy when he was born. In those days white folks all had their black folks. Black folks had their white folks. Once, in a railroad car, a Nigra girl called to me. 'You got five dollars, white boy?' Course I had."

Young Bowland, married now, scuffed his oxfords on his flowered rug. "Jeez, Georgie."

Green couch. Green chair. Blond end table. Room for the radio. Coffee table paved with dark red Catalina tiles. The last of the sun, gold-yellow, caught eight inches of hardwood floor. The room so small their knees, from couch, easy chair, striped occasional, almost touched the tiled table. Just beyond this living room in Eagle Rock, California, the dining room; a bridge table, two colored napkins, green, two pottery plates, red. A sideboard, Fostoria glass locked away. To the left, two bedrooms and a bath. Beyond the dining room, a kitchen with a swinging door. A smell of string beans. Of pork.

"She'd left me. The only girl who ever left me. I had a job as a check assorter at the time, down in El Paso, midnight to eight in the morning, so I could have the days to visit my sister, Nell. She was still pretty good then. Remember, Bowlie?"

Lucinda drew her breath. Cousin Nell. Every family had its saints. Sappy eyes rolled to heaven. Silly blouse. Sunken chest. Ready for the san. Nothing remarkable.

"When I met the girl I brought her to see Nell. She took one look at her and fainted to the floor. Still. Still, Bowl. When she left in the night I couldn't do for it. I couldn't let it happen. I took the train home to Dallas. My daddy was right there on the porch, seems like just where I left him. I told him everything. He listened to me without a word, then he got up, and hitched his pants the way he did, and went into the front door. When he came back he had the gun. 'This has already killed one man and one woman, Georgie. I reckon it can kill another if it has to.' "

The men remembered: not the deaths, but the room the old man had gone into: crammed with horsehair furniture, kerosene lamps, pictures; one of Sir Galahad, one of Sam Houston. And behind, a long, green, weedy yard, with a tire swing and a fort and a creek at the end. A screen porch with trays of corn bread, cooling, and low bowls of clabbered milk, and soft bacon under dish towels, waiting for the next meal. Dallas. Oak Cliff.

"He handed the gun to me and he said the strangest thing. He said, 'Georgie, you're the youngest. I don't want you to ever get daunted. Just don't ever get daunted.' That would have been the farthest thing from my mind, as you know. I took the gun, checked to see if it was loaded, then jumped right back on the train to El Paso, where I'd last seen them. When I got there, they were gone. That's when I took—the same train, must have been, out of there—and the sky turned that milky green. I was out of my mind by then. Ready to kill."

Lucinda stood up, pulled her skirt down, swung out to the kitchen to check on things.

"... *Boy!* Does she always dress like that? Where's the drinks, Bowlie Boy? Where's the *alcohol?*"

Cousin Georgie leaned forward, his hands out for display on each knee. His brown curly hair was parted in the middle, his face clean-shaven. He wore a three-piece suit, guarded by his father's gold watch. His eyes noticed everything, the corners of the room, his cousin's face dimming in the twilight, the knickknack shelf with things that had been in the family for years, and glazed figurines—wedding presents—from Lucinda's side.

"To think you'd land in this! Your mother'd be proud. Remember when we'd pick up nickels rolling that baby carriage filled with booze up and down the streets of Oak Cliff for Ted Tedford . . . was it *Red* Tedford?"

Bowlie nodded. He remembered all of it, the grimy Negro girl in the boxcar raising her skirt in the stinking straw, the flies, the boys outside whispering, waiting their turn. Remembered crawling under the board dance floor out in the park on Saturday nights in summer. Some boys looked *up,* to see what girls wore bloomers and who cheated in the humid Oak Cliff night and left them off. Other boys turned their concentration *down,* searching for coins in the loose sand, small change dropped from bachelors' pockets. He remembered it all, but he didn't think much of it. He'd come west four years before, found his job in a music store, wooed Lucinda at the shop. She said his accent was cute, saved her salary for this house. A bargain at four thousand, her father had chipped in. Lucinda was a gardener. Asters in back as big as dinner plates. Nasturtiums along the driveway. Azaleas. Church.

The ghost of a question, formed in the tiny room between the two young men, a comparison; a way of seeing. To forestall it, Bowland said, "We were sorry we couldn't get back to Nell's funeral. But with money the way it's been—"

"I took my sister's body on the train, back to Dallas. Sat by the pine box in the baggage car. All the songs she used to like, I sang to her. 'I Wish I Could Shimmy Like My Sister Kate.' 'Thousand Mile Blues.' She couldn't mind. I buried her by Mama and Daddy. A whole cemetery there, full of *us,* boy. Cochranes and Records and Lawses. A party of their own out there." His voice quavered. Bowlie reached over with a sudden gesture to turn on the lamp.

The door swung open. Lucinda came forward, carrying a round tray made of twine looped and twisted on a circular board until the twine had covered it, lacquered to a bright finish. Two handles, made of lacquered rope. Three small jelly glasses half filled with Welch's grape juice shimmered. A saucer held six Ritz crackers, very lightly spread with Kraft pimiento cheese.

"Ah," George said. He leaned over, took a glass, brought it to his lips for one small sip. His cousin's eyes stayed on him.

George went on, almost gaily. "It's a good thing you weren't there for Nell's last days. Her sweet ways were gone. I came in every morning after work, before I went to bed, before it got hot. I changed her linen there in the hospital, I changed her gown. I sponged her off. It was easy. She couldn't have weighed more than eighty pounds. Do you remember when *Bob* died? That was another thing entirely. Eighteen years old, ten days out of high school, the first day on the job—the sanitation commissions, that's *sewers* down in Dallas—" He smiled at Lucinda, who sat stiffly in her occasional chair, well out of the circle of yellow light. "First day, he manages a scratch on the back of his hand. Ten days later he's down with typhoid, two weeks later he's dead. *You* came over to the house, then, din't you, Bowlie? I remember Mama lighting a torch of newspapers and sailing through Bob's room with it held high over her head, the ashes and the fire falling around her, to cut the sickroom smell."

"Dinner's going to be ready soon," the girl said to her husband. "Pretty soon you'll have to say good-bye." Her irritation snapped in the air. Even her husband appeared shocked, but George went on, even brighter.

"That's probably the first time Daddy said to me, 'Don't ever get daunted. If they land you in Egypt somewhere, don't even worry about it.' It don't make no never mind *where* they land you, is what he said, and I live by those words. With Nell and Bob gone, and Mama and Papa—"

"Bowlie," the girl said. *"Please."*

*"This one,"* the visitor told Lucinda, cocking his head toward his cousin, her husband, "shot me once! He ever tell you that? I *bet* he did! He and Bob and Red Tedford and I had our daddies' rifles out. We were just fooling around, like boys will. But Mama hated guns and she said, 'Git these things out of the house and *into the yard!*' Do you remember, Bowlie, how Mama usen to say, 'It's no disgrace to be poor if you can make poor be *noble* and *fun?*' Do you remember how she used to cook bacon? How you could wrap it around your finger? How when you'd come over to stay for the night you'd say, 'Aunt Lavinia? Can I have some of that wraparound bacon you make so well?'

Lucinda stood.

"Sit down right there, Lucie, honey, and let me finish telling you about this. We was playin' the way boys do, pushin' and shovin' each other around the parlor and Mama about had a fit and said, 'Boys! Git out of here. Git out! Git!' Well, Red was cast down, and he started shufflin' toward the back door, just as if I were to start to *castigate* Bowlie right now and iffn he was to slide right by those dinner plates with a look of shame. But *Bob,* he *loved* Mama, and he knew she loved him, and she wouldn't have him long, but how was he to know that?

So he started waltzin' her around the room, sideways through the furniture. I says to Bowlie, 'Git on out of here like my Mama says.' He says, 'Nobody here's got the right to tell me what to do.' Mama says, 'Bowlie Boy, I'm tellin' your mama soon as I see her what *you* think of respect, what *you* think of the Good Knight!' Some might have thought she meant good night, g-o-o-d n-i-g-h-t, but she was wavin' over Bob's shoulder at our picture of Sir Galahad. Bob laughed but Bowlie didn't think it was funny. He stood there looking as stupid as might be, and I poked him with Daddy's .22. He wrestled it away from me and what with one thing and another the gun went off and went in right here, just under my collarbone."

George patted his chest directly over his heart. "It went straight into my breast. Mama gave a mighty scream and collapsed into Bob's arms. She thought she had seen her youngest son die right there. She would see every one of them into the next world, or, more strictly, she would have the pain of it. I sat down in a straight chair, just like the one you're sitting in, Lucinda. I was fixin' to die. They stood and watched me. Mama cried."

George reached across the tiny room, grabbed Lucinda's hand, put it flat against his thin chest. "Just under my ribs, if you were to look, you'd find a bullet. They couldn't figure how to get it out so they put a poultice on it and let the skin heal over. I read some Joseph Hergesheimer when I was waiting for the tetanus to set in. I read some James Branch Cabell. The darling of the intellectuals. It never came though. The tetanus."

When George smiled his thin, freckled face moved so completely that his ears—big, pale, freckly ears—lifted by almost a quarter of an inch. He smiled now, and waited, relaxing back on the cheap couch, completely at ease, immovable.

"The girl," Lucinda said. "What about her?"

"Girl?"

"The one you followed. On the train."

"Oh, honey. That was a terrible night. I had already gone

seventy-two hours without sleep. I had buried my sister. I had been betrayed by the girl I loved. She had run off with a rich man. A banker. When I heard that he'd taken her on over to San Antonio I almost lost my mind. I bought a quart of rye whiskey. No, I had brought it *with* me, from Dallas, Oak Cliff, after I said good-bye to Daddy. I sat up all night drinking and crying, looking out the window at the awful desert sand. Thinking of my life. The train pulled in at dawn. I went straight to the barber for a hot towel and a shave." George smiled at Lucinda. "There *are* times," he said, "when you want to look your very best. You don't want to look like a ragpicker. Do you remember what Jurgen's beautiful mistress said? When she begged him just to *pretend* that they were conforming? And that then together they could have a wonderful life? But Jurgen said *no,* he could never pretend?"

Bowlie snorted. His cousin continued, looking at Lucinda. "I went into a drugstore and ordered up a Green River. I waited for the clock over the bank to reach seven-thirty in the morning. There were three hotels in town where they might have been staying. I went to the best one, walked in, told the boy behind the counter that I was Western Union. 'Go right up,' he said. I knocked on the door. *Western Union!* Then I was in there with them, standing at the foot of their bed. The morning sun took her face. It was crumpled, all along the right cheek, from the way she'd been sleeping. *He* turned pale, pulled the sheet up to his chin just the way you see in the movies. Afraid of the gun, you see. 'Get out of bed,' I told him. 'Go stand in the corner.' I wanted no truck with him. She knelt up in bed, naked as a peach. 'Whatever you do,' she said. 'Whatever you do.' "

George fell silent. Lucinda waited until she could stand it no longer. "What happened? What did you do?"

"I said to her, 'Whatever *you* do, you'll never find a boy who loved you more than I.' Then I put the safety catch back on Daddy's pistol. I took another train with the last of my money, heading west, coming out to Los Angeles. I couldn't stand the sight of any more Texas. I hung back from coming here until I could get on my feet. Family can be a burden in these hard times."

"We only have two chops!"

George cocked his head. He seemed not to have heard.

"That's why . . . I've been hesitating about dinner."

George shrugged. "Honey, it's *my* bad manners. I plumb forgot the time. It's been so long since I spent time with family. I should have looked at my watch!"

"It won't take any time to make up a batch of biscuits. I know I've got a can of Spam out there. And some other little things."

"*I* know why you were waiting! My cousin told you sorry tales about me."

Bowlie Cochrane looked at his shoes and smiled. "Not going to be part of this," he remarked, but his wife blushed deeply in the lamplight.

"Maybe it was just me," she said. "I'm willing to admit that. Do you smoke?"

Again George cocked his head and listened hard.

"I like for Bowlie to smoke outside. There on the side porch. I like for the house to stay clean. But if you boys would like a smoke . . . Bowlie, you could show George the yard."

Once they were outside Bowland shoved his cousin brutally in the ribs. "You son of a gun! Talk about a pistol. Christ. Kee-rist. Come on out to the garage."

They stepped onto a skimpy cement driveway. A huge moon lit their way to a rickety frame building. Bowlie swung the door open, groped for the overhead string, snicked on a light.

Behind cans marked gasoline, a jar of clear liquid stood by two jelly glasses, like the ones on the twine tray. "She don't never come out here." He filled the glasses to the very brim. They drank them down and shivered. "That's something," Bowland said. "Good as Tedford's. Better." He poured again, then laughed, bleating. "Would have given five to ten," he said. "Would have laid hunert to one. But this is the only time, Georgie. I mean it. Don't mess with us. Don't mess with her. I work at her daddy's store. Make fifty a week. Don't mess with the chicken."

"How *long,* Bowl?"

"'Til times get better. That's what I say. We'd best get back to the porch. *She's* got an eye! Oh, Lord."

They pulled out cigarettes. *"She* don't know the difference. Between one smell and another."

Behind them, lit by yellow light, Lucinda set another place, changed pottery to china, brought out the Fostoria. They lounged on the side porch, against wooden posts, watching her hustle.

"Pretty girl. Nice, too."

Bowland snickered. "Oh, Lord."

"Why don't you write your mama, Bowl?"

"Never going back, that's why."

George turned away from the framed light.

"I don't care if I do either." But between the two boys yawned an abyss. Bowland's mother lived in a home with worked rugs, crystal vases filled with fruit, a mowed front lawn, her membership in the Daughters of the Confederacy up to date. The Depression hadn't touched Aunt Belle and Uncle Tom. Bowlie'd run off, but he'd come back when Lucinda popped babies. Any fool could see it. George had lost a sister and a brother. His house had burned when he was just a baby. The house he had grown up in was rented and unkempt. Sir Galahad made no headway against Hard Times. His sister Nell spitting blood into newspaper cones—that burnt sugar smell. His mother dead, some said by her own hand. His father had advised: "Don't ever get daunted." Then he'd turned, put his fist through the screen door, taken three steps into the dark. Fallen. George stood on the porch, waited, went in and found the gun, left. The girl in San Antone, whom he'd cried to,

begged to come back with him, had laughed—in the same kind
of merciless morning heat his sister had died under; asked him
a pointed question: Did he have the money to support her?
When was the last time *he'd* had a meal?

How did you live when life was insupportable? When the
body you found in the upstairs screen porch was your
mother's? When the first breasts you touched were your own
sister's, pressing, pressing down on them to stop the cough that
never stopped? When your brother cried as you rolled him off
the sheets he'd soiled, and you had to take them out to the caul-
dron—on the boil for two weeks now in the backyard—because
there was no one else to do it, Mama in bed crying, Nell away
in the san, Daddy drunk, Belle keeping her distance for fear of
contagion? And those black folks everyone said were "there for
you in time of need" weren't there either, so afraid were they
of typhoid. Of TB.

"I mean it, Georgie. Just for tonight. I know how you are
with the girls. I mean to keep this one for my own. But *boy,*
you had her going there. Wrapped around your finger. Wraparound bacon. How long you been out here anyway? What do
you plan to do?"

"I've seen hard times before. The first winter Nell was
sick. We didn't have a lot. We did have a barrel full of—"

"—potatoes. I heard the story."

"Every night my mama would send Daddy down to the
basement for four potatoes—there were still four of us then.
We'd eat them with clabbered milk—"

"I know, Shortstop. He always got the best four."

"That's right. He'd say, we're living off the fat of the
land. So don't worry about it, Mama. Don't . . . How about
another slug before dinner? Think you could manage it?"
Again the two went to the rickety garage, drained two jelly
glasses, gasped. In the bright light George looked at his cousin.
Belle's blood. His dad and Belle's husband had been the brothers. Bowland's face was white, white. His pale hands like clab-
ber. A belly on him. His round face split by a stupid grin.

"Got to take a piss now. Water Lucinda's asters. Got to make *some* contribution. Coming along?"

"No. You go."

Bowlie moved out to the far border of the backyard. George walked briskly back to the side porch, went on inside. Lucinda bent over, placing a tiny pot of marigolds in the center of the table that gleamed now, with polished silver, cloth napkins, candlelight. He recognized the quick marriage between poverty and plenty she had made in the last forty minutes: the pan of browned drop biscuits, a little plate of diced pork chops and Spam in an aromatic mound, made to look larger and more attractive with one thinly sliced tomato scalloped around it. Here were more Ritz crackers; cheese dug out of a jar and mounded, one olive on top. Here the string beans, limp from overcooking, in a small Fostoria serving dish. And— an aesthetic afterthought—a box of sugar doughnuts cut into eighths. Three glasses, filled almost to the brim with milk, cream thickening at the top.

He stood just behind her so that when she straightened, she stood against him. He was light as a butterfly against her. He grazed her neck with thin, feverish, youthful lips, let his left hand take a position in the air so that when she moved, her breast created a breeze, a cushion of air against his palm. "You're beautiful, honey. Beautiful," his whispered words a part of that breeze.

She took it, one, two seconds. Then, without a word, moved from him to the kitchen. The swinging door closed. Using his fingers George picked up one, two, three, four cubes of pork, pushed them in his mouth, swallowed. "Ow," he said. He finished off the pork and half the Spam. Then, moving in a blur, he stuffed his mouth with biscuits, took two more, crammed them into an inside pocket. Swallowing, he took four doughnut cubes, stuffed them in, jammed both hands onto the plate and into the side pockets of his suit jacket. When Lucinda opened the door again, her face composed, carrying a last-minute dish of Kraft Dinner, she heard the screen door

lightly close. She crossed to open it, businesslike, to tell the
boys to come in to dinner. And faced her husband, who said,
"Where's . . . ?" She blushed.

Then they both looked at the table.

Townsend Avenue in Eagle Rock marked the very end of
the Red Car line. George knew this, from an earlier scouting
trip, and he knew when the Five Car started. He ran, lightly,
not in a hurry, breeze grazing his cheeks, liquor burning his
belly. He hopped on the car just as it lurched into motion and
sat in the outdoor section, his face hanging out like a dog's to
catch the rush of fresh air. Three days ago he'd landed a job on
the *Highland Park Press Dispatch,* working City Side. His first
paycheck came in ten more days. He'd disdained an advance.
"Back in Dallas," he'd said loftily, "I did all right. I don't
need the money. Back in Dallas I made as much as a C-note a
week."

By midnight he was out (with a photographer) meeting
up with other guys, letting the night happen. He'd covered two
"domestic violences," one bungled burglary, when a phone call
from a buddy at the *Herald* brought him to an apartment out
on Normandy. "Something *you'd* like, George!"

In a cream-colored bachelorette with the Murphy bed
swung down, a man sat on its edge and sobbed, brokenhearted.
"Don't," he said. "Please. Don't take my picture. Go away.
There's nothing for you here. I already called the doctor. He's
coming. Go away, please."

The man had a shirt on but was naked from the waist
down. He slumped over, trying ineffectively to hide his dick,
which was stuck snugly, like a dog's, in the long, gleaming attachment of a vacuum cleaner. A man from the *Times,* his
elbow on the cream-painted mantel of a false fireplace, stared
with detached interest. "We get more of these than you think,"
he told the new guy, the Texan.

George saw how it went. He was meant to join the circle
of reporters, lay down a bet to see how long till the attachment
fell to the floor. But he couldn't do it. "Say, boy," he said, and

sat down beside the crying man. "I've seen worse back home. This ain't nothin' at *all.* Don't mind them. My daddy had a saying about things like this. Those boys don't make no never mind. Here, wait." He rummaged in his pockets, brushed off his vest, speckled with powdered sugar. "Take a look at my daddy's watch. And this here's a piece of doughnut. Take it. Take it."

# CONTRIBUTORS

LEE K. ABBOTT has published four collections of short stories, *The Heart Never Fits Its Wanting, Love is the Crooked Thing, Strangers in Paradise,* and *Dreams of Distant Lives.* He teaches at Ohio State University in Columbus, Ohio.

LISA ALTHER was born in Tennessee in 1944 and now lives in Vermont. Her first novel, *Kinflicks,* was published in 1976. She is also the author of *Original Sins* and *Other Women.*

RICHARD BAUSCH is the author of four novels and a collection of short stories, *Spirits and Other Stories.* He is a recipient of both National Endowment for the Arts and Guggenheim fellowships in fiction. He is on the faculty of the writing program at George Mason University in Fairfax, Virginia. His most recent novel is *Mr. Fields Daughter.*

CHARLES BAXTER lives in Ann Arbor, Michigan. He is the author of two collections of stories, *Harmony of the World* and *Through the Safety Net,* and a novel, *First Light.* He teaches at the University of Michigan.

MADISON SMARTT BELL is the author of five novels, most recently *Soldier's Joy.* He has taught in various creative writing programs, including the Iowa Writer's Workshop, and currently teaches at Goucher College, along with his wife, the poet Elizabeth Spires. His second collection of short stories, *Barking Man,* will be published by Ticknor & Fields in 1990.

FREDERICK BUSCH is the author of, most recently, *Absent Friends,* a collection of stories published in May, 1989, by Alfred A. Knopf, and a novel, *War Babies,* published in September, 1989, by

New Directions. His sixteenth book, *Harry and Catherine,* a novel, will be published in March, 1990, by Alfred A. Knopf.

ETHAN CANIN is the author of *Emperor of the Air,* a collection of short stories. His fiction has appeared in *The Atlantic, Esquire, Ploughshares,* and other magazines, and has received the Houghton Mifflin Literary Fellowship and a National Endowment for the Arts grant. He lives in San Francisco.

MICHAEL DORRIS is the author of a novel, *A Yellow Raft in Blue Water,* and *The Broken Cord.* His short fiction has appeared in *Mother Jones, The Georgia Review, Southwest Review,* and *Seventeen.* In 1989 he was awarded an NEA creative writing fellowship.

MICHAEL DOWNING graduated from Harvard College in 1980. His first novel, *A Narrow Time,* was published by Vintage Books in 1987; his second, *Mother of God,* will be published by Simon & Schuster in May, 1990. He teaches writing and literature at Wheelock College in Boston.

LOUISE ERDRICH grew up in North Dakota and is of German-American and Chippewa descent. Her first book was *Jacklight,* a volume of poetry. Her second, *Love Medicine,* was the winner of both the Book Critics Circle Award for Fiction and the Los Angeles Times Award for best novel of 1985. She is also the author of *The Beet Queen, Tracks,* and, forthcoming in January, a poetry collection, *Baptism of Desire.*

AMY HEMPEL is the author of a volume of stories, *Reasons to Live,* published by Alfred A. Knopf in 1985. Her second collection, *At the Gates of the Animal Kingdom,* will be published in the spring.

ANN HOOD is the author of the novels *Somewhere Off the Coast of Maine, Waiting to Vanish,* and *Three-Legged Horse,* all published by Bantam. She lives in Brooklyn, New York.

JAY NEUGEBOREN is the author of ten books, most recently *Before My Life Began,* which won the Edward Lewis Wallant Memorial Prize for Best Novel of 1985, and *The Stolen Jew,* which won the

Present Tense Award of the American Jewish Committee for Best Novel of 1981. He is the only author to have won six consecutive PEN syndicated fiction prizes. He is currently writer in residence at the University of Massachusetts in Amherst.

JOYCE CAROL OATES is the author most recently of *American Appetites,* a novel, and *The Time Traveler,* poetry. She is a past recipient of the National Book Award for her novel *them* and has won several O. Henry Prizes and Pushcart Prizes. An editor of *Ontario Review,* she lives in Princeton, New Jersey, where she is Roger S. Berlind Distinguished Professor of the Humanities at Princeton University. She has been a member since 1978 of the American Academy–Institute of Arts and Letters.

ROBERT OLMSTEAD was born in New Hampshire in 1954. His work has appeared in *Black Warrior Review, Granta, and The Graywolf Annual Four.* He is currently writer in residence at Dickenson College in Carlisle, Pennsylvania, and is a graduate of the creative writing program at Syracuse University. His first published collection of stories is *River Dogs.* He is the author of a novel, *Soft Water,* and the forthcoming *A Trail of Heart's Blood Wherever We Go.* He recently received a Guggenheim Fellowship for 1989.

FRANCINE PROSE is the author of seven novels, including *Bigfoot Dreams* and *Household Saints.* Her most recent book is a collection of short stories, *Women and Children First.*

MICHAEL ROSEN is the literary director of the Thurber House in Columbus, Ohio. He is the author of *A Drink at the Mirage,* a poetry collection published by Princeton University Press in 1985, and the forthcoming *Collecting Himself,* an edited volume of uncollected prose by James Thurber to be published by Harper & Row in the fall of 1989. His poetry has been published in *The New Yorker, The Atlantic Monthly, The Paris Review, Shenandoah, Grand Street,* and many other journals.

RICHARD RUSSO teaches at Southern Illinois University in Carbondale. He is the author of *Mohawk* (1986) and *The Risk Pool* (1988).

CAROLYN SEE is a book critic for the Los Angeles Times. She is the author of *Rhine Maidens; Mothers, Daughters;* and *The Rest is Done with Mirrors.* Her novel, *Golden Days,* was published in 1987. She has received a Guggenheim Fellowship to complete her next novel, *Making History.*

MONA SIMPSON is the author of a novel, *Anywhere But Here.* Her short fiction has appeared in *Granta, Harpers, The Paris Review, The Pushcart Prize: Best of the Small Presses,* and *Best American Short Stories.*

SCOTT SPENCER is the author of *Last Night at the Brain Thieves Ball, Preservation Hall, Endless Love,* and *Waking the Dead.* His new novel is *Secret Anniversaries.*

ANNE TYLER was born in Minnesota and grew up in Raleigh, N.C. Her first of eleven novels was published in 1964, and her stories have appeared in such magazines as *The New Yorker, Redbook, McCall's, Harper's, The Southern Review, and Quest.* Her most recent novels are *The Accidental Tourist* and *Breathing Lessons.*

o   o   o

For additional information about Share Our
Strength, write or call:

Share Our Strength
1511 K Street N.W.
Washington, D.C.   20005
202-393-2925

o   o   o